THE HANGED MAN

By Alex Fiano

GABRIEL'S WORLD □ *BOOK ONE*

∞

WHAT WOULD YOU SACRIFICE TO DO THE RIGHT THING?

Troublemaker Press
Bronx NY

The Hanged Man by Alex Fiano

First book in the *Gabriel's World* Series
2012, 2019 Alex Fiano
Distributed by Troublemaker Press
ISBN-13: 978-0-9969943-4-7
This work may be copied for the purpose of commentary up to 500 words. Contact author for further reproduction.

To the Gabriel's World audience: I thank those readers worldwide who have taken an interest and liking to Gabriel and Joel and the Gabriel's World stories, my friends who have supported *Gabriel's World*, and my unpaid intern FRO. – A.F.

∞

Gabriel's World offers a compelling community of queer and allied characters, in stories that explore the extremes and complexity of good and evil.

Welcome to our World:
Homepage: GabrielsWorld.com
Email the author: gabrielsworld@outlook.com
Twitter: @gabrielsworld
Instagram: gabriels_world_queer_fiction

Gabriel's World: It's Time for New Heroes

Reader Extras: Gabriel's World now has recaps on the *Gabriel's World* website for the chapters of each book. The recaps offer chapter summaries, commentary, trivia and other insight & info, going into the plot and characters in-depth. Read Recaps of the chapters on the Gabriel's World website: **https://bit.ly/2wUy6dJ**

Books by Alex Fiano

The Hanged Man

Two-Faced Woman

The Book of Joel

Dead for Now

Hardcore

PREFACE

In 1968, Olympian John Carlos asked Dr. Martin Luther King why he was going back to Memphis to protest for civil rights, when his life had been threatened. Dr. King said, "I have to go back and stand for those that won't stand for themselves, and I have to go back for those that can't stand for themselves."

INTRODUCTION ♦ THE HANGED MAN

In the tarot deck the twelfth card of the major arcana, the Hanged Man, represents a person in a state of suspension, contemplating sacrifice, possibly surrender. The Hanged Man is between two worlds, two choices.

ONE ♦ THE MAGICIAN

The first card of the major arcana. The Magician represents a person with an almost mystical ability to solve problems and rectify karma. The person must realize his or her full potential and act upon it.

∞

Friday, July 9, 2010
9:07 am Buckston, NJ

WALKING OUT OF THE small-town Jersey police station, I'm immediately faced with a throng of reporters. They're waiting at the bottom of steps outside the building. A barrage of questions hits me like I'm a pop-up target in a sideshow booth.

"Mr. Ross, how do you feel about your arrest?"

"Do you have anything to say to the Church?"

"Do you know the Church is planning to sue?"

"What do you say to the allegation you did this for the publicity?"

"Do you regret interfering with the family's privacy?"

I give the reporters the evil eye and say nothing. The videos of the incident at Teresa's funeral yesterday are going viral on YouTube. A couple of the Buckston cops showed them to me while I was waiting in the squad room last night. I'm not a narcissist so I don't enjoy watching myself in this context. Especially in the current fallout over what I was doing at the time, what I was saying at the time...

Why I punched the preacher in the face.

The reporters continue their slings and arrows, undaunted by my silence. "Do you think you'll lose your license?"

"Are you against free speech?"

"Are you responsible for your friend being outed?"

I ignore them all and move down the stairs. My friend, Sergeant Teresa McKinney, died in combat from a hidden IED outside of Baghdad; her funeral was held yesterday in Buckston. A so-called church group called the Fundamental Righteousness of Baltimore protested her funeral, as they have been doing over the last few years with dozens of other dead service members. Their protests involve vile slogans of homophobia, anti-Semitism, and Islamophobia. Not all the military whose funerals they protested were gay, but some were. Teresa was. Whether gay or not, what this group does is beyond low, beyond unethical, beyond sick. Nevertheless, a controversial Supreme Court decision has allowed them the legal right to do so. Nobody likes this group, its leader Reverend Mel Bunton, or the exploitation of the First Amendment.

I couldn't stand Teresa's family suffering through the incessant chanting and screaming outside the cemetery gates. I left the graveside service and went to the street to tell the fundamentally righteous assholes to shut up. They gleefully got in my face--Rev. Bunton standing so close I could feel the saliva. He and his flock tried to provoke me by calling me *faggot* and then insulting my dead friend with further obscenities. And I lost it. One might think my loss of temper wouldn't be publicly vilified under the circumstances. However, judging from the perspective the local news stories have taken--that I acted to exploit the incident for my benefit--nothing I say now is going to be construed in my favor.

A tall, white, fortyish man in an expensive tailored business suit catches my eye. He stands well behind the reporters, smiling at the goings-on. He nods to me; I realize he's my appointment. I had come back to the police station to pick up my belongings following a night arraignment, and he had arranged to meet me here. He steps away from the crowd and gets into a black for-hire car with New York plates, parked a short distance from the station.

Behind me my attorney and close friend Michaela Connor stays near the steps and draws the press away from me by making a statement. My case is Adjourned in Contemplation of Dismissal-- meaning it will be dropped if I stay out of trouble. Michaela, a striking black woman in her early thirties, explains my legal situation to the press and also offers a proclamation of outrage on my behalf for them to chew on. This gives me the chance to hustle away from the melee and over to the hire car. I duck inside before the reporters can realize I've left the scene. The car accelerates, and begins heading for the George Washington Bridge and New York City.

The car has a tinted Plexiglas window between the front and back seats, giving us privacy. The man in the Brioni suit is Raymond Booth, also an attorney. He reaches to shake my hand. "Mr. Ross."

"Call me Gabriel. Pleased to meet you, Mr. Booth. At least, I appreciate the ride back to the city."

"My pleasure. This is a good opportunity to talk. Are you okay after staying in jail overnight?"

I try to smooth the wrinkles out of my clothes, noting the bruises on the knuckles of my right hand from slamming against the preacher's bony jaw. "It's a small-town lock-up, not so bad. The cops just didn't like the publicity of the whole event. I guess it hasn't ended yet."

Booth laughs. "No, I'm afraid not. I noticed at first the feedback was all supportive of you. When I heard of it and saw you in those videos, I was thinking how much you rock. But somehow this has turned into an Inquisition of your motives."

Raymond Booth's dark hair is styled in an expensive cut, framing a smooth movie-star face. We have the same dark Irish coloring but his pricey clothes make my off-the-rack black suit seem even more rumpled than it is. I'm acutely aware I need to shave, take a shower. But Booth doesn't seem to mind. And I don't mind being told I rock, under the circumstances.

"My motives were *res ipsa loquitor.*" Meaning, the thing apparent on its face.

Booth smiles, hearing a non-lawyer quoting legal concepts. However, I've worked as a paralegal and investigator for attorneys, so I can use the terminology properly.

"I thought so." He pauses to open the interior window and ask the driver to pull over for coffee before getting on the bridge, then turns back and smiles at me. "A story takes on the narrative of whoever tells it. I believe an 'unnamed source' in your industry is spreading the word you're prone to exploit cases. Anyone you know?"

The car stops in a Starbucks parking lot, and the driver goes inside. Booth is scrutinizing me, and I'm checking him out as well. I can size up people quickly from my experience and training.

I like Booth thus far. He had learned Michaela represented me for the assault charge in Jersey, and when she told him I was being released this morning, he asked if he could pick me up to consult about a job offer. I was fine with that. Booth is a name partner in Kline, Booth and Cheng, a firm specializing in high-end art litigation, intellectual property rights, and art-related tax and insurance issues. The firm has a pristine reputation.

I consider his question though I'm 90 percent sure of the answer. "You've done some digging yourself to find that out, I take it. The source is probably Gerry Doniger, I used to work for his investigative firm. Actually, his partner Manuel Smith was my mentor in the business. But when he died, there was no love lost between Gerry and me. We've clashed before. If I fell in the East River, he'd be out on a boat--chumming for sharks."

Booth smiles again and leans back. "I like your honesty. You're blunt."

I shrug. "Before I left the station this morning, I checked my messages. Four of my regular clients have informed me that they no longer need my services. Because I couldn't stand hearing some bigoted prick saying my 'dyke' friend was going to burn in Hell. I made the choice to do what I did; I knew it wouldn't end well, but he assaulted my friend's dignity. I'll pay for standing up to him, but I can live with that for her sake. So what's to lose by being honest? Since you did some fast work to find out where I was today, Mr. Booth, you deserve as much."

"Make it Raymond." We collect our coffee from the driver and begin the trip again. Raymond leans in a little closer. He has a hint of good musky cologne; I'm always aware of good and really bad colognes. Under different circumstances, I'd ask what it is.

"I want to hire you precisely because of that attitude. New York has plenty of good firms. Large high-tech businesses with ex-CIA and Special Forces people and small operations run by former cops. You don't fit in those categories, but you have a good reputation. You mentioned on your website you help the LGBTQ community; I like that. I need an investigator, and you intrigued me. Not just in taking a risk--no doubt many would be willing to bend a law on my behalf--but your principles. I go by instinct, and you attracted me."

I resist smiling at the double-entendre and put on my professional expression. "Fine by me. Tell me about your problem--something related to sexual orientation or...?"

"No, I just liked that you mentioned it. Personal reasons..." He holds my gaze for a beat. Although I feel like an unkempt bum at the moment, I'm flattered. He smiles again. "My problem, though, is business-related."

He takes an iPad from his briefcase and shows me an elegantly subtle website for a nonprofit organization, the New York Foundation for Art and Culture. "I'm on the board of directors here. I have been for five years. Something happened recently to another board member that I found highly disturbing."

I search in my messenger bag for my own iPad, which thankfully is intact and working. I can't afford a replacement. "Who was the other board member?"

"Eleanor Whitford. I'll arrange for you to speak with her."

"Okay. What happened, exactly?"

"She overheard a conversation in the Foundation that upset her a great deal. I'll discuss the other persons involved after we sign a retainer agreement. I need to maintain confidentiality, and of course in working for an attorney you'll have that privilege. But the context was *another* board member who apparently has been associating with a known war criminal." He taps the iPad for emphasis.

I look up, with growing interest. "Serbian? African?"

"Nazi Germany."

I pause in my writing. "*Really.* My God, those people have mostly died off. Who's left?" I feel a little rush of excitement. Long ago, my mom had told me that if she could have, she would have dedicated her life to finding Nazis and other war criminals. Sometimes I feel I need to carry on her idealism.

"This particular person is still alive as far as I know, and he's on the list at the Simon Wiesenthal Center. Granted, I'm not well-versed in the topic of Nazi-hunting and I'll need you to see what you can find out. I've spoken with some lawyers who know you, and they tell me that you're a very good researcher. I've also read your articles about hate groups."

He's referring to my part-time gig writing for a New York-based online magazine. "Thank you."

Raymond leans closer again. "Gabriel, you can imagine how I feel about knowing someone connected to the Foundation is *friends* or something with a Goddamned Nazi. I can't let that go."

"And the conversation Ms. Whitford overheard implied that relationship?"

"From how she described it, yes." He shakes his head. "Since powerful people in town are connected to the Foundation I don't want to deal with a larger firm. I wanted to find a solo investigator with integrity."

Now I have to grin. "And the public accusation that I took a family tragedy and used it to get my name in the news doesn't detract from your decision?"

He raises an eyebrow. "I'm familiar with bad press and how competitors can try to tear a person down. I'm going with my instinct about you. It hasn't failed me thus far. Anyway, if you're willing, I'm hiring you."

I'm willing. By this time, we've gone back over the George Washington Bridge into upper Manhattan, and I make arrangements with him as the car travels downtown to my building on Avenue A. It is across the street from Tompkins Square Park in the part of Manhattan known as Alphabet City. Raymond is heading to his own place, on Vestry Street in the Tribeca neighborhood.

I go up to my apartment and check on my cat Archie. Archie is black and white, tuxedo-style markings. With exquisite feline sensitivity, he knows something's been up with me and rubs against my legs for a few minutes. Then I shower off the jail, and draft a retainer for Raymond. I send a PDF version of the retainer to Raymond's email. He's supposed to return it to me by fax or by email, with his credit card info.

As the evening wears on I catch up with some friends on the phone, listen to many bad jokes about my behavior, and review more messages. I call my friend Jim Pollan, who's also my New York attorney and a mutual friend of Michaela's, and give him the story of the ACD. Jim loves bad judge stories. The New Jersey judge had actually made a condition of my sentence that I was not to return to New Jersey--banished from the state. Which is illegal, of course. Mikki laughed about that nonsense--once out of the courtroom.

My voicemail is clogged with calls from local and online newspapers, bloggers, friends, my asshole father, and ordinary citizens--with them, heavy on the nutjob element. The messages range from fervent approval to scathing criticism to threats on my life. Nothing I'm worrying about tonight.

On the other hand, I don't hear back from Raymond. Considering he went to the length of picking me up in New Jersey today, I had thought he would respond immediately. However, the hours begin to tick by, and I don't hear anything from him on the fax, email or otherwise. I call his cell under the pretense of checking to see that he received my email, but he doesn't answer.

The following day, Saturday, the morning goes by without any further word. I begin to be concerned--what if he changed his mind? My current personal economic situation is a microcosm of the nation's economic crisis--bad news verging on disaster--sort of a David Gray song in real life. People aren't investing as much in professional investigators these days, although I have built myself a decent business. I can do financial fraud investigation as well as insurance claims, missing persons, cheating partners, and I have a good reputation in spite of what happened in Jersey. Nevertheless, the industry's hurting and I've been doing more investigative work for assigned counsel in New York and New Jersey, which means I wait months to see a paycheck since they get paid by the state.

In the meantime, my bills are turning into demand notices and I'm feeling the kind of unease that can easily slip into desperation. Raymond's retainer is a nice sum to take care of having to forgo luxuries like food and electricity, and the job will put me back on track instead of being the subject of public scorn.

I spend the rest of the day worrying, but also contacting my other clients who have called out of concern or antipathy. Depending on their attitude, I either calm their fears they hired some sort of out-of-control hothead or inform them their final invoice will be sent with payment due.

On Sunday morning, my phone rings shortly before ten a.m.; the caller ID says Booth. *Thank God*, I tell myself. *He just took a day off.* Then I notice the Booth is Antoinette, not Raymond.

"This is Gabriel Ross."

"I can't find my brother." The voice is female, sharp and intense with emotion. "What the fuck did you do with him?"

∞

TWO ♦ THE QUEEN OF SWORDS

The Queen of Swords represents a woman seeking the truth and emotional honesty. In her quest, one should use caution in disagreeing with her as she wants everyone to feel the way she does.

∞

"WHAT ARE YOU talking about," I ask Antoinette Booth.

"My brother Raymond. What do *you* know about where he is?"

I try to catch up with her words. "You're Raymond Booth's sister? I don't know where he is. What makes you think he's missing?"

"Because I can't find him. What the fuck do you *think*?"

"Ms. Booth, I understand you're upset, but please explain why you are calling me? Why do you believe I know where Raymond is?"

I hear her sigh. "Look, I know who you are. He told me that he was going to hire you. About the Foundation, right? He took you home from New Jersey on Friday. I'm a paralegal; he had me research you after he saw you online--when you hit that guy. I needed to see him Friday night but when I went to his place, he wasn't there. I haven't seen or heard from him since."

I take a moment to digest this. "He didn't mention you but yes, he did drive me home and we talked about a job. I don't know anything beyond that. Does he often leave without notifying you?"

"No, he *never* does. And I'll be in deep trouble if he doesn't come back soon. I don't know exactly what you told him about his problem, but maybe he had to disappear all of a sudden on your suggestion. That's why I wanted to talk to you. Telling him to disappear put me in a bad way."

"I didn't do that, honestly. I'm sorry."

A few seconds of silence on her end. Then her tone changes to pleading. "Will you meet with me? Maybe you can find him. It's important." She's smoking while she talks--I hear her inhale sharply every so often. "He just wouldn't have stood me up. Look, I'll explain when we meet."

My worry over Raymond has increased over the course of the call, and I want to do something. "All right, I have a job today, but I can meet with you. There's a café on Amsterdam between 73rd and 74th called The Beat Box. Can you be there at eleven?"

"You don't have an office?"

"No, I travel too much." A regular office costs too much in the city. I see clients at their residences, businesses or nearby coffee shops. I also have a part-time business office rental when needed--one of those mini-office places that offer a mailbox, cubicle and conference room--but I do my research at home.

"All right." She hangs up. With her words still buzzing in my brain, I give myself time to breathe deeply and clear my mind--the Zen Buddhist art of *zazen*. I hope meeting with her can shed light on what's going on with Raymond.

Shortly thereafter I leave my apartment building on Avenue A and see a young white man with tribal tattoos up and down his arms doing a job I often do, process serving. He looks at me. "Gabriel Ross?"

I don't answer and move down the steps to the sidewalk. He checks a paper in his hand. Our eyes meet again. I feel a flash of anger upon seeing the paper is a blow-up of my recent booking photograph. However, he doesn't let my anger stop him and holds out a set of blue-backed legal papers. Some people would let them drop to the ground, but that doesn't work. I accept them without comment and shove them in my backpack, heading for the subway.

At the café on Amsterdam I take an outside table, order coffee and toast, and text my client, whose one of those not concerned over my current notoriety. He texts back that he's ready to go with the program. It's 10:30 a.m., about the right time. Across the street I see the target arrive on foot to a residential building, ring an apartment and get buzzed in. As all this happens, I take pictures with a digital camera. I notify my client that the plan is on. I relax for a few minutes and wait for Antoinette.

However, she doesn't show up at 11. Ten, fifteen, thirty minutes tick by. I give up on her. Time is getting too close for my other plan in action to begin. I remain at my table with my coffee and watching the apartment building through my sunglasses, occasionally texting with the client. I'm wearing khaki shorts, sandals, a Phoenix Suns t-shirt--Grant Hill's number, 33. Just a regular guy relaxing at a café on a Sunday.

A woman appears in my line of sight on the sidewalk. "Are you Gabe Ross? I'm Toni—Antoinette."

She's pretty; good bone structure in her face. Nicely-styled white linen sleeveless dress. But she has distinct circles under her eyes below heavy eyeliner. Her wavy blonde hair hangs limply in a chignon. Her skin is pale in a way that suggests she has some unhealthy habits.

Toni leans over the chain barrier between the tables and the sidewalk to shake my hand, and I catch her scent of Marlboros and Opium.

"Yes, but Gabriel if you don't mind. I never liked Gabe."

Toni walks around the barrier and sits at my table. I'm still keeping an eye on the building while I talk. "Have you heard from Raymond?"

"No, nothing yet...funny, you're like Raymond that way. He hates to be called Ray. God, I haven't had anyone to talk to about Raymond missing; I don't want to worry our mom, or my son. I'm just a mess. See, Raymond controls a family trust for us, and he was going to write a check for me on Friday night. I was supposed to see him at six that evening. But like I said, he wasn't there...Are you watching for something?"

"Yes. That's why I wanted to meet you earlier. I'm on a job here." I check the time on my phone; I don't wear a watch. A couple years ago in a fight on the subway, my watch was smashed and left a scar on my wrist. I lost the inclination to get another one. "Nearly 12. In about five minutes, a guy's going to be flying out that front door."

"Why?"

"Because his girlfriend's husband is calling right now to say he's canceled his business trip and will be home in twenty minutes. I'm sure the boyfriend lives near here. I'm going to see if I can trail him and find out where he lives."

"Oh."

"I don't usually take people with me on a job, but when he leaves, I have to go." I zip up my backpack. "Is Raymond married? Involved?"

"Not married. He's gay; you probably know that. He's not in anything serious right now, just some losers here and there. See, I really need that trust money for my son Adam. He's almost fourteen. I have him in a private school; Raymond pays the tuition. It's more attentive to letting a child express himself and develop potential, you know?"

Across the street, the front door opens and a blond thirtyish white man in a rumpled blue Oxford shirt and jeans hustles out the door and turns right, toward 74th.

Toni puts a hand over her mouth. "Oh my God, it's just like you said!"

I've taken pictures of him leaving, and I grab my bag and stand up. "If you want to go with me, we can talk while I follow. Pretend we're a couple." I leave the check and extra-generous tip on the table (generosity isn't just the right thing to do; one never knows when it will be reciprocated with information) and leave with Toni following me. We cross the street and stay a half-block behind my target.

I continue my conversation, not too loud. "You say he's been involved with losers--does anyone in particular stand out, who might have hurt him?"

She laughs quietly. "Raymond doesn't have those types of relationships. He's too bighearted with boyfriends, but he wouldn't put up with violence from anyone. Damn, we're actually following this guy. This is kind of fun, better than my regular job."

"If Raymond's generous, he might have been conned." The target turns west on 74th, toward the Beacon theater. We continue at a safe distance.

"He's not that sentimental to fall for someone's line of bullshit. He's a good attorney and awfully cynical. I'm sure he's scared off a few men with his demeanor. I'm not saying he never feels but he's very self-reliant and powerful in his personality, you know what I mean? We're both like that; neither of us stays in a relationship for long."

She takes out a pack of cigarettes, so I do the same. We light up while walking. "Does he have any medical problems?"

"He has a bad back. He's had to lose time off from work. It was starting to bother him again last week."

"You sure he isn't just laid up for a few days, getting over it?"

"Yeah. When he feels bad, I go over to his place and help him out. Sometimes I bring Adam over. He and Adam are really tight. He'd tell me if he was home. He's aware I worry. He knows I need the check, too."

In my peripheral vision, I can see her trembling a little. Her amusement at the tail job has receded. "I work in a law firm in Brooklyn. They're going to lay me off next month. The economy sucks so much. I don't know how we're gonna live. I haven't found a new job yet. Raymond thinks I'm not the most responsible person in the world due to my history with Adam's father and other stuff. But he doesn't want us to be on the street, right? He was going to write out another check. He was even going to see if he could get me into his firm. We'd be a hell of a team."

I give her some time to get herself under control. I feel more empathy because of her mentioning about her son. I was very close to my uncle as well. In the meantime, the target is heading uptown on Broadway. "Are you thinking of calling the police?"

She nods. "I actually called today. They told me to call back Monday and file a report."

"I take it you have a key to his place."

"Yeah. I didn't look around much, just to see if he was there. Everything looked okay."

"Was there any sign of him leaving or taking a trip? Suitcases missing, that kind of thing?"

She shakes her head impatiently. "No, nothing like that. Can you do anything to find him?"

"I can try. Do you know anything about the situation in the Foundation?"

"The problem you were going to work on? Not really."

"What does this Foundation do, exactly?"

"Art conservation. Also, it's supposed to fund artists in underserved communities, and Raymond is big on underserved communities--I think he feels guilty because he's part of this high-end firm, you know?" She smiles.

Our man has slowed suddenly. He looks at his phone like he's getting a text. The married girlfriend warning him, perhaps. I stop to look in a store window. "He's going to turn around." I reach over to hold her hand, make us look more like a couple.

Sure enough, he puts his phone away and turns around to survey the street behind him. I start to point to stuff on display in the store window but then Toni reaches up to kiss me on the mouth. I'm surprised but I go with it to keep the cover. A few seconds later, I risk a glance down the block and see our man has continued on towards 76th.

"I thought I'd help with the disguise." She lights another cigarette.

"Thanks...He seems to have bought it. You were saying about the Foundation?"

"Well, he doesn't discuss everything about the place, but something serious was bugging him and he wanted a professional investigator. Like I said, he heard of what happened last week--what you did with that religious guy." Toni looks up at me, narrowing her blue eyes. "But even if he didn't hire you yet, there's a chance he told someone else he had, like he did me. Someone bad who had it out for him because he thought Raymond *had* hired you."

Finally, my target has reached his destination. A building on 77th between Broadway and West End. I wait for him to enter and then go over to check it out. Through the locked glass lobby entrance, I watch the elevator numbers above the doors light up and stop at the tenth floor. Two apartments on that floor. I make note of the respective residents' names for further research, and then lead Toni another block west to the benches and trees aligning the West Side Highway.

We sit on a bench and stare at each other. Her attempt to incur fault by telepathy irritates me. I have no reason to feel guilt, and yet somehow I've taken on a responsibility. Part of my irritation is that I want to know what happened to him. A decent man, an interesting case, and it seemed to disappear in smoke.

"So you could search for him, right?"

"Do you want to hire me, Toni?"

Her mouth turns down at the word "hire." "You can't just look for him? I know if he was in trouble and you found him, Raymond would just add the cost of this to the job you're going to do for him." She frowns intensely. "*You're* worried about him too, aren't you?"

I don't respond to that. "I can't work on the hopes that he'll pay me. Maybe he doesn't even want to be found."

She's having a hard time holding herself together. Something else is going on with her. I guess that she is making heavy investments in various pharmas. Probably not anything like meth, as her teeth are still good. Not crack, because she doesn't have the out-of-control jitters. Maybe a combination of prescription meds. Stress is a trigger. When she's doing okay, she can hold herself together, as evidenced by her ability to dress well. When she's under stress, she decompensates, turns into chaos. I've seen it, worked with it, and lived with it before.

She's working herself into a mode. Substance abusers who must get their necessities out of others are very talented at the mode of manipulation. The mode is, in order: seduce, wheedle, beg, steal and hurt. "I understand that you don't do this for free, right? I mean, I know the economy is crap now and everything. But I feel something's happened to him; maybe he lost his memory, temporarily?"

The hopefulness in her voice is a warning to me. I light another cigarette, earning dirty looks from dog walkers and stroller-pushers. "Toni, I know what you are going through, however there is no guarantee as to what's happening with your brother. I would have to be hired by *you*, not on a contingency basis that he might be willing to pay later. What I'm able to do for you now is offer you a reduced fee." I shouldn't do that, but I don't want to lose the connection to the case.

"What would *that* be?" She pouts with a pronounced sullenness.

"Fifteen hundred. That's a significant discount off an initial retainer in this type of case."

She digs out her cigarette pack, finds it empty, and reaches over to pluck the cigarette from my mouth to inhale. "Don't you feel any responsibility?" Hands the cigarette back coated in lipstick.

"I appreciate your situation, but I have to have a retainer from you." I hold out my pack to offer her one for herself.

However, she's failed to melt my cold, cold heart and that makes her angry. Ignoring my pack, she stands up and glares at the street--eyes red, hair becoming disheveled, stamping on the empty pack she dropped on the sidewalk. She starts to walk off. Then she looks over her shoulder past my head, deliberately not in my eyes. "I'll get back to you later." She moves on without a goodbye.

I remain on the bench a few minutes to wind down. Toni is draining, as if producing an intoxicating mist from her personality.

Back home, I confirm which 77th Street resident is my cuckolded client's rival by comparing names to Facebook photos, and send my client the info. Then I read the legal papers I was served--an assault suit by the Good Reverend Bunton--and fax them to Jim. Finally, I lay down on my couch for a while listening to U2, Matchbox Twenty, Erasure. Rest doesn't come but a tension headache does. I prop my iPad on my chest and search online for whatever I can find about Raymond. I review the Foundation's website, but it has little to help me. I call Raymond's number again, fruitlessly. Archie joins me on the sofa, and settles on the iPad when I'm too tired to keep my eyes open and drift off.

Sometime after five o'clock, a sudden pounding on my door startles the hell out of me. I know it's not the Jehovah's Witnesses--when they sneak in the building, they tap on the doors lightly as if they are a friend, to fool the resident into opening up.

The knocking comes again, impatient. I walk up to the peephole. Toni is on the other side. I start to say "How the fuck..." since I try to keep my home address private. And this is a buzzer building--for all that security that offers. But I give up and open the door. "What a surprise."

THREE ◆ THE SEVEN OF SWORDS

The Seven of Swords represents operating in secret; events happening behind someone's back; finding out necessary information.

∞

SHE SHOWS ME a fistful of cash as she walks in. "Here's your money."

I shut the door behind her. I don't take the cash, but gesture for her to sit on my sofa. Her hair is now hanging wild and frizzy; her make-up has been reapplied even more heavily.

"May I ask how you know where I live?"

"Looked you up, of course. Please--you know it isn't hard. What's the point anyway--you *wanted* the money--I *have* the money." She slams said money on the coffee table and the rubber band around the bills breaks, causing them to cascade across the surface and some to land on the floor in a green mess.

That little action gets silence from both of us. Archie comes out and sniffs the air around Toni, then paws some of the bills to see if they might turn out to be a good toy. Toni looks at me, blushing slightly.

I sigh. "I'm going to make some coffee. Hold on for a few minutes."

As I leave for the kitchen, she lights up a Marlboro. I have to go back to give her an ashtray before she decides to flick ashes on the floor.

Once I bring back coffee for us, I sit in the armchair to the right of sofa. "I thought you had trouble raising the cash."

Toni begins tossing in cube after cube of sugar. Plink, plink, plink; drops spray the table. "I got a loan." She exhales a cloud across the room.

"From a friend?"

"Does that matter?"

I shrug. None of my business. Maybe she obtained the $1500 from pawning something--if that item was worth $10,000. Or she maybe she has access to Raymond's bankcard. Or a boyfriend to hit up really quick. But the question is moot. The cash is there on the table--most of it--with droplets of over-sugared coffee soaking in. Do I want the job or not?

"I'll write up a retainer." I take my coffee to my office in the second bedroom and fire up my desktop. Meanwhile, I can see Toni getting on her knees to pick up the bills and put them in a neat, organized pile, blotting them with a napkin. She calls over to me in a contrite tone. "Sorry about this."

I fill out the retainer, then go back and explain the terms to her. She listens carefully and then gives me the spare keys to Raymond's apartment. She also knows his computer and email password, as she's done work for him and had to use his computer.

I collect our cups. "I'm going to go over there now. You want to go with me?"

"No, I better get back to Adam, see about my mom." Having calmed down considerably, she's now trembling a bit.

In spite of her difficultness, I am appreciative of her trust and hold out my hand. "I'll call you later on if I find anything."

She suddenly gives me a hug. For a second I hold her, hear her breathing and sense the whirlpool of energy and emotion in her held briefly in check. Then she breaks away and leaves.

The timing of Raymond's attempt to hire me and his disappearance is suspicious, but I don't rule out other possibilities. People disappear for a myriad of reasons: on the run from the law; on the run from people who want to hurt them or have been hurting them; con artists who've been caught or are leaving before they're caught; and the classic leaving the family to start over. But I don't feel Raymond fits in those categories.

At about six o'clock I'm at Raymond's penthouse apartment on Vestry Street. It's in a renovated building eight floors high with loft-style apartments. The apartment has an alarm system, the type turned on and off through an electronic keychain device. The place is nicely set up--polished wood floors of deep rich oak. The walls are bright white interspersed with faux brick. A few frameless canvasses of Expressionist art are the main decorations. The oversized furniture is neutral rough-weave fabrics and blond wood. He has several shelves of books and electronic gadgets. The rooms have a faint aroma of exotic incense.

In my work, I try to search the rooms and belongings of missing persons to pick up the personality of the individual. My point is to get a sense of what is out of sync that may have led to the disappearance. The first point I take in here is that Raymond's apartment is neat and clean. No chaos of being tossed, or of belongings being packed in haste, just as Toni had observed.

His desk is a teak table in the living area pushed adjacent to a brick wall. On it, I see a checkbook from the trust, resting on a bank statement. That backs up Toni's claim that he was going to write her a check on Friday.

A short list of groceries to buy is on his marble kitchen counter alongside a bottle of wine out of a full rack. Maybe planning dinner that night, after seeing Toni. So with whom?

What I don't find are his wallet, keys and cell phone. So, let's say he steps out after dropping me off around noon. Toni said he was going to meet her at six, following her work. A six-hour interval, more or less. He's not shopping, doesn't have his list. Possibly went somewhere on business or had an appointment. Maybe he's seeing a friend, just for coffee or lunch. Raymond's trash tells me he eats out a good deal, and buys loads of coffee from a place called Cafétière Maléfice.

The goldmine of anyone's life will be in a computer unless he or she is off the grid. I start up Raymond's Mac. Some of his files are law-related, some are personal items: letters, photos, music. In his browsing history I get his Gmail account. I check the inbox, the sent folder and the trash folder. I read emails from his colleagues, former classmates, and friends. I record the email addresses in my notes. As always, I'm of two minds about this. On one hand, it's a terrible invasion of privacy. On the other, better the invader be someone like me who appreciates the gravity of the situation, respects what's there, and is doing it for the benefit of the person involved.

Despite Toni's assertion about Raymond not being involved with anyone, Raymond has nine months of intimate emails with a man named John Harrison, whose email is NurseRatchedNY. But no other recent email, IM log, or Facebook message of a romantic or sexual nature outside of John/NurseRatched. So Toni's not entirely truthful. That tells me something of her attitude toward John Harrison.

I see my own professional website in his browser history, as well as the infamous YouTube videos. One interesting item in the searches besides my name is the term "*Odessa.*" Odessa was the name of an organization assisting famous Nazi figures in escaping after the war and settling into luxury lives in South America.

It was at best a loosely organized group of people (including priests and politicians) who helped some German, Italian, and Croatian war criminals escape. A true well-funded network as depicted in the movies didn't exist. However, it did help Nazis on the run calling in favors and taking advantage of some incompetence, indifference and confusion after WWII. They were also helped by the focus on new enemies in the oncoming Cold War. But the search tells me Raymond was trying to find out more about the alleged Nazi war criminal.

After searching his computer, I flip through the papers on his desk, and find an envelope on his desk from GPSXtra. It's a tracking service for the GPS system in smart phones and Blackberries. Phones now hold so much personal information that losing one is a serious problem for professionals in sensitive positions. I pull out the bill, realizing the service could tell me where he is right now. I go back online to the GPSXtra website. A map loads on the screen with the location of the phone.

At first, I wonder if some mistake was made--according to the map, the phone is in the neighborhood. On impulse I get up and walk around the apartment to make sure he isn't really in the apartment and I just don't see him: checking the closets, the shower, and under the bed. No, he's not here. I go back and zoom in on the map--the GPS is accurate as to a block location, and the phone actually turns out to be on Desbrosses, one street up from Vestry. The date of the last reading was today.

Feeling some excitement, I get myself out of the loft and on the street, walking up to Desbrosses. I see the coffee shop Cafétière Maléfice on the corner. It's still open.

On a hunch, I go in and wave the counter person over. "Do you have a lost and found?"

The young man at the counter has long black hair brushed straight back in a ponytail, horn-rimmed glasses and a trace of an accent. He leans his arms on the counter, tilting towards me and frowning quizzically. "Yes, did you lose something?"

"My friend did--his Blackberry. He might've left it here Friday."

"Oh, you mean Raymond's?" He pulls out a box from under the counter and takes out a dark red Blackberry.

"That's it." I call Raymond's number on my phone, and the Blackberry in the man's hand rings. "May I have it? I'm working on his behalf."

"Hmm." The young man continues to gaze at me, then his eyes widen. "Oh, I know who you are. You were in the video, weren't you? The one in New Jersey." He smiles at the recognition. "I don't understand why people are upset with you. I would gladly shove those picket signs right up that preacher's ass."

As much as I don't wish to discuss the videos ever again, I smile modestly out of tact--and work it in my favor. "Well, thank you. Raymond thought I did the right thing as well."

Having verified my credentials based on fame, he hands over the phone. I examine it while thinking of the implications. A Crackberry would be inseparable to Raymond; he'd have been here to get it by now if he was still in town and functioning okay.

The young man behind the counter continues watching me. He tries to cover this by taking off his glasses and polishing them quickly.

I smile at him. "Hey, are you from France, or Quebec?"

"From Quebec, yes."

"I like your accent. Thanks again for the phone. What is your name?"

"Nicolas. He's a nice man, Raymond." He blushes slightly.

I hand Nicolas a $20 bill. "This is for keeping the phone safe. Did he meet anyone here on Friday, by any chance?"

Now Nicolas shows a trace of discomfort. He holds the twenty but doesn't put it away, as if he's not sure he should. Time to level with him. "Raymond's sister and I can't find him, and we're worried."

"Oh, you and Toni? What happened?"

"We aren't sure. That's why I'm asking; I want to make sure he's all right."

Nicolas nods. "Sit down; we're closing in a minute. Let me get you something so we can talk."

I sit at a long, cushioned bench stretching against the window side of the shop, facing to the counter. Nicolas changes the satellite station from classical to rock. I look over the place as Coldplay starts. Six small tables are in front of the bench and brick-faced wall, and one or two chairs are on the opposite side of each table. Nicolas comes over gives me a cup of espresso, and sits next to me.

"He *did* meet a man here."

"Expected or a surprise?"

"Expected, I believe. I don't know this man. He wore black sunglasses. Like the Blues Brothers, or the Men in Black. And a black cap on his head, no logo."

"How long were they here?"

"Ah, about 20 minutes. I was curious, I admit. This was not his usual guy."

"You mean John, his boyfriend."

"Yes. But Raymond, he wasn't talking to this man to pick him up. I don't think he liked this man."

"Why so? You were watching his body language?"

"Yes, when I could. Busy on Fridays, always. But yes, I pay extra attention to Raymond. He's *séduisant*, you know? Attractive. Hot, for an older guy."

I raise my eyebrow, and realize I'm unconsciously imitating Raymond doing so. "So Raymond wasn't attracted to him. Maybe they were talking business."

Nicolas shrugs. He moves closer to me. "I was a little worried. He became sick, Raymond."

"Really? What exactly happened, Nicolas?"

"He was sitting there..." he points to the next table closest to the door. "On the bench side. The other man had his back to me, to the counter. This other man buys them both coffees. Then they are talking for a while. After a few minutes, Raymond just doubles over. I'm taking care of customers but I was going to go over and see if I could help. The other man gets up and says something like, "I'll take care of this." He walks Raymond outside. I didn't see where they went or anything, though. I couldn't leave."

I consider that for a minute. "Did Raymond look afraid?"

"Just sick; he seemed about to fall down. Later I went to get the coffee cups and found the Blackberry on the bench."

"How old was this other guy? Was he white? American?"

"Yes. Sounded American, what little I heard. He was over 30 I'd say, and under 50. Five-nine, five-ten."

I feel a surge of adrenaline in having a target. Well, well Mr. Sunglasses-and-Cap. Who are you? You get the coffee--and slip something in it. Even serious knockout drugs like Rohypnol take at least 15-20 minutes to work by ingestion. So you talk to Raymond until it takes effect and then hustle him outside--to what? I look at the street--cars driving by, people walking, as if a ghostly image of Raymond and the man who made him disappear might show.

"I don't suppose he paid for the coffee by credit card. Or that this place has a security camera?"

"He paid in cash. But yes, we have a camera. We keep the videos for five days. Come on. I'm the manager here, so I can show you."

He leads me back to an office, then digs through a box on a shelf and comes up with a CD. He loads it into a computer on a cluttered desk and plays it, scanning ahead. The camera focuses on the register from a fairly high angle. The register is perpendicular to the front door facing the corner of Desbrosses. I put on my own John Lennon-style reading glasses to examine the video closely.

I recognize Raymond walking in the door at 12:57 p.m. Not long after he returned home. He's changed into a short-sleeve chambray shirt and khakis, sandals. He waits in a line of three people.

The man in the black cap and sunglasses comes in the shop. He's wearing a black button-down shirt and jeans. He does not raise his head when he approaches Raymond. His face isn't clear. All other customers look straight ahead and their faces can be discerned. This man seems to deliberately keep his head low, as if he knows a camera's in the shop. They have a few seconds of discussion and Raymond goes to sit at the second table--I'm guessing the man offered to buy Raymond's drink. The man with the cap waits on line to order, and moves to pick it up at the far end. He dips his hands in his pockets and puts change in a tip jar. His right hand has the fingers slightly curved and held together in a stiff way. To my eyes, holding something to slip into Raymond's coffee with the tip as cover. A pill or packet. He puts sugar in his and Raymond's and stirs thoroughly. Then he goes back to the table with the two cups and sits, facing away from us.

We watch them talking, or at least Raymond talking and the other man appearing to. Raymond looks at some papers the man gives him. While he's reading, he slumps a little. He jerks back as if trying to struggle against passing out. He pushes at the table to stay upright, but then slumps again. The man in the cap picks up his papers, stands, and quickly walks around the table to Raymond. Nicolas starts to walk toward the table. The other man gets an arm under Raymond's shoulder and supports him while moving them both out the front door. He seems to turn right on Vestry with Raymond, but no way to be sure.

Nicolas turns away from the screen. "The man did something to him. That makes me feel awful." I agree, thinking how soon this happened after he left me. I have Nicolas rewind the video and freeze on the best shot of the man in the cap, when he approaches Raymond at the counter. A sideways angle of his face, hardly anything useful. Even his mouth is indistinct. Nonetheless, the frame is printed. It could be any light-skinned man over 30 or so, really. But it's a start.

I grip Nicolas' shoulder. "Don't feel bad. You were an enormous help to me. Please take care of the video, don't let it be erased. Do you think I can have a copy?"

Nicolas finds a blank CD and makes a copy. I give him one of my cards in return. "If you see the other man, please call me."

I don't want to go home yet, having found this lead. I go back to Raymond's apartment and use his computer to copy the CD file to a flash drive I have on hand and print out more stills from the CD. I call Toni. The video is too large to send by email, but she has a webcam and I have webcam device to hook to my iPad. I use that to show her the first part of the video. "Does this look like anyone you know?"

"God. So hard to tell with that stupid cap. Who is he? What was he doing with Raymond?"

"I don't know. But we should tell the police about it, now."

She meets me at the precinct in Raymond's neighborhood in an hour. The detective she spoke to on the phone earlier isn't in, but we talk to a desk sergeant and I leave the CD with her. The sergeant calls the detective, who says he'll meet us first thing Monday.

A little disappointing, but maybe we can get more police action tomorrow morning. Toni and I agree to meet at the precinct again at 9 a.m.

∞

Monday, July 12
Vestry Street, 8:30 am

Before meeting with Toni, I follow my instinct to stop at the apartment to check and see if Raymond has returned by any chance.

As soon as I open the door, I know something is wrong. The air is extremely cold, like walking into a freezer. The warm scent in the apartment of yesterday is replaced with the dull odor of recycled air.

I feel a flush of apprehension. "Hello...?" No response. I try again: "*Raymond?* It's Gabriel--Gabriel Ross."

Nothing. I go forward and quickly search the living room, kitchen, bath, and open the bedroom door.

I see him curled on the bed, back to me, naked. I begin to apologize. "Oh my God, I'm sorry..."

But he doesn't hear me. I realize his body is frozen still. For a brief, absurd moment, I think he's frozen to death from the A.C. My mind in shock.

My heart pounds, making me sweat in the cold. I slowly walk up to the bed. He is not just still; he's bound around his neck, feet and hands. I check for a pulse in his neck and confirm that he is dead.

I think of meeting him two days ago, sitting beside me in the car and telling me about his important case. Flirting, confident, powerful, alive. The song playing in the coffee shop, *The Scientist,* pops in my head, and its video with the reverse narrative. I see myself like Chris Martin in the video, walking backwards...out of the apartment and not discovering this tableau, not having to face up to his death. On Friday, Raymond tried to hire me. On Monday, he's dead.

∞

FOUR ♦ THE NINE OF SWORDS

The Nine of Swords represents a martyr; someone sacrificed to deception, violence, scandal, and misery.

∞

THE ABSOLUTE STILLNESS of dead bodies is disturbing, but they are harmless; only the living cause trouble. Yet I feel like I've descended into a frozen underworld alone, with a dead man who's also alone. I'm actually sweating, and it feels like blisters bursting. I know I will have to call the police. But I make myself calm down and consider the situation before I call. I want to think this through. I want to know what happened. I have to do this; I have to be in the underworld.

The first question is how he died. The bed is made; Raymond lies on top of the blue comforter, which makes his skin look blue. A slipknot loop circling his neck is connected to his wrists. The rope around his wrists is in turn connected to his ankles, tied in lark's head knots. His head is partly drawn forward and somewhat mottled--probably from asphyxiation. Bruises lay under the rope around his neck. Being careful to avoid actually touching Raymond, I examine his body, since after I call the police I won't have a chance to do so. By appearances the slipknot around his neck was drawn too tight, cutting off airflow while also compressing the major arteries and causing him to black out. The continued loss of oxygen would cause his death. From these observations, the tempo in my mind gets faster, pushing me forward. Something about the entire scene bothers me. I walk around the bed.

A few objects are piled on the floor on the other side of the bed--stuff that wasn't there yesterday. A stack of magazines, DVDs and sexual devices--a whip, a hood, handcuffs and other devices. Some of the magazines are lying open. All of the magazines concern BDSM topics. I crouch next to them without touching and observe.

I had learned to break things down visually when working at Manny's firm just out of college. God rest his soul, he had shared his wisdom and given me one of my greatest trained talents. Because I've always carried a lot of anger, my biggest drawback at that time was charging ahead without taking time to survey a scene for the details, then the overall picture--the *gestalt*. Manny taught me to slow down, to parcel each part of an area into components, to ask myself questions about those components, especially about what should and should *not* be there.

As part of focusing on my training, I also remember the words of the pioneering French forensic scientist Alexandre Lacassange: "One must know how to doubt." The scene gives the *impression* that Raymond was indulging in the dangerous sexual practice of autoerotic asphyxiation and went too far, as sometimes happens. The draw of the act is that cutting off oxygen causes euphoria, and can also supposedly bring on erection and ejaculation. Someone seeing Raymond this way would conclude that he was both into bondage--which for many is sexually satisfying in itself--and autoerotic asphyxia. But for me, it raises doubt. It more seems set up by someone with knowledge of BDSM garnered out of bad TV shows.

The tempo of my thoughts continues, building upon this premise hypnotically, like trip hop music. For one thing, too much stuff is stacked up here. My former boyfriend Joel was a sometime male escort, including BDSM activities. I was curious to learn what was involved in the acts and the psychology. Joel had told me some of what people into BDSM and fetishes liked. He even took me places to meet others who were into it.

From what I know, I would expect here a more ritualistic set-up and not so much sexual paraphernalia for different activities jumbled up haphazardly next to the bed. None of the devices other than the whip can inflict pain, but he has no marks on his body of any past masochistic behavior. No preparation like towels and lubricant. Also, he has no padding around his neck--hence the bruises. The lack of any kind of escape mechanism really bothers me.

And the magazines are another problem--they're in mint condition. BDSM magazines basically aren't in print anymore--the Internet takes care of that need. The magazine publication dates here include 2000, 2002, and 2005--at least the ones I can see without touching. But they haven't been opened, well- thumbed, or propped up during masturbation. They're pristine.

I look at the knots on Raymond's body again. He has no safety measures. A person engaged in self-bondage needs to have a self-release mechanism or risk death. If using manacles, a key can be frozen in ice, or salt can block the lock mechanism until water is poured on it. For ropes and cords, the knot has to have a trick release or a blade nearby to cut. But I don't see a blade or EMT shears near Raymond's bed or anywhere he could conceivably reach from the bed.

I use my phone camera to take pictures of the room, the paraphernalia, and his body with the knots. I see no other indicator of sex like semen stains, although autoerotic asphyxiation victims sometimes ejaculate after death.

So according to the narrative the scene is trying to present Raymond blows off both me and his sister, meets a stranger in a coffee shop and gets sick, leaves with the stranger and disappears for two days, and comes back in the middle of the night or very early morning to play self-bondage in a room as cold as an ice truck. No, I don't think so.

I go back to my car and call the police. I also call Jim for protection. I sometimes work for both Jim and Michaela, but they don't usually have to represent me as Mikki just did with the assault charge. The charge that should be dismissed in six months unless I get in trouble, like being found in an apartment with a dead body.

According to Jim's secretary, he's in a judge's chambers at the moment. I know he cannot up and leave that situation, so I ask that he show up at the apartment or the precinct ASAP.

Before the police arrive, I call Toni. She's already at the First Precinct waiting for me. I feel I should be the one to tell her about Raymond rather than the police. The conversation is very difficult because I don't tell her much more than Raymond is dead, and she understandably becomes hysterical. Finally, she says she's coming over as I see the first uniformed officers arrive.

I enable the password lock on my phone and turn it off. Then I start talking. First to the uniforms, and then to a couple of detectives who show up shortly thereafter, I explain the situation three or four times. Yes, I shouldn't have walked in the bedroom, but I didn't know he was in there dead. Yes, I was given permission to enter the apartment from the next of kin, his sister. See? I have a key. Yes, I had met him previously. No, I didn't touch the body. Yes, I do think someone hurt him but don't know who.

Toni then arrives at the building. Her overwhelming grief accentuates a misery I'm developing on my own, a sudden sadness that I couldn't help the man who had wanted to hire me. Toni is adamant that somebody killed him, and I feel the same way.

The process of legal death investigation continues through the next few hours. Toni is taken into the apartment briefly, and then one of the detectives escorts her away to question her. The second detective has the uniforms secure the area in front of Raymond's building, and to keep me detained outside, waiting next to a police car.

I'm not allowed to go to my car. I'm an automatic suspect because I found the body. I expected that, so I just watch crime techs come to process the apartment. They also get DNA swabs from me, which I allow. The precinct has notified the NYC Office of Chief Medical Examiner, so a Medicolegal Investigator from that office shows up at the scene. She goes in and out of the building and asks questions. Eavesdropping carefully, I hear her okay an autopsy. The body is brought outside in a bag to travel to the Medical Examiner's office in Manhattan.

By this time, a small crowd has developed across the street and more people are watching out windows. I can't hear what they're all saying but I imagine speculation and rumor spreading like a virus. They might think someone famous died--Heath Ledger lived not too far from here, and other young celebrities like this neighborhood. A local news truck shows up, and then another. That suggests a juicy story is developing and so the crowd begins filming with their phones. Déjà vu. I turn away rather than be part of another YouTube frenzy.

Too late for that. I'm recognized, and a few catcalls begin. One of the detectives comes out of Raymond's building and tries to interrogate me where I'm waiting, but the news reporters and general public interfere with his questioning. So he has me get in a police car to go back to the First Precinct.

I am taken to an interview room, and proceed to answer hostile questions. The two detectives team up to catch me in a mistake or a confession. I have nothing against them, understanding their position even if they can't appreciate mine. They're probably good detectives but they don't want to listen to me and my theory. Cop tunnel vision.

They demand to know why I was in the bedroom of a dead man who was bound and choked, but they seem indifferent when I express my gut instinct that Raymond was murdered. I tell them about Raymond getting sick at Cafétière Maléfice with a mysterious man taking him out--caught on video, which they should have and I tell them to look at. They don't seem interested. Both are scornful of my narrative that Raymond was not there the previous time I had been in the apartment.

Both the forty-something detectives--a black man named Smith and a white woman named Jacobsky-- suggest I killed Raymond and then came back later to "discover" the body, probably to get attention in the press--I liked media coverage, probably got off on it. Look what I did last week in Jersey. Clearly, I enjoy instigating violent situations and making myself the hero from some warped psychological need. Or *maybe* I set the murder up as a means of improving my public reputation after the disaster in New Jersey.

As a poor kid who lived in rough neighborhoods, my friends and I, particularly black, Hispanic, and queer, had been routinely hassled by law enforcement so I'm used to the methods. Smith and Jacobsky don't scare me and I'm not provoked to say anything other than I already have.

They decide on another tactic--that I killed Raymond in a sexual accident. The good cop/bad cop routine starts: "If you killed him in a hook-up, we understand. It got out of hand; he wanted you to do things you didn't like."

Good Cop is played by Smith. He is sitting across from me at the gunmetal gray table. His hands are open, friendly. *Talk to me, buddy*, his body language says. *I understand why you killed the perv.*

"If you don't tell us, people will assume the worst. You already seem like a real sleazy motherfucker from those videos. Don't piss away your chance to get the real story out--before we lose patience." Jacobsky plays Bad Cop. She's on her feet, leaning forward, getting in my space. She's the voice of doom. *Make me happy or it's the chair for you.*

I turn to look at the two-way mirror on the far wall, where someone is no doubt watching us. I'm getting past my initial shock of finding Raymond and getting impatient. "Are these two for real," I ask the mirror.

"Out of all the people Booth knew, *you* were the one with the body. What would you think in our place?" Jacobsky is snarling. "We *know* you were there. The DNA proves it."

"A DNA result in an hour? Are you *CSI Miami*?" I light a cigarette. They aren't stopping me, even though the building is no smoking. Letting me light up will convince me they're my best buddies and I'll cry a confession on their shoulders. My cell phone is on the table in front of me next to my Camels and the lighter. The detectives couldn't open it, and I wasn't going to unlock it for them, since then they would be able to search it legally. That makes them extra mad at me for being insolent.

"What is it, Gabriel? Did you find out he already had a boyfriend? I'd be angry too. I can't blame you for that." Smith, waiting for me to break down and clear my conscience.

I stare ahead at the wall, smoking.

"He did something to make you sick, didn't he? He hurt you and you were defending yourself, right?"

I take my glasses out of my pocket, and polish them. "Do you have an arrest warrant, or what?"

They ignore that and continue spinning scenarios of why I killed Raymond and what would happen to me--a known homosexual--in prison if I didn't confess immediately. If I told them how this was a lover's quarrel gone wrong, I could walk out with a sweet plea deal. One must understand that cops are allowed to lie their asses off to a suspect during interrogation. No one's going to sue them for broken promises.

My long experience in ignoring years of my father's drunken tirades against me come in handy to tune out these two.

Jacobsky begins a litany about how I should talk now, before I embarrass my family. Now I'm tempted to laugh--she obviously doesn't know my family. But she continues. "You admit he picked you up in New Jersey, after you were arrested for *assault*. You get into violent encounters."

I shake my head. "I don't *admit* he picked me up, I *state* it. He didn't pick me up for sex, as you're suggesting. He wanted to talk business. And I *state* again he was supposed to hire me and he was supposed to meet with his sister. Did you even see the video feed of him in the coffee shop? If I'm telling you anything, I'm telling you someone else--probably the other man in that video--drugged him and killed him."

"Maybe it was you on the tape, playing some sick game."

I'm getting edgier. Jim hasn't shown up yet, and these Glimmer Twins are starting to sound as if they really believe I have something to do with Raymond's death. I interrupt Jacobsky. "Charge me or let me go for God's sake. This is ridiculous."

"We'll charge you." Jacobsky leans close so the video camera in the room won't pick up her next words. "And maybe we'll lose the paperwork for a few days. See how you like the Tombs on your own with no lawyer to bail you out."

The Tombs is officially called the Manhattan Detention Complex, a temporary downtown jail for arrestees awaiting arraignment or trial. Built on a swamp in the 19th century, it's been sinking literally and figuratively ever since. It's the place of suicides, riots, fires and fights. Cinderblock and metal cells each hold upwards of a couple dozen drunk, angry, scared or mentally ill persons. People think of Riker's Island as the New York City jail, but an arrestee goes to Riker's after being held in the Tombs. Riker's is a country club by comparison, but granted it's a comparison of a pretty low standard to start.

I'm now mentally preparing to cause trouble. I don't appreciate threats, and I know they can carry it out and get me lost for a couple weeks. But then door swings open and an older white man in a suit gestures both of them to leave the room.

I can't hear what they are talking about, but through the small square glass window in the door I see Jacobsky and Smith's faces, and they are not happy. They argue with the other man, and then both of them turn and walk away. The man opens the door again. "You can leave, Ross."

He waits, holding the door open. I stare at him in surprise. Just like that. Of course, I know legally they have no reason to hold me anyway, but I'm not being sprung by the NYPD's Civil Rights Division, even if one existed. "Who are you?"

He hesitates, scanning the room. "Lieutenant Robert Clarke."

I stand up. "What happened? Why all of the sudden I can leave?"

He comes in the room and unplugs the camera, then turns and meets my eyes. "Are you stupid? Don't question things. Just go. Go home and count your blessings."

I put my cigarettes and phone in my jacket pockets with my glasses. "Did you catch someone else?"

Clarke turns his back to me and slowly winds up the cords on the machine. "Ross, you know Lt. Greene, right?"

"Yes, I do. We're friendly." Andrew Greene is a good cop who just received a long-overdue promotion supervising a homicide squad. He is my one friend on the force in the NYPD.

"Well, he and I go back a few years, so I'm telling you this: walk out now and go home. The case is closed. When the system wants a closed case, don't question it."

Of course I still want to question it, but I leave anyway. Clarke does not look at me as I pass him.

Outside the precinct, I start to unlock my phone to call Jim, and then see him heading up the block. He's a trim dark-haired Jewish man a couple year older than me, and usually appearing aggravated. He stops to look aggravated at me now. "I see you are somehow walking free."

"I don't know why." I shake my head. "They were pretty sure I did it." I light another cigarette. "As a matter of fact, I find being thrown out now very strange. I want to go back and talk to the Captain in charge. I want to find out what--"

Jim has my arm and is dragging me down the street, to the amusement of several uniform cops standing around. "I may have come late, but at least I can stop you from being a fucking idiot. No way in hell you are going back in there. Are you insane?"

I protest with what Jim calls the stupid naïveté of the innocent. But he knows what he's doing. At the corner he flags a taxi. "We'll get you locked in at home so my blood pressure can go back to normal." Jim rubs his eyes. "First you stir up shit in New Jersey, now you're finding bodies in your own turf. On the bright side, at least you got me out of the Kaiser's courtroom early before he could start in on me why I haven't made all my clients plead guilty and save him time from actually presiding over a trial."

I have the taxi go back to Raymond's neighborhood so I can retrieve my car. On the way I call Toni, but she's not answering. Jim is still grumbling over criminal court judges and certain clients who aren't helping him earn a living--meaning me. I ignore this.

"Can you find out anything about why they let me go?"

Jim rolls his eyes dramatically. As a defense attorney, he believes cops, Feds, and Homeland Security are chomping at the bit for an excuse to imprison and torture troublemaking private investigators. Of course, I haven't exactly disabused that notion lately. "Why don't you just ask the cops to take you down to the basement and whale on you Giuliani-style? You do understand you're supposed to stay out of trouble for the assault to be ACD'd? Yet I hear your name on the local Fox news station again. I hope the jackass judge in New Jersey doesn't watch TV."

"Nuts; you're a damn drama queen like all defense attorneys. You enjoy talking to your spies in the NYPD; it makes you feel all Woodward and Bernstein."

"Cops will lie for the practice. Okay, schmuck, I'll ask--I know you won't leave me the fuck alone until I do. In the meantime, try to practice your so-called 'Buddhism' and don't hit anyone else or dig up more dead people in the near future. It won't help in defending the lawsuit."

"Don't worry. I'm as judgment-proof as you can get short of being on the street."

Although we laugh about that, inside I know I'm not done with this case. I need to find out what happened to Raymond. On that thought, I head home to brood.

∞

FIVE ♦ THE ACE OF WANDS

The Ace of Wands represents a rebirth of ideas and energy; developing a new identity in that idea, gaining a fire in the spirit that will attract others.

∞

Monday, July 12, Continued
Alphabet City, Avenue A 2:10 pm

AT HOME, I FEEL LIKE the scent of death is permeated in my skin. This is psychological; Raymond hadn't decomposed enough for that particular unforgettable odor. But I still have the need to shower for a long time and try to transition back into life. Then I pour a large whiskey and soda to drink in front of the TV, hoping to put myself to sleep. I never like to get really drunk. Too often during my adolescence my father would return home hammered from whatever Army base he was stationed and try to fuck me up--criticizing, berating, belittling. I'm not going to do that to myself or anyone else. Instead I try to forget about what happened today.

But in my dreams, I relive finding Raymond's body; each time he's in a different place. In the apartment, in the black car, the coffee shop, the police interrogation room. At one point, he shows me a video of himself on the coffee shop computer, saying I stole his life, his consciousness, his world. *I was trying to find you*, I tell him. *I wanted to work for you.*

I wanted to extinguish the evil and tell the truth. How could I know what happened to you? After each dream, I wake up sweating, and then lie down staring into space, afraid to sleep again.

∞

Tuesday, July 13

On Tuesday, I send Toni flowers and most of her retainer minus a minimal fee. She calls me after she receives the flowers to say Raymond's body is to be released. His memorial service and funeral are taking place this coming Friday and she wants me to come to the service. A week from when I met him. Toni's voice is slow and heavy, but I can't blame her now for being medicated.

True to what Clarke said, the police do not follow up with me. I keep hoping that they will look into the man in the videotape, but I see nothing in the news. The stall on the case mystifies and angers me.

But in the meantime, the media has a blast in an otherwise slow news week. Because some idiots decided I'm controversial, Raymond's death is exploited. *Lawyer Offs Himself in Kinky Self-Sex Ritual,* one of the local tabloids proclaims tastefully. With the subheading adding *Preacher-Punching Detective Finds Body of Missing Man.*

The local television stations aren't much better. "...Booth's body was found by local private investigator Gabriel Ross, who is already a notorious figure for assaulting a controversial preacher in New Jersey last week. Sources tell our News Department that Ross has a habit of inserting himself in cases that may earn him publicity...."

"...authorities have not explained why Ross was in the lawyer's apartment, and the elusive private eye has refused to comment..."

"...so this is the guy who's claiming he was fighting bigotry, but now he's in some kind of sex scandal. That just shows..."

Raymond's connection with me makes his death news, with the 'kink' element added. The YouTube videos of my fight with Rev. Bunton go viral again. Reporters persist in calling me. I try to turn the situation around by telling a couple of reporters that I don't think Raymond's death is an accident--I hold back about the coffee shop video for now. But my opinion is further portrayed as evidence of my "radical" activism and "penchant for causing public disturbances."

A couple of news programs even stretch the story by bringing in BDSM experts to offer viewers a titillating view into sex clubs--which have nothing to do with this--and unsafe practices like asphyxiation. Really it's just an excuse just to gawk at a sex club, Raymond's death serving as the entrance fee. I know not all journalists are like this, but the feeding frenzy of getting something, anything, first creates a pack of jackals who desperately want to tie me into Raymond's death somehow; creating a story that I was the cause of his death, I was his pick-up, I was investigating *him* for something terrible he did. I don't tell any journalist about Raymond wanting to investigate the Nazi connection at the Foundation, but the Foundation's name appears in the stories. No one connected to the Foundation comments, so the reporters go back to snapping at my heels.

Although the blood work won't be completed for a few weeks, someone in the Medical Examiner's office leaks the cause of death as asphyxia by strangulation (of a sexual nature) and the manner of death as accident. The NYPD doesn't comment on that bit of information, but again an anonymous Department source says the case is considered closed. When I'm asked if I agree, I say no. Media commentators construe my open disagreement as merely an attempt to drum up business for myself.

My anger continues to simmer during the week as I become more convinced Raymond was set-up. Some of the several hundred books shelved and stacked in my apartment are on medical, psychological, and forensic topics. I take out Brent Tuvey's book on forensic profiling and feel partially vindicated in reading on autoerotic asphyxiation death scenes. Raymond's doesn't match the profile. His bedroom and body had no safety measures and no evidence of prior injuries from past experimentation, or even padding to prevent a telltale ligature mark.

∞

Friday, July 16
East 96th Street, 2:00 pm

My self-assurance feels quixotic when I attend Raymond's service in an uptown Manhattan funeral home. Raymond's colleagues, family members and assorted acquaintances have gathered in mourning. The attendees also include a few members of the sightseeing public and some press. The dividing line between the sacred--the spirit leaving the body--and the profane--the obsession with the material. I'm here to pay my respects but I feel I'm wearing an invisible sandwich board proclaiming my suspicions.

Toni stands next to the casket with an Asian man in his forties, an older white woman and adolescent boy. When the man speaks to Toni, she pointedly looks elsewhere. He starts to touch her arm, and she jerks it away. He sighs, which I can hear from several feet back, and then he walks away. I use that opening to approach her and give my condolences.

She leans on my shoulder, red-eyed. I see a new burn scar on her fingers, as if she held a cigarette too long. "I'm glad you're here. I didn't want this to be public, but I didn't have the choice over the matter. *He* did the arrangements." She gestures to the Asian man, now speaking to a group of people across the room.

"Who's he?"

"Allen Cheng. Raymond's partner. But forget him. You never got to meet my son. This is Adam. And my mother, Julia."

I offer my sympathy to them both. Adam gives me an intense look much like his uncle, whom he resembles. I flash back on my own uncle Dominic again; he also died suddenly in an accident. Julia accepts my hand with grace and thanks me with a reserved sadness. A sense of guilt makes me hear her words as: thanks for causing her son to be thrown in the front-page news as some kind of deviant.

Toni walks away with her family. I finally face the casket to view Raymond as the undertaker has restored him. His face looks cosmetically peaceful and flat, his body in repose. I can't match it with my recurring nightmares. I expect him to open his eyes and stare at me again. *Well*...he'd say. *What will you do about it? What kind of man are you? If you feel bad about me, are you going to walk away or search for the truth?*

At least the reporters don't come to the casket, giving him some dignity. I murmur to myself, to him. "...the multitudes of devas and human beings of the present and future I now sincerely entrust to you to deliver with your great, miraculous power and skillful means so they will never again fall onto the evil paths of existence." From *The Sutra of Bodhisattva Ksitigarbha's Fundamental Vows*. Then I start a Buddhist chant..."*Om mani padme hum...*"

I realize someone is standing beside me now and stop chanting. A white man in his early thirties. He wears a black jacket over a white shirt. His expression is sad and lost. He's medium height, thin, olive skin tone, dark straight hair, and dark eyes. He doesn't look at me when he speaks in a flat affect.

"You found him."

"Yes, I did. Are you a friend?"

His face takes on a pained expression. "Raymond was my significant other. I suppose no one says 'lover' anymore and 'boyfriend' doesn't do it justice. Toni doesn't want to admit it, but it was still true. Maybe we would've even gotten married."

"Nurse Ratched." I say this without thinking, realizing he is John Harrison.

He stiffens and turns from staring at Raymond to glare at me. "How do you know that? Were you sleeping with him?"

His hostility might put me on the defensive, but I know grief makes a person lash out. "No, of course not. That never happened. I was trying to find him after he disappeared on Friday."

"So you say. We were planning to have dinner Friday night so he could talk to me about picking you up from jail. Raymond said he was hiring you because he *admired* you."

"I don't know that he admired me, but I was planning to work for him."

"He went to Jersey to pick you up, didn't he?"

"Yes. We talked over his business concerns. I didn't hear from him afterwards."

Harrison looks me over scornfully. "How do you know my Gmail address?"

I shift around, uncomfortable. "I saw it in the course of searching for information to try to find him."

"Did you like it there? Did you think you would stay there after he picked you up?"

I have no answer to that; his raging emotion leaves me silent. John turns back to Raymond. He touches Raymond's face and hand with an intimate gentleness that makes me feel like a seedy voyeur. I move to allow him privacy, sit down, and repeat the chant to myself, closing my eyes and shutting out the room. After some time I look back at the casket. John has left.

I consider taking off as well. I feel nothing but grief and recrimination. I get up and walk to the doorway, surveying the viewing room. I see Toni speaking animatedly to her mother and son, and Allen Cheng talking with a small group. I recognize a couple of them from the Foundation website, including the director Ethan Nelson. Nelson catches me observing him; a spark of something shows in his eyes. My dark feelings turn into curiosity, and I start to consider the possibility of finding out something instead of just leaving.

But then someone else is suddenly standing in front of me. "Gabriel Ross?"

He's a man of Indian descent a few inches taller than my 5'9 and about my age, with a deep voice and an upper-class British accent. His skin is tan. Curly black hair in a ponytail, neat goatee. He's wearing a blue linen shirt and black linen jacket and black pants. He has dark eyes with long lashes.

"Yes, I suppose I am--depending on who's asking."

"I would like to speak with you, if you don't mind. My name is Alex Shenoy Barclay. I'm a reporter with the New York *Herald Standard*." The *Herald Standard* is the haughty newspaper rival of the *New York Times*.

I realize he's part of the small contingent of reporters present, waiting to squeeze the last juice of the story. *Sexually suspect scandalous attorney is surreptitiously laid to rest. Pugilistic private eye with a penchant for pummeling preachers crashes party.* Film at 11. Stop the fucking presses.

I'm a little disappointed Barclay is a journalist, since he's attractive. But right now, I despise the press. I give him my best evil eye. "I don't think so. You people have some balls to be here, you know."

I start to move around Alex Shenoy Barclay but he steps in front of me. My eyes lock with his in annoyance. He's ever so slightly amused, and in our exchange of looks I get a flash of chemistry. Forget it, I tell myself. He's a Goddamn reporter. Probably looking for another quote on Raymond or my "public disturbance" activities. I put on a cold expression--which isn't easy the longer I look at him. "Hey, I've had enough of the Fourth Estate for one lifetime."

"I can understand; I saw what's been said about you. Not what I'm trying to do." He smiles sympathetically and briefly grips my arm. A little tingle there with the flirtatious touch; my mouth gets dry.

"I'm not here for exploitation, I think something's up with his death. I wanted to check out the persons involved; one of our staff photographers is here as well, and I asked her to be discreet for the family's sake."

I hesitate, trying to see sincerity in his dark eyes.

He's still smiling. "What were you chanting to yourself?"

"Excuse me?" I notice then that Ethan Nelson is watching us in his peripheral vision. "Let's go to the lobby."

"Of course."

We walk out together. No one is in the lobby at the moment, which makes talking more comfortable. He hands me a business card. "I walked by you before. You sounded like you were chanting."

"A Buddhist mantra. Associated with Avalokitesvara." The bodhisattva embodying compassion.

He smiles and holds out his hand to shake. "Yes, I thought so. I know that one."

I put his card in my pocket and take his hand. My years of playing poker help in pretending touching his hand isn't fine as hell. His gaze suggests he knows anyway.

"Why take pictures of the funeral?"

"I doubt we'll use them in any story. I just wanted to have them on hand. As I said, I'm not here to harass you. I'm interested that you disagree with the police and ME's conclusion about the cause of death. Did you happen to read the item in the New York *Scene*?"

The *Scene* is a NYC weekly distributed free in plastic newspaper bins on street corners in lower Manhattan. The paper has a reputation of being edgy and antiauthoritarian; it's known for scathing reviews of every Broadway show that opens, a hatred of the mayor--regardless of who the mayor happens to be, and muckraking political stories. The *Scene* is good at making a fuss through innuendo, and the editorial board is not afraid of threats from public figures. "No, I didn't. What did it say?"

"A short bit on page three, the *Thin Blue Line* column. An anonymous source--the best kind--said that Raymond Booth was murdered and that the police are not looking for the murderer because Booth was gay and died in an unorthodox manner."

"Okay, and?"

"I thought *you* might have been that source."

I shake my head. "No, I wasn't."

"Do you believe that?"

"That I wasn't the source? Yes, I do believe that."

He gives me a half-smile. "Do you believe Raymond Booth was murdered?"

I hesitate a moment. "As I've said before, yes. I don't know the police department's motive for dropping the investigation, though."

"Do you have a particular reason to believe he was murdered? Is the police evidence wrong?"

"The *interpretation* is wrong about his death. The police aren't following up on..." I stop from saying anything more. Barclay raises his eyebrows. For a minute, we stare at each other, and clearly with something stronger than professional interest. I want to say more but I'm hesitant. I'm so tired of being screwed over by the press. I imagine he could be flirting just to get me to get me to say something and then eat me alive...in print, I mean.

Hmm. Shouldn't have had that last thought.

"The other rags in the city have really cocked it up about you. I understand if you don't favor speaking right now."

I have a thing for voices and accents; his British slang gets to me. I decide to tell him. "Raymond was on tape in a coffee shop shortly before his death. It shows--to me, anyway--that someone drugged him and kidnapped him."

From the look on his face he hasn't heard of this. I give him the lowdown on the Cafétière Maléfice incident.

He writes in a little notebook. "I'm going to check that out straight away. Any other problems you know of?"

Nelson drifts by the doorway to the lobby, which puts me on guard. "Nothing I'd talk about now. I was ready to leave; the funeral has been pretty tough."

"Maybe we could talk at a later time?" I hear an undercurrent to the suggestion. Ahem. Maybe the press isn't *that* bad.

"Well, maybe. Why?"

"I have a feeling that you're right. I'd like to discuss it with you. If you want, what you tell me will be off the record."

I fumble in my pockets for a business card. "Here's my number."

"Is that your office or mobile?"

"It's both. I'm not hard to find."

"And yet you're the proverbial good man." Unexpectedly, he holds out his hand again after putting the card in the breast pocket of his jacket. A warm, strong grip that lasts a fraction long. He briefly puts his other hand over ours, another indicator of his interest.

I watch him walk out the funeral home front door, and continue watching him through a window. I can hear music coming from a truck on the street, something exotic and mystical like Sufi music. He glances over his shoulder and catches me looking at him and smiles, making me smile back.

If he is being honest, his approach is surely a welcome change from the rest of the media jackals. I calm down from my romantic inclinations and make a note to find that article in the *Scene*. So, Toni and I are not the only persons who think Raymond was killed. Alex's conversation gives me a shot of encouragement; now I feel a need for instigating some action.

At that moment, Raymond's partner Allen Cheng pokes his head into the lobby and catches my eye. I take the opportunity to introduce myself. He already knows who I am.

"Raymond mentioned he was hiring you. I asked around about your reputation."

"He sure as hell was busy trying to hire me that day. Did he say much about it?"

Cheng shrugs. He wears a suit as good as Raymond's on the day I met him. Black silk fabric with faint lighter black stripes, platinum cuff links. "No, he was going to talk to me some more, but we had difficulty finding spare time. You know how that goes--you work for lawyers."

"Yeah, I'm well aware of the time issue. Did he mention he wanted a matter investigated concerning his Foundation? Are you on it as well?"

"I knew it was *about* the Foundation. I'm not on the board but some other Foundation people are here."

"I thought so. Can you point them out to me?"

Cheng appraises me thoughtfully. "You want to meet them?"

"I'd like to talk to them."

"You're not working on his case still?"

I meet his skeptical look with an earnest face. "Raymond disappeared and was killed before he could actually hire me. But I'd still like to follow-up on some matters."

I see he's intrigued. He gestures for us to go to a more private corner near a coatroom. Away from the funeral attendees, he folds his arms and focuses intently on me. "So what are these matters you are looking into?"

∞

SIX ♦ THE PAGE OF WANDS

The Page of Wands represents information, drive and foraging ahead--but needing to be careful not to be lost in the whirlwind of the journey.

∞

I MATCH CHENG'S BODY language with my own intensity. "For one thing, the matter of his death. You probably know I don't believe he killed himself by accident or design."

"You found him." Cheng cocks his head with a little smile. "Didn't you believe it was a sexual pick-up gone wrong?" A faint hint of sarcasm tells me *he* doesn't believe it.

"Hell no. He was killed. Did the police talk to you at all?"

"A detective called me the day you found him. He asked if I knew of Raymond's sexual habits or anyone who'd want to hurt him, which I don't."

"Did this detective mention that someone had possibly abducted him?"

Cheng fails to answer, looking shocked. I give him the same info I had just told Alex Barclay. "I'd bet money on Raymond being murdered--if I had any. He was set-up, and that likely means the killer knew him. The killer may even be *here.*"

Cheng regards me with a hint of, dare I say, respect. "Hum. That's quite a hypothesis. Who's paying you on this?"

"No one. My job for Toni in searching for him ended with his death. Let's say I'm satisfying my own curiosity."

Cheng shakes his head. "You need to be careful concerning that."

"Why so? Do you have objections?"

"Not in principle. But...come talk to me at the office sometime. For now, regarding the Foundation Board..." He leads me back to the doorway of the large viewing room, and in an undertone points out Foundation board member Eleanor Whitford (the woman who brought the Nazi matter to Raymond's attention) and Ethan Nelson, who has been dogging my footsteps. Cheng also identifies a few other board members including one who is rudely staring at us, name of Dr. Kelly Cole.

After thanking Cheng I decide to go over to Cole first, since his glare is freaking me out. He's in his fifties, tall, White and thin. "Dr. Cole? I'm Gabriel Ross; I was investigating a case for Raymond. Do you mind if I talk to you for moment?"

"I don't think this is a good time to be talking. We're at a funeral."

"I could speak to you at a later time?"

Cole's face is expressionless, but his voice is hostile and pointed. "About what?"

"Raymond and the Foundation."

"You are way out of line even being here. The Foundation's concerns are for the board members. People like you need to stay out of our business." On that happy note, he departs for the other side of the room. I make a mental note to find out what car he drives, and key it.

Toni comes up from behind me and snakes both her arms around my right one. "What was that?"

A tendril of hair has come loose from her chignon. I tuck it behind her ear. "I wanted to understand his working relationship with Raymond. But I don't think he had one."

"He's a prick. I'd feel sorry for him--his wife just left him and his daughter keeps getting picked up for shoplifting. But he's such a tight-ass bastard."

"Yeah, I got that impression."

She lets go of me sits on the corner of a padded folding chair. "Why were you asking about Raymond?"

I'm wound up enough to speak without thinking. "I'm still interested in what he wanted investigated."

Toni rises halfway and grabs my arms; she seizes upon my words with excitement. "Does it have anything to do with him being killed?" Her voice raises a little on the last word and a few people glance at us. Cheng subtly shakes his head. I get the signal. Don't say too much to Toni. Clearly she and he are in conflict. But I have a feeling it's too late.

"I can't say, but I'd like to know."

"I want to as well, Gabriel. Somebody here killed him, I just feel it. Don't you *feel* it?"

I try to calm her by touch, getting her to sit back down. I speak softly. "Yes. This isn't the place to start an investigation, but I wanted to get a sense of who these people are..."

"Go for it. Raymond would have done the same. None of those Foundation people even care that he's dead."

"What about Ms. Whitford, though?"

"Yeah....I suppose she'd be the one exception." We look around and I see Whitford with a group of other people. I squeeze Toni's hands. "Don't get yourself upset. This is a tough day. Let me handle this--I'll go talk to her."

But Cole is one of the persons gathered around Whitford, and he gives me a nasty look as I approach. "Are you serious?"

I ignore him and turn to Whitford. She's probably 70, white, in a long black dress and sweater. She has clear eyes and elegant upswept hair. "May I speak to you privately, Ms. Whitford? My name is--"

"You need to leave her alone."

Whitford looks from Cole to me. I lean towards her ear and say *sotto voce*, "Raymond tried to hire me for your problem--the Nazi."

My words startle her a little. "Just a minute..." She turns to the others and excuses herself. Cole's eyes widen in surprise? Anger? Who cares--fuck him.

Whitford walks with me a distance away from the others and we sit on a couple of empty chairs. "Those were other board members. I don't want them to eavesdrop."

The other board members appear nonplussed but go back to talking. Ethan Nelson, part of the group, continues to observe us. His scrutiny raises my hackles like Cole raised my ire.

"Raymond told me he had found someone to help us."

I nod. "I was, but he disappeared. I'll be honest; I'd still like to work on this."

She clutches my hand out of sight, between the chairs. "And I'd like you to. Please call me. I can't really let anyone else know about it, because in a sense I no longer know who to trust."

I get her number, and I memorize it rather than write it down.

"Can you tell me anything now, regarding names?"

"I'd rather not, at least not here."

"Is Dr. Cole involved?"

"No, I seriously doubt it, but he is very protective of the Foundation. Don't take him personally, please. But I do believe something dangerous is going on." Her expression is apologetic. "You'll forgive me for having to step away abruptly. I'll explain later."

Whitford stands up and backs away from me and assumes an angry expression, speaking louder. "I don't appreciate your tone, and I think you need to mind your own business and leave." In an indignant manner, she returns to the group.

I'm taken aback at first, and then recognize her parting line was for the benefit of others. I shrug visibly and look disappointed to help her cover.

I figure the rest of the board is a no-go until I talk more to Whitford, and maybe it's now time to leave. Before I can stand up, a man sits down next to me. Ethan Nelson.

"Hello." His tone is far friendlier than I'd expect. But then, he's been watching me long enough.

"Nice to meet you, Mr. Nelson."

"You know me? That's good. Call me Ethan, please. I see you have concerns with Raymond. This is a sad day, isn't it?"

"I'd say so. Why do you think I have concerns?"

"You're asking questions about him. Can I help you in any way?"

"I'm sure." I turn in my chair to face him. Nelson is a medium-sized white man almost six feet, short black hair, around 45. He's wearing a muted gray suit and distinctive, grassy cologne. He has a small scar near his right eye he has a tendency to touch.

"Well, I'd like to hear more on Raymond's work with the Foundation."

He seems thoughtful. "As a member of the Board of Directors, he was more active than most. He participated in approving projects, and activities for fundraising. He took the lead on certain events such as auctions and art exhibits."

"I see. Did you get an impression of any trouble at the Foundation?"

Nelson drops his helpful demeanor for a second as he shifts around in his seat, but recovers quickly. "What exactly are you investigating?" He's very self-possessed and deliberate in his movements, but his eyes flicker at my words.

"I'm looking into his death."

His eyebrows arch, he absently touches the scar near his eyes again. "I thought that was established as a personal matter. Tragic, but I don't see how it concerns the Foundation."

"One never knows. If you'd like to help, my question is a start."

Nelson leans forward. "Really, Mr. Ross. I don't see the connection. Are you suggesting that his death was not an accident?" He now has deep concern on his face.

"Who can tell what's going on in *that* place..." Toni has come up next to us. Inside, I try not to wince; she has a determined look, and I feel like that is my fault. "You didn't like him. No, don't give me that con artist charm. He didn't like you either. He probably had good reasons."

Nelson smiles politely. "I'm sorry over Raymond, Antoinette. But you're mistaken. Raymond and I had an excellent working relationship."

"*Bull*shit." A faint mist of saliva is expelled with her words.

I stand and try to draw her away, as an argument isn't going to be helpful in this setting. "Let's talk outside, Toni."

But she shakes me off. "Excellent working relationship? I don't think so. He was better than you, all of you." She looks around to include the few people standing in the room in her invective. "Whatever was happening there, he would have found out. You smirk at me like you're a big shot. Give me a fucking break. If Raymond was still alive, he'd throw you on the street, you fraud."

While Nelson's expression towards Toni is condescending sympathy--for onlookers who are trying to pretend like they're not listening to this--something else has been triggered in his eyes, making them fiercer. His hands twitch almost imperceptibly. I can imagine that if they were alone, he'd slap her.

"Perhaps we can talk again." I give Nelson a version of his own polite smile, and manage to steer Toni away.

But she isn't done. Over her shoulder she glares at the remaining people in the room. "You think you're getting away with it...We'll find out what you did to him...Gabriel's going to find out..." She sweeps her hands out, knocking over a few chairs. Nelson doesn't even react to that, although her hand comes within inches of his face.

I hustle her off a little more forcefully, noting that Cheng is visibly flinching. A few reporters who were on the verge of leaving stop to gawk. I see Julia coming to collect her, and I turn Toni over to her mother with relief. She then collapses in tears. Good opportunity to make my way out of this festival and figure out how I can follow up on the shit that's been stirred.

As I walk by one of the reporters smirks. "Can't let a funeral go without trouble, can you, Ross?" The others laugh.

I give them the finger and leave. I take the subway home, using the ride to listen to Massive Attack, which always fits on train rides, and unwind from being in the house of death. When I get back, I get online and turn up some of Alex Barclay's articles as well as the story in the *Scene*. He's a good writer and mostly handles complex white-collar crime cases. I find his Facebook profile but resist friending him for now. I enjoy his profile photo, though.

My cell phone rings, and turns out to be Alex himself.

"I was just reading some of your work."

"Were you?" He sounds pleased. "Well, I'm hoping you can help me out. I spoke to Nicolas at the coffee shop. He says a police detective took his CD of the video you mentioned, but you might have a copy?"

"I have the file. Strange, I already gave the police a copy of it. But in any case, I can email the video file to you. Did you contact the police as well?"

"Yes, I was able to briefly speak with the detective on the case. But she said she never saw a CD; neither her nor her partner. They asked Nicolas for it on Tuesday, but he said he gave it to another detective on that same Tuesday. No one seems to know who that is."

"Interesting, because Toni and I gave it to the precinct desk sergeant to give to the detectives there. And yet they don't have it, and someone took it from Nicolas as well." Somehow, this doesn't surprise me. A cover-up is working here, and that has some daunting implications.

∞

Seven ♦ The Knight of Swords

The Knight of Swords represents delivery of actions and ideas by the pure of heart, but he may be challenged in a war-like manner requiring the deliverer to armor himself.

∞

THE NEXT DAY Alex has an article on the video I sent him. Few other news outlets follow up on it, as it doesn't fit the narrative emanating from official sources. In the *Post,* the anonymous NYPD mouthpiece used in previous stories suggests that if the video is genuine, it shows the man in cap and sunglasses was a hook-up gone wrong. But the *Scene* is outraged after picking up the story and begins to indict police officials from the Commissioner on down. I make a note to myself to contact the paper.

I'm pleased a story has finally been printed that makes sense-- as well as vindicating Alex's intentions. That keeps me in a good mood doing some work around the city for my remaining clients during the day. My work keeps me out fairly late, until nearly ten. Then I drive back to my neighborhood. Rain started earlier in the day, and is now a downpour. I start the impossible routine of finding a parking space through an endless series of concentric circles around Avenues A, B, and C. My phone rings while I'm still looking.

"Mr. Ross? My name is Peter Bordeaux. You were recommended to me by an attorney. I need someone who can help me on a discreet matter involving my wife."

"Okay. Can we set up a meeting?"

"Could you possibly meet me now? I hate to ask, but I work in the restaurant business so I have odd hours. She's actually working now while I'm off, and I wanted to be sure she wasn't on to what I'm doing, if you know what I mean."

"Sure. I suppose I can. Where are you?"

"I hope not far from you, the Lower East Side. Actually, on Clinton Street between East Broadway and Henry. It's 201 Clinton. I'll pay you for your time, since it's late. But I really need to do something about this. It's killing me."

The address actually isn't that far away, a dozen blocks or so. I'm tired, but the necessity of working means I should look into it. I've done this before.

"Who recommended me to you?"

"John Atwater." Another defense attorney with whom I've worked.

The man continues, "He helped out a friend of mine, also with a delicate matter."

"All right. I'll be there around twenty minutes or so, depending on parking."

"Get a garage, I'll pay for it."

I'm thinking of doing that when I return from this meeting, considering the space problems in my neighborhood. That resolution makes me feel better about heading back downtown to the Lower East Side, just off Canal Street. A few blocks from Clinton Street I put the car away and then walk up.

The rain makes things a little difficult to see. Somehow, I forgot to bring an umbrella earlier the day. The streets in this area are darker, since it's after business hours. Not teeming with life like in Alphabet City. I pass by the Educational Alliance nonprofit, across from a branch of the New York Public Library. Both are closed. I check my phone for any updated messages.

Around the corner, I shut the phone and look for 201, assuming the address will be an apartment building. It's across the street from where I'm standing.

But it's not residential. It's an empty storefront, and covered in a metal grate.

Even in the warm rain, I suddenly go cold. Nothing is around, or so it seems. No one on the streets, no lights on anywhere nearby, no traffic on Broadway. My trouble instinct kicks in.

I remember seeing a bar still open back near the garage. I can go back there and call this man--if he exists.

But it's too late for that. I can feel them materialize even without seeing them. They move from the shadows around me on the dark street. I hear a discordant tone inside my head, a jagged guitar note or drum beat precipitating trouble.

Three men, two to the left and one to the right. They're already starting to circle. Instinctively I back up against the wall of the building behind me. These men wear dark t-shirts and running apparel. I don't see knives or guns. That tells me I've been lured out for a beat-down.

I'm angry at myself for falling for this, for needing the money enough to unheedingly step in this trap. But I have to clear my head due to the danger of the situation. I size up the three white men: one big and thick, one smaller and sinewy, and a medium-sized one. Just like the Three Bears fairy tale. Being against the wall keeps them from completely surrounding me.

They expect me to run so they can grab me easier, and I'm not going to. I've been in fights before, and they don't know me. My resolution is that they will not walk away in the same condition as they arrived.

I've learned in street fighting experience I need to avoid them knocking me to the ground as long as possible, where it's easier to stomp people into unconsciousness and brain damage. Spending too much time with one person leaves you open for the others to crush you. So I keep them all in sight, dropping my backpack behind me. Then I raise my arms in a Baguazhang Single Palm Change stance.

That throws them off a bit, as usually a target tries to escape; in that situation two grab the victim while the third starts the beating. So they hesitate for a moment.

Then the leader, the big one, steps forward to start. He swings viciously and I duck the punch at the last second. His fist grazes my jaw. But he hits the wall instead of fully catching my face. The pain from that makes him double over; without taking time to be pleased about it, I circle around and follow that with a kick to his groin.

In the wake of that move, the smallest of the three tries for a kick to my midsection, which is stupid on his part. I take on the kick with my left arm and hook my right under his calf. The moves are harder as we're slick with the rain coming down, and I can't see as well as I'd like. Nonetheless, by instinct I can I bend his leg, yank him off balance, and swing him into the third man.

That gets them down for a moment, and the big one is back, sort of--jabbing with his other hand and wobbling some. He's taller, and can take some pain. But he hasn't been trained. Several people, including my uncle, have taught me to fight. All the big guy can think to do is swing at my face. I drop my shoulders, bypassing his fists, and get him with a left cross and right uppercut. Then I aim for his body. He brings his arms down to protect my jabs, leaving him open for another left cross. When he falls over from that, my knee connects with his face. That sends him to the street with his head bouncing on the pavement and into a puddle. Good.

Doing that leaves me open. The second man, the medium-sized one, grabs my backpack and slams me on the head with it, then tries to get a strap around my neck. For a second, I'm stunned. My pack has books, none of which goes well against my skull. Still, I can grab the strap and yank him into my space, where I hit him hard in the ribs with my elbow.

The small man is back and trying to grab at my arms. I go inside the pull and head-butt him--my forehead into his nose, which he doesn't expect, but nearly makes me fall as my head is still spinning. He holds his face, but he's red with anger and maybe 'roid rage. I see it in his eyes. He grabs at my arms and we both go to the sidewalk. He attempts to get me in a chokehold. I've fought back from this maneuver since I was 12, and the rain works against his being able to get a grip. I buck up and throw him off balance, then roll away. Now he's facing the ground and I jump on his back, yanking his arm up from behind.

I pull on the small one's arm until the medium guy tries to jump on me, so I yank the small one up and shove him into the other one. The big idiot is out for now, sitting on the curb in a daze. The other two try to figure how to jump me, because I continue to circle. Moving targets are difficult, and attacking at once means they get in each other's way. My attention shifts between them.

The third man tries again with his kick. His balance is off, and I let his rage work against him by dodging the kick, grabbing his leg, and slamming him into the wall behind me.

The medium one, around my size, contemplates me carefully. His hands are better placed as he comes to me, not too close. He knows better. The big one thought his size would be enough, and the small one is just stupid. Just like the fairy tale, the medium one is the best. He's been trained in punching, jabbing, and dodging. Both of us are bleeding, but we ignore it and face each other. I'm playing for time hoping that we'll be noticed and draw a crowd. Way fewer people out in bad weather. If anyone's watching from windows maybe they'll call the cops.

Maybe. You wouldn't think you could feel alone in this city, but it happens.

For a few moments the medium man and I are closing in on each other, both weaving away from each other's arms and legs, both landing hard blows but not hard enough to stop. He tries for my face to throw me off, and I try for his legs to throw him off, because he's not as good with his legs. It keeps him from being able to do anything serious because he doesn't want me getting a hold on him. The small man and bigger one have been out of the game, and I pray, un-Buddhist like, that they are hurting. But they're not completely out. Which is why I know I'm only delaying what they're planning to do, maybe being paid to do. My fight training has helped in keeping them at bay for this long.

My head is now swimming some from the blows and the adrenaline; it throws me off enough in my reflexes to be caught from behind again. Something hard, metallic, hits the back of my legs. Maybe a baton that one of them had hidden. It knocks me off my feet to my knees, onto the asphalt.

A low, angry voice from one of them. "You'll learn not to get involved in shit you have no business being in." I don't know who says it, because I'm trying not to fall down completely.

For a moment, in a situation where I've taught myself not to be afraid, I have a brief despairing feeling of being alone in this desolate street and facing death. It could happen. They could beat me to death right here and no one would come in time. What would my life mean?

A blow to my face wakes me from that brief reverie. I instantly taste blood. I fall again, and bring my arms up over my head and face. Protect what's vital, ignore the pain.

Whatever thing hit my legs before is now slammed against my ribs and on my arms over my head. New sharp, wrenching pain from kicks to my right leg, and my back.

A siren in the distance--finally. As I felt them arrive, I feel it as they leave. At least, no one's hitting me anymore.

I'm aware I'm actually in the street at this point. I force myself to get on my knees. Don't faint. Get to the sidewalk. Every part of me hurts incredibly, and I throw up before I reach the curb. I see blood splattered and mixing with the rain. I get to my backpack. Hold on to it for some sort of comfort. Up the block a police car goes by, the source of the siren, but apparently doesn't see me. Fuck. What if they were going somewhere else? What if these assholes come back?

I'm feeling like I'm about to black out, and I'm scared of internal bleeding. I try to find my phone. It's lying on the sidewalk next to my backpack. Call Danny. My best friend, Danny Martinez. 911 isn't going to help, I think in a daze. Get Danny. We've both been through fights before in the Bronx when we were teenagers.

I can't see the phone anymore; I try by touch guessing where he is on my call list. I hear his voice, concerned, but I can't make out the words.

"Clinton...East Broadway. I was jumped." I think I say it. I must have. The phone slips out of my hand and I try to fight going out.

Somewhere in a dream, I hear a siren closer to me. It could be a minute or a year later, I have no idea. I hear radios, calls for an ambulance. Voices asking me what happened, if I was robbed. I can't respond, even open my eyes all the way. I just feel like it's safe to pass out.

∞

A major metropolitan hospital is an archipelago with chaotic streams swirling around deathly still islands of waiting, boredom and illness. People stare endlessly at each other in the most revealing of poses. Covered in blood, half-naked, tubes in and out.

Ignoring the freak show, Jim is standing on one side of the stretcher and Danny on the other. I've just been wheeled out of a CT scan. I only really woke up when they pulled me out of the machine and put me back in the hallway, to await being returned to the ER area. I have a surge of panic from not knowing what happened up to now, but reassured by them being there.

Danny touches my face gently. "Jesus Christ, you had us scared."

I can see now how he and Jim really are scared. Jim grabs my arm. I almost yell from the soreness, but hold it in so I don't alarm them further.

Jim asks, "What the hell happened?"

I'm starting to feel every place I was hit. Face, head, legs, back, ribs, arms. Nauseous and dizzy, even lying down. "I was jumped. Three guys on the street."

"Gay bashing? The cops doing anything?"

I look from Jim to Danny, who's frowning at my face. I must look wonderful. He's my age, around six feet and well built. Handsome with wavy dark hair and goatee and Nuyorican attitude, which he shows. "Where the fuck did the police go, anyway?"

An orderly arrives to take me back to the ER. Jim and Danny walk beside the stretcher on the way.

I respond to Jim. "I don't think so."

"It wasn't a mugging, though."

"No." I swallow hard, trying to regain equilibrium. I remember what one of the attackers had said. *Learn not to get involved.* It was a warning.

Back at the ER, curtains separate me from a couple arguing on one side and a woman loudly moaning on the other. In plastic chairs a few feet away, a jump-suited and handcuffed prisoner leers at everyone passing by.

"I seem to recall the police were there, and they were writing down some shit, so I guess it's reported." Suddenly I need to vomit again, which causes both of them to turn away. Afterwards, I lie back down, wishing for morphine for my aching head and other places. The female half of the couple behind the curtain to my right mutters aloud about my vomiting. "God, that's disgusting."

Danny pokes his head through the curtain. "Shut the fuck up, why don't you?" Then they curse each other in Spanish and Russian.

To add to the potential international incident Danny's inciting, Jim stops and argues with a passing nurse to get the doctor back here unless the hospital wants to risk a major malpractice lawsuit.

The nurse in turn insists that a doctor is coming. No doubt sometime between two and 24 hours from now. Probably the latter since Jim told the nurse he was a lawyer. I consider how much of this treatment my very cheap emergency insurance covers, which makes my head hurt worse. Danny and Jim sound like angry bees to me, and the noise becomes a little fuzzy. I close my eyes.

"I was set up. Someone lured me out."

I can't stand lying down, despite the pain. I need to see what's going on around me. I force myself to sit up, getting another wave of nausea.

"Who?" Jim steps in front of me to block me from moving.

"I'm don't know, man. Someone who said he wanted to meet me for a case. I was an idiot to fall for it. Now I want to find out who it was."

"Take it easy. Let's ensure your head is in one piece first." He and Danny keep hold of me on either side, either to comfort of to keep me from trying to get up and falling off the stretcher. They're trying to calm me down and let me retain my dignity, but getting themselves worked up by doing so.

An intern finally arrives to settle them down a bit. The hospital wants to keep me overnight for observation as indeed I have a concussion, bruised ribs and contusions, but no internal bleeding. I'm disappointed at that, especially as I'll remain waiting in the ER potentially several more hours for a bed to open. On the plus side, a nurse finally gives me a Percodan for the pain and nausea.

"Help me with this, will you?" I'm trying to pull the hospital gown off my torso. Danny helps get it over my head. "What are you doing, man? You need to relax."

"I can't relax. I'm afraid what might happen while I'm asleep. How about you two find my backpack and my books? I have to have something to read."

While I'm talking, I see Alex coming into the ER. He spies me and comes up to my stretcher. "Jesus, you look terrible."

I'm a little shocked to see him show up, but in spite of that suddenly uplifted. He's in a tan shirt and black slacks with an expensive raincoat. I'm sitting up--barely--naked under the gown crumpled on my lap. My still soaking wet jersey and jeans are in a plastic bag on the end of the stretcher. In spite of his opening remark, I have to laugh, which hurts, and I introduce him to Danny and Jim.

Alex then turns back to me. "They heard what happened to you in the newsroom; one of my colleagues recognized your name and called me. I'm sorry this happened. I wanted to come by and make sure you were okay." He scrutinizes my face.

"Just how terrible do I look?" I know I have a huge bruise on my jaw, I can feel it. I've been cut under my ear; it's been patched up. That's what I know about, at least.

"Well...really not too bad. You take a punch well." He smiles. I notice his glance briefly flickering over my torso, which carries the marks from the attackers' hands and the baton. But in spite of the injuries, I'm in good shape from my martial arts and boxing routines. I don't know whether he's looking at the bruises or otherwise.

"It's on my business card, if you didn't notice."

Jim and Danny catch the music of our conversation, exchange glances and decide to go out and recover my backpack from the nurse's station.

I tell Alex the details of the attack, earning more proclamations of sympathy. I'm feeling better already, either from the Percodan or the flirting. Alex leans over and gently touches the side of my face.

"Jesus Christ, three of them. I can't believe you're still walking. You must be something."

I shrug. "I was lucky. If they had serious weapons of any kind, this wouldn't be the same story." But silently I thank those who taught me how to take care of myself.

Alex still looks impressed, and I decide I should allow him that. I start to tell him of how the fight was handled so he can admire me some more, hopefully, until my head starts swimming from the medication.

"You're tired. You won't be able to read the books your friends are supposed to be getting you."

"They're giving us time to talk in private. The books are probably soaked as bad as my clothes. So you had mentioned an idea about professional collaboration?"

"I'd be very interested in collaborating with you." He reaches out to touch the tattoo on my left bicep. "Yin Yang, hmm? In a sun. I haven't seen that one, it's nicely done."

"My own design, however clichéd. I'm into Eastern spirituality. Once I'm out of here, we can meet up and collaborate."

He laughs. "You feel more positive on the press now?"

"I'm starting to. Depends on the person I'm working with, if you know what I mean."

"I think I do. You have any more tattoos?"

I pull away enough of the gown on my lap to show him the side of my left thigh, which has the Japanese Kanji characters for strength and character. He touches that tattoo as well very briefly, tracing one of the characters. "You should have the *om* symbol next."

"Because it's eternal and sacred?"

"You know about it."

"Some. I've read the *Bhagavad Gita.* Where should I have it placed?"

"I'd have to consider it. Perhaps look you over for the right place."

We both have to smile at that.

"You know the symbol, then."

"You have a pen?"

Instead he hands me his smartphone, with some drawing app enabled. I trace the symbol the best I can with a sore hand.

He looks from the phone to me with a glint in his eyes. "Impressive...you must have it in here somewhere already." He touches my head again.

"I'm glad to see you're okay. Unfortunately, I can't stay. I'm afraid if I keep standing here with you not dressed, I'd get us both in trouble."

"I could live with that."

His hand goes over mine. "You need to recover from this. Get better. I'll call you." He nods goodbye to Jim and Danny, who have returned.

Danny unzips my pack and takes out a Sara Paretksy novel. "So, what's up there? How is it a bunch of guys can beat on you and put you in the hospital, and you get a date out of it?"

"I think that's the least I could get, under the circumstances." We all trade insults for a while then the two of them reluctantly leave, Danny promising to stop by my place and see that Archie is okay. I'm just as reluctant to see them go, instantly lonely. Then my other best friend Veronica Gianni calls. She's out of town and on her way back, and having heard my message wants to make sure everything is okay. "I'll be there in a couple hours. Can I do anything?"

"Sneak in a pizza?" I'm starving. Although dinner hour has long passed, a sympathetic aide hears my conversation and sneaks me a tray of food. Of course, that's exactly when a bed turns up, but the aide lets me eat in the stretcher and talk on the phone while he pushes me to the elevator and up to the seventh floor to my room.

∞

Sunday, July 18

The next morning, I give a statement to a couple cops who visit, and then I'm released with a handful of prescriptions. Veronica has recovered my car from the garage off East Broadway to drive me back, with Danny helping. I have bruises and cuts seemingly all over. A few stitches on my arm and on the cut side of my jaw under my ear. I'm recovering from the concussion and various sources of pain. I call the lawyer "Peter Bordeaux" claimed to have gotten a referral from, John Atwater. He's never heard of Bordeaux, and is horrified to hear what happened.

I'm home for the rest of the day, zoned out on Oxycontin. Jim stops to visit briefly and he and Danny lecture me on this and that. The Oxy helps me pretend to assent to their advice. Veronica, who has taken off work for the day, sticks around to take care of me. She's also a private investigator who works part-time for a large firm. A very strong, beautiful olive-toned woman in her thirties, who identifies as bisexual and genderqueer, choosing to use female pronouns. The firm keeps her because she's so skilled at espionage, although she's as little corporate-minded as I am. She keeps the job for the benefits and equipment she can borrow. Every so often she goes rogue as I do. We consider ourselves soul mates and that we were connected in a former life. I tell her about the case with Raymond and show her my evidence--the video and the pictures I took of Raymond's body--for her opinion.

"I agree. He was set up, you were set up." She strokes my head. "You'll get to the bottom of it, after you get better first. Check out those magazines and junk, someone had to bring those over. The whole scene doesn't make sense."

I'm gratified she agrees with my theory. "But no one's hired me to do this."

Her smile for me is always brilliant. "Does that stop you? Something is telling you the situation is off. A higher power asking for your involvement."

"Or challenging me to stay away."

"You don't back off from challenges. You're always fighting the Devil one way or the other. Now I can nursemaid you, but what you really want is someone who knows you to tell you this..." She gestures to my injuries, "...was worth it. It's tied to the case. If you feel you have to pursue the case, then follow your instinct."

Sometime later, I find a voicemail from Toni. She's checking on my recovery, and also reminding me about Raymond--as if I could forget. I almost need to soothe her more than myself.

Alone at night, I feel frustrated. I play around with my Tarot cards with Veronica, looking for a hint what to do now. I keep turning up the Hanged Man, symbolic of suspension between worlds, decision-making. I feel like I know what this is telling me to do. I just have to develop a plan of action.

I don't stay alone, at least over the next day. Jim's wife Ella and his sister Evelyn, who are also my friends, show up to cook and nurse and generally make a fuss. Evelyn was a Sudanese refugee adopted as an infant by Jim's parents, and Ella is of Japanese descent. Both women are just past 30, and they for some reason adore me, much to Jim's detriment when he and I clash. Jim finally got around to telling them what happened and I suspect he'll pay for that later, and I'll in turn pay for his payback.

After some medicated sleep, I feel human. I brave a look in the morning to see what's been in the news. I'm in the news again, this time about the attack. Not surprisingly several stories--but not in the *Herald Standard,* or *The Scene,* quote the perpetual anonymous source who suggests I arranged to be beat down for publicity--thanks Gerry, you fuckwad.

But Alex's article is very sympathetic and carries the implication that the attack on me is curiously timed. I have to agree; someone wants me to know what I'm in for if I continue to investigate Raymond's case.

I slowly begin to work again during the day, doing some background checks for a client. Three canceled contracts from former clients arrive in the mail, the ones who scuttled after the New Jersey incident. Little more to do right now for income. I've been cash-poor before, but I'm aggravated by the unfairness.

Later in the day Veronica comes by to check on me, giving a critical eye to the bruises. "Be careful typing; give your hands a chance to rest."

"Do I look like I'm writing anything? Just checking. On my phone."

I scroll through the new messages. "Oh, my God."

"What?"

"An email with the address *SmokingDharma.*" I look at her with my eyebrows raised.

"What's the significance?"

"It's whom I've heard use that term before."

I open the email. She looks over my shoulder.

Are you okay? -J

"Oh my God!"

"See, I told you. He's alive."

"Well, of course."

I give her my stern expression. "And you haven't been in touch with him?"

"Not for over a year...you know I was after you two broke up, but then he changed his email and didn't tell anyone."

"Typical." This is Joel, my ex. He almost never wrote anything even when we were together, text or email. When he did, he kept it as short as possible. This is the first contact from him in two years. I'm surprised to hear from him, but it's not a bad surprise, although I can't say our relationship ended well. In fact, it ended with me literally walking away from him back in March of 2008.

"So what do you think this is?"

"You have to decode. He heard what happened, and wanted to know if you were all right. Omigod, you have to write back right now." Her tone implies possibilities I don't want to get into. He disappeared after we broke up, and I think it hurt her almost as much since the three of us were extremely close.

"Don't get excited, baby. I'm glad to hear from him, but that's all." I open a reply to the letter, and think for a while.

Veronica digs her fingers into me, impatient. "Just write, already."

"Ow. Hold on. I'd like to check the email headers to see where he is, but he's probably using a proxy..."

"Write." She pokes my shoulder. "Or I'll do it for you."

"I can't trust what you'd say." I smile and write in the subject line: *Open the email and respond for Christ's sake,* which gets Veronica laughing. Then I compose the message.

Thank you for checking. I'm okay. Where are you? I would like to know how you are doing. Please call me.

I pause. *Veronica is here and says hello.*

"Thanks."

"Oh, I'm using you, my love." I send the email.

"How so?"

"We know him. He's not going to write back soon, maybe not at all. I want to know if he reads it. And what his mindset is."

We then get into playing M*A*S*H trivia online. Twenty minutes later, she looks at her phone. "I have a text from a blocked number."

"Check it."

She shows me. A smiley emoticon with devil's horns. I know it's Joel's greeting to her. "See? He loves you. He's just been his infuriating self in disappearing. Maybe..."

She raises her eyebrows. "Maybe? Maybe he's going to come back."

I look down at my phone and shut it off a little too quickly. "I'd be glad to know he's all right."

I don't rise to any hints, or any hope, she expresses. That's not some place I can go, as the hurt is too real still even after two years. In any case, although I am pleased at hearing from him, I'm also dealing with a hollow feeling from my current situation. Like the Hanged Man, in suspension. I think about what Veronica told me the previous day. We're both used to working our own way regardless of whether anyone else thinks it's a good idea. I feel she's right, and I need to find who killed Raymond. The warning isn't going to take.

∞

EIGHT ♦ THE FOUR OF SWORDS

The Four of Swords represents rest and retreat—to gather one's self and continue a struggle after being revived.

∞

Monday, July 19

THE NEXT MORNING I'm able to get up and practice zazen breathing and moves in the martial art of Baguazhang, although it hurts. Circle walking. Practicing the Swimming Dragon, a basic exercise just to get my sense of balance back.

Then I get out of the apartment to visit the Nichiren Buddhist temple around the block, where I sometimes meditate or speak to the monks. After that, I walk to a boxing gym in the neighborhood where I practice. I've slacked off recently, but my ability to hold off the attackers as well as I could reminds me I have to keep my skills sharp. One of members, a casual acquaintance, shows me some kickboxing moves after I tell him about what happened. His footwork reminds me of the kid I used to know when I was around twelve. One of the ones I thanked in the hospital ER. His name was David; he was sixteen, and sized me and my situation up very well--he was also a gay kid from a broken military home.

David taught me some hand-to-hand combat moves. He also inspired my interest in Eastern culture, philosophy and physical techniques of martial arts. He would talk about a Chinese master named Wang Shu Jin, when all I knew was Bruce Lee. Jin was a Daoist master of *chi* and Baguazhang. David made him sound like a legend: a man who could train anybody and lose to no one. David himself had somehow learned all kinds of esoteric points regarding *chi* and developing inner power regardless of one's size, age, or health, and some techniques of Baguazhang. He shared with me a good deal of what he knew. Patiently, calmly, when all I really wanted to do was practice baseball and basketball. Somehow, something told me to listen to him, and he was the first person outside my uncle Dominic to give me the skills to survive to being an adult.

Then my mom and I moved away, as per usual; I never saw David again. But I won't forget his kindness. He taught me to gain control of myself just as I was moving into a phase of school conflicts in Michigan, Minnesota, and the Bronx, where I was born and where my mom moved us back when I was 15. A few years ago, I found a Baguazhang and Taoist master to help me learn more. While we worked well together, I had a conflict with him some months ago. It was my fault, but I haven't been to see him to do anything about it.

Rather than dwell on that, I go to the library for some research.

∞

"*Hunting Evil. The Real Odessa. Finding Eichmann.* Good rehabilitation material. Is there any room for our food?"

I clear my books off the dining table. I should have hidden them before Danny came over. As I take Chinese food containers out of a bag, carefully as my hands are still bruised and sore, Archie jumps up in a chair, waiting expectantly for his share. He's oblivious to Danny's sarcasm.

"So what's the deal with those?"

"I wanted to get some background on Nazis war criminals."

"You have a new hobby, or is this connected with work?"

"It might offer me an idea of which one could be connected to Raymond's Foundation."

"Really?" Danny portions the food between our plates and gives Archie some strips of beef on a soup container lid. "So you're working on his case?"

"I can't just sit around and do nothing."

"I understand that. I know work is slow. But you can volunteer at the Milk Center. Or we catch a Yankees game or even take a weekend trip."

"That isn't what I meant."

"I *know* what you meant." He points a fork at me. "I've seen you do this before."

I first met Danny when I lived in the Parkchester section of the Bronx. We met in John Philip Souza High; a couple years later, we both decided to drop out. Both of us were good students, but didn't care--skipping class was a regular thing. We fought with other students pretty frequently (a way of life in high school at the time), traveled to Manhattan to try to convince gay clubs in the Village to let us in, and got into minor-league trouble around the Bronx. Not serious trouble like dealing or gangbanging, but a few incidences that suggested we were on our way to being sent upstate with the hardcore neighborhood juvenile delinquents.

My mom Katerina Ross had tried hard to keep me on her path. She was a librarian and art lover and cat lover and a gentle but inwardly tough spirit. I was distant from her in my teens when she started seeing my father again after they had been separated for several years. I didn't want anything to do with either of them. So, I stayed at Danny's place (thank God his mother liked me, because his brothers hated my guts) or at Dominic's apartment--the one I now have.

Dominic kept after us. He was my mom's younger brother, a college professor of art history who had made himself an academic success. He was also gay and tried to give his hardhead brat nephew the benefit of his experience. He made Danny and I go with him to the Harvey Milk Center, a LGBTQ youth outreach center, from sheer force of will. He insisted we take the G.E.D. exam, and made us apply for college where he taught at SUNY Midtown. I found out later that around that time he signed me onto the lease for his Alphabet City apartment, which I didn't fully appreciate until I was able to take it over after his death.

Danny and I had been the two smart gay teenagers in school who had to defend ourselves in the heat of the AIDS crisis prejudice. Dominic taught us to connect with rather than run away from others through the G.E.D and college experience. Danny took that to heart and studied poli sci and sociology, then moved on to graduate school and eventually becoming the director of a tenants' rights organization.

Meanwhile Dominic helped me reconcile with my mom shortly before I started college, helped me find internships in the city and in Rochester, and after I graduated with a degree in history and psychology helped me move on to my life of intrigue and mystery by getting me an introduction to Manny. Manny was gay too, and started working as a private investigator in the early Seventies. Although by virtue of his generation very discreet in his professional world, he always would help out someone in the community if needed.

I see a lot of mixed history when I see Danny. We're closer than brothers and getting on each other's nerves worse than a married couple. At the moment, Danny pretends to be casual. "Any job prospects?"

"I'm finishing some articles for *Cultcha*, that will earn spending money. The controversy actually gets them more web traffic, so there I'm golden." *NY Cultcha* is the online magazine I write for on occasion. I've written movie reviews, blogged on politics, Eastern philosophy and LGBTQ issues.

"Well, if you're interested, I've got some important work to do with investigating buildings uptown; I can use a back-up guy to just kind of keep an eye on things."

"Thanks. I'm not too proud to be your bodyguard."

"Bodyguard? How many times did I save your Irish-American ass from being kicked all over Westchester Avenue when we were 16?"

"None. Unless you count running to call your mom saving me."

He throws a soy sauce packet at me. We eat for a while. Then I light a cigarette and search for a Yankees game in my iPad.

Danny joins in a cigarette. "What's really on your mind? Did this guy's death get to you?"

"Yes, it haunts me. But I can still look into the Nazi business that brought him to me in the first place."

"At the moment, you just need to survive. You can't work for free. You did the best you could and that's that."

"I'm well aware. But think about it. Why would the cops close the case so soon? Who was leaking the information from the M.E.'s office? How did the CD with the security video disappear? This shit is getting weird."

"All right. Let's think about it, then. Why do cops close cases?"

"When they get a confession, or a conviction."

"And that didn't happen here." He dishes Archie some more leftovers and then starts cleaning up. "So why else?"

"When no crime occurred...or, when they know who did it but can't prove it."

"Or aren't allowed to. Remember when we were hanging out the summer before we went to college? Over on 229th Street in Wakefield? Just playing ball and the cops rousted us?"

"Yeah, I thought our moms were going to kill us. Those two cops smacked us up in the squad car for mouthing off."

"We didn't know half the guys we were playing; you were with me to visit my cousin, and some strangers showed up to join the game. Suddenly, three squad cars show up and kick our asses."

"It was that one guy from the West side. At the station, they searched him after beating him senseless; they pulled all sorts of shit from his jeans. Crack, probably heroin too. Never saw that guy again."

Danny draws on his cigarette and points it at me. "What else do you remember?"

"The cops didn't bother to apologize for hitting us, nor did they tell our mothers sorry for mistaking us for a drug gang...what are you getting at?"

"Um...shit, maybe I didn't tell you the rest of the story. I talked to my cousin Eddie later on. The guy was from Morrisania. He was dealing of course, but the cops in Wakefield set him free later."

"Are you kidding? He was a little Frank Lucas in training with all those drugs."

"Yeah, and he had protection. From a precinct captain in Morrisania. The word didn't get to Wakefield right away."

"So, case closed. What you're saying is someone's being protected in Raymond's case. Like in Son of Sam; close the case in spite of all kinds of inconvenient evidence about other killers, to avoid embarrassment."

Danny rolls his eyes. "If you want to drag one of your many conspiracy stories into it as a frame of reference, then sure."

"I will, thank you very much. And the press goes along with it...just like, if you'll allow, Son of Sam." One of my hobbies is researching alternate theories of famous crimes. Lincoln, JFK, Jack the Ripper.

Danny nods. "But where do you start on a conspiracy like that? Who has the ability to engineer a cover-up?"

"The Foundation. It has to be a starting point. Raymond told me a Foundation member was associated with the Nazi war criminal. If they can do that, they can influence a police investigation. And arrange to snatch the CD that the detectives never saw."

"A decent working hypothesis. A powerful person or persons have managed to quash the investigation. I can believe it. But what can you do? If this person can influence police procedure, and let's throw in having some punks trying to beat the shit out of you, what more can *they* do? So, accepting that life's unfair, leave it alone now."

His tone is a warning but I'm not worried about his disapproval. He's a mother hen-type and disapproves of my actions quite frequently.

The next day I start reading my new books and learn more on the known Nazi war criminals. Some had gone in hiding like Josef Mengele, and others slipped through the cracks with relative freedom, such as Otto Skorzeny.

But on Friday, as promised, I meet with Danny at his request in his office in the New York Tenants' Action Group (NYTAG). Danny's all business-like: "You ready for that job?"

Volunteers work feverishly in the large outer office, making a racket along with the radio in the background. "Tell me about it."

He proceeds to detail how he is going to have a crew film the conditions of certain slumlord buildings for a program intended to be part of a PBS series. I'm not sure why he wants me there. I don't do bodyguard work. Not because I can't fight, but because I'm not a tall man who looks like a football player. An intimidating physique is necessary to get regular bodyguard work and also not to be challenged on the job. I suspect he's doing this just to keep me busy.

I'm pretty sure I'm listening, but at some point, Danny taps the desk. "You still with me?

"Of course. What did you think?"

Danny goes to check on the front room and make sure no one is getting in trouble, and turns around. "The case is closed, Gabriel."

"Excuse me?"

"Your mind isn't here, it's on Nazis and Raymond Booth." His voice gets softer. "Let it go, man. You've been lucky so far; why push it?"

As my friend, Danny deserves the truth. "I think I can do some looking around. I kind of owe him."

"*Owe* him? Am I wrong, or did he never pay you?"

"No, his sister did."

"Then you don't owe him. Or her. You did your job. Sorry he was killed, don't get distracted."

"Would you really stop if it were you? One of your tenant cases?"

He sits on the arm of my chair and puts his hand on my shoulder. "No. And, I've been threatened by drug dealers and landlords who were fronting for the mob. I know neither of us like to give us, and it scares me. I don't want to go to another funeral."

"To quote Britney Spears, I'm not that innocent. I can trust my judgment on this. And it was my skill that protected me the other day. I haven't lost my competence."

Danny gives up with a sigh. "Well, let's put your skills to work." He returns to discussing the plan for getting in and out the buildings. The participating residents will let us in, but landlords' thugs for hire or resident criminals may hassle the crew. I'll be armed and mostly serving as a lookout. Despite my participation in the discussion, Danny continues eyeballing me with skepticism. When we're finished and I'm leaving the office, he gives me one of his special *I-know-better-than-you* expressions and immediately picks up his phone. I have an idea what's coming.

Back at the apartment, I dispose of a mouse corpse Archie has proudly left for me. I spend some time assuring him what a fabulous mouse serial killer he is, and then prepare to indulge in more Nazi-book reading.

But before I can turn a page, I get a call from Jim. "Hey, what's up? Turns out I was assigned a new case. I need an Omnibus motion on some search and seizure issues. You can handle that?'

"Really? I don't suppose this has to do with Danny calling you today?"

"I never said Danny called me."

"You didn't have to, counselor. You two are about as subtle as Gladys Kravitz on *Bewitched.* I'm still doing my research on Raymond's case, regardless."

"Don't fuck with me, boy. I took on another case today in the Kaiser's court on the premise you would do the research."

"You might *ask* me first. I could use the money, but I can make my own decisions about it."

Jim begins to bluster, and I consider that I still need him to check his police sources.

"All right, all right, I'm doing it. I can do a fucking Omnibus motion in my sleep for Christ's sake."

"Good, won't be any different from your usual work then. I'll email the indictment over."

∞

Saturday, July 24
Alphabet City, Avenue A, 9:43 am

The following morning I'm deep into the motion for Jim when I hear a loud knocking at the door. It's Toni, who has made it past the building security system yet again. I open the door; she hugs me then closes her eyes.

"You look tired," I tell her.

"I haven't slept." She stays in my arms for a moment. Then I take her to my small dining table and pour her coffee. I note that she's medicated but functioning, although her eyes are bloodshot again. We don't do much small talk. She pets Archie and lights up.

Finally, she's ready to talk. "I'm here for a couple things. I'm Raymond's beneficiary on his life insurance. As soon as I got the death certificate from the funeral director, I applied for the benefit. The fucking company just notified me they're not going to pay out because of the sex act part. They say he caused his own death."

She hands me a copy of denial letter from the insurance company, Raymond's death certificate and the autopsy report. Apparently, the blood work came in and revealed nothing. Yet I can't believe that's the whole story.

"Then there's Cheng. I told you he was Raymond's executor. He's also the trustee of Raymond's estate. He does not give a shit if I live or die. I still need money for Adam, since I won't be working soon. The trust has money, but he's holding on to it like it's his. I'll never understand why Raymond had made *him* trustee instead of me."

I finish reading the papers. "I'm sorry this happened. What did you have in mind?"

"You need to prove that it wasn't an accident...that someone killed him." She stamps out her cigarette angrily. "Remember? You said you didn't believe he died accidently."

"I don't." I get my iPad. I had transferred my photos of Raymond's room to it earlier.

Toni leans on me, digging her nails into my shoulder, trying to see what I'm doing. "What is this?"

"Raymond's bedroom—don't look at it." I push her away gently. Reviewing the pictures doesn't change my mind. "His bedroom's too damned staged."

"What do you mean?"

I explain to her why I feel the items around Raymond's bed raises my suspicions.

Her expression is more intense than ever. "I haven't been back in his apartment yet, or even gone through his stuff. I don't think I can with Cheng in charge. Didn't you say something to the cops about it?"

I lean towards her, making my voice calm but strong. "I did. I told the police I what I believed. They were not interested."

"Well, why didn't you tell the news people?"

"I've talked to reporters. Only a couple of articles have bothered to give me some credence. The others fucked up what I said. They just printed their sensationalist bullshit."

Toni's voice gets shaky. "Don't you *want* to do anything?" She buries her head on my shoulder, still digging in the nails.

"What can I do, Toni? I don't have influence with the police. I understand why you feel injustice here. I feel it as well. But the case is in effect over." I glance at my coffee table, which holds the books I'm reading about Nazis, refuting my words. It's not over for me, it's just beginning.

She gets on her knees in front of my chair, her hand on my leg, squeezing. "Doesn't he mean something to you? His dying?"

"Toni, I believe you, and I agree with you, but I'm in a difficult situation. I just got the shit kicked out of me for getting involved in this."

Her eyes widen. "That attack on you was connected to Raymond?"

"I'm pretty sure of it. I want to be Raymond's advocate, but he's *your* brother, you must be his advocate."

She touches the bruises along my jaw. "I still want you to prove he was murdered."

"You want to *hire* me to prove Raymond was murdered."

"Yeah."

I lay my hand on her head. "Are you prepared to pay me another retainer?"

From the look on her face, she clearly is not. She starts to cry on my leg, and mutters she could give me the rest of the money I had returned to her, except that she had heavy expenses for her son...but there was the insurance. "If we prove that his death was murder..." she strokes my leg absently. I override her.

"Being paid upfront is the only way I can do it, Toni. I'm not the *A-Team*."

She stays silent on my leg for a minute. Inside, I try to maintain my composure. I'm in a terrible conflict. I want to continue the investigation, yet I know that professionally I can't give in to her seduction.

Toni spots my tarot deck on the coffee table and grabs the cards and starts shuffling and laying them out on the floor at my feet. I don't like that--crazy vibes for the cards--but I let her continue. She points out in the cards where she sees Raymond, me, herself. Fortune for us, more luck around the corner.

In spite of my empathy, I'd like to politely throw her medicated ass out of the apartment. I feel for her, enough to allow her to push boundaries. But I can't get shipwrecked on her Fantasy Island.

I try logic. "To challenge the insurance denial, you'll have to hire an expert in causes of death. You'll be in arbitration and if the denial is upheld, take it to court. A lawyer might take the case on contingency for one-third of the insurance, but you'll likely still pay for the expert. This could drag on for a few years."

She acts as though she doesn't hear me, taking out her phone and making a call to her son. "Adam honey? I'm here with Gabriel. You met him at the funeral, remember? Yes, he's a sweetheart. He helped out your uncle. He's going to help out again. You want to say hi?" She holds out the phone to me.

Since it's my own apartment, I can't just walk out. I take the phone and try not to sound irritated for the kid's sake. "Hello, Adam."

The young man sounds cordial, apologetic. "Hi...Mom's not feeling too well right now. Don't be mad at her."

"I'm not."

"I know you've done what you could. Sometimes it's hard for her to be realistic."

"Everything's fine. Are you okay?"

"Of course he's not okay." This from Toni. I step away from her and ask Adam, "You holding on?"

"More or less. I *would* like to talk to you again sometime if you don't mind."

"Adam, I've been through what you have. You're welcome to talk to me whenever you need."

I return the phone to Toni, who continues telling Adam not to worry over their problems and bills, and that I'll find out who killed Raymond and help the family. Her blatant manipulation burns me.

Yet while I'm trying not to get infuriated, I flash upon an idea. It's as if the devil on my shoulder realized I've considered letting the case go, and came up with an emergency appeal. Yes, I could just let this go and blow her off. I could get back to regular work. Or I could delay that and try out my idea.

When she ends her call, I adopt a mellow tone to facilitate her departure. "Toni, I want to follow up on something on Monday. We'll see how it goes, and I'll get in touch later, okay?"

She looks delighted at having won a point. I get another hug at the door and a kiss on the cheek. She tells me I'm her savior.

I rather doubt that. Especially as my idea is calling Allen Cheng's office on Monday and asking if I can meet with him.

∞

NINE ♦ THE ACE OF PENTACLES

The Ace of Coins represents a beginning of a business venture: a new source of income, an offer to consider.

∞

Monday, July 26

I'M GUESSING CHENG is still intrigued by our previous conversation. When I call, his secretary checks with him and then tells me I can see him for a few minutes if I come right now.

I dress nicely for this. A few years ago at Syms--a discount department store where money-challenged people like me could get decent clothes, I purchased a grey Joseph Abboud Profile suit. I combine it with a white shirt and purple silk tie. I don't get a chance to wear this suit often. However, a man needs a good suit for certain occasions. I have found the treatment of a man in a suit is distinctly different from a man in a leather jacket, Converse shoes and jeans.

The firm is on East 78th Street in a renovated building with a quiet luxurious style. I rise to the 35th floor in a large elevator lined with cracked green mirror glass and playing muted classical music. I'm listening to my own on my iPod, taking it out just before I get to the office.

A male receptionist scans me like an airport metal detector. I swear he's checking me out as I hide behind a *Metropolitan Home* magazine, no doubt admiring the suit or so I like to think. Eventually, he leads me back to Cheng's office, and holds my gaze just a bit.

Now I face the secretary, an older female who has seen too much to be impressed by my incredible Joseph Abboud suit and the Jack Spade leather slim brief I'm carrying as accompaniment. I get another scan, this one more to sense if I might be a terrorist with a grudge against her boss. Then I am admitted to Cheng's office.

Cheng stands to shake my hand. His suit is much nicer, of course. Donna Karan, one of those advertised in *Esquire* that most *Esquire* readers couldn't afford. My face doesn't look as bad as it did a week ago, but it still shows the scrapes and contusions of the fight. I see him taken aback a little when he studies me.

"Nice to see you again, under better circumstances. I hope you're doing better from what happened. Are you still trying to satisfy your curiosity?"

"That's right." I sit in one of the plush burgundy chairs. "You had told me at the funeral that you didn't really know what Raymond wanted investigated at the Foundation."

Cheng shakes his head. Of course, he's a lawyer. He's not there to tell me anything. I'm there to tell him.

I'm not unduly put off. "I do, but not all the details. Raymond was killed before we could start the case."

He nods. "That seems moot right now. Although I've seen what the papers have said, what you've said. What happened to you."

I'm undaunted. "It didn't discourage me, in any case. Allen, let me share some ideas with you that explain the basis of why I'm here. Since you are the trustee of the estate, and from what I understand a good friend of Raymond's, I felt you were the person to consult."

Cheng leans forward. "Certainly. Please tell me what's on your mind."

I take out a legal pad out of the brief and begin my pitch from my notes. I have a folder ready with various documents as exhibits. First, I explain how I became involved in the case, and the beginning of my investigation--the interview with Nicolas, and then finding Raymond's body. He listens intently the entire time. I watch him carefully when I tell him about the scene around Raymond's bed.

He picks up a pencil and chews on it. Interested. "What makes you think it was staged?"

"I know about these kinds of deaths. I'm not an expert you would have in court, but I can tell you that this isn't the right narrative."

He holds my gaze, tilting his head to the side and smiles. "Narrative. That's one of Raymond's words."

I nod. "He used it with me. Allen, you may have heard that Raymond's insurance company denied Toni's claim on Raymond's policy. Even if the death was accidental, the claim is denied because they say his death was his fault."

"I knew he had the policy. It wasn't part of what I'm handling. She told you about it?"

"She asked me my opinion of his death, since she did not accept that verdict. I do not accept it either. I'm not trying to be dramatic, but I believe this is a case of homicide, and I have told the police my opinion, although they didn't give me credence."

Cheng gets up this time and goes to look out his window while apparently considering what I said. "You think Raymond was murdered."

This is key. If Cheng has any inclination at all that something is wrong with the case, he'll stay with me. If he just wants the situation to disappear, he will usher me out ASAP.

To bolster my opinion, I show him my grisly photos of the scene and photocopied research from Tuvey's book for my exhibits. I also point out the air conditioner was running full blast, which could very well alter the time of death calculation. Without insect activity, time of death calculation is conjecture at best.

My explanation takes almost a half hour. I also mentioned what happened in the fight. Something about being beat up tends to let authority to my words. During this time, Cheng comes back to his desk to review my notes and evidence very carefully. He asks questions and plays devil's advocate. His posture is relaxed, open. He sits down with his hands behind his head, listening.

"What would you intend to do with this, Gabriel?"

Now comes the really tricky part. "One option is to use this for Toni to challenge the insurance company's decision. Not with just what I have, though. To challenge an insurance decision at arbitration I would need more evidence, so I'd contact an expert on psychological autopsies. What we compile should discredit the conclusion that Raymond was either suicidal or practiced this type of sexual act. We'd need other experts to challenge the aspects of the autopsy and crime scene. But also, I'd reexamine what Raymond wanted investigated, to see if I could get a lead on who might have killed him. The timing is too suspicious for me. I think it's connected."

He nods. So far, I'm making sense.

"However, Toni does not have the fee necessary for a retainer. My rates are not over the top as a one-person operation. But I can't afford to take on her case pro bono. She wants me to investigate based on receiving part of the insurance money, a contingency basis. But that's not doable for me. If the arbitration doesn't go her way, then the next step is litigation. That could take years to resolve."

"Yeah, that is pretty much what would happen."

Now the tricky part of the argument. "But this doesn't just affect Toni. Raymond's reputation has been denigrated, and that may or may not affect your firm. But to find that he was set up and murdered could help mitigate any damage."

Cheng tilts his head back and gives a little smile. "You want to get the firm involved?"

"I was hoping as the executor of the estate, you could perhaps authorize funds for a limited investigation. This would be to clear his reputation. In this high-end line of work, I imagine that counts."

Cheng lets his guard down for a moment, with a grimace. "Yes, we recently had a very good client leave, because he felt that his deals needed to have a pristine context and his lawyer having been sexually, uh, experimental tainted that. Actually, the art world is just as dirty as anything else. But it's all about the narrative, as Raymond said."

"As a bonus, it would alleviate his sister's needs."

Cheng puts his hands flat on the table. "Nothing will *really* alleviate her needs. But you are correct about Raymond's reputation. However, as a fiduciary to the estate, I would have difficulty justifying expenses just to clarify the manner of Raymond's death."

I wait, as I believe he's not dismissing me. I'm right. After a moment, he leans back in the chair. "Yet it bothers me too. I'm looking at you and I see a man who just paid for what he believed. I may have an alternative. Can you give me a few minutes?"

"Sure. Please take whatever time you need."

He nods and stands up. "Thank you. I'll have Darlene bring you some coffee and something to read."

Good thing Darlene finds me a magazine to read--*Esquire*--since Cheng is gone over 30 minutes. I actually have a couple books in the brief, but figure reading a novel in his office would look insolent.

Cheng is in a more energetic mood upon his return. "Gabriel, I have a proposal. The firm is willing to fund your investigation, with a set of parameters."

"I see. What are the parameters?"

He takes out a white legal pad. "First, we will draw up a retainer agreement. We'll offer you an initial retainer of $5000.00 and reimbursement of expenses. You will periodically send reports to the firm of all expenses and use of the retainer. This will be confidential, as we are considering this a legal matter on Raymond's behalf. I can authorize the firm to act in his interest.

"Second, you will continue to be funded so long as your activities and results are progressing in the goal of collecting enough evidence to demonstrate that Raymond's death was not suicide or accidental death. This would at least be enough to lobby for a change of the official autopsy report. We can handle that aspect. In doing so, I'll forward a list of experts to you to consult about the case. We will draw checks to pay those experts. Third, this has a current time frame of one year. If we can get the truth out sooner than later, this might work. You can pick up the contract and retainer here tomorrow."

"All right." I clear my throat. "I understand what I find will be confidential, although I may need to share some aspects with other professionals who may be able to help me. You would need to trust my discretion and judgment to a certain extent. Any *public* disclosure would be run by you first." Here I'm thinking of Alex and the prospects of collaborating with him.

Cheng gives me a very serious look. "You may use your discretion, except for the most sensitive information."

Just what I wanted. "And finally, I would still want copies of what I turn up for Toni to use at her arbitration; I know she is a giant pain in the ass, but I still feel my own sort of fiduciary duty towards her."

He has a slow, sad smile. "Be careful on that, Gabriel. I saw how it was at the funeral. She can be sympathetic, no doubt. She's also extremely manipulative and has no problem enveloping you in her drama. I watched her push Raymond to the limit of his love and patience. We don't mind the evidence being used for her insurance claim. If the insurance company's decision is overturned, so much the better for our case. But she will try to make you fight her windmills. Remember that. She should not be given inside information on the progress unless I approve."

"I can deal with that. To begin with, having a statement for the media regarding the investigation would be a good idea as an informant might contact me."

"Ordinarily, I wouldn't like that." Lawyers don't like anything they can't control. "But I don't think this is a state secret, and you might be right about getting a tip."

"I'll work on a statement and email it to you. And one more thing. I need to speak with you and with the employees of the firm about his death."

This time he laughs. "So you get me to hire you, and then you'll interview me and the firm as potential suspects, and then you'll charge us for the pleasure?"

I shrug. "Would you expect differently? I can't dismiss possibilities, even that a client or employee of the firm had something to do with Raymond's death."

"All right. You can arrange this with Darlene. I had nothing to do with Raymond's death, but I'm glad you're thorough."

He digs out another key to Raymond's apartment and hands it to me. "Now that I think about it, can you also do an inventory of what's in his apartment? That would be a separate arrangement to pay by the hour. Send me a retainer to be paid by the estate."

"No problem." We shake hands. I try to suppress my elation of being back on Raymond's case.

I don't waste time. A couple hours later I email Cheng my draft statement, and a couple of quotes I would give about it if asked, as well as a retainer for inventorying Raymond's apartment. I also ask him if he wants me to pursue work on the video from Cafétière Maléfice. I doubt much can be done even with facial recognition technology, but it's worth trying if he wants to pay for it. I'm familiar with the technology, as I've advised clients on using facial biometrics in security systems instead of passwords. Pose deviations--i.e., not looking straight at a camera, still present problems even for advanced technology, as does the use of disguises.

Later in the day, Allen Cheng emails back his approval of everything. Hopefully, I can get my electric bill paid off now.

I start out re-reading the *Scene's* stuff. The police-oversight column *The Thin Blue Line* has reiterated its contention that the police wrongly attributed Raymond's death to an unusual sexual act, when evidence exists that he was murdered. I'm gratified seeing this in print, but I'd also like to know what led them to the idea. They say the NYPD has not responded to the accusations. Not surprising. To not respond may help the story go away, and also indicates the stories aren't worth acknowledging.

Calling the *Scene,* I reach Carl Mankiewitz, a staff writer and editor in charge of the *Blue Line.* His tone is suspicious. "Are you the same Gabriel Ross who found Booth's body?"

"Yes. I have problems with the official police story. From what I read you do as well."

"Huh. You didn't return our request for an interview."

"I told your reporter what I believed had happened. Look, I haven't been treated very well by the media. I didn't want to see anything else I said be twisted around."

"So why are you calling now?"

"Why do you think his death wasn't accidental?"

Mankiewitz snorts. "We don't reveal our sources."

"We're on the same side."

"Yeah? I don't know about that. In this city, anyone can be paid off. In fact, according to our source, you might have been one of the ones who murdered Booth, and you're throwing red herrings to thwart real investigation."

"Really? Your source wouldn't be John Harrison, would it?"

I've caught him by surprise. He doesn't answer. I go on. "I'm actually continuing to investigate Raymond's case and I still think he was killed. I have a statement on my new investigation, and I would like you and one other publication have it early."

"Huh." Silence for a minute. "What other publication?"

"The *Herald*. For Alex Barclay."

"Huh." More silence. "He's okay, so far as mainstream reporters go. Anything on your attack? You got hurt kind of bad, didn't you?"

"I'm still walking around. It's not stopping me. Off the record, I'm pretty sure it was connected to this case. You know Alex Barclay suggested as much; you could too. I wouldn't protest."

"You think it was connected? To shut you up? What if it happens again?"

He has a point. I've jumped back into work and not thought about what comes next after a beatdown.

"Yes, yes and I don't know. Just have to see what happens."

"Mmmn. Okay. Give us the statement and a quote and I'll see what I can do."

I read him the statement over the phone as well as one of the quotes I had prepared. I don't give any real details but express outrage over the official lack of interest in the case. Mankiewitz takes the opportunity to ask me about the New Jersey incident. Whatever I say will be used against me in the lawsuit, so I don't so much discuss what I did but rather what the Church and Bunton have done against humanity.

After that, I try several times to call Eleanor Whitford to follow up on our funeral conversation. She doesn't answer so I leave her a voicemail asking her to call as soon as she can.

Then I send the statement and a different quote to Alex. I also ask him if he can send me the photographs his colleague took at the funeral, not for publication. I don't know if that's pushing the limits of our connection, but he gets the photos to me within a couple hours by email. He also lets me know he's going to be out of town for a week or so, but did I want to have dinner with him the following Thursday? I do.

Talking to Whitford is out for the moment, so I pursue another lead. I agreed with Veronica about the BDSM magazines in Raymond's room. As they were in near-mint condition, whoever set up the scene bought them from somewhere. Possibly online, but the city has used bookstores that sell vintage magazines. I start checking them out.

Not too many used books stores are left in New York City but some diehards remain, including a couple of stores I've been in before a few times. I call each and ask if they sell vintage periodicals. If they do, I ask if they sell adult periodicals. If they do, I ask if any of those periodicals are "specialty items." I want to sound like a collector. Three stores are good possibilities to visit later. One uptown on Broadway and one near St. Marks Place that I'm familiar with, and one off Houston in the Village I don't know as well.

Then I initiate a technical part of the investigation, setting up the psychological autopsy. A psych autopsy is a data collection tool on the likely mental state of a deceased person. Part of the collection involves interviews of persons who knew the deceased, his medical history, and so on. This biographical information, personal information (relationships, life habits, drug/alcohol use, and stressors) and other data–family history, legal records and writings of the deceased, can be organized into a report that helps determine the manner of death (i.e., suicide or homicide or accidental).

I research and contact some expert witnesses including those Cheng gave me, to interpret the facts in Raymond's case. I find a forensic pathologist who specializes in sexually-related deaths and a psychologist who is an expert on sexual pathologies. Their testimony will be useful in showing that Raymond was unlikely to be a person into that sort of misadventure.

Once that part is put in motion, I need to have a conversation with Toni. I get a hold of her at her firm and arrange to meet her around lunchtime at the Brooklyn Courthouse on Adams Street. I have to explain why I'm working for a lawyer she considers to be an enemy, and how this will ultimately help her.

Toni is not completely a loonybird. I think she knows in her heart I can't work for free, but she is so absolutely sure Cheng is out to get her. But now she's subdued because her firm is enacting the layoffs this week. I start out by reminding her that what I find will ultimately help her in the arbitration with the insurance company.

We are sitting on one of the benches near the Courthouse. Several stands are set up selling farm fruits, vegetables and baked goods. But we're eating pizza. She has her hair up and make-up perfect, wearing a satin baby blue work suit. I'm wearing my casual work attire of button-down shirt, jeans and Converse shoes.

"What does this mean for me? I have to appeal the claim denial."

We hammer out a plan on how she can frame the appeal for now. Getting down to business revs her up a bit. She touches my hand. "Do you really have to work for Cheng? How do we know he's not involved in Raymond's death?"

"We don't, but that won't affect my investigation. With not having to worry about being paid, I can spend more time on this."

She shakes her head. "He's going to turn you against me. He's never liked me and believes I'm a space case or something. Will you abandon me, Gabriel?"

"No. You see I'm here, right?"

"Will you, you know, keep me up to date on what's going on?"

"Of course."

She seems doubtful about my sincerity, but gives me a quick hug.

The day is not finished for me yet. With my renewed sense of purpose, I head back to Manhattan to visit the used bookstores.

∞

TEN ♦ THE KNIGHT OF WANDS

The Knight of Wands represents being ready for battle; preparing for a fight. The Knight uses intuition in his preparation and follows through on hunches.

∞

IN THE UPTOWN STORE, I ask the middle-aged white male proprietor if a person fitting Cap-and-Sunglasses' vague description recently bought a giant stack of BDSM porn. The difficulty in asking questions of people is usually two-fold: 1. Businesspersons don't like to reveal information on customers and lose said customers; 2. People don't like to give information that will end up with them being witnesses in court. If you ever need to clear a room, tell the people there you'll need them as witnesses in court.

Luckily, the general mix of humanity in the world includes do-gooders, the nosy, the unaware, and those who just fall to my charm. Getting them to talk just depends upon the approach. It's social engineering--how to make a person give you the information you want.

Uptown bookstore person remembers I've been in the store as a customer and bought several movie books. Using that leverage, I start out with just a blunt question. I can't promise confidentiality because the police may end up needing to know. So, I tell him some of the truth--that my questions are in relation to a missing person. My calm demeanor helps. Also working for me is the fact missing persons tend to make people much more cooperative than murder. The bookstore person tells me that no such person has been around that store recently. I believe him.

The St. Marks place has a facially tattooed and pierced young white male assistant who illustrates his notebook of poetry in between taking customer's money. He does not need to be finessed. Anyone alive who keeps him from his art is annoying to him, including me. I get curt answers and a sullen expression. But he cooperates, even calling the owner, when he gets the idea I will stay and bother him until I'm satisfied. No purchases that fit the bill here, either.

I move on to the West Village bookstore. A fortyish medium-toned black man with a close-cropped widow's peak and narrow beard is the proprietor. Other than buying a few books from time to time, I've never had much more interaction with him.

When he's finished with another customer, I introduce myself.

"Jason Evans." He hands me a bookmark and a card. "You like the Nero Wolfe and Lew Archer stories. I remember you buying a stack of each."

I'm rather pleased he remembers this. Jason wears black horned-rimmed glasses but is interested in my John Lennon-style reading spectacles. I let him try them on. He listens to my question about the magazines and nods. "Sure, to help find anyone." He then looks at me sternly. "Not to hurt someone, right?"

"No, to help. I'm a Buddhist and an ethical professional."

"Really?" He cocks his head. "I have some books you might like. D. T. Suzuki. The life story of Do-gen."

I smile. I think he's testing me. "I'd like that. I have Katsulis' *Zen Action, Zen Person*, and I'd like more on Master Do-Gen."

He smiles back. "You'll like it. Anyway, to your question. I do carry magazines because purists will pay extra for hard copies of erotic material and that brings in cash. Specialty items are a necessity in these times to be competitive."

I nod in agreement. "My favorite hang-outs as a kid were movie theaters and used bookstores. I always felt my imagination could fly in reading a book in a way that could never happen in school."

He laughs. "When I was young, my favorite hang-out was a used bookstore behind a church in Brooklyn. I used to sneak out of Sunday school and go visit, even though if I was caught..." he smiles at the memory. "I'm going to double-check here on the computer, but I know exactly who you mean. A couple weeks ago, no...it was three, a white man came in. He was around thirty. Pretty nondescript, plain jacket, sunglasses, one of those wool hats younger people seem to think is hip. I think he was doing it to cover up, though. He asked for material relating to bondage and similar acts.

"I showed him some stuff. I keep it in a back room so people don't handle it and ruin it, and kids don't go looking. He bought everything with no more than a passing glance. He's not a collector, not like the comics and graphic novel people. He was in a hurry and paid cash. A few hundred. He didn't want to be on a mailing list, so I'm sorry I don't have a name. But he was here on a Wednesday. July 7."

I have a set of prints from the photos Alex had sent me. Various persons who were at the funeral. John Harrison, Ethan Nelson, Dr. Cole, Allen Cheng and others. Also, a separate picture of Raymond, and fuzzy man with sunglasses at the coffee shop.

"He wasn't any of these persons."

I also have photographs of the magazines themselves. I show these to Jason as well. "Yep, those are the ones I sold. I had them catalogued." He shows me his Excel file on that and makes a copy for me. While it's aggravating not to be able to connect the purchase with someone definite, at least it wasn't Raymond or his boyfriend. And it means more than person was behind this.

The magazines were bought just before the weekend where Raymond was murdered. That tells me a great deal. This set-up was planned out beforehand, even before Raymond thought of hiring me. The man sounds younger than the one in the photo, but he could have had help.

"Jason, you've been more than helpful than you know. I'll take a look at the books you were talking about."

He walks me over to the Buddhist books, and also brings out a book on Buddhist art. The books are all great, but pricy. The art book is $55 alone. I can't really afford it, but I buy them all.

Jason starts ringing the books up. "This going to help in your murder case?"

I raise my eyebrows. He smiles tightly. "I read a lot, Gabriel. The *Daily News* and the *Post* had some fun with you. So did the commentary on YouTube with what you did in New Jersey. You're a troublemaker, they say. Although the *Herald* doesn't seem to think so." His smile gets wider. "Luckily, the *Herald* is my favorite paper."

I take the carefully-wrapped books. "I hope you see that I'm not what I was portrayed to be. To be blunt, I was beat up for my trouble."

His eyes narrow as he looks at the marks still on my face. "Yes, you did. Proved yourself the hard way. If I thought you were what you've been accused of being, I wouldn't have spoken to you. What happened in Jersey...those people in that Church bring a bad name to Christianity. They should have left that poor girl's family alone. Is this all part of the other matter, with the attorney?"

"Sure is. You'll see in the *Herald* soon."

"I hope to. I wish you luck on this. Come around again. A man like you, who needs books and loves books, should deal with an expert in books."

"You're right about that," I shake his hand again and give him my card. I tell him about a book club I belong to. He invites the club to meet in his store and I promise to follow up on that.

Books save me again, and add to my evidence in the case. I'm pleased as I write up my notes at home, until I get a text from Jim asking about the motion. I decide to pretend my phone is dead and work feverishly to finish the motion that evening and stay out of trouble.

Danny, Jim, Ella and Evelyn treat me to dinner on Thursday. Veronica and Michaela have also been invited. I'm suffering from lack of sleep due to dealing with Jim's stack of paperwork, but I'm up for a good meal.

I chose an upscale brick oven pizza place I know. While we're eating, the women ask me what I'm doing, and I give them a thumbnail version of the case. I'm also indirectly letting Danny and Jim know about it. They have to be polite in mixed company, and the women are as fond and protective of me as I am of them.

Danny gives me a pained smile. "I still need you for the grant work, bro."

"And I'll *be* there for it. I'm used to doing more than one job at a time, remember."

Jim adds his two cents. "I think you have some legal work to finish, too. I have to have time to check your grammar."

"Have I ever not finished? I correct *your* grammar, Mr. Dangling Modifier. And I just got the retainer check today from Raymond's partner. I could even buy this dinner--but I'm not."

Jim folds his hands on the table. "And your chances of success for this venture?"

"A good as any case I've had. Have you heard any feedback from your cop friends?"

"I don't have cop friends. I have contacts who are susceptible to well-placed bribes."

Ella takes an interest in this. "What do you want to ask the police, Gabriel?"

"Well, I asked your husband to use his fine legal mind to find out why I was released and the case was closed. I have some interest in making sure I'm not still a suspect."

Ella frowns at Jim. "Why aren't you doing that?"

He rolls his eyes. "Stop brainwashing my wife, Gabriel."

"We're supposed to find out more about this, counselor."

Evelyn joins in to give Jim a hard time. "Gabriel needs your help, Jim. He was arrested, almost put in jail, beat up and in the hospital. You didn't even tell me he was until he was released. You need to help him."

Jim sulks for a while. We ignore this, and Michaela asks me just what the police has done up to this point.

"Mikki, they've taken the information and the descriptions I gave them. But they aren't going to find these people until they screw up again somewhere. Maybe I'll find them first."

Michaela smiles. "Going Clint Eastwood on them?"

"I'm not saying. I don't want to put you into an ethical quandary as an officer of the court."

Now Evelyn's frowning. "Do you have any police protection?"

"Not in this lifetime. I have the distinct impression my attackers are not on the 'A' list of crimes to solve."

"Why don't you think the attack was from gay-bashers? This has been happening more in the city lately."

"I know, but what the man on the phone said, using Atwater's name...it screams setup. Someone researched me."

"And paid those men to do that?"

"No doubt. I think they were hired for this; probably the man who called me was too. Whoever hired them was giving me a clear message."

Veronica joins in. "Maybe the guy on the video. Because you went public rather than drop the case."

"Who was that?" Michaela is next to Veronica, and turns to her. "I need to catch up on all this."

"He has a security camera recording from the coffee shop in his neighborhood, with some strange man kidnapping his client. I saw it, it's really creepy."

"I found out some other guy bought the magazines that were left by Raymond's bedside."

"Really? That's a solid lead then."

"Right. That's what's so frustrating. I'm doing this, and I don't have the contacts, outreach, hours etcetera that they have. I'll need luck on my side to get to the truth, but I'm moving forward."

Jim reaches across me to pull the pizza platter over closer to him. "Or, you could tell the police your lead instead of obstructing justice."

"How am I obstructing justice in a closed case?"

Evelyn turns to Jim. "What have you got against this, Jimmy? Gabriel said he was being paid for it. He's not going to neglect your work."

Jim lays down his pizza. "All right. Before you all gang up on me, I've known Gabriel for over ten years. Dan has known him longer, but we both know him pretty well. Yeah, he won't fuck up the work he does for us--"

"Thanks, Jim."

"--But, what you two don't take into account is that this is not just about going after an honorable objective. I do that every day, but do some people go to jail who shouldn't? Yes. Can I do anything about it? Goddamn little when the prosecutor or judge has an agenda. That's the system. Gabriel thinks he's an outsider, so he doesn't care about the system. He knows deep down this won't change the situation. It will just get him on a blacklist and extra problems when he just needs to earn a living right now."

"Doing the right thing is so fucking bad? Is that it?"

"Goddamn it, Gabriel!" Jim slams his hand down on the table, making everyone jump. "Can you afford to be a pure ethicist? I work 60 hours a week to make sure we can afford the cheapest fucking health insurance, much less saving for emergencies or retirement. Even thinking about having a kid is tough. You're single, but you can't piss on your career forever. Life gets harder, not easier. At 20, you can afford to be the universal idealist, but now look at your situation."

He takes a breath. "You're a great investigator, one of the smartest people I know. Smarter than all of us, and better at working a crime scene and finding people than most cops. And what do you get for that? Your former boss has dragged your name through the dirt and made you a joke, and you didn't do anything wrong. But you have to beg your clients to stay with you."

"I don't beg anybody."

He shakes his head. "It's always begging in some form. I know you're right about Raymond Booth, but what does it matter? Is it worth your life? If you're right, it means *someone wanted to fucking kill you!*"

A waiter comes over, looking us over with a worried expression. "Um, is everything okay here?"

"No problem." Danny smiles at him. "We're doing a run-through of our new off-Broadway play. Sorry we got loud."

"Okay then." The waiter regards us suspiciously as he leaves.

Danny drops his smile. "Another point. Just because someone wants to hire you to do something, doesn't mean you should take it. That partner of Raymond's is using you. The firm can write off the cost of your work. If you find something great, if not, oh well. But if you get killed do you think he'll give a shit?"

I cross my arms. "I deeply appreciate your interpretation of events. So, in the future before I make any business decisions I should run it by you two for approval as to the proper balance of pay versus social consciousness? Give me a fucking break. My work for Jim most of the time involves churning people through the system he says he's so powerless against. And you're hiring me to watch the halls for drug dealers while you're documenting the roach hotels of the city. And if some asswipe tries to come at your team, who risks being shanked? Me. Don't play *Father Knows Best* with me, I don't have much to lose when it's my job."

I see the women are upset at our exchanges. I drop my angry tone and attempt to placate them. "Come on, you all know Danny and I go at it like this all time, and Jim's getting cranky in his old age. They have some idea that I can't take care of myself."

Danny points his finger at me, which always annoys me. It's why he does it. "You know you have us as family. If something happens to you, do you think that wouldn't tear me and Jim up? Or everyone else here, even if they believe what you do is 'romantic' or encourage you in your madness. When we're at your funeral all we'd be thinking about is what we could have done to stop you."

A silence falls over the table. We busy ourselves eating. Danny has no problem in having vicious fights and then switching modes. He waves over the waiter for more wine and asks Evelyn about her classes. She runs a program for young women to get into nontraditional trades, held at City College. Ella then talks about a PBS project she's working on as video editor. I listen to them, but I'm still aggravated and after a few minutes decide to go outside and smoke.

Standing out in the balmy night allows me to calm down. Then Jim steps out of the restaurant and stands next to me.

"Smoke?" I hold out the pack.

"Please. If I want to kill myself, I'll use a gun..."

"Suit yourself. I have those, too."

"Give it a rest for a minute. Let's be friends again, or I won't get any from my wife for a while."

"Who says we aren't friends? Just stop giving me marching orders."

"Yeah, well...." He runs his hands through his short dark hair. "I did call a couple of people."

I blow smoke away from him. "You just weren't going to let me in on it."

"They didn't really *know* anything, but it was how they said it. Like they didn't want to even hear Raymond Booth's name. I got the impression that a curtain has come down."

I sigh. "We could talk to Greene."

"Your cop buddy?"

"He's not in the First Precinct, but he can probably find out something. Cops gossip enough. The lieutenant who kicked me out seemed to know I'm in good with Greene. I might as well ask. The worst he can do is say no."

"Fine. If he's willing, I'll go with you."

"Good. By the way, I was notified a complaint has been filed with the New York Department of State Licensing. Reverend Bunton has accused me of unprofessional conduct and damages. The State wants a response prior to investigation."

Jim grimaces. "You better let me write it; you'll piss them off somehow." But he's relieved the tension has eased and we can go back in the restaurant and have a less argumentative evening. After dinner, I call Greene.

I'm not an ex-police officer like most private investigators, including my former boss Gerry, so I don't have a network. Greene is the exception. Manny introduced me to him some time ago.

I'm in luck and he's in at his office in Manhattan North homicide. "I heard you were promoted to supervisor, about time."

"Thanks. I'd ask what *you've* been doing, but..."

"Yeah. I'm working to get past that now. I hope it doesn't make knowing me a problem."

"You're like Godzilla, destroyer of worlds. But you were hit pretty hard yourself, didn't you? You better protect yourself, man....so how may I trouble myself on your behalf today?"

I explain to him about what happened at the police station after I found Raymond and what Lt. Clarke told me.

Greene's been tight with me for some years since I helped him out one time with his young niece who's a lesbian and also a cop. She had picked up a wild one-night stand who made off with her service weapon after their hook-up. That is the worst kind of trouble a cop can get into. Greene had asked me to see if I could find the thief. I tracked her down in a couple days and scared the gun out of her. The niece dodged the bullet of having to report the theft to the Department.

So while my question of why the Booth case was closed does not look appealing, he agrees to meet with me and Jim the next day. Not in his office, but a diner nearby just to be discreet. Greene is fifty-ish, black, fit and streetwise from a long career of navigating departmental politics.

Greene looks at Jim, who's considering the prospects of a pastrami sandwich on the menu. "Your lawyer doesn't seem too interested."

"He isn't. But just in case anyone in the Department is still considering my potential as a suspect..."

"Don't worry, they aren't."

"Good, we can go." Jim puts the menu down.

"Shut up, counselor. Andy, is there any idea why they suddenly dropped the case?"

"Clarke was right. Someone called in a favor. I think it went as far as the M.E.'s office. But not the Chief M.E. He's a stand-up guy. Whoever put in the hush would expect you to be grateful you dodged a bullet and just forget it."

We pause to order lunch. When the server leaves, I lower my voice. "Who has the pull to stop an investigation?"

"Really, it comes down to the brass closing up a case to not embarrass the Department, or a person on the outside with heavy influence."

"Politician?"

"Not necessarily, but a possibility." Greene shrugs. "Really, I can only find out so much. If the case were re-opened, it would be an embarrassment. We have budget problems too, and a botched case doesn't look good to the public."

We don't have much else to go into. Jim is relieved that I have no more immediate legal issues for him to worry about. When we depart, I go back to his office to help him with paperwork. "So we're pretty clear that this is a losing battle. If you want, I'll talk to that Cheng guy and get you out of this."

"Um, I can handle my own battles. And I'm not quitting."

He flashes me an angry look. "Did what Greene say not register? I'm not one for overarching conspiracies, but if he's right about someone getting the P.D. to shut the case, I don't think that party would appreciate your continued existence."

"I don't think they would anyway. So I might as well stay on the case. If anything, this convinced me I'm on the right track."

"And at the risk of your life? Is it worth it?"

I consider that. But I already know the answer. It's what I have to do.

∞

ELEVEN ♦ THE PAGE OF CUPS

The Page of Cups represents the arrival and restirring of emotion, sentiment, feelings. A relationship is revisited and stirs the past.

∞

Saturday, July 31

AT RAYMOND'S APARTMENT, I begin sorting through his belongings. Cataloguing turns out to be complicated. You don't realize how much stuff even a small apartment has. Raymond owned expensive clothes and kitchen toys, books on politics, history, classic literature, gay issues and art. Just his huge collection of DVDs, classical, blues and jazz CDs alone is exhausting to list.

After a couple hours of this tedious duty, I examine his Mac again. Disturbingly, his files and his emails have been erased. By whom? Possibly by the killer returning with Raymond's body. In any case, his browser history still exists. I search for any websites or discussion groups, blogs, etc. involving BDSM. Persons with fetishes will usually look for those fetishes online, possibly in a club. Raymond has no applicable history. I find some regular porn sites, nothing special.

I don't find anything else hidden in the bedroom. Other than the suspiciously new magazines still by the bed, he has no fetish porn or other sex toys, nor any place where the ones by the bed would seem to be stored. I search for hidden areas in the apartment where secret videos or pictures may be stored. Nothing. I'm satisfied his apartment has been exhausted as a source of evidence on his death, and I go back home.

As I approach my building, I notice a man waiting alone on the steps of the Russian Orthodox church next door, looking away from me. Ordinarily I wouldn't care, but again I realize I should be wary of people; I should be looking over my shoulder. Then he turns his head and I recognize him. Joel, my former boyfriend. Or lover, as John Harrison would say.

He stands up, giving me a familiar subdued smile. My instinct is to smile back, with a rush of emotion running over me.

Before even speaking we embrace each other. I feel the buzz of energy he always has under his placid exterior. His leather jacket smells of cloves.

"Still smoking the kreteks? Jesus."

He laughs, takes a box of Djarum from the inside of the jacket. "You still do the Camel Light Wides? I know you haven't quit." His voice has a natural wryness and an undercurrent of something deeper. I've always thought he talks like Andy Bell sings.

"Too stressed for that." I take out my own box. Joel leans over, hesitates a second, and then quickly kisses my cheek. He has a goatee, the same dirty blond color of his hair. I can't grow a light goatee. The dark Irish part of me makes my facial hair a couple shades darker than my light brown hair and I look sleazy instead. But he looks good with it.

Joel is almost the same height as I, making our gazes all the more closer. He stands near as we smoke, and plays with the drawstring of the hooded jacket I wear. I feel like some emotional flashback button has been pushed. It started with the email, but I didn't pursue it. I didn't get involved with anyone during the time we've been apart. I didn't want to go through the effort of starting and losing again.

Plus no one I met was like him or had the chemistry that was between us. That deep a feeling took a long time to suppress after I finally walked away. The chemistry and intimacy, is in his eyes as he watches me. I can't help but smile again.

"So what's going on?"

He laughs again. "I could ask you the same. Can we go inside?"

"Sure." I gesture to my building's entrance. The building has a nice rust-color façade. The inside is a small foyer with mailboxes, staircase, small elevator behind the staircase, and a locked door to the basement and the alley behind the building. I have a key to that door the super doesn't know about, to use when I don't want to leave by the front door. We go up to my place on the sixth floor, looking at each other the whole time. He keeps his hand on my arm, gently. We're both comfortable with silence, but it gives me a chance to review what I feel about him. Just as with seeing the email, I'm rather surprised that I'm so pleased with seeing him, but I also feel a hell of a lot more that--a flux of mixed emotions.

Archie stretches from one of his favorite spots in the window as we walk in, and jumps down to greet us.

"Hey." Joel gets on one knee. "He remembers me."

"He's a capricious little son of a bitch."

Joel turns his head up to me. He doesn't say anything. I take a draw on my cigarette. He knows I'm not talking about the cat. In spite of being glad to see him, I suppose I'm still angry.

He's heard a lot worse. He scratches Archie's ears. "Hi, buddy. You cool with Joel, right? You know I got something for you." He takes a bag of his pocket containing a catnip mouse. Archie immediately starts to bat at the toy. "Whoa. Just like a man, wants instant gratification. That's okay, son, have a ball." He opens the bag and tosses the mouse in the middle of the living room floor.

He stands up and smiles at me. "So who do I have to fuck to get a drink around here?"

His posture is a bit of a put-on. We're both nervous. In the kitchen, I find a bottle of Australian Shiraz-Cabernet and open it. I'm only on good terms with one of my ex-boyfriends. And for me, when it's over, it's over. I don't think about them much. Joel is different. He'll always be different. I had wondered, even agonized, over and over what happened to him; where he went after I walked away. When I come back with the bottle and a couple of glasses, he's moved to sitting on the floor in front of the sofa. I pour a glass and hand it to him. He twirls it between his fingers. "I see you're still a lousy dishwasher."

I indicate a wastebasket in the corner of the room "Complaint box is over there."

He smiles and holds up his glass and I clink it gently. I sit on my extra-large ottoman, which is next to him. Archie also settles near him, cleaning himself.

Eventually he takes off his jacket. He looks around the apartment noting what's changed. He contemplates a painting across the room from the sofa, a Buddhist mandala design. He painted it at my request; it was how we got together. I took it down for a couple months after the relationship ended, but brought it back because it is a stunning painting and I still use it to meditate.

I watch him looking around. "So you're here...what's up?"

He smiles and shakes his head. "Gabriel...always ready to get down--to business."

"What am I supposed to do, invite you to move in until you decide you feel like talking?"

He says archly, "You wouldn't want me to move in unless you can have a GPS up my ass 24/7."

I deserve that for what I said before. We're both overstating the case and we both know how to hurt each other. I say into my glass, "I was never like that when we first met."

Our eyes are locked. I see a different emotion in him, one that he must have gained in our absence. Sorrow. In spite of being irritated by his smartassedness, that affects me. It makes his expression heavy and he looks down at his wine. "You're right. You were very accepting and patient. I supposed I fucked you up."

My ears burn. "No, I...never mind. It's not useful to go down that road. So what's up with you being here?"

He finishes his glass and reaches for the bottle. "I was worried about you, jackass. You know I heard what happened, that's why I emailed. I came back as soon as I could, not as soon as I would have liked to. I wanted to see if you were okay, if you needed anything."

For a moment I feel very much like a jerk. I'm questioning his motives without justification, because I'm nervous. I'm silent while he strokes Archie. Joel has taken care of me before when I was ill; he has a deep well of compassion.

"I appreciated the email, like I said. I would have liked you to write me back."

He doesn't answer, getting up on his knees to scrutinize my face closely. The stitches are gone but I still have healing cuts and yellowish bruises. Worse where the baton hit me.

I set my glass down on the coffee table. "You didn't come back just for me?"

He ignores that as well. "Let me see where you were hit."

"Uh, okay." I take off the sweatshirt, and the t-shirt underneath. The bruises are still somewhat dark on my arms and back, the back of my legs, across my ribs. He's frowning over what he sees, and makes me get up to look at my back.

His expression is similar to Alex's in the hospital, but more intense. So much so, I feel the need to reassure him. "It's okay, it doesn't hurt much now."

"They used something on you."

The tension in his voice affects me. He's upset and trying not to show it. He touches me softly around the bruises.

"Nothing broken. I kept them off me for most of the fight."

"I know. I know your skills."

But his expression doesn't change. For a moment, he meets my eyes then looks away. "I didn't write because I was coming back. To see you."

After a second he collects himself, as if he didn't mean to say that. He faces me again, and changes his mode, grinning wickedly. "You must be okay, because you're still uptight."

I smile in spite of myself. "You are the only person I know who makes me that way. With anyone else, I'm the most chill guy in the room."

"Keep dreaming. There is nothing chill about you. You can't even say "chill" and sound right. You're intense, like a jaguar. I admit it made for good sex."

"Thanks for the character reference." I try to sound casual as I put on my shirt and pick up my glass, but I can't. "I'm glad you came by, in any case."

He's taken my place on the ottoman, watching me. "I was impressed with what you did in Jersey. It reminded me of that time on the subway when those stupid kids were hassling us. I showed the video around and kept telling people, I *know* this guy. You have some fans in Europe. That was the fun part, but what happened here was bad. The cops find anyone?"

"Not yet. I'm sure they're looking as hard as you'd expect."

"I *don't* expect anything from them. You have any ideas about it?"

"Something to do with the case I'm working on."

"The stuff in the news with the attorney?"

"Yeah." I'm starting to feel the wine a bit, which makes me relax more. I begin telling Joel about Raymond's case. As I'm talking and walking around, getting agitated all over again, he picks up a pad of paper and a pen from my coffee table. He has a habit of drawing while others talk. Joel is an incredible artist. To me, he could make a name for himself but he doesn't do much to sell his art. I recount the case from the beginning. Raymond picking me up at the jail, finding his body, what happened during the attack on me, and why I didn't think it was accidental death.

I get wound up in my story and have to take a break to calm down.

"Baby, you're angry. I understand that."

"I'm tired of people telling me to stay out of the case. It makes me want to hide out for a while."

"Danny's on your case? Or is it James? You're right that you're too old for wet nurses. But you bring out that urge to protect that all do-gooders have."

"But not with *you*."

His smile is pained. I've said the wrong thing. "I'd protect you all right, but not to tell you your business. The urges you bring out with me are baser. And you used to like that, because I was an antidote for when your friends would be complaining that you wouldn't let them run your life."

"I don't want to get in a debate of you vs. them. I just want to trust my own judgment."

He responds softly. "Your judgment is fine, it always is. I believe you that Raymond's death was murder. I think you're right to investigate it. I'd never question that. You have my support."

"I'm glad. I don't really have an expert in the field to confirm my suspicions regarding the autoerotic part."

"I know something of it, though I'd never willingly try that. That kind of accident might happen to someone new to doing it, but I'd think that would be someone younger. Most of the time when someone dies from it, they're younger. Around 30."

I show him the photos I took. He turns over the legal pad and takes the photos.

As he looks them over I say, "You could be one of my expert witnesses."

"No one's going to listen to an expert witness who was in the sex trade. This isn't *My Cousin Vinny.*"

"You can be an expert *on* the sex trade."

"I'd rather not. You mean well, but you forget not everyone is accepting about it like you are. But if you want my personal opinion, this situation doesn't look right. This guy was smart, a lawyer, right?"

"Yes. While the two don't always go hand in hand, he *was* very smart."

He hands me back the photos and returns to his pad with another enigmatic smile. "So, we use logic. Like you taught me. A smart person can still act foolishly, and he could've been into dangerous stuff. But I think being smart, he would have researched it. How to do it the right way, what precautions to take. He wasn't 14. A guy like that would even hire a professional to show him how."

"You're right; I didn't think of it that way, but that just makes me surer now."

I take the chair at my writing desk by the sofa and we sit for a while, me thinking and him drawing. I feel my emotions rising again. He's suddenly in my place, much like he would be when we were together. When I first met Joel and began our relationship, he had a tendency to disappear every so often--a couple days, a week. I saw it was a protective measure of avoiding intimacy because of his fucked-up childhood.

While I empathized with him and gave him space during our two years or so together, my feelings were so strong for him that it killed me when he'd take off. I'd miss him and not even know if he was coming back. Then he'd show up unexpectedly. Gradually, he stopped doing the disappearing act unless he felt...I don't know. Unsure. Scared. Distrustful. Eventually I thought I had overcome that with him, but I was wrong, as I found out in an unpleasant incident. That made me walk away and I thought I'd really, truly never see him again. All of this revives the dormant anger in me.

"Where the fuck were you all this time? You know I wanted to know..."

My outburst makes him look at me over the pad. "Did you? I had to go somewhere. I had no reason to stay here, right?"

I don't answer. I don't have an answer. I don't even know why I asked because he's right. And wrong.

He goes back to drawing. "If you wanted to know, you could have found me. But you made it clear You. Were. Done." More than a hint of reproach.

"I could never find you when you wanted to disappear." I look down at my wine. "I knew you were in Europe. Your friend Chris told me that much. I *did* look, Goddamn it, I had to. But how am I going to find you in Europe off the grid? You didn't trust me enough to ever tell me where you went when you'd take off. From the first day through the whole time we were together."

He goes back to drawing for a minute. And then out of the blue: "Are you seeing anyone?"

The question startles me. "Not really."

He smiles. "Not *really*. Hedging your bets? Were you hung up on Raymond?"

"Excuse me?"

He shrugs. "I don't know if you hooked up with him or not. But I think you weren't really *involved* with him. You didn't have a chance try to fix his flaws, secretly follow him around town and investigate his every move."

I feel myself getting flushed. I set my glass down hard, sloshing wine out the glass. "If you're going to go down that road, get the *fuck* out of here."

That doesn't bother him; he rarely gets provoked. I suppose he hit a nerve because I did think Raymond was attractive and John had in essence accused me of being involved with him. And the tension between Joel and I unnerves me. I glare down at the spilled wine. "I never got involved with a client."

"Whereas it was my profession, is that right?"

"Don't bust my balls. I never threw your past in your face when we were together. I was just clear about not having unnecessary risks in our lives--really, your life--by you continuing to escort. Am I supposed to feel guilty?"

"I don't believe in unnecessary guilt. I also don't believe in trying to save people. I'm all right with who I am."

"I'm all right with who you are as well. And I wasn't involved with Raymond."

"Okay." He pets Archie, who is demanding more attention. "And anyway, I don't escort anymore. Not since you left." He gets up and goes to the kitchen, and comes back with paper towel to mop the rug where the wine spilled. "I know you better than that anyway. I'm just giving you a hard time. Are you interested in anyone these days, or not?"

"Why would you ask?"

He cleans around my glass. "I need to know my competition."

"Are you serious?"

He takes my hand and wipes off the drops of wine. I'm acutely aware of the familiarity of his touch. Of course, I should have realized why he was here. Just because I don't feel that I could get involved with him again doesn't mean he'd feel the same way. What throws me is that like me, he never approaches anyone who has rejected or left him. But here he is.

His voice is quiet, but now without his sardonic attitude as if reading my thoughts. "I'm here, right? And our connection is still here." He puts his hand with mine on his chest. I feel my face slowly flush and burn again.

"I'm not stressing you now, but we have unfinished business."

I'm defensive. "No, we don't. If you must know, I met a reporter for the *Herald Standard*. He seems like a nice guy."

"Really? What's his name?"

"Alex Barclay."

"Oh, him." Joel disposes of the paper towel, and then sits at my laptop on the writing desk next to the sofa. He starts looking up Alex online.

"Yeah, I see you've been Internet-stalking him. You forget to clear your cache again? Hmm. Professional, educated. Quite the upgrade." He continues reading for a while. "You know, I read his stories that mentioned you. That's how I knew what happened. But I didn't know he was writing those stories to get you to fuck him."

"Jesus, you have no right..."

"Got to you, did it?" He regards me for a long moment, to the point of awkwardness. I struggle for something to say to change the subject, and find nothing. As if knowing that, he smiles.

"I have to go for now. I just moved back, and I need to get my stuff. I really am glad you're all right, and I'm sorry this happened to you. You want to play cool, I can do that. I'm here for you. If you need anything..." He writes a number on the pad.

As he writes, I get up. Then suddenly he's right in front of me again, pressing the sheet of paper in my hand. "Remember how sometimes I'd help you with your work?"

For an instant, our eyes carry a thousand silent communications. His being very close throws me off; he's watching me in a way that makes me unable to speak clearly.

I hear myself agreeing to his suggestion. "I might at that, with some surveillance or whatnot."

He smiles, but eyes then go to the scar developing on my jawline and his face gets dark again.

"What's the matter?"

He makes the effort to cover his feelings. "It makes me angry, that's all. I *would* protect you. You have no idea." His fingers entwine in my hair for a moment and let go.

I go to the door as he lets himself out and shut it after him. I then go back to the pad to look at his number. It's underneath a drawing of Raymond as a Gustave Doré-style angel. He's been reading the news pretty well to remember what Raymond looked like. God only knows what he meant with the drawing.

But I also know I can use his help, and I'll probably take him up on the offer. My relief that he's okay, that I know where he is, is more evident now that he's not here to see it. I decide not to think about the reason he's back, too confusing for me.

The following Monday I'm preparing to visit with Ethan Nelson, with whom I've made an appointment at the New York Foundation for Art and Culture. While I'm getting my stuff together, my phone rings.

"Gabriel Ross." It's not a question. The voice is strange, not really human, like a voice run through a modifier.

"Yes. Can I help you?"

"I have a suggestion for you that you would do well to take." Definitely the person is speaking through some sort of device. The tone is deep and slightly wavering. No telling the gender or accent.

"Who might you be?" I speak in a friendly manner.

The person ignores the question. "My suggestion is this: you should cancel your investigation. You can give any excuse. No one will censure you for it."

Censure. What a fancy word for a machine-like voice. Perhaps it's the Nero Wolfe model. I'm not that upset by the message. As a private detective who has sometimes handled newsworthy cases, I have received any number of nutty calls. Because of that, my cell has the ability to record with a click of a button. I click. "I'm glad to hear I won't be censured, but why should I quit my investigation? Are you going to threaten me with something? Waterboarding maybe?"

The voice snorts, maybe amused. "This is not a threat; it's a suggestion. I think recent events should convince you. If you cancel the case right away, within two weeks you will receive twenty-five thousand dollars. You don't make a lot through your business right now. This should get you back on track."

So someone's run a credit check on me and my credit service didn't alert me. That's not right. "I appreciate your interest in my well-being. But I'm doing my work. I don't get paid *not* to work, unless the client chooses to end the case."

"Mr. Ross, that isn't a good road to travel, philosophically. Did your trip to the hospital give you any idea of that? You like movies, don't you? Well, you will understand this cliché: *you are in over your head.* Step off the case or you will not be taking any more cases in the future."

"I thought you weren't going to threaten me. Lying is a sin, you know."

Click. Whoever this is has no sense of humor. After a minute of being pleased with myself for my decorum, I have to absorb that someone just threatened me with death to leave Raymond's case.

∞

Twelve ◆ The Ten of Wands

The Ten of Wands represents a question of burden: has too much been taken on in a project? A goal is in the distance, with potential relief for the burden—but can the journey be made?

∞

Monday, August 2

I REPORT THE THREAT to Allen Cheng's office, mostly to see if he changes his mind about the investigation. I also look up the number of the mystery caller since it did show in my Caller ID. The number traces to a company that rents phone numbers for a limited period of time, usually for people with Craigslist ads or similar reasons for dealing with potential crazy persons. Dead end.

I'm not off the case, according to Cheng. He is not intimidated by the threat, but is concerned for my safety. I'm just glad my door has good locks--a high-security strike plate and an extra Medeco Residential Maxum bolt lock, as well as an alarm system. After setting these up, I'm ready to go.

I don't drive, since parking in the Foundation's Midtown neighborhood is a nightmare. I take the subway instead.

The Foundation is in a three-story building with a solid black granite front and the name emblazoned on the flag over the door. A brass plaque announces it was founded in 1944, during World War II. Display windows hold posters of past events the Foundation has sponsored. The building itself takes up the space of three regular-size storefronts. The entrance has two tall brass double doors. The doors are covered with a black grille front with buttons for an intercom. The public isn't going to just walk in here and put their grubby fingers on anything. I press the intercom button, and look up at the security video camera above the entrance. I'm sure someone inside is checking me out. After a good two minutes, a disembodied voice asks if I can be helped. After stating my name and purpose, I'm finally buzzed in.

I wait in a high-ceilinged, wide low-lit marbled lobby. A couple of plush chairs are set on an Asian rug in front of a desk, but I don't get the impression this is a waiting room. I can see some doors down two different hallways, but no people.

Then around the bend from one hallway comes Nelson, briskly walking towards me.

"Hello there. So you came. Thank you for arriving on time." He's impeccably groomed, wearing a tan shirt, black slacks, and a dark brown jacket. He moves with total self-awareness, as if he's playing a part in a stage drama. Relaxed, his mouth is set in a perpetual purse, framed with deep smile lines.

"Please follow me. We'll go to my office."

I follow him to an elevator. Inside he sizes me up again, and in the confined space I catch the scent of the grassy cologne he wore at the funeral. "I forgot my manners." He holds out his hand for a strong shake. "I'll bet your job is very interesting. Did you go to school for that?" The elevator doors open. He leads me down the hall.

"I didn't; it was a journeyman sort of process."

"*Journeyman*, really? Well, school *is* difficult. I had three years as a doctoral candidate at Cambridge, Semantics of Sociology degree."

Although he isn't obvious about it, he's still watching me in his peripheral vision. No doubt learned from that highly impressive Semantics of Sociology degree.

His office is past a miniature alcove done in brown and gold tones, and through frosted glass doors stenciled *Ethan Nelson, Director*. He waves me to a large burgundy chair across from his desk and oversize executive chair, and seats himself. Dramatic avant-garde music plays softly.

"My secretary and most of the staff are out today. Not much going on this week."

"I see. What about security?"

"We have a couple people, a skeleton crew. But the building also has an elaborate security system installed, connected with a firm off-premises. Their monitoring system is high-tech enough that they can get the police here faster than a security guard could get up to the next floor."

"Is that security needed? I can't see the Foundation being at risk like a bank."

Nelson seems affronted by my questioning the superior security of the Foundation. He answers as if he's responding to a cross-examination on the stand. "In fact, many valuable items come through here. As a charitable Foundation, we don't just handle monetary gifts. Sometimes a member will arrange to donate a priceless painting to a museum, and the painting will be stored here temporarily until the transfer is ready to be complete."

I try to poke at him a bit. "So the *Mona Lisa* could be in the next room, then."

He tents his fingers with a short smile, and speaks in the manner of a correcting a slow-witted child. "The *Mona Lisa* is in the Louvre. That's a museum in Paris, France."

I smile too, and consider for a moment punching him in the face. I went to the Louvre when I was a teenager with Dominic, who knew more about art than this asshole ever will.

While I am choosing not to punch him in the face--for now--he goes on. "There isn't much going on until a month from today, when we prepare to open a new exhibition project. Some our members have managed to save some priceless scrolls and *objets d'art*--excuse me--trinkets--from Iraq and Afghanistan during the conflict. These items will be on display."

I appreciate his going to the trouble to dumb-down *objets d'art* for me. "That's going to be soon?" I find the project rather strange, since these 'trinkets' belong to their country of origin. But that's not my affair.

"In six weeks. A private affair for fundraising. We're all very excited."

He swivels restlessly in his chair, again studying me intensely, although other than his eyes his posture is relaxed. "So what brings you here, Mr. Ross, after that debacle at the funeral?"

I shrug. He too sees the faint marks on my face. I've gotten used to people looking and pretending they aren't, but he doesn't comment. He does absently touch the scar under his own left eye.

"You invited me to get in touch with you. You worked with Raymond Booth rather closely regarding the Foundation. This was one of his favorite projects, am I correct?"

Holding my gaze, leaning his head on his hands, Nelson doesn't answer right away. He stays silent nearly to the point of awkwardness before he speaks. "Of course."

"So you could tell me if you are aware of anyone who might have posed a threat to him."

"*Really.*" He puts his arms down carefully on the armrest. Although his gaze has been intense, he now seems more than superficially interested in my words. "Why would someone *here* pose a threat?"

"I'd rather not go into the details. But suffice to say I'm reasonably certain."

He smiles slowly, looks out the windows for a moment, then back to me. "I thought the police closed the case. But you are suggesting there is more to his death?"

"Maybe they don't get the last say."

"You disagree with the police's conclusion." He leans back and swivels again slowly side-to-side in his chair, then leans back and crosses his legs. "It must have been terrible to find him like that." He tries to look sympathetic but for some reason his eyes are brighter at the mention of death. I don't like that.

"Yes, it was," I reply. "I hope you wouldn't mind helping me on this."

He's still swinging from side to side, and stops to check his watch, reminding me that he's an important man. Then he looks back at me. "You're rubbing your wrists. Are you having trouble with your hands?"

I consider his tone very carefully. It's supposed to be sympathetic, but to me it sounds like a saccharin version of sugar. "I was in an altercation. You might have heard."

He covers his mouth with his hand, slowly, as if he's thinking. "Yes, I believe I read something about that. The city can be so violent sometimes. Your work must be pretty dangerous, then, which makes your choice to pursue it intriguing. And to be honest, I would *love* to help you. Actually, why don't we talk while I give you the tour of the place?"

But as we get up, he pauses. "Could you wait outside the office for just a second? Then I'll show you around..."

I wait in the hallway for ten minutes. I don't hear much. A drawer opening and closing. A short, unintelligible telephone conversation. When he comes out smiling, I notice he's ever so slightly jittery and has a tendency to scan the area constantly. Back to the elevator, down to the ground floor. During the trip, he yaps about some bullshit events the Foundation held during the year, which I pay no attention to. I'm picturing him in a cap and dark glasses. Although really, he and John Harrison, Kelly Cole and Allen Cheng would look nearly the same wearing the cap and glasses if their heads down.

He leads me to a large exhibition room, a giant open area. In the center are three sculptures. A multicolored globe with relief images of people being beaten and tortured in various countries at war ten feet in diameter. It's flanked by statues: one of Icarus, the other of Diogenes. Nelson, continuing to show his elitist snob character, is surprised I know who they are, the character of myth and the philosopher of the streets.

We walk on through the exhibit room to a small dining area. His tone turns more business-like. "What *exactly* do you want to know?"

"For one thing, how did you get along with Raymond?"

"Honestly, Raymond and I were in sync for the most part. If he had issues, it was that he was a little too idealistic. The Foundation has to be realistic in this economy. During our board meetings, the rest of the members understood, but Raymond sometimes would have some back and forth."

"Anything serious?"

"Absolutely not. Are you familiar with nonprofits? Yes. Well, you know directors and members range from the hands-on to the almost invisible. Raymond was very much hands-on, almost like he was a staff member. But that showed his dedication to the mission, and helped in fundraising. I truly admired him for that."

Liar. He tries for admiration in his voice, but it comes out flat.

One of the dining room walls holds several framed photos of the Board members. He walks over to stand with me and points out pictures of himself with various members, and also local luminaries--politicians, news people, and celebrities. I notice how proud he is of this photographic evidence of his importance and how he gazes at his own image with undisguised admiration.

I spot another photo with Eleanor. "Is Ms. Whitford available?"

"For what?"

A slight sharpness to his tone. I turn to look at him innocently. "To speak with, of course."

"Ms. Whitford has not been feeling well lately. She had no problems with Raymond, in any respect."

"I'm sure. I understand they were close. More the reason to speak with her."

Nelson doesn't like that; his expression gets cold. He moves over to an expensive pod machine and begins brewing. "I'm sorry; I'd put you in touch with her, but she is, and I hope I'm not giving away TMI, a bit depressed lately. She has little family left and her health isn't great. I think she has lost some interest in the Foundation. She was even more depressed over Raymond's death. I'm being a bit protective of her, I know, but I don't want her disturbed." The hiss of the coffee maker punctuates his words.

He hands me a china cup of coffee. My silence to his litany is apparently taken as assent to the smoke he's trying to blow up my ass. "Poor Eleanor. She had-has-such a working knowledge of history and art, invaluable to the Foundation. I've had to kind of take over recently since she's been ill. The board is all she has, and I don't want them to vote her out, you know?"

Ill? She was fine at the funeral. I frown at him. "I guess you would know. You have the doctorate. I can't imagine the work necessary for that." Internally I wince at my own words, but I want to test him by buttering him up. I put envy in my voice: rough kid from the streets, out of the league of the supposedly well-educated gentleman.

He responds to it visibly by smiling and assuming a thoughtful expression. "My dissertation was on *The Problematic Theme Structures of Social Equity*. At Oxford. It was a long, hard road to get where I am today."

"Oxford, very impressive. You were well-received I take it."

"I heard some government officials were interested in using it for policy mandates."

I'm *so* sure. I sip at my coffee and keep my voice casual. "I thought you said before that you attended Cambridge."

He frowns and his neck tightens. He pauses to cover his irritation with checking an imaginary spot on his tie. "I did my dissertation early at Cambridge. I expanded it for Oxford."

More bullshit, and I make a mental note to see about a so-called "Semantics of Sociology" degree. Nelson's face is now traversed with tension lines. He changes the subject away from his illustrious education. "Gabriel, tell me. Why do you think Raymond was murdered?"

"Circumstances suggest it. I've kind of gotten messages to that effect, you might say."

A brief, uncomfortable silence, as I watch him, thinking about that message today. What did he say when I arrived? *So you came.* Did he expect me not to, perhaps because of the phone threat?

Coffee time over, we start to return to the elevators. As the doors open, he turns that dark gaze on me. "Such an interesting profession where you get to dig up the ugliest of human behavior and...*deal* with it to earn a living. I have no doubt you're under-appreciated." He has faint smile on his lips.

I don't rise to the bait. "Everyone is under-appreciated. Certainly you must be, what with the responsibilities of the place."

His eyes get distant. "Oh, now you've got me." He seems to be considering what I said. Even in his suspicion, he's absorbing every bit of praise concerning himself. Narcissist. "Even in the position I'm in, sometimes it is hard to get gratitude for all you do, for all you deal with day in and day out."

As we get out and head back to his office, his tone gets harsher. "Sometimes, when you're dealing with trust-fund babies who've never actually worked for a living, or you have to troubleshoot and deal to get something *they* want, you realize they don't understand what you're doing, or the pressure and finesse necessary to make everything go right..."

We sit down; I lean forward in my chair. "There's so much hard work and hard decisions to be made here; the pressure of keeping the whole concept afloat is incredible."

"Yes, there are people who really *don't* understand the way the Foundation should be run, and will subjugate it, or ruin it, in order to promote some outdated premise."

Suddenly he snaps back into the present. "Since this is your forte, what do *you* think about his death? Don't you think it's a crime of passion? Isn't the simplest answer the most logical?"

"Not always. I think that the options are open as to motive and method."

"But if he was truly hurt by someone else, then perhaps it was, well, a pick-up. Look at the circumstances of his death."

"I have, carefully. By the way, where were you that weekend?"

"At work and at home. Yes, I was alone if that's what you're asking."

"Hmm. I appreciate your candor."

"As I said, I honestly want to help." He knows how to lie. Appearing cooperative, making eye contact, being friendly, but he's also fidgeting, his eyes are dilated, and his voice is rising a little in pitch. He's used the word honest or true several times to convince me. But what works most for a liar is the human need to believe what they hear, not to examine what's said closely. I'm naturally suspicious, and I'll go the other way--to disbelieve on instinct.

That makes me want to provoke him. I have to eventually, so I take a calculated risk. "Then tell me, would any persons associated with the Foundation possibly have been in the Nazi party?"

His eyes become sharper and darker. "Excuse me?"

"Nazis. You know, World War II, killed millions of people. Some of them were able to leave Germany after the war and go into hiding."

"And you think someone's in hiding *here*?" He rolls his eyes in amusement. But his voice is a bit too loud and off-key.

"I believe my question was clear. Do you know any associates of your board members to have been in the Nazi party?"

"Was *that* Raymond's problem? I had no idea he was getting these delusions." He smiles again, running his fingers over his mouth, practically face-palming in fake utter disbelief.

"Interesting you say that was Raymond's problem. I never suggested that."

"Well, why else would you ask....didn't he hire you..." We look at each other in silence for a moment.

Nothing was ever printed about Raymond having hired me. The news outlets don't even know he picked me up in Jersey. Only that Toni hired me to find her brother.

"Raymond never spoke to you regarding a problem here, I take it."

"Nothing involving Nazis, no. Nor UFOS or Bigfoot for that matter. It was a pleasure speaking with you today, Gabriel. But I have to get some work done. Let me say this. I had no conflicts with Raymond and I have no Nazi connections. I understand that he and Dr. Cole, whom you met at the funeral, did have something of a feud. Perhaps *he* knows. But please come back anytime."

"Certainly. Thank you."

I feel his eyes on me as I leave.

∞

Seven of Wands represents working to maintain one's equilibrium and to gain superiority over a difficult situation.

∞

Wednesday, August 4

IN THE MORE EXCLUSIVE parts of Westchester County just north of New York City, several small, genteel towns are tucked into wooded areas of breathtaking loveliness. Pricey estates rest on scenic elevations of craggy rock, overlooking streams and other waterways.

In one of these estates Ethan Nelson waits in a hallway outside the owner's library. He arrived on time but is kept waiting a half hour. He's used to that.

The owner of the house is called Mr. Jacobs, an alias. Nelson knows the man's real name but is under instruction to refer to him as Jacobs.

Nelson waits without fidgeting. He concentrates on what he needs to say during this meeting.

Finally, the library door opens. Jacobs stands in the doorway and gestures Nelson to come in.

Nelson sees that another man is present. Around seventy, gray hair, British-style dark gray suit. Jacobs does not introduce him, but Nelson nods toward him and waits for Jacobs to gesture him to a chair. No presumptions must be made; a strict code of decorum prevails.

The library is almost large as a basketball court and has twenty-foot high ceilings. The windows are framed with thick drapes. Bookshelves stretch down the walls, interspersed by antique furniture and rugs. The library is soundproofed. Nelson can't decide if it's wired for sound and video. He thinks not. Having records can be dangerous, as he knows.

Jacobs is a white man around fifty. He is the very physicality of the WASP-type. His expression is cold. No greetings to Nelson, but right to the point. "Is this situation resolved?"

Nelson smiles confidently regardless of Jacobs' stone-faced expression. He never feels pressure or nervousness of being called on the carpet. "I don't think any serious problems exist."

Jacobs purses his mouth. "Really? The private investigator has still been asking questions. Apparently, he knows *something* is connected to the Foundation. Maybe this was handled too little, too late."

Nelson briefly glances at the older man sitting close enough to hear, but not directly participating in the conversation. Jacobs is seated at a large massive desk that wouldn't be out of place in Versailles. Nelson's chair is set pointedly in front of the desk and the chair is small, without arms. He suspects Jacobs's chair is slightly raised, all the more to give the impression of power a judge's bench might have. The older man is in a much larger chair off to Jacobs's right. His legs are crossed and he smokes foreign tobacco.

All of this sends a message of exactly what kind of status Nelson has. He's well aware of his place, although he has hopes of moving beyond that. He speaks carefully to impart his confidence in the situation.

"Yes, no doubt Booth told him *something*. But if he really knew anything important, would he be asking questions? Doubtful, very doubtful." Nelson taps his head. "Ross is emotional and foolishly impulsive. He has a thing about Booth's death; maybe he just wasn't paid enough. Or he's nosy, or maybe he even had the hots for Booth. Who knows? The point is I can read him like a book, and he's already stupid enough to have gotten himself in trouble on camera before he even became involved in this affair. Someone like that is very easy to manipulate. Trust me, no one will take his inquires seriously."

Jacobs knows Nelson is an expert on manipulation. His past work in setting up situations to provoke others in committing certain actions has been unquestionably successful.

Yet his instinct nags at him that this particular situation had a flaw somewhere, something Nelson overlooked or misinterpreted. He is not relieved much by the reassurances. Nelson appears appropriately calm and deferential. But Jacob senses his doing so is a little harder today. Jacobs is also very good at reading character.

The older guest speaks now; his voice has a mild Swiss accent, his English is flawless. "We do not need any more examination of this matter. The fallout can be serious."

The Swiss man's demeanor is cultivated from years of privilege and experience. He is used to affairs being settled quietly behind closed doors and tasks being taken care of with a waved hand and unspoken agreement. He is uncomfortable with persons not in his social class, especially on business. But people like Nelson are a necessity.

Nelson would ordinarily confront anyone who challenged his competency. But not here. His demeanor is also in-born but with a different quality. Although far outside the Swiss man's social set he is immune from intimidation by class, money or even physical danger. His gaze is equally intense but he directs it at the floor or Jacobs's desk, and keeps a small smile so as to not appear disrespectful. Nonetheless, in that gaze is a mental hardness that no amount of money or privilege could duplicate.

Jacobs follows up on the Swiss man's remarks. "The attempt to have Ross intimidated didn't work, obviously. Not if he's convinced Booth's partner to hire him. There are still stories in the papers. Then you report that he showed up at your office. You actually agreed to speak with him."

"I would have seemed suspicious if I didn't."

"Who cares? What is Ross to the Foundation? Why give him an opening?"

"I understand your concern." Nelson controls his voice so no scorn shows. "But in doing so I discovered he believes he knows something about Nazis. That tells me what Booth told him--and what he didn't."

Neither of the other two men changes expression. Nelson is not bothered by their blank faces. He doesn't need social niceties. He has to make his case. No other outcome can happen.

"In addition, I found out that Ross has his fallible side. He shouldn't have even *mentioned* Nazis. He was trying to get a rise out of me. That's another weakness; he thinks he's on the side of 'justice.' It tells me how he's vulnerable."

The Swiss man still doesn't look convinced but his expression is less severe. He almost gets conversational. "I will tell you this. Right now, the political situation in Germany is delicate due to the debates over the economy. We are trying to arrange certain business there right now but some radical groups are making trouble by reviving the old principles from Hitler's time. They are stirring up the Greens and the Social Democrats to protest. Some of the radical leaders are crude in their tactics with statements that come close to Holocaust denial and so on; they're only seeking attention. But because the liberal public gets...aggravated at any Hitler-admirers, it could hurt as a backlash to our goals in general. So if Ross's investigation turns up any connection to Nazis, that is trouble we don't need."

Jacobs taps the desk with his fingers. "But ultimately, the investigation needs to be stopped before *any* more trouble develops. I think how Booth was taken care of had some rough spots."

Nelson takes longer to control his face, staring at the floor again before he can look up with almost as blank an expression. He clasps his hand together. "I understand that this was not the usual method. We came across the situation with Booth by my intuition that he was nosing around. I had to handle him in a short time frame, since he had already contacted Ross. The public aspect was unavoidable. But the nature of his death was such that people don't want anything to do with him; it discredited him. I think the risk was worth it."

The Swiss man looks at Jacobs, who thinks a minute before speaking. "With the media, that's true. At least for most of them. We'll need to look into the others. Sometimes the story needs to be set in motion, and then the truth creates itself, so to speak. You can keep track of what Ross is doing? Head him off?"

"Yes. He's under surveillance. Right now, I'm making that constant with the associate you sent me."

"Good. Nelson, don't make the mistake of underestimating people. You don't need to take the same action with Ross as Booth. Not yet. At least, I do not want anything with Ross to draw attention to us."

"I understand. People have failings. Booth had failings and Ross has failings. I was able to take advantage before and I still can. I'm not going to fail *you.*"

"And Booth's sister?"

"She'll probably self-destruct. No one else will deal with her once Ross is out of the picture."

"Let's hope so. I expect better results." Jacobs looks up and away, a flash of annoyance in his face.

"I would say..." Nelson smiles humorlessly. "...that if this matter is resolved as expected, that might serve to demonstrate my competence to help you with more important projects."

Jacobs still stares into the distance. Not giving Nelson the courtesy of meeting his gaze. "More important projects? You have complaints about your status?"

"No, I'm not saying that at all. But I feel that in a larger context I'm not being utilized to the fullest extent of my capabilities. The tasks I handle involve important issues, but are often a matter of brute force. I could do a great deal more if I was in a position similar to your line of work or even overseas..."

Jacobs shakes his head once. Now the Swiss man looks away, distancing himself from this aspect of the conversation as Jacobs responds.

"I think you should understand your situation better. You're in a position of prominence, not brute force. You're in this position due to your previous tasks. I don't think now is the time to move elsewhere. Remember we approached you for very specific reasons to work for us. I don't think anyone recruited you with the promise of membership to a non-existent executive training program. Even if that were so, you don't have the background for what you want. But if you show your competence as you promise and you'll be more amply compensated. That's what it's all about."

Nelson's body tenses imperceptibly. The silence of the library echoes on him. It's all chess playing, he thinks. "The matter of background is superfluous. Anyone can fix that. It's about opportunity."

Jacobs thinks for some time. Nelson remains seated without moving. The only one who seems relaxed is the Swiss man, who lights another cigarette.

"All right, I understand about ambition." Jacobs finally turns back to Nelson. "I'll take that into account when this is successful. You can leave now."

Nelson feels a victory inside, which he does not show. He nods and gets up to leave. No goodbyes or thanks are expected or wanted. A nondescript man in a black suit waits to walk Nelson back out to his car.

The other two men sit for a moment in the library, which now has music playing in the background.

The Swiss man listens for a while. He considers Jacobs. "You don't seriously intend to recommend him for something more...elevated? That is not going to work."

As Jacobs was cold and imperial to Nelson, his manner becomes slightly deferential to the older man. "Seriously, no. But humiliating him is not effective. He's a very valuable person, in his place. His own weakness is grandeur, and hopefully that will not be a continuing problem. This isn't the Mafia or the CIA. I wouldn't have a showdown with him unless absolutely necessary."

The older man stirs uncomfortably. "He knows too much himself."

Jacobs taps the desk again. "I don't know what he knows. He's only told so much. But he came out of nowhere, and manages to get done whatever needs to be done. He has no vices other than his ego, I think." But something still nags at him.

Around ten years ago, Jacobs had been introduced to Nelson in passing. Then five years later, a London colleague had arranged for Nelson to be set up in the East Coast for certain work, that led to his current position in the Foundation. The colleague had assured Jacobs that Nelson could take care of serious problems. And so he had. Jacobs did not trust him; he trusted no one outside his own circle. But he relied upon Nelson. Still, he was unsettled that a background check on Nelson produced nothing. Nelson had effectively wiped away his past.

Nelson's value lay in three important traits: unquestioned loyalty; a skill for manipulative cunning; and indifference as to what happened with the targets. Yet for Jacobs, who himself was drawn into his circle of colleagues as a young man, the traits were also minefields. Loyalty lasted until the job was dissatisfying. Now Nelson's ambition made his loyalty ever so slightly in doubt. His indifference was not simply sociopathic; combined with his intelligence he was miles above an ordinary hired killer. Attempts at manipulating him would be futile, and he'd never show if he knew what was happening or not.

Jacobs remembered several years ago when a rich man on Long Island had accidentally killed an underage girl during a rough-sex party in his home. The rich man was spoiled, childish and not smart. But he was connected. Nelson was sent to do what he could as fast as he could that very night.

Within the next few hours, a young man who had been drifting through the same Long Island town on a lark was approached by a couple of lissome young women with offers of exotic sex and drugs. The young man passed out during the would-be bacchanalia and woke up to find the rich man's victim next to him on the beach. Suddenly the police were upon him, having been called from an anonymous tip. The young man ended up pleading to manslaughter and sex abuse. He had no reason not to believe he had actually done the crime during a drug-related black out. Nelson had known where to go to find such as patsy, and arranged with the women to handle the pick-up.

In another instance, Nelson handled the robbery of a small museum as cover to *return* a painting. The original had been stolen and duplicated while on traveling exhibit, and the forgery displayed for years. Later, under trying times, the thief had attempted to offer the original as collateral for a business loan when his Ponzi scheme started failing. Circumstances necessitated keeping the thief from causing the museum scandal. The original painting was replaced during the "botched" robbery in which little else was stolen and for which no one was apprehended. The thief later died of an apparent accident falling drunk over a hotel balcony.

Jacobs keeps in mind that this situation is simple. Booth was an attorney prominent in his field but unknown otherwise. He's now dead. Ross is a private investigator barely keeping his head above water. Realistically, he is not a threat, especially if Nelson does his job. Jacobs will give him that chance, but he's already mulling an alternative plan just in case. In case Nelson does have a problem, and if the situation with Ross is not as simple as it appears. But one way or the other, Ross will be stopped.

∞

FOURTEEN ♦ THE FIVE OF WANDS

The Five of Wands represents preparing for competition and struggle. For this, one needs to be in full control of one's mind in case of mental as well as physical battles.

∞

Thursday, August 5
Alphabet City, Avenue A, 11:15 am

I HAVE AN APPOINTMENT to see Dr. Kelly Cole during his office hours. I'm a little stretched for time this week. I have my current roster of clients to handle, dealing with the experts who are now working on Raymond's case and reviewing their reports, and brainstorming on the case myself. Jim is breathing down my neck about his projects as well. Danny will be adding his project soon, but his excursion is a little over a week away. But I need some help with the pressure. After thinking about it some, on Monday after seeing Nelson I called Joel to take up on his offer of help.

Before I leave to see Cole, I get my current files out. Joel has come over and we go over a list of errands. Since he's extremely good with computers and technical issues, he starts playing with my iPad, laptop, desktop, and phones to optimize them. Joel has natural investigative instincts plus some skills I taught him back when we were together. I give him my passwords and spare keys.

Whatever our personal issues--which are unspoken between us at the moment--he's a good soul and utterly trustworthy for business. He can stand in for me wherever necessary; he has done that before. When I review the files with him, we pick up as if he had never left. This is especially important with Raymond's case, because I need Joel to meet a couple of experts and grill them about the information they're providing.

Joel lights up one of my cigarettes while we talk. "Why are you seeing Cole? Just to exclude him? Sounds like Nelson is the better suspect."

I look at the notes I've printed out from my office in the second bedroom of the apartment. "I'm strongly feeling that way, but I have to cover everything."

"I got you. But Nelson knows you know."

"He knows I'm suspicious, that's all. He thinks I'm stupid. And that he can talk himself out with whatever lies he sets up."

"Right. That got to you, and I know why you incited him. Although you need to be careful about what gets to you. But with his slip-up, it was...not evidence, what's the word you love to use?"

"Indicia."

"That's it. Indicia that he knows what Raymond was doing. Then if he set up Raymond and got someone to help him with that...he probably also had someone to threaten you on the phone and paid those guys to jump you."

"Right, I need to be careful."

He watches me long enough for me to stop futzing with my files.

"Okay, Joel, what's on your mind?"

"He's not going to stop, is what I'm sayin'. In one way, it will confirm this and in another, he'll try to kill you."

"Don't worry. Like I said, I'll watch my back."

He breathes out smoke slowly. "You don't know how, baby. You have good instincts about people, but you also have that quality...like a cat, you see a bird and want to pounce out of righteousness without looking in the shadows."

I give him my skeptical look. "Overstating the case."

"This is a time for overstating. I've been in those shadows. Hiding, not to hurt. But I've run into those who hurt. I don't want you hurt again." He gets up and puts his hands on my shoulders. "Be like me, sometimes...okay?"

I know what he means. Melting into the background to observe rather than be a target. "I'll work on it, I promise...but with the job here, keep track of your hours. I'll pay you the rate I have for outside contractors--"

He plays with my jacket collar. "Don't worry about it."

"Of course I'm worrying about it; you need to be paid."

"I'm cool. Just go to your thing."

I spend a few minutes trying to get him to accept some kind of monetary compensation, but he just ignores me. I don't have time to keep arguing about it. Clearly he's not short of money, which means he's doing this just to help. Sometimes that costs more in the end but I can't worry about it today.

Cole's office and lab are on the eighth floor of Manhattan South Hospital. The hospital's pathology department is reputed to be one of the best on the Eastern Seaboard for research--or so the website tells me. The hospital is affiliated with Columbia and is a top-rated teaching facility. Dr. Cole is an anatomical surgical pathologist and one of the teachers primarily responsible for the top ratings in translational research. His secretary leads me to his lab. The lab is fairly large with several microscopes, hazardous waste disposal containers, cutting stations, sinks, and machines for analysis.

Dr. Cole is wearing a lab coat that ties at the back, bending over to wash his hands in one of the sinks. He greets me in a neutral tone. "Mr. Ross. I see you are continuing your investigation, as it were."

His voice has a distinct deliberateness, a differing timbre for each word. He picks up a metal tray covered with a cloth and carries it to a refrigerator. He then takes out a covered dish with something dark red and gelatinous. He carries this to another table and begins to slice samples. I don't want to look too closely at what he is cutting.

"Frankly, I'm surprised you agreed to talk to me. I get the impression at Raymond Booth's funeral that I was morally repugnant to you."

"I'm curious. As a scientist, if you believe in empiricism you have to deal with that which is morally repugnant, if in fact you are. I never said as such. I saw your statement in the news. I saw you were beat up as well. Rather severely. I can see it still leaves marks on you after two weeks, so it was severe. Yet you pursue. If you don't mind my asking, why are you doing this? Is it some kind of lawsuit involved?"

"No. Raymond's partner, Allen Cheng, hired me to look into the matter."

"Really." He stops and stands up, casts his translucent gaze somewhere into space, then looks at me. "I can't imagine why. Did you talk him into it?"

"He agreed with me that Raymond's death is actually homicide."

"Do you have a good basis for this or are you just trying to get money from Cheng? I remember reading about you finding Raymond's body. You seem to be involved in a lot of controversy."

I refrain from rolling my eyes. If he's trying to insult me, which he is, he's out of luck. I've been called worse than just money-grubbing.

"Yeah, right now that's true. But it's because I'm doing something on principle, which people often don't understand. I do have a reasonable basis for my supposition. I'm also trying to find out if he had hostile relations with anyone who could be a suspect."

He points his scalpel to his chest. "Such as me, you mean."

"Sure. That's only logical. But look, I'm not here to be hostile, Dr. Cole. I'm just trying to find out information about Raymond and what he did particularly at the Foundation. Ethan Nelson in fact suggested I talk to you."

"Did he now? Are you asking..." he lifts the scalpel like a sword for emphasis, "...if I was one of Raymond's enemies, or something to that effect?" His expression doesn't change into abject fear at the prospect of my considering him a suspect.

"From what I was told, your relationship was not amicable. You tell me. Were you on bad terms with him? Was anyone else on bad terms with him?"

He lays down the scalpel and begins to set up one of the machines. "You know, I'm rather overwhelmed with work here. The hospital says it has budget problems and can't help. I have to depend on the good graces of student volunteers looking for extra credit, despite the progressiveness of my research. That's rather sad, don't you think?"

"The hospital doesn't provide you with a staff?"

"Part-time. The hospital devotes its budget primarily to those who bring in income. Not those who might be involved in important research with direct clinical applications for the future."

I'm quiet as he begins whatever test he needs to get done. Eventually he speaks. "Anyway, bad terms. Yes, and I expect this to be confidential. Our former director left because Raymond felt he did not have enough dedication to the Foundation. While I understood Raymond's position, in order to ensure that the grant requirements are met, we had to get moving on certain things. While Raymond was out due to a back injury late last year, we searched for a suitable candidate for director and Nelson was recommended to us."

"And how did Raymond get along with him?"

He takes time to study me over the dead man. "I don't know the particulars of his relationship with Mr. Nelson. There may have been a personality issue at that, but you have to understand this happened frequently because Raymond was used to getting his way-- like lawyers do--and if someone was challenging him in any manner he could be churlish about it."

Having set up his test, Cole goes back to his dish with the mystery organ. "So why do you think Raymond was murdered as opposed to suicide or accident? Autoerotic accidental suicides happen frequently, believe me. I've read scientific papers on it. A couple of famous rock stars died that way."

"For one, the scene of death appeared to be staged. For another, I haven't found that he had any true interest in BDSM, and he had no safety means of escape. Also, he was seen with a person right before his death--a man was dressed to avoid being identified. A witness said Raymond became ill and was taken away by this person."

Cole is slicing again. "Not a bad deduction, but how do you know he wasn't actually in a sexual situation?"

"I think it's too coincidental that some person was with Raymond, and Raymond appeared ill just before he disappeared. I find the fact the air conditioner was turned down extremely low in his room suspicious."

He raises his eyes to mine. "The air conditioner? You're thinking time of death."

"The rate of decomp would be slowed right? Maybe throw off an accurate time at least?"

"Yes. That has been done before, and time of death is hardly an exact determination in all cases. Even stomach contents aren't reliable. The Canadian case of Stephen Truscott showed that. The best indicator of time of death is insect activity. What did the report say about that?"

"Very little. No real insect activity was found. He perhaps was either alive for three days or kept somewhere cold and where insects could not get to him."

He nods. "So you have found aspects that may or may not mean homicide. I'll give you this: I'm not convinced, but what you mention is logical. But why do you think I might have been responsible?"

"I think he would have known the killer. Most people know their killers, in the standard murder motives of money, jealousy, or to cover another crime. And as I mentioned, Nelson seems to think you might be worth asking about it."

He shrugs, rolling his eyes slightly. "Mr. Nelson does not have the capability of reading my mind. My relationship with Raymond was not severe enough to necessitate murder. I will receive no money or increase in standing in any way due to his demise. He had nothing over which I was jealous; he was homosexual and I'm not. I haven't committed a crime so I couldn't have killed him to cover up a non-existent crime."

Cole seems sincere. He's not trying to convince me of anything. He's matter of fact.

"Why might Nelson have said so? Does he not like you very much?"

The organ he's working in my peripheral vision is making me ill, since I have Raymond on my mind.

"I'm not going to speculate about why he might have said that. If, *if* he was implying I was involved in Raymond's death, he's sorely mistaken."

"Do you remember where you were from Friday the 9th through Monday morning, the 12th?"

"Yes. I was working here, and then I was home. I live on West 84th Street. My daughter was with me during the evening. My secretary can verify I was here during the day."

I walk away from his workstation and go to look out the windows. "Do you know if Raymond had any particular concerns with the Foundation, outside of the directors' competence?"

"Meaning what? I hope you don't think I'm going to go into the Foundation's business with *you*."

"God forbid." I continue to watch the traffic down five stories below. "However, he did have concerns. Maybe he raised them to you or one of the other Foundation members. Ms. Whitford, for instance."

I hear a clatter of the surgical instrument being dropped on metal. "Really, Mr. Ross. Rather a cheap ploy. So I'm supposed to think you have information, and inadvertently confirm it."

I turn to face him. "No, it's not a ploy, it's fact. Maybe he didn't tell you, though."

"Mr. Ross, even if you are genuinely concerned about an area that is not your business, this would be a matter for the police. I know of no one having a motive to kill Raymond, and I doubt our Board members do, either. Nothing is wrong with our Foundation."

"Not the Foundation itself, perhaps, but I'm talking about the board members. Do you know of any who might have had contacts with Nazis?"

He crosses his arms and scowls at me. I see the reappearance of the cold anger he had at the funeral. "The Foundation helps a good deal of charitable organizations in this city, and that is very important in times of severe recession, as we have now. We don't need trumped-up scandal for an institution with a spotless reputation. I thought you might possibly have something worth discussing, but if you're going to resort to calling our members Nazis..."

"I'm not trying to smear the Foundation and I didn't call anyone a Nazi. I'm just trying to find out some answers about what happened with Raymond Booth."

In response, Cole goes to the door of the lab and calls for his secretary. When she steps in, he says, "You see Mr. Ross here. He is a private detective engaging in questionable business. If he calls you or approaches you for any information about me or the Foundation he is not to be entertained. You can hang up on him or call security as needed."

The secretary looks at me with an expression of sternness, for having bothered to engage in chitchat with me earlier. She also seems a tad embarrassed. I'm not. I give her a polite smile and look back at Cole.

"You didn't answer my question."

He shakes his head at me. "*Nazis.* There are no Nazis in the Foundation."

"I didn't say *in*, I said in contact *with*."

He glares at me, and his arrogant professor/doctor demeanor seems to be ready to freeze me solid. I meet his eyes with my own conviction. "It can happen, you know, Dr. Cole. People can be involved in bad things. You're telling me you've never run into stranger things in your line of work? Answer me this: did Raymond routinely chase imaginary conspiracies?"

Cole suddenly slumps. His face even goes slack. For the first time he looks unsure. "I don't know. I wouldn't like to think so. Why do you ask about our board? Do you have any evidence of such a relationship?"

Interesting that Ethan Nelson didn't ask the same question. "I can't go into it, but I have good reason to think so."

"And you are hypothesizing that a Nazi connection is also related to Raymond's death."

"Possibly. I would like to find out more if you could help."

Cole picks up an instrument and stares at it, turning it around in his hands.

I take a step closer to him. "Maybe something going on at the Foundation bothers *you*."

He looks at the secretary, who is hovering around the door. She and I wait to see what he decides what he's going to do.

Finally he looks back at me. "I can't help you with a Nazi I don't know exists. If I hear something--well, I'll have to see. In the meantime, if you are considering persons who would benefit from Raymond's death, don't forget he was in a relationship. I didn't know much about it, but isn't that where the police look first? Understand I didn't talk to him about his relationship but I heard the other end of some phone calls." He turns his head, as if embarrassed to be reporting vulgar gossip. I can see his eyes are troubled.

What I said bothered him. A problem with the Foundation, perhaps. He knows or suspects something but doesn't want to share, doesn't trust anyone.

"Okay." I turn to walk away. "You can call me if you change your mind about what you believe."

The secretary steps aside with a more sympathetic expression.

I head out for some the work I need to do for the day, and late in the afternoon go back home to change clothes. Joel has left notes for me about his progress. He's professional in his work; that I can always count on. I'm rather glad he hasn't stayed in the apartment, as tonight is the date to meet Alex for dinner. He had suggested a Latino-Asian place in NoHo, a neighborhood north of the Village.

I find some excitement about the meeting even though it's supposed to be business, remembering--nay--reliving the flirtation in our earlier contact.

I meet Alex in the lobby of the restaurant. He's wearing a white button down shirt and an extra-long blue jacket. I have a long leather jacket over a grey Henley. When he greets me, he takes my hand with both hands.

The evening starts out more like a date than a business meeting, but I'm not complaining.

"I like your taste in jackets."

Alex reaches across the table to feel the sleeve. Up close under calmer circumstances, I can appreciate his looks and voice even more.

"Thanks. I invest in them more than shirts. A good jacket can cover up cheap shirts." I laugh, finding humor in my own situation especially as Alex is wearing an expensive shirt. Something tailored, by the look of it.

"What made you want to get into investigation? Were you police?"

"No, I'm not the cop type. I was good at not minding my own business as a kid, and I liked the idea of doing it for a living plus the idea of finding wrongdoers, fraudsters, missing persons. I read too many detective novels and got kind of romanticized about it."

"Is not having a history in law enforcement a problem?"

"No, not for me. I worked too hard to be good at what I do. I was lucky in having good mentors in Rochester and here in the city who showed me the ropes."

"I think you've done well. I checked you out here and there, I admit. And you write too, with the online magazine. Very well, very passionately. You're a good talker. Do you do marketing? Have you considered getting on radio programs to talk about your work or writing?"

"I work so much that I don't end up having a lot of time for marketing...but you're right."

"I think you should look into it. Now, what about this person who's talking about you to my colleagues at other papers? The person from your industry?"

I laugh. "Gerry. The partner of my former mentor. He was a former cop, actually. He even had some sweet deal to train a town police force in Afghanistan with our tax money. I heard he did a crap job."

"Why is he saying things about you?"

"He always hated me. He didn't like his partner Manny, much either. Manny got me in the business full time, and really was my mentor. But Gerry couldn't stand me from the start. I'd chalk it up to a personality issue but I think he was bent somewhere. Manny probably was aware of that, but when he started having health problems, that took over being able to check out his own partner. But when Gerry came back from his contracting bullshit in Afghanistan, I happened to be writing some pieces for *NY Cultcha*. I have a friend who's in the service. He gave me some inside info on the contractors over there and how a lot of them don't know shit about what they're doing. Gerry thought I was personally targeting him. Whatever." I shake my head. "We all have enemies, right?"

"And new friends." His smile captures me for an instant, and then we peruse the menus and order drinks. I have to admit that sitting across from him in a completely different atmosphere from the funeral home and hospital; he's making my knees weak in a seriously good way.

As if he senses that, he smiles. Trying to be casual, I mention that his accent reminds me of actor/comedian Eddie Izzard, my favorite famous person of British ancestry, along with Welsh singer/songwriter David Gray. He finds my remark amusing but agrees with me on how fabulous Eddie is. Alex turns out to have been born in Kent and lived there until he was twenty then moved to Chicago to work for the *Sun-Times,* then New York. He's met Roger Ebert, one of my heroes.

"My mother was born in Mumbai back when it was Bombay. My father is British, a journalist who worked for the BBC and then for American news organizations. I don't know how they got together; she was given an incredible amount of grief for not marrying a man from her caste, and then my dad is not an Indian or Hindu. But they got over it, not wanting to leave her without family, and here I am."

"Are you Hindu?"

"She raised me that way. Sometimes I'm agnostic. Depends on how I feel during the day. Since you were chanting at the funeral, I take it you're Buddhist?"

"Yes, since Gnosticism isn't really around anymore Buddhism will do. Irish boys aren't known for their proclivity to Buddhism, but I'm already the black sheep."

"Really? That's a shame. I think your family would be proud of being a self-made man."

I take a healthy swig of my Sam Adams. "I'm not being fair." I show him a photo of my mom and my uncle in my phone. "They've passed away so I don't have any family left. But they were mine and I was theirs. I still have people I'm related to, but..." I put the phone away. "You don't want to hear about that tonight."

We continue talking. At one point I mention my mom taught me Tarot cards, and he asks me if I would read them for him. As it happens I have a deck in my messenger bag, an elegant deck with cats. I take out the deck for a quick three-card outlay for Alex. Past-Five of Swords. Something that has served as sort of a psychological prison, a long-time struggle; Present-Eight of Pentacles. Pride in what has been achieved, but be careful of it going too far; Future-Temperance--try to achieve balance and not do too much. Alex smiles over the reading. He doesn't comment if the readings are accurate or meaningless.

At the end of the evening we both hesitate, as if not sure who should suggest meeting up again--as if this could be a delicate matter. I decide this is a good sign. Sex is far more easily negotiated than what might be conducive to a relationship.

I ask him, "Do you like cats?"

"Cats are brilliant. Hindus appreciate the dignity and character of animals."

"What about atheists/agnostics?"

"They think cats are smarter than humans."

"Fine, because I have a cat and he will think he's smarter than you, and I wanted to invite you over to talk more about my case, and maybe just hang out. If you didn't like cats that would be difficult."

He smiles at my somewhat-rambling speech. "No worries. I'd be keen on that."

"Excellent, because I thought of something you could brainstorm with me about. I'm trying to figure out what Raymond was trying to figure out. The case has a connection to Nazis..."

"Nazis? Really?"

"Yeah, maybe we could figure it out a little more."

"Why not tomorrow night? Have some good wine, a little music in the background. Put on some David Gray. He will counter the unpleasantness of Nazis in books. This is a plan."

He has to work some more on a story tonight. But before we separate outside, he takes my arm and pulls me in close to him. "I have to do this. To be honest, I wanted to do this the first time I saw you."

And then he's kissing me on the street. That cliché about no one else existing becomes true for the seconds his mouth is on mine.

"You're going to leave me with that?" It's all I can say, trying to sound smartass about it.

"Give you something to think about." Even after he leaves, I have to take a minute to remind myself I'm supposed to go home as well.

The restaurant is not that far from my building. The night is clear enough and streets populated enough I feel comfortable walking back south, from 6th Avenue down 8th Street, which becomes St. Marks Place. I'm lost in thought.

Going past the New York University campus buildings and University Place is when I start to feel different. Edgy, without real reason. I pause and light up a cigarette in order to give myself an excuse to look around. It's just after nine and I'm near the eastern edge of Washington Square Park. Summer, so not as many students around. Broadway's coming up in a couple blocks, but these streets are a lot quieter.

I can't say how I know something is different. I don't see anyone suspicious in particular; all kinds of people are around. Yet the *qi* is disturbed. Someone is watching me. I have a sixth sense about that, unless I'm really distracted. I feel it now. The first time I felt this was at nine years old, sensing and catching someone following me home from baseball practice.

Looking around without appearing to do so, I can't help but feel vulnerable. Anyone who wanted to take a shot at me could do so from any direction where a person could hide--doorway, rooftop, or car. The thought gets me moving again. But I'm still scanning the area.

I hear my text alert buzz, and take my phone out.

It's Joel. *You're right, someone's following you.*

I'm immediately disturbed and angry. First, knowing Joel's here somewhere which can only mean *he's* following me, and second, that someone else is around.

I text back quickly. *So you can see me?*

You and him, sort of. Go to the Starbucks on Broadway.

A few minutes later, I turn the corner and duck inside the Starbucks. I feel better being off the street.

I get black coffee and wait by a counter inside, away from the window. A moment later Joel shows up. I don't know how he makes himself invisible to get in and out of places so discreetly but he's a master at it.

Still, I can't help but show my annoyance with him, and he recognizes it when he comes up to me.

"Yeah, I know," he says in a low voice. "It's not what you think."

"What, then?"

"Like I said, someone's following you. You knew he was around; I saw that when you were on the street. You weren't obvious. I just know you very well. I'm glad you can still tell, because I sure as hell could."

"Really? Maybe I was sensing *you*." Backstory: after we met, Joel had followed me a couple times. He accused me of doing that to him just a few days ago, but I only actually did that once, on the last day of our relationship. When he followed me it wasn't to be a stalker, but from habits developed as a youth. He was a throwaway kid who survived on the streets by being very cautious of everyone and everything--even me, when we were together. It was his way of making sure the world is safe. Sometimes on a dangerous job he followed me without asking to make sure I was safe.

That was then, four years ago. I don't think I can re-adapt to it under the circumstances. Just knowing he was probably nearby when I was with Alex infuriates me.

He guesses what I'm thinking. Damn him, he's good at that. "No. I'm not sweating you. I don't care about what you and Harry Potter are up to. I'm concerned that someone is watching you full time, which means they're going to try something."

I take time to drink my coffee and calm down. He's sincere. I'm pretty sure of it inside. But he has a way of getting to me.

"Okay, what did you see?"

"Not much. Someone's there but really, really in the shadows. You know I'm good at that, and this person is better--almost. I know what to look for. But I couldn't see him, or her."

"And this person has been around since when?"

"Since I've been back, at least."

"You've been doing this again, following me?"

"Calm down, Gabriel. Don't act like we don't know each other or didn't take care of each other back when. Yes, I have been. I'm not letting you be attacked again."

We watch each other for a moment. I have a pretty intense glare but he never backs down. "You don't like any implication you can't take care of yourself. I know you can, but you need help. This doesn't mean you can't handle the case, it means I need to watch your back so you can."

His argument is disturbingly logical. "And you really, really think someone's there."

"You would too, Gabriel, if it wasn't me telling you. You think I'm saying this to cock-block you somehow. I'm not that kind of person. Nelson has people helping him. One of them is following you, knows about you."

My mind can't sort this out. Because like he said, it's him saying it. "How do you know? How do you see this person?"

He leans on the counter, looking around the shop. "Can you explain instinct? No. If I could get a picture of whoever it is, I would. It's movement, it's patterns on the street, it's a disturbance in the Force. I don't know how to put it. You know what I mean. We're street people."

"I can't walk around in fear of this."

"Okay, whatever. But just be aware." He straightens. "You should go back home. I'll leave once you're in your building." He abruptly walks away and out the shop.

When I follow a minute later, Joel is nowhere visible. I go back to Avenue A, feeling better as my home streets are more populated. The sense of being followed disappears. Joel didn't ask me to text him or call when I was inside, he never does. But after I go up the stairs to my apartment, I text him anyway that it's clear. I'm surprised when I get a "*k*" in response. For him, an extraordinary effort.

Then I pull the curtains closed.

∞

FIFTEEN ◆ THE FIVE OF CUPS

The Five of Cups represents staying in sorrow over past events; the person is having difficulty seeing what else is around him, emotionally miserable, not able to see any benefits.

∞

ST. SIMEON'S HOSPITAL is in an old gray monster building in the upper Thirties. It used to be a private Catholic hospital but was taken over by the city fifty years ago. The campus has some newer satellite buildings for teaching and cancer treatment, but the main hospital remains hovering like a fortress over Third Avenue. The gray stone is streaked with black on all 12 floors, from years of polluted rain.

After the strangeness of last night, I'm starting to feel like I'm traveling through alternate worlds and each place I visit is a different reality. I'm repulsed by being in a hospital again, making Joel's advice from the previous evening stand out starkly.

I'm here to see John Harrison, meeting him where he works on the seventh floor. Like with Cole, I'm surprised that when I called him, he agreed to meet me. But I jumped on it.

He had asked me to text his number when I arrived and after I do so, he responds he'll be down shortly. While I'm waiting, I not-admire the decorating scheme of gray-green paint contrasting with the dirty orange floors. I don't like hospitals, even brand-new shiny ones with television screens in the elevators and grief counselors. But something about the older hospitals is more comforting in their griminess. You get the sense not much is expected of you, whether employee or patient.

Harrison walks up to where I'm waiting on the first floor next to information. He wears a simple burgundy set of nurses' scrubs with a black thermal jersey underneath, and an ID on a lanyard.

"So," he says, folding his arms. "Let's go down to the lunchroom for this." I follow him down the cavernous hall populated with artifacts and tables of insurance company representatives.

Harrison has faint circles under his eyes, indicative of back-to-back shifts. He's on the thin side, and his face is rather delicate. His haunted eyes make him seem more vulnerable. He smooths his black hair out of his face and leads me to a table in the back of the cafeteria, saying hello to various co-workers on the way. We sit down.

"Thanks for meeting with me."

"I'm doing this on the off-chance you might be doing something useful. But you understand I don't really want anything to do with you."

"Sure, I appreciate you talking to me anyway. But why the hostility?"

"I know Raymond wasn't always faithful. A lot of men don't care about that, and whatever works for them is fine. But I did. That didn't stop him. Little mini-affairs. I always had to worry he was getting emotionally involved over some new guy." His look at me is pointed.

"Okay." I clasp my hands together and set them on the table. "You're under a mistaken impression that *I* was involved with Raymond that way. Didn't happen. He was going to be my client before he was killed, and that was all."

He smiles a little, with suffering still showing. "Well, about him hiring you...actually I was the one who sent him the video of what you did in Jersey. At first, I just thought it was funny. Then he said he was thinking about getting an investigator and you might be the one. He said how much he was interested in seeing what you were all about."

Harrison leans back and looks away. "See, when we had tensions going on about something, he'd get passive-aggressive by pointing out the attractive aspects of other men. So recently after we were arguing about whether or not I was going to change my career, he told me he was going to hire you. How he liked your confidence, your integrity, oh, and that you were attractive in a Rob Thomas kind of way. You know what that's like, for someone to hurt you like that so casually?"

I'm embarrassed. "I'm sorry. I hate to say this, but that sounds pretty dickish." I feel even worse that some part of me is a little complimented by this interest from a man now dead. I can picture Joel giving me shit for this, like I'm Dana Andrews in a gay version of the old movie *Laura.*

"He could be that way."

"I didn't do anything with him, though. I swear."

He shrugs, thinking about it. "All right. If I'm wrong, I'm wrong. You *would* have, though. He's a seducer. I suppose I'm being unfair to you, I know you were beat up. That newspaper seems to think it has something to do with Raymond being killed. Look, I have to get something to eat. What about you?"

We get up and collect some food from the steam table, bring it back. A couple of co-workers stop by to ask him things. Harrison gets into his food, but continues talking.

"Raymond was who he was. He could run hot and cold. You have to understand; I wasn't always interested in his work. And by "wasn't always," I mean never. So we got on each other's nerves like any other couple. But he didn't like to lose. He wanted me to give in and be what he wanted, and I wouldn't."

"What do you remember most about Raymond?"

"Man," he says, shaking his head. "I try to just remember good things. I don't think about it much. I just work. I'm not good at dealing with...grief, I guess. But when he was relaxed, you know, he was very affectionate. I like to just think of him and me watching TV together, and hearing him laugh. I liked to make him lose it and be silly and not be such a lawyer, you know." He fiddles with the plastic utensils for a minute, rearranging patterns, lost in his mind. For a moment, I think he might cry but he just gets a distant look in his eyes that darken his face. He then rolls his neck as if getting out kinks.

I look away to the dull mint green walls. St. Simeon was one of the hospitals that were supposed to be part of the implementation of total free health care in NYC, the way free tuition for the CUNY system was supposed to be the implementation of total education. Somehow, it fell apart in the 1970s.

I'm catching John's mood about being steeped in the melancholia of the past. I have to shake that off.

"What were the contentious parts of your relationship, if you don't mind my asking?"

"One of the most frustrating things with him was that he would get the idea he knew better than other people. I know he wanted me to do something other than be a nurse. He wanted me go to med school. But I don't want to be a doctor. Too much liability, not enough reward. I like where I am; there's a continuing nursing shortage so I'll always find work. Maybe he wanted us to be together and do something like Doctors and Lawyers without Borders, some kind of social work fantasy. He offered to pay for school. He didn't want to insult me but I think that he felt like I should be doing better in professional status because of his high-class social circles."

"This is might be a difficult question, but I need to know about Raymond's sexual proclivities."

Harrison nods. "Because of the autoerotic thing. We've seen that here; you wouldn't believe what comes in the ER that has to do with masturbation activities. Or *who* comes in. But Raymond had no interest in BDSM. I'm not into it but I don't have a problem with it. Lawyers and finance execs get into bondage for the power issue. Gay and straight. But not him. He had no use for that. He wasn't shy about saying what he did like, so I'm pretty sure he wasn't hiding anything from me."

"I appreciate your being honest. I don't think this was an accident. I also don't think it was suicide. So I'd like to clear this up-- was Raymond depressed or possibly suicidal? You'd know the signs."

"Absolutely not. I have issues with depression on and off, but he never did. That was difficult sometimes because he wasn't sure how to cope with me when I was down."

"Would you mind signing an affidavit to this? I could email it to you, and you mail it back to me."

"What is this for?"

"I'm investigating Raymond's death on behalf of his estate, for Allen Cheng."

"Allen, okay. Is this in any way for Toni?"

I had been making notes in my iPad. His tone makes me look up. I remember that Toni had been dismissive of him at the funeral, and didn't acknowledge Raymond as being in a relationship when I first spoke with her.

"If it was, would you not want to do it?"

"She and I do not get along, to put it lightly. Raymond tended to feed her habit."

"Is she on something?"

"Vicodin, probably. She could still turn it around, but if she doesn't, she'll kill herself. You can probably see that already if you're asking."

"You've been in conflict with her?"

"From day one. I think she just wanted him to herself, to focus on her issues. Any time he was going somewhere else--let's say, we were taking a weekend out of town--she'd come up with a crisis to get him involved. I was getting tired of it and to his credit, he was making a real effort to leave her problems for her to fix. So, she hates me because I took some of the attention away."

He smiles wryly. "You know, or maybe you don't, Raymond had me in his will. He had redone it a month or so ago and we were serious in spite of our problems. Nothing that extravagant, but I thought it was a loving gesture. But Toni's already told Allen she's challenging it."

"Ouch."

Harrison shrugs. "I wouldn't expect different. I don't even feel like fighting the issue but Allen said he's defending against any will contest because he helped Raymond with the will, and as the executor he knows what Raymond wanted. God help the man, he's the one who has to dole out to her from the trust. But he's got the balls to shut the door on her when needed."

"What's that trust about?"

"Their father. He was a lawyer as well, did pretty good with investments. He wanted them to be able to take care of themselves, and for Toni's son. But he didn't trust her. Toni's always been irresponsible. We're pretty sure she put the wrong father on Adam's birth certificate, a guy who was dead, so she wouldn't have to share custody."

"Well, I can't say this won't help her. I'm working for Allen, but as a consequence if the cause of death is established as homicide she can and will challenge the insurance denial. I hope you will still work with me."

"Let me think about it. I'm not crazy about the idea of having my life in a public record, but if Raymond really was murdered...what do you believe that was all about?"

I slide over to him one of my business cards. "Here's how you can contact me. I can't say for sure why he was killed but I'm pretty sure he was. I haven't run across any evidence to the contrary. Why is another matter. What do you know about his work with the Foundation? Any conflicts?"

"Some problems there made him angry. I went with him to a couple of parties or whatever that they had, but I didn't like the people very much. Generally, I tuned out what Raymond had to say about the place which led to him to telling me less, you know? Mostly what I saw was that Raymond really didn't like Ethan Nelson, the director. He also had dust-ups with Dr. Cole. But they're just both *really* opinionated and kinda snobby. He said he was going to have you look into the problems there but he didn't specify what the problems were."

"But he was friendly with Eleanor Whitford."

"Yeah, she was a cool lady. About the only person at that place I could stand."

"Was his problem with the Foundation something she had come to him about?"

"Maybe. Yeah, I think so; she was calling him a lot right before he died. The books he ordered might have had something to do with it."

My attention gets sharper. "What books were those?"

"Some old series on the occult. He had them sent to my place from Amazon. He knows nothing about the occult but he wanted to go through them."

"For what, do you know?"

"I don't really know. Had to be about his foundation issue. I said I'd try to help this time, just because he was so upset about something there. So he said he wanted me to research. He had the books sent to my place because he wanted me to look through them when I had time."

"Any chance the research involved Nazis?"

"Yeah! Nazis, he wanted any mention of Nazis. I didn't really get a chance to read them, though. Weird stuff."

"Any chance I can borrow those books?"

"Sure. I live near Chinatown." He gives me the address. "I'm home by eight tonight. If you want to come by then."

"I will. Thank you."

"Yeah. From what you describe, I have trouble thinking it was an accident or anything either. But at the same time, I know it doesn't make sense, but I can't imagine someone going into his place and killing him."

From my bag, I pull out the still photo of Cap-and-Sunglasses. "Does this guy look familiar?"

"You think this guy did it?"

I know John is grieving, and doing his best to cover it. But I see his face become dark, deep with anger. "It's likely. I'm sorry to show it to you, but..."

"No, I understand. I read about the video in Cafétière Maléfice. You can't see his face. Bad angle for a security camera. Could be anybody."

John has a smaller frame than the man in the photo. I don't think it's him. And his emotions are so evident. He hands me the photo back with a great deal of control.

"Were you working the weekend he disappeared?"

"Yeah, sometimes I work six shifts a week. I worked Thursday through Saturday that week."

"Did you go anywhere else?"

"Like where...Oh, I get what you mean. I might have killed him, right?"

"I'm not saying you did. Having an alibi helps, though."

"Well, that's a problem, then. Thursday, I worked the day shift, 8-4. I stayed home that night. Friday and Saturday I had the night shift, 4-12. I didn't do much during the day but sleep and watch TV. I tried calling him Sunday but he never answered. I didn't hear about what happened to him until the day he died. From the news. Does that hang me with you?"

"No. I don't think you had anything to do with it. I'm sorry to have to bring it up, and that you heard about Raymond from the news. That sucks. But I appreciate your help." I get up. "I know you need to get back to work."

His tone is very strained. "I'll see you tonight for the books. And Gabriel, please find this person who killed him."

I nod. He quickly wipes away tears springing in his eyes, shakes my hand and goes off. I mentally write him off my list of suspects and leave the hospital. I have some work to do before I go to pick up Raymond's books from John. I'm looking forward to seeing how those may shed some light on the mystery.

Later, I meet John at his building, and he has me come up with him to get the box of books. My hands have healed pretty well and I don't have trouble with the box. He seems in better spirits, and tells me he'll probably help with the affidavit. I can't help but be pleased that some clue is in books, my favorite possessions other than Archie. I'm also pleased I can get Alex to help with this tonight.

∞

SIXTEEN ♦ THE TWO OF CUPS

The Two of Cups represents two persons coming together in a deep emotional attachment. Perhaps it's a union, two making a world of their own. Emotionally, the stakes are high.

∞

BACK HOME, I MAKE A LIST of the books. Ten volumes altogether, on Ancient Magic, Alien Visitors, Other Dimensions, Prophecy, Mysterious Creatures, Sects and Secret Societies, Investigating Evil, The Spirit World, Human Powers and Words and Symbols. The used encyclopedias are from the 1970's, edited by the New Times Publishing Company. I remember these books. In my youth, I used to read them at the public library. Although Mom had an interest in the occult my father would have smacked me for having the books in the house. But he can't now. The reward of adulthood.

Alex has come over to my place. When he arrives, he kisses me and that weak-kneed thing starts with me again. I could just drop everything I was supposed to do right now, but instead I allow him to come in and look around and meet Archie. We talk for a bit about his follow-up story in the *Herald Standard* mentioning how I'm back working on Raymond's case; it has a quote from me on I feel Raymond's death will be uncovered as more sinister than accidental. I'm hoping the story will spark some interest and reaction.

Alex flips through the New Times books, impeded by Archie flopping on any open page. Since I know about these topics, he asks me about several concepts and writes down anything interesting. In a moment of black humor we decide to eliminate for now the potential topics of UFOs, Bigfoot, ghosts and Satan. While we're joking about what might remain that the Foundation could be into, my phone rings. The number is blocked so I guess the caller is not my previous threatening caller. Just in case, I answer with the recorder on.

The voice is male; the voice is pleasant, but with a serious, hesitant tone. "You're the Gabriel Ross who is investigating the death of Raymond Booth?"

"Yes, I take it you must have read some news article."

"I did. You are right in what you are doing; I wanted you to know that."

"I'm glad to know I'm right. Can I help you?"

"Not really. I just felt the urge to reach out."

I catch Alex's eye. He is preparing to use my computer to access his database and frowns at me. I switch the phone to speaker. "You think Raymond Booth was murdered?"

"It's a solid assumption."

"Do you have any particular knowledge?"

"Not of his death specifically. I know what he was up against. His death was a message. Not to be too cryptic, but some deaths have a dual purpose. Not just to silence the victim, but to remind others that looking for the truth will lead to a lonely death under ugly circumstances. Like JFK. Really, like Oswald. Why do you think Ruby shot him in public? It was a warning to anyone else involved."

I'm intrigued by his analogy. "Aren't there like fifty-five hundred JFK researchers? With all kinds of vastly divergent theories as to why JFK was assassinated?" I can say that because I've read most of the JFK books; it's always been an intriguing conspiracy to me.

"Yeah, disinformation as usual. Think about this--was anyone actually convicted for JFK's murder? Quite a feat for a closed case."

I give Alex credit for not laughing or looking amused at this exchange. I'm not laughing either. Somehow, I don't perceive that this caller is a nut. "Okay, if I read your line of reasoning right Raymond was killed both to shut him up, and to warn others."

"Exactly. People are going to remember that he died in a sordid sex act, rather than his being a good lawyer. And in your investigation. I know you were beat up, but if you don't mind my asking did you get some kind of message warning you away?"

"What makes you think that?"

"I have a hunch. You probably did. You don't sound too surprised. The message was serious, so be careful. You must realize that already."

"If you know what is going on who is it behind all this, then?"

Alex leans forward questioning me with his eyes. His expression is obvious--did I get such a warning call? I shrug an affirmative.

"I can't tell you directly who killed Booth. But the circumstances are, let's say, familiar to me."

"And can you help me out on this?"

"If I tell you too much you won't believe it. Research is its own purification and vetting process. And you are researching this, right? Have you run across anything strange?"

I decide that this person is worth a gamble. "Yes, Nazis. That's fairly strange." My eyes fall over the books at Alex's feet. I see a topic that hadn't been eliminated in our semi-serious perusal of the books. It fits with what we're talking about and I add it on impulse. "And...secret organizations."

The man on the phone sounds impressed. "You have done some good work. I'm not surprised. I read what you've written online. I had a feeling you might be the kind of person who would see beyond the cover-up. Keep following that line of thought. The weirder stuff is what I'm talking about--the more out-there stuff about the Nazis."

"You mean the experimentation--"

"No. Not the human rights abuses or genocide. The Holocaust is history and public history, except for the idiots that deny it, but never mind. What I'm talking about is the *esoteric* part--the part that scholars prefer not to discuss. Keep looking. I wish you luck."

"And who are you? How do you Raymond's death is connected to a bigger issue?"

Silence for a moment. I think maybe he's hung up. "Hello?"

The man speaks slowly, hesitantly. "I don't want to say too much. I read a lot. I know something of the people behind this. Sometimes I see a news story that catches my eye. I've been around...similar situations. I read about your incident with the preacher--good for you on that, by the way. Then I saw you were being criticized for being involved in the death of the attorney. It reminded me of other deaths. Suicides that weren't actually suicides. People discredited for no reason. I read what you said in the news. And you were attacked. But you kept on. That was why I had to call. I felt for you."

"Yeah, the attack might be connected."

"I know. You were lucky. They won't stop so long as you keep investigating this. I can't tell you to do so, that's your decision. But...I wish you luck."

"And can I speak to you again?"

A pause. "You might, if you can find me. Keep researching, and if you turn me up, I'll talk to you."

Click. The connection ends. Nobody does a proper goodbye these days.

"What the hell was that?" Alex looks deeply concerned.

"Welcome to my life, babe. I am the king of getting weird-ass phone calls." I save the recording. When I look up, his expression hasn't changed.

"Gabriel, were you really threatened?"

"Yeah. The other day. You have to understand, Alex, I get many *meshugganah* people calling about my cases if they're in the news. And since the New Jersey incident...I have hate mail on top of hate mail. This is par for the course. Not the first time I've been threatened, either."

He's not reassured. "And apparently the fact that you were attacked is to be expected, according to this bloke."

"I suspected as much. But what am I supposed to do? I'm staying on the case. And I could use your help. What do you use for a database, Lexis?"

Alex still looks upset, but nods. "Yes, that's part of it. But we also have a specially designed article retrieval service for the paper. In order to make connections and background research as fast as possible, the service searches cached sites, blogs, foreign sites, video sites, and every available public database as well as all the ones we subscribe to. I helped develop this. My other degree is in library science."

"God, I'm getting hard just thinking about having such a database. Sounds better than sex."

I get him to laugh, finally. He says, "I hope I don't inadvertently replace the idea of sex. But I'll still help you."

"Oh, I think sex could still be on the table, with a little persuasion. But my laptop's over there. Have at it."

Alex takes my desk chair and logs in remotely to his *Herald* account. "What did you think of what he said? Not completely hatstand?"

"I assume that means crazy in British talk? The man sounds like he *cares* about this a lot. Just in his taking the chance in calling me about it in the first place. I could have just laughed him off. I also thought he sounded a little scared. I wonder if he investigated it himself in some way. Maybe I'll take him up on his offer to find him. But now I really want to know what we can find in the database. Your library degree is intimidating."

Alex calls up a search page. "You have nothing to feel outclassed about. I've heard how smart you are."

"From whom?"

"It gets around, I have my sources. Now, what do you want to check next in these books?"

I look at the pile of encyclopedias that Archie is sleeping on. "I have a feeling that this involves secret societies, if it involves Nazis. The original Nazi party had many occult connections and influences. The problem is how far the possibility can be taken. History and reasonable theories are overtaken by wild speculation because it makes good shows on the History Channel--Nazis and secret technology that being developed and was mistaken for UFOs..."

"You seem to know about this stuff already."

"I happen to enjoy conspiracy theories. Speaking of *esoteric*, how about Hitler's supposed search for the Spear of Destiny, the one that pierced Jesus' side when he was on the cross?"

"I believe I saw a mention of that in one of those books. Also the alleged genetic experiments to reproduce a clone of Hitler, although I think maybe someone just took the *Boys from Brazil* too seriously..."

I get one of the books from under Archie, who meows faintly in protest and then stalks off for a snack in the kitchen. "Who knows what inspired Ira Levin to write it. The truth is in there--the ratlines where Nazis were helped into other countries, records were changed behind Harry Truman's back when he forbade party members to be allowed to emigrate here."

"True, half of NASA was staffed with those Nazi party scientists coming in after the war when Communism became the new evil obsession."

"So what are you looking up, if you don't mind my hovering over you?" I look over his shoulder.

"I can deal with it. I found a few names in the books I want to check. Maybe with your love of conspiracies, you will have heard of them." He leans back a bit. I pull my ottoman over behind his chair and put my head on his shoulder, and my arms around him.

"I'm surprised I don't already have this collection of books. These were published during the big occult revival in the 1980s, but my father didn't want me to have them--went against Catholic ideology. Not that I was Catholic, but he was. I once promised myself to get all the books I couldn't get when I was a kid. I guess I forgot to look for more once I started working as an adult."

"You should get them now. I'll buy you some. What is your favorite conspiracy?"

I lift my head long enough to point to my bookshelves. "Probably JFK is hands down. I thought it was funny the caller mentioned JFK. I can never believe the Warren Commission's conclusion, and I see no problem in questioning authority."

Alex smiles. "In Europe and Southeast Asia conspiracies are far easier to believe, because this shit really happens. I don't know why in America conspiracies are supposed to only be for those mad as a bag of ferrets."

"Because they are all lumped together. If you even mention questioning an official version of a story you're a nut. It doesn't help that television shows on conspiracy topics always choose to feature a so-called 'expert' who is a nut. Makes for good television, but bad for fair play. Certainly not all conspiracies are valid, and believing in one logically doesn't mean accepting them all. As *if* all those persons who think Oswald was set up also *have* to believe the Clintons killed Vince Foster, or that Obama was born in Africa, and that HIV was a government-designed virus. I say all conspiracies stand alone on their own merits. Now you got me on a rant."

"I like hearing you rant." He lifts his hand briefly to stroke mine resting on his chest. "Well, we have some results here."

I watch him scan the information, enjoying doing so. He meets my eyes in the reflection of the laptop after a moment. "You know, this is getting more interesting I have to admit. Look here, have you ever heard of the Tertullian Society?"

I look at the story he's reading, a book review from the British supernatural phenomena periodical *Fortean Times*. "I read that magazine. The Tertullian Society. Very little, but if I recall correctly, they were a small group who were supposed to be evil in some way. Because they weren't very big, they didn't get the press of the Bilderbergers. Does it say more there?"

"The review doesn't add much; just slams the author."

"I wonder if Colin Wilson wrote about the Tertullians."

"England's Colin Wilson? What *didn't* he write about?"

I lean over his shoulder. "That review doesn't mention Nazis, though."

"You read too fast, Gabriel. Give me a chance. Look at this, here's another story that has the connection." He shows me a website in French.

"Thanks." I don't hide my sarcasm. "I understand completely now."

He laughs. "I'm sorry, I couldn't resist."

"Hey, if it was Spanish, I could translate it."

"Brilliant. But I happen to speak French. This is an online magazine, sort of the French version of your *Fortean Times*. The point is to put a political spin on arcane topics. "A bit spiky--a bit *French*," as Eddie Izzard would say?"

"If you think I can rant on conspiracies, don't get me started quoting his stuff."

"I won't argue. But to return to our article. The author is arguing that the Tertullian Society was one of the sources for the ratlines--that helped Nazis get in the U.S. But see here, not the scientists--rather a few Nazis who were later in key finance positions on Wall Street, influencing certain government policies international and domestic for the next sixty-five years; well, fifty-five, this article is ten years old."

Archie jumps up to my computer to see if he can walk on the keyboard, then demands a head scratch from Alex. I use the opportunity to collect the encyclopedia volume on secret societies.

"Damned if the Tertullian Society isn't in this. That's funny, because they aren't like the Illuminati in terms of popularity. Jesse Ventura wouldn't bother to do a show on these people, too obscure. But they turn up in this encyclopedia, so random. Somehow Raymond got this far, or almost."

"That's what this article says as well. It isn't a large New World Order sort of thing at all; they're actually very small in scope. And no one is sure where exactly these people are--and somehow that makes them more sinister." He turns back to me. "I don't like that since you were just warned about them."

I wave that away. "So, according to this article the Tertullian Society was an influence on Hitler with its ideas of pan-Germanism, racial superiority, and justified fascism. A dude named Friedrich Schroeder personally mentored Hitler when he was still in Vienna. But nothing was heard about the group when war ended and it supposedly died out."

"Yet according to the French piece it's supposed to be around today. At least long enough to have helped the Nazis get a foothold into global financial affairs. So if they are really around, that gives an idea of their political stance."

"They ain't Greenpeace." I start pacing around the room. "Raymond believes a Nazi war criminal is associated with a Foundation Board Member. He orders these books, which mention a Nazi connection to the Tertullian Society. The French article says the Society still exists. So..."

"The Foundation is connected with the Tertullians."

"Right. And this elderly lady, Eleanor, seems to know something or found out something--because she asked Raymond to look into it. Now, Raymond, being perhaps a hot head--a *lawyer* in other words--is either too obvious about what he's doing or steps on someone's toes."

"So he's killed because he might have exposed the Society?"

"Murder is usually over money, sex or exposure, or all three. If exposure could inhibit money or power in some way, then I suppose it's possible, if any of this is feasible."

Alex stops his computer scrolling. "You said you visited the director of this Foundation."

"Ethan Nelson. He has an attitude, that guy. Cocksure. A real dick."

"Do you think he is part of this?"

"I wouldn't dismiss the idea. I don't like him, but no one's going to be convicted on that. Depends on the circumstances of how the Tertullian Society is connected to the Foundation--maybe it has always been there. Maybe the connection is remote."

"But he--Nelson--knows what you are doing, what you are investigating?"

"Um. Something like that. Subtlety isn't always my strong point."

Alex doesn't say anything. I consider his silence. "Are you wondering if I'm putting myself in danger?"

Alex regards me intensely. "*Putting* yourself? Remember, I saw you just after you were beat up. You're already in danger. We both think that Raymond was murdered, right? As does your friend and admirer who called earlier."

"Absolutely."

"And not due to some unfortunate self-strangulation sex act."

"Maybe the situation is not Occam's Razor simple, but the evidence for suicide is not there. Conversely, evidence *does* exist that someone did abduct him or did something with him."

"Just saying if this someone has killed once the second is quite easier. And you've been attacked and threatened."

I pull one of the curtains aside to look down at Avenue A. "I'm not worried. Statistically, most threats are baseless." Granted, I don't mean that. Again, I hear Joel's concern reflected again. But I don't want Alex to get upset as well.

"Maybe, maybe not. But just be careful."

"I appreciate that you care."

He gets up and walks over to the window where I am and slips an arm around me. I smile to myself.

"Since we're into the arcane now, we should check your cards. Might you have a new love interest in there?"

We go back to my table. I shuffle the deck and draw out a new card. Two of Cups. "All signs point to yes."

"Good thing that worked," Alex says. "I'd have had to throw the deck out the window if it said otherwise." He makes his point by leaning in to kiss me. I am more than willing to forget about the Foundation and the Tertullian Society and Raymond to give in to that kiss, to slide my arms around him, to feel him pull me closer. Music is playing in the background, and he gets up to slow dance with me, until the desire becomes too much not to indulge.

We both recognize that moment. The music has changed several times, and is now into Al Green. It fits right in with what we're feeling.

Still standing together, his fingers unbutton my shirt. His lips graze my face. This is a slow seduction. We stand against each other for what seems like an eternity. Then I in turn unbutton his shirt. As my fingers move, so do his hands in caressing me. Our breathing starts to sync in becoming shorter. He kisses my neck and in doing so presses against me. I feel him hard, and this strips away any vestiges of shyness.

Being with another person in sensuality is literally like being in another world. Everything else is closed off. We can't move any further from where we are, and somehow just make our way down to the living room rug. His body becomes familiar to me, and somewhere in the shared intimacy emotions arise. That sense between persons that the sex is not just sex.

I'm so drunk on him I have no idea how eventually we get to bed, but we do.

Sometime around three in the morning, I wake up. I'm at first surprised how good I feel with him there. Archie is on the night table next to us. What I don't like is that Archie is staring intently out the bedroom door towards the living room. I hear a low growl from my watch cat, who has even more intuitive instincts than I do.

I have a thing about being on alert for break-ins, due to some rough stuff in my childhood. But now for other reasons as well. I'm instantly on alert trying to determine what is going on. I hear a scratch, like something faint against the front door. Am I hallucinating? No, Archie hears it too. He doesn't like strangers in the hallway, even the UPS person.

I slip out of bed, pull on my boxer briefs, go out the room and gently close the door. I walk silently to the living room. A tiny crack of faint light under the front door, from the light in the hall. I swear I see the knob on the door turn a fraction. I watch the light. While I'm watching it blacks out briefly, as if someone is moving by the door. Now my adrenaline is high.

I quickly go back to the second bedroom, take a key from a niche I carved into the top of the door frame, and unlock the first file cabinet drawer. Then I take out my locked gun box. The key to the box is taped behind the cabinet. I've practiced doing this many times. I retrieve one of my handguns, a Sig Sauer P250 357, slam in the clip, make sure the safety is off and go back to the door, look through the peephole.

Nothing in sight. But if someone's there, and I can feel it again, he or she could be waiting elsewhere. The elevator and staircase are not within the range of the peephole.

"What's going on?"

I just manage not to jump, trained by reflex not to panic when holding a loaded gun. I look over my shoulder. Alex is right behind me. Naked, concerned. He takes my arm. "Are you okay?"

"I thought someone was out there."

He's looking at the gun. His face becomes very tense. I can almost see the thoughts going through his mind. His eyes raise slowly to meet mine.

"Just being cautious." I keep my voice low.

Alex does not like the gun, that's so clear. He lets go of my arm and moves around me to unlock and open the door despite my protest. He steps in the hallway, exposed to whatever may be out there. I can't let him do that and move past him with the gun out.

No one is in the hall that we can see.

I turn back to him and see his expression still grave.

I try to shrug casually. "Maybe I was hearing things." I wasn't but I want to get him back inside.

He doesn't respond, but starts to go towards the stairs. I put my hand on him.

"Nothing's here, but let me look, okay?"

I move down the hall past my neighbors' doors and to the elevator. Nothing. The staircase is to the left of the elevator.

"Is it clear?" He's still by the door.

I check the staircase, which goes to the roof. Joel is sitting on the top step.

I start to raise the gun, but stop when I recognize him. I keep my tone neutral while looking at Joel but my look isn't neutral.

"Yeah. Nothing here." Good thing Alex can't see me, or him.

I go back to Alex and lead him inside the apartment. "Damn, I need a cigarette. I hate that, but I'm out. I'm going to run to the place on the corner."

"You want me to go for you?"

"No, I'm more dressed than you are." I smile with some wickedness I don't have to fake too much, and go to put my gun way, pull on sandals, jeans, t-shirt, get my wallet.

Alex is searching the bedroom. "I don't see Archie."

"He's smarter than me. Probably behind the bookshelf, it's his hiding area. I'll be back in a few minutes."

I move fast and leave the apartment, locking the door behind me and going back to the staircase. Joel is now sitting on the middle steps, smoking one of his kreteks.

I go up to the railing, where his head is just above mine, keep my voice low. "What the fuck are you doing?"

"He was here."

For a moment, I think he means Alex, but realize he means whoever is following me.

Joel continues, "I startled him off. He's fast; he knocked me away to get down the stairs. I let him go. I doubt he'll be back tonight."

I see a scrape on Joel's face in the dim light. I didn't hear anything, but it could have happened while I was getting the Sig Sauer.

"You saw him this time."

"White, early to middle thirties. Dark glasses on, though. Cap. Black clothes, thin, a couple inches taller than me."

"You sure he was actually here?"

Joel moves closer to the rail, matching the scorn in my tone. "I don't care if you're fucking...*him*. That's not why I'm here."

I turn away from Joel and head down the set of stairs to the fifth floor. A second later he's behind me, which makes me move faster.

I know I'm absolutely wrong, but I can't help but consider if Joel is lying. He'd never do that. I know this. Being sneaky or trying for sabotage isn't his style. But I'm so aggravated by his being here I'm thinking things I shouldn't.

"Where are you going?"

"Out for cigarettes. It was an excuse so I could tell you to get the hell out of here without him hearing."

He gets in front of me, making me stop at the second floor. "You really think I made this up?"

I meet his eyes. I don't think that if pushed to answer. But I don't want to say it. My emotions with him are suddenly so raw. I can feel my heart pounding, and I can almost feel his too, seeing him get angry with me because I can't admit it.

Really angry. He turns away and goes down the last staircase. "You better check that you don't have a full pack sitting up there where he can see it, or he'll know you're lying."

Then he's gone out the door. I walk down slowly. Angry and regretful at the same time. Of course, I see him nowhere outside. I get my cigarettes from a corner store and walk back, with my mind in flux.

When I'm inside the apartment, I see my almost full pack of cigarettes on the coffee table, and put it away in a desk drawer. In bed, Alex is sleeping. I get in; he draws me closer and I'm able to get some comfort in sleep.

∞

SEVENTEEN ◆ THE PAGE OF PENTACLES

The Page of Pentacles represents one becoming a student, engaging in learning in order to take on more responsibility.

ALTHOUGH THE NEXT DAY is Saturday, Alex has to leave before lunch to follow up a story. When I start to work, I discover he's left his database still logged in. With a bit of a forbidden fruit thrill, I do a search of my own. One of my research skills is brainstorming effective search terms and possible connections.

I find a few more mentions of the Tertullian Society, and way too much on the ancient church father Tertullian. I print the Society ones, and then go on to look up conspiracies involving fake suicides, as my mystery man had mentioned last night. I hope to run across him too. He seems to think it was a possibility. Why? He said he had seen this stuff before. So, he could be in law enforcement, or he could be a journalist.

This becomes a fascinating hunt through the underworld of conspiracy theories. The service turns up cached websites long dead, and what I think of as ghost town sites still online but left alone and not updated since the late 1990s, as well as online versions of Zines and newsletters following rumors and making speculative connections. My intended work this morning falls to the wayside. I don't bother to answer when Jim calls, not wanting to be distracted.

An old story from 1996 catches my eye; a journalist named Kent Varney is the author. The article is in a long-defunct magazine called *InsideNews*. The article described how a couple of grassroots civil rights organizations had an ongoing global search for Nazi war criminals. They were using newly developed software touted as being a potential investigative tool through monitoring Internet traffic. The article mentions that some deaths may have been connected with the story, including a murder set up to look like suicide. The software was suddenly taken off the market due to government litigation.

Varney had published several articles in various other trade magazines, and wrote fairly well. I was surprised he had not broken into a bigger forum but don't we know--success is tricky in every profession. The widest-read magazine in which Varney had been published was *Fortean Times*, a publication that has already served me well. Varney also independently published a couple of books on Amazon concerning government policy and fascist forces in Europe. Currently, he has a well-trafficked blog writing on ancient historical wonders and mysteries. A background check shows he now works at a Colonial history museum in DC. The museum's website has a short video with him explaining the meaning of various early U.S. flags. His voice sounds very similar to my caller.

I send an email to the address in his blog, saying I found his article in *InsideNews* to be interesting, and could I call him.

Within a few minutes of sending the email, he calls *me*.

"My God, you're even better than I thought."

"Thank you, I think. Is this a game for you, Kent?"

"No, no way. Look, I don't know what made me call you before. I felt for your situation, as I said. You seem like a good man. I had a real urge to reach out. Believe me, I'm not playing games or wasting your time."

"Well, looks like you were right about having run into this before. How did your story start?"

"Hold on, let me get back to my office....okay. This first started back in 1991. I met a man at a computer convention. I was working for a computer magazine at the time. He had designed software for the government, but was never paid for it. He was in the process of suing the government about the whole thing. The software used a sophisticated detection system for language to troll newsgroups in the Usenet system. You remember when those first started?"

"Yeah. The groups with something dot alt something. Like for science fiction or technical discussions."

"Right. Well, some of the first worldwide users of those newsgroups were hate groups--white supremacists. The software program the guy invented searched out those discussions discretely--it had some way of getting around actually subscribing to them--and it searched for threats or illegal information being disseminated, like on how to avoid taxes or build a bomb. So this seemed like a good thing, right? But while he's having a problem getting his licensing approved, he's also being asked to alter the program to secretly spy on other groups as well. University students, as example. He doesn't think that's right, so he doesn't do it.

"So guess what happens? His government buyer contact has the software copied and gives it to some other hotshot programmer to reverse-engineer the code, and then creates a new copy set up to do the spy work. This other programmer also changed the software to be able to set up fake accounts that could be used *spread* certain rumors or disinformation. I think the government is still doing something like that now, through the military. My contact never was paid for his work, even though he ended up with something like six federal lawsuits against the government. A judge said he was in the right, but he was still forced to declare bankruptcy. Later he hears that the software has been altered again. This time, the software has been redesigned to track foreign web postings, and financial information."

"I don't remember this in the news at all."

"Oh it wasn't. That was the time leading to Desert Storm, and only tech journals were even bothering to pay attention. Now, even back in 1990, the sheer amount of information obtained from the Usenet needed a more than a few people to handle and translate. More people mean higher risk of a leak. In talking to some people the original software designer had recommended, I turned up another guy, a low-level software analyst who was intrigued enough to investigate some of what he heard on his own. The analyst tells me that he began researching a man who was said to be a troubleshooter for secret organizations. The troubleshooter was in his late sixties at the time and also known to be an unofficial CIA op.

"So I start looking into this the CIA guy, who claimed he was a 'private security risk assessment specialist.' Then I find out that the analyst turned up dead in his car, a handgun suicide...except that the gun was in his right hand and he was left-handed. The official verdict was still suicide. You see?"

That makes me think of the call to warn me off the case. A death and a warning. And if I don't heed the warning? That's why I'm being followed. So Joel says. No, don't do that. He's right, and he's looking out for me.

"Meanwhile the software is still out there. The developer tried to sell it commercially, which is how the Nazi-hunters got ahold of it. Then the government takes the software through court injunction claiming, unbelievably enough, patent violation on the developer's part. The case became bogged down in court as only government litigation can.

"I was more than a little nervous after the analyst's death. I still did meet with the CIA contact. He was quite a character. Unfailingly polite but malevolent; it just rolled off him. He denied being involved with Nazis or the software. Then came the phone call. A man told me to go back to writing about computers or I might wind up in a similar situation as the analyst."

Kent excuses himself to answer another call. When he returns I ask him what happened ultimately with his investigation.

"I'm sorry; this brings back some bad memories. I wasn't the only one threatened. My wife at the time received those calls as well. My mother, too. I still went on and found some interesting connections. Then a couple things happened. Someone ran my wife off the road in Bethesda. Then the computer magazine canceled its contract with me. I had to sue them in fact. They settled, but it took almost six months to get another writing gig. My name was poison. I tried to get some big-time magazines interested in the story so I could go on, but no one bit. I was surprised, actually. A couple lesser-known mags were willing to take a look. But they couldn't pay, and I had real bills to take care of for my wife's recovery and to keep the house and so on. I had to give it up. Then life took over, right? This was a hobby that had no payoff. I'm not scared for myself, but I also couldn't put my family in harm."

I think about how his situation was a bit similar to mine. "So you let it end then."

"Right. Now my mom is passed away, and I'm divorced and we sold the house. But, the trail is stone cold. Writing is a hard way to make a living. I'm doing okay, but even as a hobby I wouldn't go back there. But I was still affected by what happened to you. And I feel like you're on the same trail, in a way. What do you think you can you find out?"

"I don't know; I don't know where it would lead me. But more information must be available, especially online."

"Bullshit information, sure. Look, the other sources I developed, they gave me connections to some serious major scandals. You may have heard of any one of these stories. But just on the surface, see. Not the connections between the incidents. Each story is presented as a standalone gig. No one wanted to follow up. And in a way, I understand that. You understand how crazy it sounds that some over-arching system is controlling certain aspects of the world. The Illuminati, the Vatican, the Trilateral Commission, the New World Order. Whatever, it all sounds insane. And I don't know that any such thing exists. When I read about it, I keep running across anti-government militia types--Fed Reserve, IRS, government microchips, religious wackos. I'm not with them and I don't want them with me."

"I know what you mean. You start trying to question something and you're now in the same category as the people who think the pope and the president are lizards from outer space."

"Exactly. That in itself makes me wonder....what you find online is also a lot of disinformation. I sometimes think the Internet as a whole was set up as a disinformation service to be able to control what story becomes the 'official' one."

"I thought the Internet was the Wild West."

"Even the Wild West had Wyatt Earp, right? It's not as wild as it looks. Listen. I've had a lot of time to think about this, from what my sources told me nearly twenty years ago. If you were something...in *power*, would you be scared of fringe groups? No, just the *New York Times* or *Rolling Stone* or *Time*. Do any of them report the fringe? Hell no. If anything, they have the stories that reaffirm the status quo.

"If you question an official story, you're a conspiracy nut, right? Wearing tin hats and protesting fluoridation or whatever. Right-wing lumped in with left-wing, the birthers and the truthers all in the same category. Anyone doing real research has to fight the label of *conspiracy theorist*, and you can't do that when respected publications keep printing articles on how all conspiracy theories are full of shit."

I have to laugh at how he thinks like I do. "Yeah...skeptics always say that people who believe in conspiracy theories do so because it comforts them to have a rationale for why terrible things happen. I always thought that idea could go both ways. That people who refuse to look beyond the official story do so because it comforts them as a rationale for why terrible things happen."

"Right! So, if you are in *power*, what would you do? Have even *worse* information online, so to make anyone questioning the government--or really, the power holders *in* the government or elsewhere, look utterly discredited. Sometimes you look like a nut, sometimes you don't, right? Now it's worse, though. Used to be you could question something obvious like the Warren Commission, and that wasn't disrespectable; look at the stats that said more people believe in a conspiracy about JFK than don't. But I swear, I think these lizard hunters and false flaggers and birthers were set up by someone to make *any* inquiry look bad--because the media lumps them all together. Have you noticed how many articles have been out, and even books now, on debunking conspiracies? And they focus on the birthers, but they include any other story like JFK. So who the hell wants to be connected to the birthers? Or the Posse Comitatus types. So stay away from anything reeking of conspiracy if you want any respect. Plus, after 9/11, you don't want your Google searches being reviewed by Homeland Security, right?"

My head is spinning. There's nothing like a slightly paranoid person talking to a very paranoid person. I feel like Laurence Fishburne is handing me red and blue pills--a favorite metaphor of truthers. I can hang up and forget I ever learned this stuff, or go full-tilt tin hat.

"Kent, when you called me before you said you were familiar with what happened to Raymond and I understand that, but...what made you think what happened to Raymond was like what happened to your analyst? I agree with you, but nothing about Nazis was in the news. Yet you think Nazis are involved."

"Well." Kent falls silent for a moment. "Uh, some details in the story were familiar...I recognized a name, so to speak."

I think about it. No one other than Raymond and I are in the story. And Toni, but I can't imagine it's her.

"You mean the Foundation, don't you? Raymond was on the board."

"Um, well. I wouldn't bet against it is all I'll say."

"How did you hear of the Foundation before?"

"Well, the details are a little vague in my memory at the moment. I have notes, but they are in storage. I don't mind showing you, but I'm not sending them electronically."

"But you would show me in person, maybe?"

"Yeah. If you come down here, that means you're a serious person. I don't mind showing you, if it will help. It may not. The stuff is deep."

"Is the Foundation in your notes?"

"I honestly don't remember. Might be, might not."

I consider which is easier. Trying to convince him to fax or send me the notes, or go to DC. If I was him, I wouldn't like to be put to the trouble of digging out old files for some yahoo who called me. "What if I pay you for the notes?"

"I'm not saying I wouldn't like the extra money, but I don't want to just send my notes to anyone. It's my work, my holy grail. I know I can't do anything with it, but I need to talk to you in person if I'm going to give it to you."

"Why would you trust me, Kent? How do you know I'm not disinformation myself?"

He laughs. "Oh, I don't know. Somehow, I doubt anyone behind to your lawyer's murder would have handled the preacher the way you did. Not the status quo. I have to leave this--my notes--to someone to work on, because I can't. You're my choice now."

The idea of Kent's notes is growing on me. A short trip to DC is still money I don't have, and need to justify to Cheng. I tell Kent I'll have to get back to him if I can swing the expense.

I call Alex to tell him that Kent may have some information on Nazis and possibly some other stories. I don't mention the notes for now, until I meet up with Kent and see if he will actually let me have a copy.

Alex is all for the idea of visiting him. "Do it. If this is good stuff, it could lead to a book we could work on together. I'll give you the travel money if Cheng won't."

"I don't want to take money from you, but thanks. You think this is worth a book? If it is, it's Kent's book, not mine. He did this research; he lost his wife through this."

"We'll bring him in on it if he wants. We wouldn't leave him in on the cold. But see if the stuff checks out first before saying anything."

I laugh. "Believe me, I'm not going down there promising a book deal. My main concern is if this connection between the CIA bad guy and the fucked-up software and whatever other big-league scandal proves who killed Raymond."

"What it proves now is that Raymond had a basis for wanting the matter investigated. If you have enough connections to Raymond, the questions are raised even if you don't have a specific person who actually killed him. Once you have the alternative story out there, it can't be taken away. It's getting the story out in the first place that's the hard part. It could lead to something, Gabriel."

"Kent's wife was run off the road by some hired gun. I don't want *you* to be run off the West Side Highway."

Now it's his turn to laugh. "Don't worry about me. Hindus are taught how to deal with demons, like Hanuman fighting Ravana, the demon king of Lanka."

"It comforts me a great deal that you are familiar with the *Ramayana* and can analogize it to this situation. Especially as you are also an atheist."

"Agnostic. So you know some Hinduism as well; this feels so karmic then. Doing the right thing, like your Buddha. I spent a couple of my formative years in an ashram my mother sent me to, to study Hindu philosophy."

"*My* Buddha. The original one was Indian, you know. So what do the agnostics do in this situation, then? Did the ashram teach you that?"

"We carry a shiv. I have one of those, too."

∞

Monday, August 9

I have to go out to pick up checks from Cheng to give to our hired experts for the psych autopsy. I also want to get some data from a photogrammetrist I had put on the expert list. Her work was to determine physical characteristics of the man in the video. She had a hard time being definite, but it's something.

When I get to my car, I find a note on my windshield. This is not an annoying postcard for some club, or a cheap business card offering bullshit jobs at fantastic pay rates, but a note with my name on it. I pick it up carefully and unfold it with my fingertips.

It's actually several sheets of paper with photos printed--of me. Recently. In places I recognize having been in lately. No words, but in each picture my eyes are cut out.

I feel cold. I try to shake it off inside. Not every day does one get such an ominous sign on one's windshield. At least without having stolen someone's parking space. I have extreme unease mixed with bravado. The presence I sensed on the street, outside my door is probably the same as whoever put this on my car.

But my business plans are not changed. I'm not going to be prodded into stopping because of this. My anger grows as I go about my tasks. Finally, after I'm done, I stop by the Foundation. On impulse, I want to talk to Ethan Nelson again and see what his attitude is. When I buzz the Foundation front door, he actually comes down to see me. He moves in close, so I can't get by him and wreak havoc inside. Once again, he is rather strongly doused in his grassy cologne, which makes me back up a step.

He should have no reason to think I'm hostile, but something has changed. He doesn't bother with the gracious host attitude. "Gabriel. What do you want?"

"Are you threatening me?" I hold up the papers with my blinded face.

He smirks. "Maybe you just aren't a popular person. You should rethink your career. The problem with you is that you're smart but you don't apply it properly."

"I don't think so. I think I'm doing my job pretty well. You have no idea about the kind of person I am."

"Really?" He leans against the doorway. In the resulting shadow, he looks tired and his eyes are red. His overall pallor and nervous twitch makes me wonder for the first time if he does drugs. "Am I underestimating you, is that it?" His mouth is set in a way that seems familiar to me...the person in the video with Raymond. That reminds me. I take out the photogrammetrist's report.

"You over-estimate yourself. You're about 5'11, right? Just about the same size and shape of this person. Is this you?" I show him my blow-up of the man at the counter in Cafétière Maléfice.

While Alex's and the *Scene's* articles mentioned the video, they didn't include a picture. Nelson doesn't betray surprise at the image. Instead, he assumes a superior look. But I see his eyes are drawn to the man in the picture. Almost enraptured, like when we were in the Foundation dining room looking at the wall of fame.

"There are many white men in this city and the rest of the world who are 5'11. You can't prove that was me in that shop. If that's your reason for harassing me, expect another lawsuit soon."

I give him a small smile. "You know, most people would ask who the person is, where this was from. And what exactly I'm accusing them of before saying I can't prove it."

His mouth falls open a crack. I imagine his mind bouncing around like a pinball. He made a mistake. A tiny mistake that can't be used against him in court, but a mistake nonetheless. Caught up in his own image like Narcissus. I seize upon that mistake.

"All those other white men in the city and rest of the world weren't covering up a crime in an organization where a board member was murdered. Think about a jury deciding that and the risk of you being recognized for your lovely self here. Go ahead and sue--I'd love to have discovery on you and your background. Harlan Ellison once said, "There are some people one should never screw with." For you, whoever you think you've intimidated before, no matter who you work for that wants to controls the world, I want you to know *I'm that person.*"

He drags his eyes from the picture and looks me over. Like most distinctly evil or disturbed persons, the eyes are the hardest. Whether or not eyes are the window to the soul, people without a sense of shame have no problem staring into someone's eyes to the point of discomfort. I match his stare. To engage in a stare-down, you need to mean what you say, call the bluff. If you are just blowing smoke, the psychopath will stare you down. If you are sincere, you can match the stare. I don't have a problem staring him down.

He has eyes without boundaries. I imagine I see hate there-- hate for having even in a tiny way bested him. For a minute, I see where he could be a worse threat, a nightmare, if he set his mind to do so.

His face rapidly undergoes a process to return to neutral. Sweat breaks out on his face. If he is jonesing, he'll need a hit soon. His voice loses some smoothness and gains an edge. "You should mind your own business. I'll make sure your license is gone. Try your shit way of making a living peeping in bedrooms then. You'll be fucking lucky to work at Starbucks cleaning the bathrooms. You're white trash who can't hold a real job because you can't deal with normal people. You think you're going to do anything but regret having been here?"

I can't help being a smartass. "Regret what? Not writing a dissertation on *The Problematic Theme Structures of Social Equity* at Cambridge, or Oxford, or was it DeVry? Do you even *have* a degree to manage the rich persons' *objects d'art?*"

His expression gets blacker. Challenging his superiority is dangerous. "You can't win in a game with me. You really have no idea of the meaning of 'who not to screw with.' You know nothing about me and what I can do to you."

"I know you don't want me to find out more about you. But I'm going to. I'll bring you down, asshole."

He shakes his head. "You've made your own fate with this one."

"Go fuck yourself." Not eloquent, but serves as the last word. And now I have to live up to this.

∞

EIGHTEEN ♦ THE EIGHT OF SWORDS

The Eight of Swords represents a female figure in a constrained position. Being trapped presents a difficult choice--move and one may be cut in order to be free. Don't move and one is strangled by the ropes that constrain. Freedom must lie with not fearing the cuts.

∞

Monday, August 9, Continued
Alphabet City, Avenue A 11:30 am

GETTING BACK HOME, I'm still in the throes of adrenaline from confronting Nelson, regardless of how foolish that might have been. I want to forget him and revel in the developments within my personal life.

But it's not that easy. Joel has been here; he's dropped off a stack of paperwork--interviews, notes, records for the cases I need. Enough so that I now have time to catch up with Jim's research. I also find all my dishes and glassware re-washed and stacked on the kitchen counter. He has a note pinned to the refrigerator to the effect that rather than growing my own penicillin, I could try being hygienic instead.

This makes me smile some. I guess he isn't angry anymore, or this is his way of working through it. I feel the conflict stronger about his being here and my new thing with Alex.

Calling Danny is out of the question. He'd love to hear about Alex but would give me forty shades of Holy Hell for allowing Joel back in my life. He was there for the breaking up and the aftermath. No, I don't need to let him know that just yet. I call Veronica instead. I tell her about Alex and she asks for as many details as I'm willing to give. Then I change the topic.

"I know you know Joel is back."

"Of course, we've been talking."

"He's helping me out."

"We can hang out like we used to."

"Not exactly like we used to; remember two minutes ago I mentioned a new relationship?"

"Well, you know you can be in love with more than one person."

That's Veronica. She's up for anything. What I love about talking to her is that she forces me to argue against myself. "Whoa, whoa, whoa. I said nothing about love. I think I'm falling for Alex, sure. But Joel...I love him, I'll always love him for himself, if you know what I mean. But I'm not in love anymore. Romantically. Remember how difficult it was to get past those feelings?"

"Yeah. If you did."

She's not convinced. I tell her about my conversation with Joel when he returned. "Okay, so sure, we may have missed each other but you know, I'm not off the freaking grid. He had my contact info if he had something to say."

"You know how he is. But I'll tell you, he's changed, I can see a maturity and gravity in him. He'll make amends."

"Veronica. I can't handle this. He's a beautiful man but no way. No way. What was between us was too much."

"I think we could talk about it. The three of us. Remember when I was your de facto relationship counselor?"

"I don't want to *talk* about it, Jesus. I'm just dealing with him as a friend."

"Well, we'll just get together again, okay?"

"I'll see about it. You should meet Alex, too."

"Of course, I'd love to meet Alex. But I'm not changing my sense about you and Joel."

I sigh again. "You're not helping."

"Not my job. You want nagging, call Danny. Which you haven't, I bet a million dollars."

"I ain't taking that bet."

Having failed to deal with my issue, I decide to ignore it for now. When Alex calls, I'm ready for him to come over.

I don't smoke a lot of reefer, but damned if it doesn't help me relax. Every so often, I need some relaxation that doesn't feel like time stolen from responsibility.

That is why I'm sitting on my living room, sharing a blunt with Alex. First we smoke regular cigarettes to warm up, although he doesn't really smoke like I do. But he lights both Camels and hands me one, just like Paul Henreid and Bette Davis in *Now Voyager.* Then, getting to the good stuff, we pass the blunt back and forth.

I can feel the regular world float away as we swim away in the music, or so it seems. I get a little loopy under the effect of a joint, but we are holding each other's arms and rocking back and forth. When he runs his hands down my forearms, all my hair seems to stand on end. Pretty soon we are closer, close enough to kiss when we are rocking back and forth. Now I can feel like I'm melting. To the point of losing when one begins or ends.

∞

Wednesday, August 11

The world is unfair when you have to leave your bed. The best part of the last few nights has been Alex. The first couple of days after we spent the night together, he wasn't able to come over due to work obligations. But since then he's been over every night. We've started a pattern of talking about our lives, cooking meals, feeling comfortable, being passionate.

The previous day I had Danny and Veronica over for dinner with Alex and that went well. Danny and I are highly critical of each other's significant others, sometimes without justification. Even before I broke up with Joel, Danny and he got along like Yankees/Red Sox fans. I still don't tell Danny that Joel is back.

The rapport between Alex and I has drawn us close this week. He has made a few references to things he wants to do with me in the future; travel and recreation plans. This morning he has to leave to work on a burgeoning political scandal. All sorts of contacts were calling him, but he put them off long enough to draw me to the light coming through the kitchen window. We stand there in the sunrise, him dressed and looking good, me looking scruffy and rumpled. He smooths my hair with his fingers.

"Some of my family will be in soon; I have a lot of extended family in England and Mumbai. I can't wait for you to meet them. I can see in the future telling others our how-we-met story, at a funeral."

I take his coffee out of his hand and set it on the windowsill; put my arms around him. "How far in the future? People will get sick of that story eventually."

"We'll keep adding to it." He kisses me. "I can see very far in the future. Something about you makes me feel home. This may be too early, but how do you feel? We're both people with heavy working schedules and odd hours. It's either sex or a relationship based on flexibility and trust."

"I can handle it. You have an idea what my work is like. If you can deal with that and not judge, we can build something. Over time."

"I know." He leans his head into mine. "You have to have time to let your guard down. That's trust. You'll find out you can trust me if I give my heart over. I'll let you have that time, because I think you're worth it. I'm not up for partying at this time in my life; I want a partner."

On that note, he had to leave. I'm still tired this morning; I have been working a tough couple of days finishing the work for Jim and gathering the reports for Allen Cheng. I've also spoken with Nicolas and John for their affidavits. I haven't shared with anyone my belief about Nelson. I have no real proof. I mull over my confrontation with him, which gave me the mental hook I needed to know he was the one who took Raymond. But at the same time, I also totally let him know I was on to him. Did it matter? I don't know. But I'm thinking on what to do next concerning him.

But now I promised Veronica I'd meet her and Joel for coffee at a bakery in the neighborhood. I haven't seen him in person since our clash five days ago.

I'm the last to arrive. Veronica gets up to hug me, but Joel stays put. I feel the awkwardness.

When we sit, Veronica changes a business-like expression. "Okay, this has to end."

I pick up my coffee cup. "What are you talking about now, troublemaker?"

"Let me." Joel puts his hand on hers.

"Doesn't matter. He's not going to be happy about it."

"What the fuck?" I start getting irritated at their exchange.

She looks at me and then back at him. "See? Let him be mad at me, not you."

Joel shakes his head at her. "He'll be all right."

"You two going to continue to talk about me like I'm not here?"

Joel faces me. Meeting his eyes is again like touching a direct current. He takes a moment to speak. "So you were okay with the stuff I got for the cases?"

"Yeah, it was great. Your work always is."

"Good. But you still have a suspicion I'm not telling you the truth about you being followed."

"No, I know it's true. It's just..."

"Bad timing? What you still feel for me? I suppose so. I can't help that. I can't tell you not to have a social life, even with the wrong person."

I frown at him, but before I can protest, he goes on. "But whatever. I told you I'm here for you no matter what. Someone's after you and you need to be aware of it. I don't want any doubt in your mind that could distract you, or make you act rash to prove me wrong."

"I'm not that stupid, Joel."

"You feel too much."

"I do not," I say, as I think about getting in Nelson's face on Monday. I try not to turn red.

"You do." This from Veronica. "You know we're alike that way. It's a positive quality."

Joel nods. "It is. But your first reaction to anything is to rebel, to tell the world fuck off. Don't give in to that now."

"Uh huh."

"See? You're still skeptical."

Veronica puts her hand on mine. "He's telling the truth, Gabriel. I saw him."

I look at her now. "You saw who?"

"The man following you. Joel had me with him a couple times in the last week, when I could."

"Why would you not tell me that?" I don't want to get angry at a friend who is a soul mate the way she is, but I feel it coming.

"Better you *didn't* know. We could see how he followed you when you're acting normal. But he *is* there, no doubt."

I take some time to think this over. "I could kick both your asses for just doing this without telling me. Seriously. I understand it's from care and love, but you're going too far not including me in on your games. I need to have a little time by myself, okay?"

I get up and leave the bakery, acutely aware we're all guilty of bad behavior.

Back to the apartment. I try to groom Archie to have something to do to calm myself. Then I give up and lie down, dozing off.

My phone rings, startling me awake.

"Ross? I need to talk to you."

"Dr. Cole?"

"Of course." He sounds irritable, as if it could be no one else. "I've been concerned over Ms. Whitford because she hasn't been feeling well."

"Oh, so Nelson was telling the truth about that." I sit up and swing my feet out of bed.

"You talked to him? Well, I don't like what he is telling me, that he's *taking care* of her. He barely knows her and honestly, she does not like him."

"Really? For some reason that does not surprise me."

"I'm worried now. She has never failed to return my calls."

"Did Nelson happen to tell you she was depressed?"

"Yes, that's exactly what he said. Now, I know she was upset that Raymond died. But you have to understand Ms. Whitford. She has always been independent, an iron lady. She would never fall apart over this. She would never suddenly become helpless and dependent. And if she did, she *wouldn't go* to Nelson."

"She didn't answer when I tried to call her a few days ago. But why, if you don't mind my asking, are you calling me in on it?"

"Does it matter?" His tone turns impatient. "I had to admit that some of what you said stayed with me. While you have an attitude, you're okay. I know I was pretty rough with you. But I had you checked out just in case *you* decided to harass Ms. Whitford, and you have a good reputation. If you are right, she could be in trouble."

I'm already up and pulling on a t-shirt and jeans as the conversation ends. A short time later, I find myself double-parking my Camry outside of Whitford's three-story brownstone on the Upper East Side, watching the place, with the radio on to take away the growing heat of the early morning air--the 10 a.m. air, anyway. The brownstone's windows are dark or have the curtains closed.

After watching for a few minutes, I get out of the car and walk up to the door. There is one doorbell. I ring it and wait. Nothing. Two minutes later, I ring again. Then I try knocking. Then I go to her next-door neighbors on either side. One isn't home. The other has a domestic worker who knows Whitford, and tells me she hasn't been seen outside the house for at least a week, and that is unusual. She thinks maybe Whitford is sick. She doesn't know if any relatives that visit regularly.

A good time to see about the courtyard in back. Walking down the block and around the corner, I find an opening in an alley that leads to the courtyards. A small stone wall topped with an iron railing blocks the area from the alley. It's pathetically easy to get up the wall and over the railing, even though it's pointed. All the yards for the brownstones appear to be easily accessible from one house to the next. Once in the first courtyard I easily make my way to Whitford's place.

Her yard has tubs of bright colored flowers blooming under the sun interspersed with ancient metal yard furniture. A couple of steps lead to the back door. The curtains aren't quite closed; through them, I see nothing moving around inside on the first floor. The second floor has two balconies. I guess that with a lawn chair moved up to help, I can climb them, too. After a moment's hesitation, I pull a chair over.

I make a jump for the bottom railing and use the momentum to swing my legs up to catch the floor between the railing bars. Peering in the double glass doors, I can just make out a figure through the gauzy curtains. After a moment, I realize the figure is also looking at me. It's Whitford, who doesn't appear to be unduly upset I'm on her balcony. I'm ready to escape back down, but she just looks at me in the manner of a cat watching a spider make its way across the wall. Interested, but not enough to stir.

I take out my picklock gun, the kind a cop or locksmith would use. I'm actually a certified locksmith and do consults on personal security. The equipment and knowledge are extremely useful for when I need to do things in the gray area of the law. Her balcony door is no problem. Inside, I note the air conditioning is on, but the room, some kind of sitting room or bedroom, is dusty like it hasn't been cleaned in some time.

"Ms. Whitford?" I ask.

"Ummhummn," she says with a slow nod.

I move closer and give her an once-over. She is dressed and in reasonably good condition, but not alert. She shows no sign of stroke, like a limp arm and leg. I suspect she is drugged as she continues to look out of it by her expression, even with a strange man in her sitting room. I get down on one knee next to her. "Who's taking care of you, ma'am?"

She appears to be thinking about it. "Ummmn."

As if to punctuate my question, I hear a door below shut. Now she looks mildly upset at this arrival.

I want to find out what's going on, but my being here could cause bad repercussions for her. So I slip out the door to the balcony and swing back down to the patio.

I go back the way I came, borrowing someone's patio table for leverage to get up the wall. "Hey," someone says behind me, which I ignore. Never stop for questions.

Back down the block in my car I watch the street. No one is outside her building, nor any other double-parked cars around. But a moment later, her door opens and I catch a brief glimpse of Nelson. So he has a key to her place.

I have an idea to get into see her. This would be where I'd call Joel or Veronica...but I can't. Instead, I call Alex for help.

We start the plan from the *Herald* newspaper office, at his desk in the enormous city edition room surrounded by constant chatter and office machines. Alex introduces a couple of other reporters to me. Then he calls Nelson.

Alex blocks the return number of his office phone and calls for Nelson at the Foundation. He says he's her grandnephew, Alex Whitford, and that he heard Nelson was "taking care of" Eleanor. He's in town to see her and she isn't answering, and he wants to speak to Nelson immediately. Alex emphasizes this is an emergency, since I'm guessing it was Nelson going in Whitford's place when I left.

Nelson calls Alex back in a few minutes, evidently from his cell. We can hear street sounds.

Alex assumes an attitude of self-righteousness. "What are you doing with my aunt?"

"Mr. Whitford, I haven't done anything wrong with her. Your aunt is ill and depressed. Really, she doesn't want to see anyone but me right now. I have to ask, if you are concerned, why haven't you been here before? Right now I feel as though I'm the only person who actually truly, cares about Eleanor."

He's totally bought it and scrambling in a hurry to cover up whatever's going on. Alex sounds stern. "Mr. Nelson, since I'm here, unless I see her I intend to call the police immediately. Family still counts for legal matters, doesn't it?"

"Well...even though Eleanor's health will surely suffer, you can come by tomorrow." I'm busy writing as this goes on; I give him some quick notes on a Post-It.

"Tomorrow isn't going to settle anything. I'll meet you at the brownstone at two. We can all talk together concerning her condition."

Nelson sounds agitated, but agrees.

Alex then tells his editor he has to leave to investigate a story, which in a sense he is. We leave and get over to the brownstone in under an hour, the two o'clock appointment being a ruse.

Once on Whitford's block again, I quickly go over some last minute strategy with Alex. He leaves my car, goes up to her brownstone, and rings the bell as I hang back out of sight from the front of the building.

I figured Nelson would stay there to cover up anything needed to hide in her house. I'm right and he opens the door. He is surprised to see that Eleanor's grandnephew is Indian. Alex is confident and persuasive and Nelson lets him in, which is the main part of the plan.

I give Alex a few minutes head start. If Eleanor is there, she will also be surprised over her grandnephew--at least that she even has one. Alex will play out any awkwardness as Nelson's fault for over-medicating her, which I think is the case.

Alex then will try to distract Nelson from locking the front door, or fake an immediate phone call to enable him to step away and unlock the door. Turns out to be the second option; he steps out of the brownstone for 20 seconds and goes back in. I follow up two minutes after. The front door is unlocked. Slipping inside, I can hear voices in a sitting room to the left.

Whitford is sitting in an overstuffed chair in the sitting room. She looks startled and confused.

Nelson, on the other hand, turns to look at me in an absolutely shocked manner, which pleases me to no end. He has incurred my anger, and I have a deep well of anger. He stands up, balling his fists, still looking incredulous. "What are you doing here?" His voice loses his characteristic measured quality.

"I told you before; I wanted to speak to Ms. Whitford."

∞

NINETEEN ◆ THE SEVEN OF PENTACLES

The Seven of Pentacles represents using one's wit to navigate out of a situation. The person must be at the top of his game, as this requires far more finesse intellectually than brute force.

∞

NELSON IS STIFF with fury. "You *fucking* cocksucker."

His language has degraded considerably since the Foundation interview. He looks from me to Alex. "And you. You're that reporter. Both of you get out of here."

"I don't think so." I step towards him and press my advantage. "Are *you* her guardian? Do *you* own this place?"

He almost pulsates with his internal rage. I can see him grabbing my throat, ripping me apart. I'd gladly go hand to hand with him, but this isn't the place. He doesn't appear to have a weapon, so I'm not worried about surprises with both me and Alex here. I crouch down next to Eleanor. "Ms. Whitford, you remember me, Gabriel Ross? I was going to work for Raymond Booth. You and I were planning to talk." She stirs at Raymond's name and opens her mouth to speak.

I smell Nelson's cologne again before feeling his hand on my shoulder to pull me away. I jump up and knock away his hand. I have a thing with people grabbing my shoulder; my father used to do that, sneaking up on me and digging his fingers in. I'm ready to deck Nelson for doing the same. Alex steps between us. This calms me down enough to say loudly to Whitford, "Would you like to talk to me?"

She looks at Nelson with fear, but says yes.

I look back at Nelson. "You heard her."

His eyes light up with some inner demonic force. "Fine. This will not last long." He smiles grimly as he walks out. Alex follows to make sure he actually leaves.

But now I turn back to Whitford. "May I sit down?"

"Yes." Her voice is less shaky.

"Ms. Whitford, do you want me to call someone? Call the police? Call Dr. Cole? Do you want Nelson to leave you alone?"

She understands me well enough, perhaps shocked into semi-lucidity from the drugs. "I don't like what's going on..."

"I'm going to tell Dr. Cole, okay? Whatever is going on, Nelson does not have to be here. Is he hurting you?"

"No... could I have some tea?"

I get up and find the kitchen. Alex is in the hall. I nod at him and he winks at me. Five minutes later I have tea for her. I let her finish the tea. Now she regained a little more of herself, but is still struggling against medication.

I ask a couple nondescript questions of when she met Raymond and how long she had been with the Foundation to get a sense of her capabilities. She answers readily enough.

"Who is that man? He's not my nephew..."

"I understand. He's a friend of mine who's helping me because we and Dr. Cole were concerned about you."

"I'm glad to hear that." She looks like she is going to cry. I take her hand. "You remember I asked you regarding what Raymond hired me to investigate?"

She nods. "I-I... heard something a little while ago. I heard something that....that really bothered me. I didn't know what to do." She squeezes my hand.

I move closer. "I understand completely. What did you hear?"

She thinks very hard through the cloud she's in. "A name, a name. I heard them talking..." She looks around again.

"Nelson?"

"Yes. He was talking to another man, a board member. Mr. Nelson was giving him something. They were talking about an evil man. I heard his name--I *knew* his name."

"A Nazi?"

"Yes. You see, my father was in England during the war; he helped the French Resistance. There were men he knew...who were Nazis...."

"And the man you heard about, he was a real Nazi, I mean, from Hitler's time? In the Nazi Party?"

"Oh yes, yes he was. He worked with finance persons on Hitler's behalf. I knew this because my father said he thought this man had killed a friend of his to escape from France. As far as we know, he escaped, see, from France to Africa to South America..."

"The ratlines."

She's gaining strength in her memories and nods in response. "...so I asked Mr. Nelson what the board member wanted, just to see if I could find out more. He had some odd story that this all concerned importing art. Later on, he started talk to me about it, and I didn't feel right afterwards, very ill. I haven't felt right at all since then. He comes around and does things, but he told me--he told me I *shouldn't* be asking questions."

"Who was this Nazi, Ms. Whitford?"

She thinks again, remembering. "Schleiden. He was trained in accounting, and helped out Eichmann; he assisted him at one time."

"And the Foundation board member who is supposed to be friend of his?"

"His name is William Christensen. I think he spent some time in Chile as well as Germany, as a financier. But I don't know how he is acquainted with Schleiden. That is what I wanted Raymond to find out. I'm sure Nelson didn't know that I knew who Schleiden was. Raymond started to ask around for me. He would have found out, I know."

"Did he mention a group called The Tertullian Society?"

Her head tilts at the name. "I don't think so, but for some reason it sounds familiar."

"Raymond may have heard of it from asking around."

She looks so tired. We've been there almost an hour. I decide to push the issue on Whitford's safety. I call Dr. Cole, and when he answers, I put him on with Whitford. She is reluctant to say anything really specific. I feel that Nelson has messed her up some through meds and manipulation. But Cole is ready to have Nelson thrown out for good.

I'm still on the phone with Cole when we hear a loud knock at the door. I figure Nelson is back and I'm ready to knock him down the front stairs. But he's not alone. An older white man in a suit is with him. The other man speaks through the chain on the door.

"I'm Dr. Ralph Howard; Ms. Whitford is under my care. You are going to have to leave."

He proves he's a doctor by showing me some ID from a hospital and some kind of document that has his name and Whitford's name. I can't really read it because he takes it back. "I'm the one who can legally determine who is allowed to speak to her."

The medical profession can cause as much trouble as the police when powers are used for the wrong reasons. I leave to ask Whitford if she knows Howard. Howard yells through the door he'll have me arrested if I don't open the door. And Cole is yelling through my phone demanding to know what is going on. I tell him he should come over here under the circumstances and duel with the other doctor.

Howard follows through with his threat and the police do indeed arrive. Nelson is smug and impervious with a doctor to back him up. Whitford is frightened by the two patrol officers entering the house and can't answer them clearly. I insist she be taken to an emergency room to see if she has been injured, and Howard accuses me of trying to rob her. Of course, the police find a respected director of a philanthropic institution and a physician more credible than a private investigator (scum of the earth petty criminal and known troublemaker) and a journalist (slightly above scum level, but still not human and on record as questioning official police reports). Still, we're able to stay without being arrested until Cole shows up and takes over the situation to fight with Howard.

Alex and I leave. He's hyped enough to go with me to the main branch of the library at Fifth Avenue, which has some of the best-archived historical material. We research more on Richard Schleiden and find out he was a lesser-known name in the Nazi echelon. He had a rank as an Obersturmbannführer (lieutenant colonel).

Schleiden indeed worked with Eichmann for a short time. He helped supervise financing of some operations, and also oversaw some execution of Russian POWs. He transferred some of Hitler's assets out of the country as the war was coming to a climax. He left Germany shortly before Hitler blew his mind out in the bunker. Afterwards, he was smart enough to be ahead of the Russians who were gunning for him on a most wanted list. He moved to Egypt and allegedly assisted the notorious Otto Skorzeny and Richard Gehlen in training terrorists to fight the new state of Israel.

He was not a bureaucratic Nazi "just following orders" but a diehard racial purist. Nonetheless, rumors spread that the CIA might have helped him change identities because he had some information on Russian troops and intelligence that would have supposedly helped our Cold War intelligence faction. But reliable word about him stopped after 1950.

Schleiden happened to be heavily into the occult, much like some early supporters of the German Workers Party and the shadowy men who mentored Hitler. His interest in the occult, although shared by Himmler, was so deep that on some level he was either an embarrassment or a rival to others close to Hitler and so was never in Berlin too long for his own protection.

Much of this information was in conspiracy-themed books--some good with footnotes, references, photos, etc. Others were atrociously written and of questionable viewpoint. Nonetheless, we save all the information, copying and highlighting, cross-referencing as we work, since I have often thought that even the most crackpot source may have a *piece* of the truth or at least a good lead.

Later on that night, I take Alex back to his apartment in the East 80s. I find a parking space next to his building but we stay in the car for a while, talking and enjoying the night air on Lexington Avenue.

Gradually, I sense something different in atmosphere again. I stop my conversation. I realize I have to be careful, as I was advised. The street is fairly dark but still a few passersby are around. And dark spaces where someone could be hiding. The more I concentrate, the more I can feel something. As if the buildings, the streets, the people fade away and a black indiscernible presence waits quietly, like a heartbeat.

I start the car without really thinking about it. Just in case something happens.

"What's going on..."

A large alley, nearly the width of a one-car garage, is to our right, and just in front of us. The light disappears from the alley like a dark hole. My attention is drawn to the alley looking for a change in the vibrations.

I feel rather than see the change. A disruption in the flow of black. I drop down to the seat, pushing Alex down as well.

Several cracks echo in my ears accompanied by a sudden starburst of lines in the windshield. Puffs of foam padding spits out from the driver's seat.

From my position hunched down in the seats, I call 911. Alex tries to get up, but I hold him against me, awkwardly bunched in the seats of my car. I make him stay down while inch up and roughly navigate away from the space in case the shooter wants to come up to the car and make it personal. Two blocks away I stop and look. No one comes out of the alley, but I have no doubt the person is gone. The bullet holes in the windshield are where my head had been.

Alex has not said a word, but eases up to look outside. "What just happened?"

"We were shot at." My voice is flat. A patrol car pulls up and I drive back to his building.

The officers interrogate us shortly, start writing a report and collect the bullet out the car, while I call my insurance to arrange a new windshield.

"Do you have any enemies," one of the officers asks us.

I'm pretty sure the answer is yes, but I doubt the police would be interested in my theory of connections. Once the officials let us go the hour is quite late. I see on Alex's face how exhausted and stressed he is. "I'm sorry." I take his hand.

"I can't believe how you are just taking this in stride."

I shake my head. I feel a sense of fatality, although I don't believe in fate. What else did I expect? I can only be glad Joel and Veronica's urges soaked in my head somehow. "Do you want me to stay over?"

He does, and after I check out his apartment and his building just for my own comfort we sleep for a few hours. He's still stressed and doesn't sleep well. I don't either, somehow taking the shot as a literal omen of my life.

I don't really register when he gets up early to answer a phone call and then tells me he has to leave; he says I can hang around as the front door is self-locking. He's in a rush and nervous, but by the time I'm actually awake, he's gone. It's barely 7:30 a.m.

I haven't had much chance to check out his apartment, which is much bigger than mine. He has very good, effortless taste in black and white furniture and a touch of color. He had told me that his mother and father had money, allowing him not to have to worry too much about the economy. But I don't want to look around the place without him being here. So I shower quickly and leave myself, to get breakfast in the neighborhood.

I go back home and write up my notes, set up a time to help out Danny with his film project, make an appointment to talk to the staff at Raymond's firm the next week, and work more on Jim's research. The shot fades from being a concern for now; my insurance sends a service to replace my windshield. But I don't hear from Alex for hours; that worries me. I leave a few messages on his phone and check my email.

Finally, he texts me that he has some problems and will talk to me after work. That fills me with more trepidation than the shooting. We meet at a hotel bar in his neighborhood. Although I'm concerned for his stress, I've also located the address of William Christensen in New Jersey. I want Alex to go with me to pay this one a surprise visit.

Alex is waiting for me at a small table in the front of the bar near the windows. His Hugo Boss blazer is neatly folded on a bench behind him. He gives me a smile but doesn't talk much while we order. I start to bring up Christensen, and he listens for a minute and then holds his hand up.

I clasp my hands together on the table. "What's the matter? What happened today?"

He sighs and rubs his forehead. "My editor had a private meeting with me. The publisher found out what happened yesterday. He has a friend connected somehow with the Foundation."

I get more bad feelings, not alleviated by his expression. "He told you not work on this?"

"That's exactly what he said. I spent most of my time trying to keep my editor from not giving me a reprimand to put in my personnel file. I've never had a reprimand or disciplinary action in my entire work history."

I don't have anything to say to that. Alex's work and mine may have the same bad hours but are so completely different in terms of environment. I suddenly feel that stark difference.

Alex reaches over the small bar table and takes my hand. "In the fall, I'm supposed to be a candidate for a promotion. To be an editor, possibly a columnist. In light of how the newspaper and journalism world is shrinking and career options are almost negligible, my editor suggested that pursuing anything connected with...well, your story...would hurt my chances of continuing at the paper at all."

I remain silent. I suppose the fact he's holding my hand is a positive factor.

"Gabriel, talk to me."

"I'm sorry I got you in trouble."

"You didn't 'get' me in trouble; I made my own decision about investigating the case. But it has me at a bad place all of the sudden."

"Okay." I nod along. "I understand that completely. I would hate to be the cause of you getting fired or other trouble. So no problem. I'll go visit this guy tonight and tell you later how it went."

He leans forward. "Let me talk to you regarding that. You mentioned your friends were giving you trouble about staying with this case. I see why. Until last night, I suppose the level of risk in the investigation was obvious--but at the same time not *real* for me. I saw you in the hospital roughed up, I saw you with that gun in your hand in the apartment...and still, until today, I didn't realize how dangerous this is. How far-reaching it is."

He pauses, biting his lip. His deep black hair is gathered behind him in a ponytail. At any other time, I would admire the contrast of his hair and skin with the white herringbone business shirt. But I'm actually staring at his shirt and noting details to calm down, because now I feel a fight or flight response in the pit of my stomach. I jump in before he can continue. "Whatever you're going to say, don't. Don't go there."

This makes him close his eyes for several seconds. Then he looks away, and picks up his cocktail. I'm having beer. Imported beer, but still even that choice of cocktail seems to distance us.

"I care about you." His voice is soft and slow. "I didn't see us as a fling, even when I first met you. I meant what I said before."

"Me too. The case has nothing to do with that."

"It will now. I have to imagine you being shot. Another attack maybe, where you're beaten beyond recognition. Who knows what else could happen? A car accident, being pushed off a building. I don't know, it sounds crazy, but my job is not really what I'm worried about. It's experiencing it--not just reading about it in a book. I can't tear myself apart watching you fighting forces you can't control. I want you to stop this."

I sit back and measure my breathing. I was planning to tell him that I thought Nelson was Raymond's killer. Now I figure that isn't going to play well. I also haven't told him about the amusing photo project left on my car. Also not going to play well. I sip my beer, count ten. Respect his words. Don't be defensive. Try logic.

"Suppose I was in the military. How would that be different? Risk is risk in any job, and you know what work I do."

"All I can say is that the military makes sense on a level this doesn't. It has nothing to do with thinking if you're right. I know you're right, I believe in you. I just don't want to see you die for it. This case is not worth it. You could do so much more with your fantastic mind than in this line of work...can you see that?"

I briefly flash upon John saying how Raymond had suggested his career could be upgraded. My reply is a little quicker and sharper than I intend. "I'm not dying for anything. I can take care of myself. I understand about what's happening with your job. I don't want you to get in any more trouble, absolutely. I don't want to draw attention to you that way. That's not the way to build a relationship. But respect me for *my* job."

He spends a minute watching me. I'm uncomfortable under his gaze, but meet it. Then he begins talking in a very careful tone. "If this is because of money, I can help you. You don't have to stay on this case just to keep from struggling with bills."

Money. The bane of my existence. Fuck it. "I'm not looking for support of that kind. Thank you anyway."

"Jesus Christ. Don't act *insulted.*"

"I'm not insulted." I finish my beer and find myself wanting to throw the empty glass. I don't want to lose him, but I'm not going to give up my work, either. "Look. We've had a really hard 24 hours. Let's just take an evening to cool our jets and discuss this another time."

I see regret in his eyes. He thinks he's made me angry over his financial offer. The thing is, I am. But not for the money itself, more for the idea I can't have control over my life. Money always means control.

"Gabriel, please don't take what I said the wrong way. I'm trying desperately to help you. This was a difficult thing, but we could work through it..."

"Sure. We will."

"You don't sound like you believe that. Why are you upset with me because I'm concerned about you?"

"Me and my not-good-enough profession."

He leans toward me. "Jesus suffering *fuck.* It's more you than the job, but I'm not apologizing for being concerned about your well-being."

"My self-respect is part of my well-being. You care about your job, you should understand."

He sighs and sits back. A moment of silence. "I don't want to continue down this track. Why don't you come over and spend the night with me. We don't have to talk about this."

For a moment, I want to. I want to just go over and act normal. But I have something to do and I feel the urgency to move on it. And I realize Alex has gone as far as he could with this. He can't accompany me in this work. "I can't. I need to follow up on Christensen tonight."

The frown he gives me in response raises my Irish. I was going to suggest I come over afterwards but his expression shuts me up. The atmosphere between us gets suddenly cool.

"Why? Why can't you let it go? Why are you in a hurry to get killed?"

I don't answer. Nothing I say is going to make a difference. He lets go of my hand, albeit reluctantly. He looks down at the table. "You do what you have to." His voice sounds quietly regretful. Whether for what he said now or this morning I can't tell. I mumble a goodbye and leave.

I walk down the block to get my head clear. Light up a Camel. I feel overwhelmed with adrenaline from the conversation.

Without realizing I'm doing it, I take out my phone and call Joel.

"What's up, man of action? You talking to me finally?"

I turn around and see Alex leaving the bar. He sees me but doesn't stop.

"Hello? Still there, Gabriel? Cat got your tongue?"

His smartass tone wakes me up. "I have things going on, for sure."

"You sound preoccupied. Want to talk about it?"

"As a matter of fact, I do."

∞

TWENTY ◆ THE FOOL

The Fool represents a person on a journey, seemingly against the grain of all others. He is often mistaken for being childish or imprudent, when in fact he has hidden wisdom and resources.

∞

Thursday, August 12, Continued

I pull up outside Joel's building in Chelsea. He's waiting for me. "So what's the lowdown, my man?"

He smiles at my contemplation of him. He shows no hard feelings for the other day.

"You want to come along with me on a mission? I need to question someone."

"Sure. I'm up for it. You're trippin' on something though. Tell me."

I smile grimly to myself. I'm still smarting over my unpleasant conversation. "You sure you're not worried you might be killed hanging out with me?"

He laughs. "I never was. I was only worried, and Veronica too, that these people would get to you. She's been real upset about you, by the way. Not that I'm trying to make you feel bad--except I am."

"Shit. I owe her an apology."

"Let me." He takes my phone and starts texting, surprising me by his growing use of texting and casualness in doing so. "I'll make it good. You'll buy her dinner and a lavish gift. That book she wants in The Strand on magic that costs $300."

"I owe you an apology too...I thought Alex could handle it, but he backed out as well. Things got too hot. Look, I can understand if someone doesn't want to get involved but I don't like being questioned on my judgment."

"I'm sorry." Joel finishes his texting and lights one of his awful cloves. "You should be used to Danny and Jim thinking they're your parents, but your romantic interest surprises me. Here you were ready to play house too, I bet. Don't look at me like that. You wouldn't be so angry otherwise. How well I remember. Anyway, I read about him, Barclay. His father was pretty well known for hard journalism."

"You read about him? Why?"

"Why wouldn't I? He has money, your boy. Dad was part of the posh set in the Brit social structure. You can tell...Harry Potter speaks BBC English. Elite on his mom's side too."

I shrug. "He didn't mention it."

"Being modest, was he? Caught on that didn't impress you. Remember, people with money are less likely to risk it. That doesn't fit in well with your mission to save the world."

"Umm. That's not true." In spite of the situation, I don't want Joel scoring points. But he knows me on a psychic level. All the mental alleyways and hidden passages I keep from others.

"He'll try to change you, talk you out of your profession. You're bedazzled right now and don't see it. You're such an Anglophile, sweetheart. You fucked this guy because he's British, didn't you?"

"Joel, don't be offensive."

"No big deal, man. I've done that shit. Brits have their charm, but don't take it too far. I know you want to be James Bond, but you can't do that by DNA transfer."

I wonder why I let him needle me. "What the fuck? Jesus. Are you here to help, or not?"

"Yeah. Part of that is helping you to recognize yourself."

"We'll worry over psychoanalyzing me later. Let me tell you more about where we're going."

I give him the rundown on Christensen as we go through the Lincoln Tunnel. I suppose that judge in Buckston would be most displeased I'm doing this.

I fall silent, feeling a little pensive. After a minute, Joel changes gears and lays his hand on mine. He's looking at my face again. The bruises are gone but the scar is still there on my jaw. His expression is angry. Not at me. But his voice is soft.

"You didn't need to apologize. We're aware of how strange this all is. But I owe *you* an apology for what happened between us before. When you left, I mean. I spent the last two years thinking about that. I'm sorry for it, what I did. I should have been here for you. That attack would have never happened."

His voice and words surprise me. He often sounds like a stoner or slacker, which he isn't. This is a different tone, mature. He's sincere, even a little scared, like he's not sure how an apology should go.

A weight I didn't know I carried in the back of my mind lifts, and at the same time confusion sets in with the storm of my mixed feelings about him.

"Thank you for saying that." The feeling between us is a little awkward. I feel like I should apologize too, but I'm not sure for what.

Christensen lives in Alpine, in an expensive suburb featuring many celebrities, sports, and music stars. His house is not one of the mini-mansions but still rests on a nice piece of land near the water, set back in a glade of trees. The style is Romanesque Revival, and looks like a gloomy gray castle in the twilight. I park at the end of the driveway.

"Ugh. What a gothic nightmare of a house. Let's go talk to *Dracul*." Joel gets out of the car and crushes his cigarette on the street.

I get out and look around. The nearest neighbors are some distance away but still within shouting distance. The Camry is a great car but does not fit in with the high-end rides here. Christensen has a two-car garage and I note a Mercedes CLS in the half-circle driveway.

I consider if anyone might call the cops on us. I haven't been forced to get one of the hideous new retro yellow license plates the DMV is fostering on New Yorkers as yet; mine is still blue lettering on white. I open the trunk and get out a bottle of white shoe polish. On both plates, I block out the letters and numbers and toss the bottle in the back seat.

Then we head for the house. Joel gives my arm a squeeze on the way to the door. He seems energized to be here. He winks at me.

I ring the doorbell in the double doors and we wait. After several minutes, a man in his fifties in button down shirt and dark slacks opens the door. "Yes?"

"My name is Gabriel Ross. I'm an investigator. I would like to speak to Mr. Christensen about an urgent matter."

"I'm afraid you'll need to call in the morning and see. Mr. Christensen is retired, and I'm not going to bother him--"

"Tell him it's about his friend Schleiden."

The man's mouth snaps shut. He turns his blank expression to a glare. "Wait here." He shuts the door.

Joel grins at me. "Fuck yeah. This is like TV, man. Like on *The Wire* or some such shit."

I smile in spite of myself. "We'll see. This fucker's going to put up some stiff resistance."

"I ain't worried."

The servant comes back. He's not happy. He jerks his head to indicate we can come in. Most of the house is dark and I don't get much of a sense of its interior. We're led through a couple of halls to a drawing room of sorts. It has three windows off to our right facing the trees. Books are placed here and there. The lighting is terrible, just a couple of green-shaded lamps. We wait for a long time, at least twenty minutes or more. I'm ready to get up and start turning over the place. But then the servant comes back with the man of the house.

Christensen is around 80 or so and looks like Ian McShane's decrepit older brother. He's wrapped in a red quilted robe. He gives us the once over and sits in a leather chair. "Who are you people?"

"I'm a private investigator. I'm looking into the murder of your fellow board member, Raymond Booth."

"That matter is closed."

"Maybe not so much. I find awfully suspicious that Raymond was murdered shortly after finding out you have questionable taste in friends."

He doesn't seem unduly perturbed. "I don't know what you're talking about. You should be more respectful of other persons."

"Really? Why did you let us in, then?"

Christensen ignores that and looks at Joel. "Who are you?"

"I'm his bodyguard. If you play rough, I'll have to knock you around, old man."

Christensen's head snaps back in surprise and he clutches at the arms of his chair. I elbow Joel in the ribs. But Christensen still isn't really upset. He slowly looks back at me. "Now, whatever you think you're doing, you should listen to me."

We wait. He doesn't say anything else. Joel and I look at each other.

I sigh. "Well? What are we listening to?"

"Sit down." He waves at the chairs. "Where did you hear this nonsense?"

Joel sits on the arm of a chair but I remain standing. "Good sources."

"It's a misunderstanding. I'm not acquainted with anyone like that."

"Like what?"

"Sit down." He points to a chair. "With Nazis."

"I didn't say he was one. You seem to know a lot concerning who you don't know."

"I assumed. The name was German. I'm too young to have been in the War, if you didn't notice. I was never in Hitler Youth. And we didn't have that here in America."

"Again, you're awfully defensive for someone not involved."

"Will you sit down? Respect a person in his home, sir."

"Why should I? Suppose I thought that your non-knowledge of Schleiden directly led to Raymond's death."

"Raymond was a good man; what a terrible thing to say about him."

"It's about *you*, not him. Raymond didn't have Nazi friends." His hands twitch. Then he strokes his mustache. "Do you want money, is that it?"

Joel laughs. "Listen to this guy. Everything's about money to rich people. Hey, does knowing Nazis pay off? Even David Duke isn't doing that well these days. Maybe the old Nazi guy is leaving him his jackboot collection or something, and he's going to sell it on eBay."

Christensen leans over and shakes his finger at Joel. "You're impudent. You don't go in a man's house and insult him." He turns back to me. "I'm trying to reason with you. Damn it, will you sit down? We can talk over your problems are, if you want."

"Why are you so anxious, Christensen?"

The servant walks behind us. "Do you want anything, sir? For the guests."

"I suppose yes, we can offer them something."

The servant gives me a dirty look. "Well?"

"No thanks."

He looks at Joel, who winks at him. "How about Matt Damon if you got him back there? I liked him in that *Bourne Identity* movie."

Offended, the man turns heel and leaves without a response. Joel gets up and follows him silently. Christensen is still looking at me, not noticing Joel's departure.

"You two aren't nice."

"You're being *too* nice to two guys who rang your bell at 9 at night, accusing you of collaborating with a Nazi. Why?"

He doesn't react right; he just stares at me curiously. "You seem serious. I wanted to help."

I walk closer to him. "Who did you call?"

"What? I asked you--"

"To sit, I know. You're doing a piss-poor job of stalling. You called someone to come over and take care of the situation, is that it?"

"I think you need to calm down. I *should* call the police."

"But you aren't. And we aren't going to hang around and wait for some hired help from the Foundation to arrive. Where is Schleiden now?"

"I'd suggest you not involve yourself in questions that can--"

The servant comes back in the room. "Sir, I believe this will help the gentlemen." His voice has a breathless edge. He gives Christensen a paper-wrapped box, and bends over to whisper in his ear.

Joel returns as well and comes up behind me. He speaks in *my* ear. "Something's up. This dude just got that package from some other fucker, outside the back door."

"Now then." Christensen looks pleased. "I think I can help you out. Since you seem to be so interested in information..." He fiddles with the object, like he's looking for an opening.

Joel's information about the package gives me a cold rush. "Someone just came by and gave that to you?"

Christensen and the servant just glance at me without answering. The older man waggles his finger again. "Be patient..." He tries to rip open the paper.

"Don't open that."

"What? You are unbelievable. I have something here to help you, and you insist..."

I take Joel's arm and back up. "Seriously, Christensen. Leave that thing alone. Come out of the room. Something's wrong here. Is the person who gave it to you still around?"

The servant looks troubled for a moment then reaches as to take the package from Christensen. "You're supposed to give it to *them*, sir..."

Christensen holds the box away from the servant, with his grip on a flap of paper. "Let it alone. I want to open it first."

I pull Joel outside the room and push him ahead of me down the hall as fast as I can move.

The blast comes a second later. We're on the floor covering our heads. I try to shield Joel from the splatter of drywall and whatever sharp objects were in the bomb. Luckily, the drawing room behind us absorbs most of the explosion, as I can see when I raise my head. Smoke pours from the doorway.

I help Joel get to his feet. The house is so solidly built not much damage has happened in the hall. We make our way back to the drawing room, crunching bits and pieces of plaster, which also falls off our clothes.

"Jesus." I survey the area. Not much is left of Christensen's upper half, as well as the chair and the pretty collectables that had been on shelves behind him. I don't look at him closely.

His servant has been thrown to the far wall on the left. I go over to him to check for a pulse. No good. Joel is pushing around debris from the wall and ceiling with his feet. "What the fuck was in this, nails?"

"They looked up the Unabomber's recipe. We have to get out of here."

"The cops are probably coming."

"Eventually. We're pretty far out; we can leave before they hear about it. I don't want to have to explain a bomb to them, if you don't mind."

Joel doesn't argue, in fact he's ahead of me out the room. At front door, I hold him back, and take out my Sig Sauer. This was one of the few times I figured I might need it.

"Fuck. We're going to shoot our way out."

"The man you saw isn't going to leave without knowing what happened with us."

I wished I had night vision glasses to check out the woods in back of Christensen's place. My Camry is at the end of his driveway. I can see the street beyond. No one is outside; no one is even looking out their doors yet.

"Head for the car, I'll cover you."

I walk next to Joel as he heads down the half-circle; I'm walking backwards, with my gun aimed at the trees.

A faint rustle. A couple of silent shots hit near our feet. Looking in the direction of the shots I can see a silhouette in the trees. My city stalker, perhaps. I don't just carry a gun, I know how to use handguns, rifles and shotguns. The one quasi-bonding experience I had with my father was his teaching me to shoot when I was young, up until when I couldn't stand him anymore. He had the Army ranking of Expert in rifle, auto rifle and pistol. He taught me all those and more. I'm farsighted, and like in baseball I had preternatural power and accuracy.

I aim at the silhouette and fire. The figure jerks back sharply, hit. I aim and shoot at his legs, and he goes down. My gun seems louder than the bomb did in this silent neighborhood.

I follow Joel to the car. He gets behind the wheel and starts it up. I slide in the passenger side and keep my gun poised. Joel pulls away.

A few dozen yards down the road, we see a person or two coming out their front doors. I hunch down and Joel pulls the hood of his sweatshirt over his head.

"Turn corners awhile."

We're pretty far away in twenty minutes, and my tension eases some. "Let's find a place to pull over. Not a gas station. Some place empty. There, behind the Stop and Shop."

My voice sounds a little strange. Joel glances at me but pulls in a shopping center. I direct him around the back, behind the store where I know employees usually park. At this time of night no one's around. At the far end of the lot beyond the loading dock, no cameras are present.

I need the opportunity to calm down. I get out a bottle of water and a rag and wipe off the shoe polish from the plates. Joel gets out of the car to light a cigarette and watch me.

"Damn. That was fun. You should have me help every night."

I scrub the plates a last time. "Two people were just killed."

"You said the one guy is friends with a Nazi. So, his knowing the Nazi got Raymond killed, right?"

"No doubt."

"So why should I feel so bad? You remember he was going to give that thing to *us* to take home like a box of chocolates, and leave Archie an orphan. Except he didn't want to let it the fuck go."

"Control freak. Did himself in. I don't know whether he was supposed to go up with us or we were supposed to leave with it or what. But now one less person is around to shed light on things." I finish the job and look up. The back parking lot borders against a small rock outcropping. Trees surround it. Even the sodium lamps aren't in this corner. A good place to hide for a few minutes.

Joel moves over to the front of the car where I'm sitting on the hood with the water. In the dark we can barely see each other. He's mostly a moving shape, offering me the cigarette.

I inhale. God, these clove things he likes are terrible. I smoke it nonetheless, to give my hands something to do other than shake. The quiet of the rock and tree layout is soothing. "It's nice here. No persons shooting. No bombs going off."

Joel gets in front of me, leaning on the rock wall. "But we survived."

"I'm sorry I put you at risk."

I hear his laugh again. "What the fuck man, don't apologize. I'm a grown boy..." He watches me smoke. "You're really upset, aren't you?"

"I think it's all sinking in. I just didn't expect this."

He leans over and puts his hand on my shoulder. "Hey. You're all right." I feel him grip harder, affectionately. "C'mon. You've been spitting in death's face up to now, baby. A little bomb isn't going to shake you up, is it? Feeling so much again. I always thought you were an empath, like Deanna Troi on *Star Trek*." His voice is soft, not critical.

"I just don't believe the situations I get in. And get other people in."

His voice gets more like a purr, soothing. "That's because you don't realize the kind of man you are. The man of action. That's the one I admire." He moves next to me and reaches out to run his fingers through the back of my hair, now sticking to my head with sweat. He ruffles out the edges.

I move away from the car, going up to the rock wall, and leaning on it to stare in the trees. "You'll admire me into a grave if you aren't careful."

"Um. Not while I'm around." His hand moves down my back. I'm just wearing a Henley shirt. The moon has come out from a cloud, giving us more light. The night has unexpectedly become chilled, or it's just me. Joel leans his head in against my shoulder.

His body gives me warmth. "It's okay." He wraps his arms around me. "You can relax. Everything's okay. I'm not going to let anything happen to you."

I tense at first; I'm not supposed to let this happen. But something else has taken over...from the stress of the night and my nerves. I let him hold me and give me the warmth. He tunes into me like he used to.

"You're shaking."

"I feel bad."

"I know. That's the part of you I always loved and still do. You're a good person, Gabriel. You wouldn't feel bad if you weren't. I just want you to relax." He puts his mouth near my ear. "Just listen to me. You know with me you're safe. We've been through a lot together."

Listening to him makes me feel better, although my heart is still pounding. I turn around, and he keeps his arms around me. The moonlight reflects our images in the windshield, embracing. I briefly see in the reflection Joel closing his eyes, with an indescribable expression. I almost feel like a voyeur of such a moment. My voice catches. "You never said anything about loving me when we were together."

"You knew, though, didn't you?"

I lean on the car. "I had hoped. I had waited to hear it."

He opens his eyes, staring at me. "You know I'm not...whatever, normal or something. I should have told you."

Something about the night seems so surreal. Hard to think only a few miles away two bodies are smoking in a house, and we could have been in pieces next to them. The shock from that makes me want to give into his comfort. He pulls me close again.

"That's it. Just breathe, relax. No one's going to bother us. We're in the best place in the world; no one around, no one knows where we are." His lips brush my neck. I feel my face flush. The events of the previous hour start to fall away while the adrenaline is still burning inside me. The night has become so surreal I can't really see anything but shadows, and I can lose myself in those shadows.

I feel more than I can think. When Joel brings my face to his to kiss me, I go with it, meet it. He's not forceful or frantic, but gentle. I can remember how gentle he was when I was in a bad way. How he would stay with me when I was really sick or really depressed. Stay by my side.

While he kisses me, he slowly slides his hands down my body while leaning against me. The warmth between us grows. I realize I'm aroused. If Joel had been more aggressive with his seduction, I would have broken away. But he remembers my moods; how I can be teased and coaxed into intimacy.

He works at me like he used to when we were together, particularly when I was angry. Going back to murmuring in my ear, stroking my crotch, bringing my hand to his evident erection; knowing I always feel a thrill over my partner showing desire.

"Feels good to do this, baby, right? Having your back, you having mine. No matter what, we always have that connection. We communicate without speaking, that's why we work so well together. What did you used to say, synchronous? That's what made it great, right? You know what this reminds me of..."

He stops to kiss me again and moves in face to face, pressing his body against mine. We start kissing more deeply; then he has his tongue at my neck. I can I taste his skin, and my hands move to him. He talks in between working on my neck. "...reminds me of when...we were in the park that one time...I got you to fuck in a public park. You didn't want to...but when we found the right place you got into it..."

His description of that night becomes more graphic, but the words slip away from me. I remember the night very well. What I remember as well is the next day, when I happened to be at home alone and found a sketchbook he had left. Flipping through it to admire the drawings he worked on so furiously, I found a Post-It note with a man's first name, a date and a time. The date was the previous day. While we had been intimate at the park at night, a few hours before he had met up with some man--a client.

My anger with him then was about...how can I say it. Trust. Not me trusting him--him not trusting *me* enough. I knew his previous life, and how his work could be as dangerous as mine, and what got him into it in the first place. He did not need to continue doing it and in fact had pretty much given it up. Almost. When he was scared by how close we became, I'm pretty certain he went off and did his own thing in that world as some means of retaining control. I understood. I didn't like it, but my philosophy is to work with what you have if it's worth it. I felt he was worth it.

But after nearly two years, I thought he knew me enough to trust I wasn't going to hurt him. I asked him to promise he would stop and work with me on the relationship, and why I wanted him to--that I wasn't going to use him or abandon him. In not so many words, he had allowed me to think he had quit. I had thought we had moved into a trust that was difficult for both of us to allow. But when I saw that note, I knew he wasn't going to allow it. That there was a part of him he would hold back from me in a lockbox.

The memory of how I felt when finding that note is like ice water in my mind. Shortly thereafter I had followed him to another client's apartment and made him come down to the street to confront me. That's when I walked away from him in anger.

The sadness of the break-up overcomes me. After I left, I had wanted to find him, make it better, do what I perhaps should have done before--talk it out. But I couldn't find him and I swore after I got through the initial heartache that if I did ever see him again, we couldn't be together romantically. It hurt too much to be in love with him.

This all mixes potently with my sadness and anger about Alex. Like I'm cheating. I'm a monogamous person; I'm not sure about him. But I know no one in a relationship wants a partner to be emotionally involved with another. Yet I feel caught between the two of them. Alex representing one world, and Joel another. And Joel's closer to my feelings, like an id to Alex's ego. Nonetheless as much as I find I can still desire him powerfully, remembering my life with him invokes pain, pain he and I both caused. I can't get past that right now no matter that I can know I can easily reignite that heat with him.

Despite the part of me that wants to very much stay with his seduction, give in to the magnetism of our combined sexuality, I move my hands away from him slowly and down to the hood of the car. He senses the difference and raises his head to look at me. I can't meet his eyes; I gently slide away.

I change my voice to neutral. "We better get out of here. Just in case the New Jersey cops are unusually thorough." I get in the driver's side and start up the car, light up to allow my body to cool down. My mind is back in neutral but my body still remembers his touch.

Joel watches me from the outside, and then returns to the passenger seat. He takes one of my cigarettes from the pack I have on the console between the seats. Typical Joel, he is not angry or reproachful at the disruption of sex. Slow to rise to the level of arguing, refusing to judge, never giving in to the expectation of a scene. Maybe that's good. I don't think I could take a scene while I'm coping with a complicated personal life and people dying around me. But it's also part of his seduction. The juxtaposition and contrast between those who give me a hard time and himself, refusing to do so.

I don't have to tell Joel to be discreet over being at Christensen's. He'd never tell the cops one word about me or my business. He'd never tell me not to do my job. That same blasé code also applied to how he had considered his body an occasional commodity, his indifference to doing anything with his art, or even consistent communication. He reminds me of a cat. Impossible to train, and ends up running your life.

But like a cat, as only cat owners know, he's fiercely loyal and loving in his own way. Since he has no awkwardness regarding our encounter, he's able to ask me what I'm going to do next and be sincere in his interest. I have an idea for the next step as my mind goes back to working mode. He offers to help. I can use it and accept.

We're back in the city. He takes a key off a ring and slips it in the cellophane wrap around my cigarettes, putting those in my jacket pocket. An intimate gesture. "A spare key in case you need to find me. I know *you* don't need a key without your lock-picking talents, but still."

I sense that giving me a key is another part of his seduction. "Okay. I appreciate that."

"I'm not going home, anyway."

"Where do you want to be dropped off, then?"

"Your place."

I tense up. I can still feel the dangerous surge of the heat between us. "I don't think--"

"You *do* think, you think too much. You're not going to be able to sleep well. I'm going to keep watch on you. Nothing else. You shouldn't be alone. I don't think you can call Harry Potter over tonight in any case." He smiles to himself.

After some time finding parking, we're back home. Archie is in nocturnal fighting mode, but no mouse corpses tonight, thank God. Still, the cat pouncing on invisible objects makes me jumpy. I want to patrol the perimeter of the apartment, go out and check for invisible assassins, but I'm too exhausted.

Joel has me lie down on the sofa. He sits on the floor leaning against the sofa and watches television. I watch the back of his head.

"Go to sleep, Gabriel." He doesn't turn around. "I can feel you thinking. You're safe. I'm watching over you. Remember I'll protect you. Let it go."

∞

TWENTY-ONE ♦ THE TWO OF WANDS

The Two of Wands represents a need for courage and bold directions in facing challenges.

∞

Friday, August 18
Alphabet City, Avenue A, 9:30 am

SOMEHOW, I DID ACTUALLY SLEEP. Joel stays around the apartment in the morning as I'm working on getting myself awake. He walks around casually naked and talking, and I try to ignore the visual part. Eventually he showers and borrows my clothes since his are streaked with plaster dust.

As he's cleaning off his high tops, I think about what I want us to do today, and how to do it.

Shortly thereafter, we head downtown to Ethan Nelson's home address. Before we leave, I call the Foundation to make sure Nelson is there. I don't talk to him, but to some sort of secretary. I tell that person that I want to make an appointment, giving a fake name and a story about an expensive piece of art to restore and donate.

I'm not keeping the appointment, of course. Around eleven o'clock, the time of the appointment, Joel and I are at opposite ends of the block where Nelson's apartment building is located, observing. It's on the West Side, a few blocks from the Foundation. About twenty stories, white stone. Simple entrance door, meant for a master key. Through double-glass doors, we can see a marble hallway with big green plants, and a brass-plated elevator.

We approach the building from our respective positions. Joel looks like a tourist in my clothes: camera stuck in a pocket, city map in his hand. He stops and looks at the door attendant hopefully, like maybe he will know where the Museum of Natural History is. He approaches the door attendant while taking an inhaler out of his other pocket, one I gave from a time when I had bronchitis.

Joel approaches the uninterested man, shaking the map open. Suddenly he wheezes loudly and clutches his chest. The door attendant asks him if he's all right, and Joel then sends the inhaler flying and crumples against him, dragging him several feet to the left and outside of the door, distracting him long enough for me to slip inside. I go right to the elevator and up to the tenth floor.

Joel should now be having a miraculous but not too suspicious recovery.

Everything about this building is incongruously pleasant. But then, other people live here too, not just Ethan Nelson. The elevator is large and clean, a white floor inside with tiny black checks. Ethan's hallway has the same floor pattern, and more potted plants. Very nice for him.

His door is a muted burgundy, with a brass knocker. I knock, just for a formality, and after two minutes listening carefully for movement, use my tools to open his lock. I step into a living room-- large, high ceilings, polished gray wood floor that slopes into a circular depression where wrought iron furniture is carefully arranged. The floor reminds me of a pond of dirty ice. Big fat gold colored round lamps off each corner of the living room. Tall windows line the living room, with the deep gray drapes pulled tight. I look around carefully to make sure no one is lurking in the shadows, and then go over to the windows just to make sure the regular world is still outside.

I turn back to see what is around me. He has several paintings of gothic-style mythological scenes. Biblical, Roman, and Greek stories. The décor of gray and heavy earth tones stands in sharp contrast to the large gilt-framed scenes of martyred saints, apocalypse, Hell, suffering, men fighting giant beasts, crucifixions, and torture. Famous figures and legends: Prometheus, Achilles, Judas, Brutus, Cassius.

As I move around taking in these huge portraits of human and unearthly pain, I feel emotion pouring off the canvas and hitting a glass wall. Nelson chose these scenes--why? He's trying to connect with life and cannot really. He has to go back into his gray and burgundy womb and only observe life.

Aside from the living room, a large kitchen is off to the right, and a dining room. A brick-covered half-wall separates the two. To the left is the hallway leading to the bedroom and bath. His bedroom is spacious, low-ceilinged, recessed lighting, softly carpeted in warm tones. His apartment gives me a feeling for him, his self-containment. But more than his psyche, I want to know who he is. One detail that stands out is the lack of anything personal in the apartment. No photos of family, friends, no photos of anything, really. No mementos, ticket stubs, cards, even a grocery receipt. He has nothing personal in the apartment other than expensive clothes and grooming products. I find the bottle of his grassy cologne.

Over an hour of frustrated searching leaves me with no more to go on this cipher. Of course, he could have personal items in storage, or in a safe deposit box. Yet I feel that he wouldn't trust the outside, either. Something has to be hidden here. I consider the possibility of a safe built in somewhere. Nelson wouldn't be worried about the police or a thief. Common hiding tricks might be out of his league. No fake outlets, books, plants and other tricks.

I check behind the awful paintings. The topics are so unpleasant it could be to drive away anyone who might want to inspect them closely. Nothing hidden in the frames. I turn away and look around the place again. The half wall is in my direct line of vision. That is the only thing incongruous. Nelson doesn't seem like the brick type from the rest of the décor. It might have come with the place.

Or it might not. I go over on a hunch and check both sides. On the dining room side, my prodding finally yields a click, and a square yard of the brick facing falls open. Inside I find a wooden box about twice as big as a cigar box. It's engraved with intricate patterns. No lock; it can be flipped open like Pandora's.

The box has the first personal items I've seen in the place: photos, IDs, clippings from newspapers, coins, a couple necklaces and religious symbols. I realize it must be his keepsake repository of sorts, small enough to grab and run away with in an emergency. The photos seem to be all of him but I don't take the time to study them. Rather, I use my phone camera to photograph the items one by one, trying not to leave fingerprints or disturb the order of the items. The items speak in a form of psychometry, telling me each has an unbelievable story attached.

I'm placing the box back in its space on the shelf when I hear some scratching noises at the door, like a key being used.

Swifter than thought I move from the dining room across the front area to the bedroom.

The front door opens. I hear footsteps come in and stop. It has to be Nelson. Now he walks slowly across the floor. Every move deliberate. He walks around the living room.

Then the kitchen and the dining room. I consider my options and decide on getting under the bed. The bed is on high legs, like an altar, and it's not difficult to move under even though the carpet here is very thick--still gray, though. I reach to work my phone out as he comes in, because of course he's coming in. Before he does I quickly text Joel a signal.

It's so silent in the apartment I can hear the faint sound of the carpet being compressed under his shoes. I see the shoes suddenly poised in front of me, black and highly polished, dark gray slacks breaking perfectly over the feet.

I try to suppress my breathing, which automatically makes my lungs itch. Nonetheless, I put my face into the nap of the carpet.

He walks around the bed. My heart beats so fast my ears pound. Now I have to breathe. I'm afraid he's bending down and looking at me but when I open my eyes, he's still standing, on the other side of the bed. I open my mouth and take the most silent breath of my life. The itch at the bottom of my lungs begs me to cough, and I start shaking from the effort of suppressing it.

He yanks open the closet double-doors like he's expecting to see someone. I hear clothes being shoved aside. Then he sighs. At that moment, his house phone rings. He picks up the bedroom extension.

"Yes...really? What did he say? Hmm. All right. Thank you."

He goes back out to the hall, and in a minute, I hear him open and close the front door. I know the door attendant has told him that someone is asking for him outside--that would be Joel. I don't crawl back out until Joel texts me that Nelson has shown his face outside. I roll out from under the bed and make the front door in seconds. A staircase is at the end of the hall. I go down five flights and find a laundry room.

Joel texts me that Nelson has gone back in. I can hear the elevator go up. Joel then lets me know the building has a courtyard in back, very large with a chained gate to the street.

Cautiously I check the stairway. No one there. I carefully go down to the first floor. When the door attendant wanders outside, I go through the lobby to the hall leading out back to the courtyard.

Joel is waiting outside the gate, grinning. I use the chain to pull myself up, and he helps me over. "Damn, you pulled it off, motherfucker."

"I think a lost a couple of my nine lives on that one."

He hugs me quickly and we leave the area to head back to my place.

Back in the apartment, I quickly scroll through the pictures. "I found some kind of information on him, I'm pretty sure. I have to decode it. But I think I'm next going to DC."

"What, you going to lobby him away or something? Pay off a congressperson?"

"No, I have someone else to visit to fill in some past history." I tell him about talking to Kent.

"Since Christensen is dead, Kent's notes may be the next best source of information, and I want to get it information fast, before he changes his mind."

Christensen's death was in the news. But not as a bombing. Just an obituary that Mr. Christensen, beloved so and so, suddenly passed away. He was a noted executive and on the board of the Foundation with the recently deceased Raymond Booth. For once, I'm not in the story. Nor am I going to the funeral.

Joel stays with me while I try to get Allen Cheng on the phone to authorize a plane ticket or train ticket. Cheng's not available, out of town.

"Damn it." I consider what I bills I can risk not paying to fund the trip myself.

Joel watches me, stroking Archie, who's cleaning his paws delicately on the dining table. "What's the deal?"

"I need money from Cheng. Fuck it, I'm going anyway. He'll pay me for it or else."

"I'll front you. Just go."

Alex had offered the same favor, although if the offer still holds I wouldn't take it. But at its cheapest, a one-night stay over in DC with airfare is $500 minimum. I glance at Joel without speaking, considering the implications.

Joel takes a credit card out his wallet and skims it across the table at me. "You're good for it, sweetheart. You don't have to pay me back, it's up to you. But if you do, I'll fuck up that lawyer if he doesn't reimburse you. He'll turn over his Rolex or eat it."

"Thanks. Can you take care of Archie, too? I'd ask Danny, but I'm supposed to be planning his bodyguard job right now. I'm going to have to avoid his phone calls, but if I get back okay I'll still make his job."

"Oh, I'll be here. If Dan the Man shows up, we can talk over old times." He looks pleased at the prospect. Confrontation almost never bothers him.

First, I make sure Kent will still see me. He's in fact enthusiastic to do so, and I make the reservations and get a flight leaving in a few hours. I start packing when my apartment buzzer goes off.

"Someone at the door?"

"Hold on." I go to check the intercom. Toni's voice comes through. I really do not need to see her right now but I'm practically out the door anyway. My shock is that she bothered to ring the buzzer.

"Just my client, the sister."

"What is she doing there?"

"Probably going to complain about something. I'll give her the bum's rush and then we're off to JFK."

Knock at the door. I check that she is alone and open it.

She doesn't look good. She isn't wearing much makeup and her face is pale and splotchy. Her hair is hanging long, badly crimped. She has a jacket pulled over her as if freezing, although the day is warm. I don't ask what I can do for her. I don't want to know. I introduce her briefly to Joel, who goes in the bedroom and shuts the door for our privacy.

"What's going on with your investigation? Do you have proof yet?"

I explain, briefly, that experts are preparing the reports and that I'm still working on the investigation.

"What else?"

I keep in mind Cheng's warning not to tell her too much. No mention of Nazis and secret societies today. "I'm looking into what Raymond wanted researched."

"Is that all? Is that all you're doing?"

It occurs to me that was all *Raymond* had wanted me to do. Her attitude is distinctly different, and it throws me off. "I've collected enough information that might be able to get a second autopsy. I think we can prove he was murdered when it's all pulled together."

"So what the hell does his research have to do with it?"

"It's a lead. Something that has to be checked out."

"What is *the research* about?"

I'm getting irritated. "What Eleanor Whitford told him. She seems to be in trouble right now, but I have some leads from her."

"What do you mean?"

"Ethan Nelson has her sedated and in seclusion under some doctor's orders."

She paces around, shaking that off. "Whatever. I can't keep this up. My money is being held up."

"Toni, I can't help that. There is a process that has to be--"

"Fuck the process. This is so Goddamned unfair. And you're fucking around with the old lady and whatever bullshit she told you. Listen, you can give me an advance on that policy, right? Obviously, you'd be paid back, with interest."

"After you just cursed me out? You have a strange idea about tact. Even so, I'm not going to do that, it's unethical."

"No it isn't, this is my money. You have to help me. Somebody probably killed Raymond because *you were looking into this.*"

"You think I caused his murder? I've done nothing but advocate on *his* behalf, which is really *your* behalf now."

"Then you should be helping me. *You're just making money off his dead body!*"

I see Joel peek out the bedroom door. But although she's yelling, she's not violent. I try to keep calm and not be drawn into the drama, but I can only put up with so much of this. Part of my annoyance is her past affection with me--somewhat manipulative but I felt also sincere. Whatever meds she uses has stripped that away; I've experienced that before--when you just become a mechanism to someone. Looking at her then makes me more sad than annoyed now.

"Toni, you need to go home and come down off of whatever shit you are on. You know I'm on your side and have been."

Her eyes darken at that. Even vague allusions to take a drug addict away from the drugs invoke hostility. She grits her teeth and grabs my arms. "Gabriel, remember my son. I have to take care of him. I'm not looking for money for me; I'm trying to take care of him. You know I was laid off. How am I supposed to live?"

"As I recall, you have income from a trust fund."

Her nails, or at least the ones not broken off, dig into my arm. "That *fucker* isn't giving me anything I need. That is not enough for us to live on. I just need something for a couple weeks."

I carefully remove her arms. "I can't do that. I told you, to do so would be inappropriate. Look, you're going to have to excuse me, I need to go out of town--for *Raymond's* business--and yours."

She retracts her claws from me and digs into her face. "Is that Nelson guy paying you off?"

"Absolutely not." Something clicks in my head. "Why the hell would you ask that? What do you know about him?"

She cocks her head, looking sly instead of thoughtful. "Is he a suspect?"

"One of several." I don't like the look in her face; she's turning over prospects. I take hold of her shoulders. "Stay *away* from him, in any case. Listen to me about that. Have patience and this might all work out. And if you know something specific about Nelson you haven't told me, you should."

"I once thought...." She shuts her mouth and shakes her head. "Fuck it. If you don't want to help me, I don't need to talk to you." She stomps to my door.

"Toni, if you want this solved, don't make the mistake..."

But she yanks open the door and slams it against the wall. Jesus. I wonder about her son and how he survives this. Maybe like I did with my father's incessant mean drunkenness, through baseball practice and sneaking out.

"Fuck you, asshole!" She yells as she stomps down the hall. Not as traditional as *have a nice trip,* but no one can say she didn't send me off with a bang.

"What the fuck is she on?" Joel comes up beside me and watches her stalk into the elevator and jab at the buttons.

I close the door. "She's high on life."

"Gonna get herself in trouble."

"It could happen. I hope not, because she's salvageable."

"Are you kidding?" He gives me a raised eyebrow. "Being the do-gooder again. What did she want?"

"Money I couldn't give her. Now she's going to hurt herself somehow."

"So you thought you could talk her out of it? Didn't you learn with me?"

I look at him. "Don't compare yourself to her, even as a joke. You've survived hard times. She decompensates. I think if she got help, she'd be okay. But..."

"She doesn't want help, she wants a fix. Chick's flippin' out. She's going postal on somebody. You can't save her from herself. Not do that and your work too."

I shut the door with a dark feeling welling up. Joel takes my hand for a moment.

"She has a choice, Gabriel."

"She's going to do something stupid."

"That's a given. But right now, you got a job to do. You can't do it and watch her at the same time. Let's go." He takes my keys.

As we leave, I put my hand on his arm. He smiles. "What do you want me to do?"

"Keep an eye on her?"

"All right, babe. For you."

∞

Twenty-Two ♦ The Ten of Swords

The Ten of Swords represents a troubling situation: possible destruction, being trapped.

∞

DURING THE FLIGHT, I retrieve the photos of the items in Nelson's box from my camera and load them on my iPad. The various identification cards have Nelson's photo, looking a little different in each one, but with different names. I start doing some research. The name Nathan James is on an ID from Seattle, WA. I find out a Nathan James was suspected of a con involving stealing personal information of women who had disappeared in the area. Whether the women were dead or not is unknown, but James was arrested but released for lack of evidence. Nicholas James also turns up on what appears to be a work ID as a federal bank examiner. The date is 2001, and that is the latest date on any of the items.

Another ID and some clippings are from a northern California college. The news stories concern Nelson. In this identity, he is "Dain Michaels." He was Senior Development Officer at the college. An old newsletter interview with Michaels implied that he was from a big money background and took the job at the school for philanthropic reasons. Another news story reports that one of Michaels' colleagues developed suspicions about and discovered Michaels had a fake resume. Somehow, Nelson was tipped off, and left just before his embezzlement of college funds was revealed.

From some other items in the box, pamphlets, religious medallions and IDs, I get an impression that Nelson pretended at one point to be a missionary and fundraiser. I can imagine where the donations went.

One postcard from Brighton, Minnesota is especially intriguing. It is very old, thirty years from the tiny printed copyright. The card is addressed to Eirik Rane, a name on no other item. The address is general delivery to Minot, ND. Mentally calculating his age, I figure this is Ethan's real name.

At my hotel, I call Kent and arrange to visit tomorrow. He works on Saturdays, and will have me over at his place that evening. I spend the rest of Friday with some more online research. I learn Minot is a fairly small town. Going through an online phone directory and websites, I call around some places asking about Eirik Rane, beginning with the local schools. A long shot, as schools are nearly as confidential as hospitals in giving out information. Nonetheless, I manage to get leads on people who knew Rane.

I find out Eirik Rane, born in 1965, is not missed in his hometown. One of his neighbors, even thirty-odd years later, is still angry. The man ensures I'm not going to quote him and then goes on a rant. "As an adolescent, life didn't move fast enough for that little fucker. His parents never abused him or mistreated him, but he went bad. He started getting a reputation as a thief. Small stuff, but a lot of it. His parents tried to cover for him, but didn't take long for everyone to know."

"Are his parents still around?"

"I don't think so. They moved out of town a long time ago, and I think they may have passed away."

A former classmate of Rane's confirms his bad reputation. "He did worse than stealing. He conned people. He had even volunteered at a local organization to help the poor, and was taking the money and other donations. He harassed a couple teachers as well."

"I had to wonder about that. One high school teacher hangs up on me at the mere mention of his name."

"We heard he found out one of the teachers was gay, and blackmailed him about it."

That seems to fit in with the lovely persona of the Nelson I know. I also find out from some searching neither Oxford nor Cambridge has a Semantics of Sociology Degree, and in fact, no other school on either side of the Atlantic does.

∞

Saturday, August 14
Washington DC, Hyatt Regency

Danny calls around six a.m., demanding to know where I am. His project is Monday. He's figured out I'm out of town and is concerned I won't be back in time. I cut him short by promising to show up when I'm supposed to. I don't mention anything that has happened over the last couple of days. But he knows something's up, and I'm sure I'll get an earful later.

Before I can start to get dressed, Alex calls. I feel a stirring of guilt. I'm tempted not to answer, but that isn't the right thing to do as an adult. We have a slightly awkward greeting.

"I saw an obit on that man you were going to see. I wanted to make sure you were okay."

Damn the news. "Yeah, he seems to be dead."

"Were you there?"

I think over my answer. Just lie for safety's sake, or make the situation worse.

"I know what happened. It wasn't the way it reads."

I hear him inhale sharply. "I didn't think so, under the circumstances. Probably much worse, I imagine."

I wait. The silence gets heavy.

"Gabriel, talk to me. Regardless of what happened, I still care about this. About you."

I move past the emotions that rise in me by summarizing the events with Christensen. A short summary, but it can't sound anything but awful. I've boggled his mind. What didn't I do that he should worry about?

Oh yeah, one other thing. "Who was this person you were with, now?"

"An old friend of mine."

"Not Danny."

"No. His name is Joel. You haven't met him."

I can almost hear him turning that over in his mind. Or that's the guilt acting on me. "I'm glad you weren't alone." He doesn't sound glad. "Perhaps we could meet tonight and talk again. Try it better this time. I thought on what I was telling you Thursday and realized I was unfair. I haven't known you long, but I felt such a connection. I didn't want to lose it by seeing you..."

"Dead."

"I don't like saying it. But that's true. On the other hand, I asked myself did that mean I didn't want to see you again if that was the price. And I knew I couldn't say that. You're not easy, Gabriel. You're a mass of intense energy and righteousness, but I've already gotten hooked."

"That's sweet." I'm rather surprised that he had been reviewing his actions and thinking about a better way to approach our situation. My anger at Alex from Thursday eases considerably.

"I didn't like how we left each other in New York, and I appreciate what you have to say. I want to talk to you too, but when I get back. I'm in DC. I'm going to talk to Kent Varney."

"The one who called you about the conspiracy theories? You decided to go, then."

"The case is getting hot. I don't want to lose any more lines of information, you know?"

"Do you need anything? Do you want me to research something? I can do that without the bosses finding out."

"I have some names to run down. I think Nelson may have used them as past identities. I'll send them over to you."

"Good. When you come back, we'll have a chance to catch up and think this through."

The goodbye is much easier.

I turn on my iPad to check my mail, and get an instant message from Joel to set up my webcam. He's bare-chested and holding up Archie, waving his paw. I suspect Archie has been bribed with treats to be this compliant. "Hey, baby. Me and the cat want to know what's up."

"I'm sorry; I should have let you know I got here okay."

"Dude, I didn't think you were going to run out on me or anything. You're stressed. Chill and get back in action. You going to see that guy today?"

"Yeah, later on."

"Let me know what happens. I'm going to follow Toni and what fine mess she gets into."

"Thank you. Keep me updated. I'll have my phone with me. With any luck I'll have something from Kent for show and tell later."

"I can show you something now, if you want."

"I know better than to tell you to behave, so I'll just say see you later."

"Stay frosty, man of action."

The strange synchronicity of both of them communicating with me gets me thinking. I used to feel that Joel never regretted his actions, but he apologized for the past. What if he is here to change? What do I really feel about him? Well, I can't unravel that mystery now.

Around ten, Kent calls from work. He invites me for a tour of the museum in the afternoon and then going back to his place. Since I love museums, I accept. I plan to just have a morning of doing nothing work-related as a tourist, see the White House gates and the Smithsonian, and then wind up at the Colonial Museum.

The swampy DC heat takes over the day, but I still enjoy my favorite sites in the nation's capital including the legendary cursed Hope Diamond. Towards the end of the afternoon, I meet up with Kent at his workplace.

He's a sweet, friendly person; white, light in coloring, around 50, a little taller and chunkier than I. He enthusiastically shakes my hand when I arrive, claps me on the shoulder, takes me through the nation's history encased in glass. I get lost in the exhibits and almost forget why I'm here. But eventually we leave and have dinner at a Chinese place nearby and then take the bus to his apartment M Street NW and 24th, a decent area.

Before we leave the restaurant, Joel texts me.

--I followed her to the Foundation place. She's here now.

--Can you wait around until she comes out?

--Surely.

Kent and I then discuss traveling on planes vs. trains, baseball, and writing. He has read my movie reviews and offers me his thoughts and writing tips. We even talk about tarot cards. He wants to know what they mean and to give him a reading. I lay out three quick cards. His is the Hanged Man, which has turned up often as late. "Making a choice, perhaps? I understand about being in suspension. I've been in suspension with this story for years."

At that, the conversation turns gradually to his former obsession. He settles in with a narrative.

"I had been tracing a few financial persons who became powerful after World War II, but were not well known publicly-- behind-the-scenes sort of figures. I was interested because these men had all at one point worked in Mexico City, and it turns out all within a block of the Mexico City CIA station. They were known to have had contacts with a couple of CIA-connected persons later implicated in Watergate.

"I thought it sounded like the beginnings of a great story or book, at least a set of circumstances that has been pretty much overlooked in conspiracy history, questions of what these financial people had been up to in post-war America."

Since the CIA connection was strongest, Kent pursued the lead to the CIA person he had mentioned before, Chandler Pentington. Pentington was ex-CIA, although clearly at the level of work Pentington engaged in (he implied strongly to Kent he had handled civil unrest, sabotage and possibly even 'extractions') he would not be completely disengaged from the agency.

Meeting with Pentington was very cloak and dagger. Out of the way bars, parking lots, highway rest areas. Very early in the morning or late at night.

"For me, Pentington is a scary person. He sometimes would insinuate that I was going too far in the investigation and would be killed by forces unknown. I even saw him slamming a bar patron against a wall for an innocuous remark. I kind of then became really be nervous about knowing him, even though he seemed to be an excellent source on what the finance men had been doing--setting up political contacts still existent today."

Pentington was long rumored to have underworld contacts, and may have been peripherally involved in money laundering, weapons trafficking, and overseas porn/prostitution rings. He was the kind of man who would be described in reports as "representing the interests" of groups of people regarding investments in one project or another. Either the people or the project would be shady, or both.

Kent goes on to say that Pentington sometimes took him to certain places where he seemed to easily bypass security, just showing up randomly at boardrooms, government offices, private clubs and such. This seemed to support either his mob contacts, or the rumor Kent heard from another source, that Pentington was possibly also a confidential informant for the Department of Justice.

We're sitting in the living room. The only problem with Kent is he doesn't smoke but I can deal with it. His cheerful face becomes clouded for a moment. "I admit I made a mistake then, telling Pentington about the rumor. He never answered me on the informant status, but he did become more threatening. He specifically warned me I could be set-up to be arrested as a drug dealer or child porn aficionado, or just be killed. He said he had contracts out on people before."

"I know how you must have felt."

"I dropped contact with him. I felt guilty about the possible danger I was putting my family into. Soon after that, my wife had the car accident and I gave up the investigation entirely. But not the research. I kept at it on and off for several months as she recovered. I didn't tell her about it, because what I learned was too disturbing. I just started collecting things: copies of public documents, copies of documents others gave me, notes from interviews, connections and maps and timelines and backgrounds that I didn't use. I haven't told you even half of everything and everybody I spoke to, but some people gave me some really deep information. I tried to feel out a book deal at one point, but no conventional publisher would touch it for fear of the allegations involving domestic and international banks, international criminal syndicates, weapons--and the elements of the government that could be implicated."

That reminds me that around the same time Kent was working on his investigation, author Gary Webb had published a series of articles in the *San Jose Mercury News*, and later a book called *Dark Alliance*. Both had implicated the CIA in Nicaraguan Contra drug smuggling from Central America and indirectly to the crack cocaine explosion of the 1980s. Webb was torn apart by the big media outlets of the day, although his basic story was not discredited and led to the House Narcotics Committee probing Contra/drug allegations. The *News* distanced itself from the stories, and the lack of support/furor to debunk his allegations hurt his ability to remain a mainstream journalist.

Kent's revelations promised to be even more explosive, and the conventional news outlets and publishers did not want to put themselves out there without solid proof--or even with it. I could imagine approaching Alex's "hear no evil" publisher with this story.

At this point, Kent pauses in his tale and with a slight air of ceremony, he gets up and motions for me to follow. He leads me to a room that was probably intended to be a second bedroom. It is set up as an office, with a desk facing a window, bookshelves encircling the walls, and a small table in the center of the room covered with papers. Currently the table has a small section cleared for an expandable file folder. The folder is very thick, at least a foot. A desk lamp shines on it. Kent certainly has a flair for the dramatic.

"This seems like an incredible amount of work for one story."

"Well, I didn't tell you all of what I've looked into over the years. I found connections to other stories, expanding from the software story. I took the notes out of storage today. I don't keep them here, because I want to give them protection. I'm almost afraid I would throw it all out, from frustration. You know, I've thought about a book just on adventures in writing."

"Why not? You sure have a good perspective on it."

"I'm afraid it would discourage anyone from the business." He laughs. "My history certainly isn't encouraging."

"Writers are discouraged every hour on the hour. They're masochistic." I spend a few minutes scanning the stories he wrote or started to write, his sketches of connections between events, reminders of leads to follow, photos, news clippings, charts, names leading to names leading to names. Most of the documents are notes, but I can't read them. "Um. These look like hieroglyphics."

"Sorry. It's shorthand. Gregg version. My mother was an expert at it and I picked it up t00. Nobody really uses it anymore so it's good to hide things. I have a book on it somewhere I can give you to translate, and you're welcome to ask me questions. I'll set up an index tonight to help."

"I appreciate that. Since we're here, I wanted to ask mostly about the Foundation and the Nazi connection. Have you ever heard of the name Richard Schleiden?"

He nods and sighs. "You know your stuff. Sure. It's in the notes. I remember that a source who was kind of hyped on this stuff told me Schleiden was a follower of Jörg Lanz von Liebenfels, Rudolf von Sebottendorff, Dietrich Eckart and Friedrich Schroeder--those guys who were the *philosophers* so to speak, of the Nazi party."

I recognize the names from what I've read, although his German pronunciation is much better than mine.

"Schroeder and Eckhart were direct influences on Hitler."

"That's right; one was a fucked-up poet, the other some kind of mystic. They were both fanatical anti-Semites."

"Jesus, how old is Schleiden? Is he even still alive?"

"I don't know--I don't think I ever heard anything about where he is now. But he'd have to be pretty old. Schroeder died in 1946, I think. I remember my source called him the 'keeper of the flame' for future occult-based fascism. The difference is--" Kent looks for a particular set of notes to point out to me. "When the Armenian genocide and the Holocaust garnered international condemnation--given after the fact--and then the civil rights movement began to gain ground, the philosophy had to be caged in new language."

"So in your opinion," I point to the notes, "Would the keepers of the keeper of the flame be political parties--like Zhirinovsky in Russia, or the National Democratic Party of Germany?"

"I don't think so. These people wouldn't be directly be openly fascist, or in far-rightist groups. That's risky. People in those parties can be unreliable for keeping secrets, and they're full of infiltrators. I think this goes beyond politics. Corruption is corruption regardless of what label one wears. From what a source told me, I see more of their influence in international finance and control of governments through financial contacts."

"Does Schleiden have any family or contacts who might know anything?"
Kent sits down and pages through his notes. "I don't know of any, I didn't have the resources to do research in German. But you wanted to know about the Foundation. Schleiden was big into art. There were rumors he stole art--so much was stolen from Jewish families, you know. Well, this Foundation was started after the war."

"1946, I remember."

"Right. It handles art conservation. Schleiden was supposed to be connected to the place. Maybe had something to do with the art he took, fenced it. Keep in mind a couple people who helped start this place died 'mysteriously.'"

"Suicided."

"Exactly."

My phone rings. Joel. I step out while Kent thumbs through the pages.

"What's up?"

"Something's up. She hasn't left but he did--Nelson. He went to pick up his SUV."

"Alone?"

"Yeah. I followed him--he drove behind the Foundation building. It has some kind of lot, but it's electronically controlled. He's backed up behind the building. If he leaves, what do you want me to do?"

I make a quick decision. "Keep after him. Even if she doesn't come out."

"I'm there."

I go back to Kent.

"Here." He points to a passage on a page of. "Sorry, I know you can't read it. An engineer in Bolivia was seen to have some of Schleiden's personal effects back in the 1970s, something with his name on it--it's not a typical name in Bolivia. But the engineer claimed to be a Bolivian native, although he looked European. Still, for some reason it was thought the engineer had the stuff because Schleiden was mugged or something. The engineer's name was Juan Linera. He was from Cochabamba, worked for Standard Smelting."

"Who was this source, if you don't mind my asking? Is this someone aside from Pentington?"

"Well...I meet a lot of people who know other people..."

I've almost forgotten about my secret society. "What about the Tertullian Society? Are they connected with all this?"

"You found out about them, huh?"

"Raymond did, at least something gave him a hint about them. I may never know what that was, but it probably got him killed, and it's almost got me killed as well."

Kent has at last become reluctant. "See, this is where I came in, so to speak. I thought this was a made-up organization. But it's not. Especially when I kept finding ties to them in my other leads from this story. They really...scare me."

"I don't blame you. Don't worry about them anymore. I'm going ahead with this. If you wanted to write about it later, I have my own contacts who could help you."

"No, no. I wouldn't do that. I don't want anyone to know about this, really. Since you want to go ahead with it, I trust you. Crazy, I don't know you but I think you understand what's going on. I give you kudos. Do what you want with it. I wouldn't write a book. When I tried, not even mentioning the Tertullians...I dropped it."

"Because the publishers weren't interested."

"Right, and someone else found out. I had another threat. Serious. A fire in an apartment I was staying in. I barely got out. I still have some scars on my legs. It's why I don't smoke. I'm afraid of fire."

"Me too; I know what you mean."

"This person called me later, no ID. Just said if I wanted to burn alive next time it could be arranged."

"The warning."

"Yeah. I'm surprised you want to go on with it. God bless you."

He falls silent. Then he snaps his fingers. "I want to help you somehow. I can't go on the record so to speak, but while you're here, maybe I could introduce you to *another* person who helped me out, someone totally out of left field. He's an insider of sorts, a former DC investigator for a House committee, and also connected vicariously to the intelligence community. Naturally, being in DC he's heard enough to set off a firestorm if he ever told all. If he's around, he can verify some of this stuff about the Nazis. He's heard contacts."

Kent leaves to get his cell phone. I wait as I hear him call. I can hear bits and pieces of the conversation. Kent is friendly to the other person, explaining that he'd like to have him tell me some 'war stories,' but also careful, claiming I'm not actually here at Kent's apartment yet. At one point, Kent's voice goes very low and sounds rather tense.

After listening to and thinking of the serpentine conspiracies for the past few hours, I can't help but be a little disconcerted by the phone call. I can't imagine being 'vicariously connected to intelligence' and not actually being in intelligence.

I look at Kent's notes and think about having too much information to live, becoming a liability to powerful forces. Am I such a liability? Maybe Raymond was. I could still just end this and turn around, leave, and forget about Raymond's problems, tell Nelson I'm giving up, or just not say anything. They'd get the idea. Looking at Kent's notes, I feel a little disconnected from reality. If this were a movie--it'd be very exciting kind of stuff. But the implication of real people who have been hurt and killed from trying to find out more about whatever is going on here is very sobering. Two days ago, I was almost killed by a bomb, the day before shot at, and shortly before that beat up. Clearly, this ain't the Quakers I'm dealing with.

Kent sounds like he's appeasing the person on the other end, assuring him of something. When he comes back, he's his cheerful self again, very hopeful of the upcoming social visit. He tells me more about the man he just called, named Martin Arthur. Arthur is coming right over in a couple minutes. Twenty years working at the heart of the Capitol, used to be an alcoholic, now he just wants to do good but of course can't go against the powers that be, etc. I nod along, still feeling unreal as Kent tells me Arthur is a great person, shirt off his back, salt of the earth. A little too much, as though Kent is trying to convince himself.

"You sure about him, Kent? Really? What did you tell him about me?"

Kent's expression gets thoughtful. He stares at his notes for a minute, resting on the table. His holy grail. "I wouldn't put you in danger knowingly. I understand the fear of being set up. But I've been in touch with him on and off over the years. He's okay with talking to you strictly on background. But look. You want the notes, right? I'm okay with you copying them."

"Yes, very much. I'm actually very awed by your willingness to share."

He shrugs. "You might be able to go where I can't. There's FedEx Office a block over on M Street. Take this out and copy it. Martin will be over here soon, and I'll talk with him first before you come over. Gauge his mood. If anything seems off, I'll text you. I think we'll be okay though."

He packs up the folder in a bag and I stuff it in my backpack, then leave. But outside I hang back just a bit in the shadows of the trees outside Kent's building, out of impulse. Ten minutes later a rather thickset man with a moustache arrives at Kent's building. In the twilight, I can't see him too well, but he has a very tense body language. He looks over his shoulders before he goes in his face is set in an intense scowl. I'm not crazy about meeting him if this is Arthur but perhaps he's just a cautious cynic, as Kent suggests.

It's nearly eight o'clock. I feel a comforting sense of calm, going to copy at a nighttime FedEx. That is not an unusual task for me. I find a copier in back so I can be away from other customers, and take out the bag. I'm thinking about where to start, since a good portion of this can't be run through a feeder.

In the midst of my reverie, my cell goes off and immediately stops. I see that Kent tried to call. I call him back, but he doesn't pick up. Then I get a text message from him with one word.

--*dont c*

Don't c. It has to mean: Don't come back.

∞

TWENTY-THREE ♦ THE DEVIL

The fifteenth card of the major arcana. The Devil represents a person dedicated to fulfilling a base desire; something within the person cannot allow anything healthy to develop, but only to encourage corruption and twisted motives.

∞

Saturday, August 14, *Elsewhere*

NELSON HAS BEEN INVOLVED with these people for several years. He has been good at getting their dirty work done. He let them take full advantage of his intelligence and resourcefulness. When he started with this organization, he just had been impressed with its reach--he was never afraid, never hesitant. He had been searching for just such an environment where he could really exercise his talents.

He has no empathy but he does have loyalty. Thus far, the loyalty has been rewarded. This organization--small, elite, and powerful, has some hocus-pocus history; he knows some of it but doesn't care. The pedigree is something to impress people who must cloak themselves with the dubious prestige of a secret society. His concern is only how it can be exploited in a practical manner.

But like any privileged social set, one can only move so far up if not part of the long-time elite. That happens in any career, he supposes. The limitations are frustrating at times.

Jacobs gave him some indication of getting him a better position, but upon further consideration Nelson doubts that will happen. The current events are being interpreted in the worst light. Regardless, Nelson still feels he shouldn't be left out. He can do more, *deserves* more considering the extraordinary risk and effort to help them out. Good help is hard to find everywhere.

His methods aren't questioned when results are needed. But he had been summoned again to Westchester to explain why Ross was still alive. He was dressed down like a low-level office worker at a yearly performance review. Somehow, what had been arranged with a specialist didn't work. The specialist was an expert in removing persons, and had an explosive device ready for such contingencies as happened in Alpine.

But Ross escaped it by seconds, with a cunning Nelson figures must be better than average. Ross handled things better than Booth did. Nelson understands now that Ross has been in the trenches and learned. Not as much as Nelson but enough to provide a challenge.

Nelson takes out of his pocket a small tin with some pills. They are a special mix, a designer formula from Berlin. MDMA and amphetamine, a lab-created expensive tab named Blue Sun. Seems like he's running out, although he doesn't remember taking that many.

Nelson still feels he has a handle on the matter. He thinks Jacobs and the others who know of it do not appreciate he has things under control. After all, there are no further investigation on any official levels, no one talking who shouldn't be. Ross is like a pinball; erratic but eventually he'll be contained. Nelson hasn't made any mistake that can't be rectified. That is what is so aggravating; those in charge won't understand that *nothing* is beyond fixing.

The original problem was Christensen. Christensen had spoken to Nelson because some obscure website had published information on his old Nazi friend, information a little too accurate-- mentioning the Tertullians. He wanted the website taken down. No problem. Nelson had arranged for a hacker to spike the site with a denial of service attack and keep it spiked until the jackass webmaster closed the site a week later. The webmaster has also had some other challenges arise in his life to take his mind off Nazis.

Raymond found out about some of it, because Eleanor happened to have overheard part of a conversation between Nelson and Christensen. Eleanor wanted Raymond to find out about the Nazi, for Christ's sake. And Raymond believed he was some kind of freaking missionary.

Raymond didn't know Nelson was able to hack into his email-- he really had no idea of Nelson's role and his capabilities. Raymond went into Nelson's office when he wasn't there, and searched his computer, finding the cache of the website on browser and reading it. Raymond didn't know Nelson had his office set up with a camera and he was able to see exactly what Raymond was doing. Then Raymond was going to hire Ross to investigate because he *just didn't have the time*, a busy lawyer and all. Too bad for him. When Nelson found out, and he *always* found out, make no mistake, he knew he had to protect other people here.

But Raymond couldn't be warned away--the stubborn missionary type. So what was done to him was the best solution for everyone involved. No more fuck-ups. Nelson did not usually get personally involved, too dangerous. But this called for finesse to make sure. Nelson had to trap him personally, and arrange the scene. Raymond's termination was a masterpiece.

At least Eleanor is not talking anymore, and Nelson has taken steps to reward himself for that. Cole is still making waves, but he can be distracted due to his own vulnerabilities. He will not put himself out that far on Eleanor's behalf. Too much trouble. Very soon, she'll send notice of her retirement from the board and move into a new caretaking facility where Dr. Howard can keep her under control. Until other, more permanent measures can be taken.

If Raymond's junkie sister hadn't gone on and gotten Ross involved...oh well. It's a problem to be solved, that's all. Ross has the same bullshit idealism Raymond had, instead of self-preservation. Nelson has a hint of something new with Ross--the other man who was with him at Christensen's house, and maybe around Nelson's own place. Ross made a serious mistake to get anyone else involved.

Nelson knows that taking care of Ross is still a priority. If anything else happens, the matter could be taken away from him.

Nelson is in his Foundation office thinking about all these factors, when his assistant tells him that Raymond's sister is there to see him. She had called for an appointment and he had said to come at the end of the day. He gets up and goes into the anteroom to tell his assistant he can leave, as he gestures for Toni to come in the office. Time to put on the sympathetic face.

Toni looks like death warmed over. She glares at him and gets to her point. "I hear you are responsible for Raymond's death."

"Excuse me?" Nelson tilts his head, as if hearing her wrong. His mind is already moving ahead to the conclusion of this meeting.

"That is what I've been told. You have something to do with his death. We're getting the proof now."

"What are you talking about, Antoinette?"

"The information Gabriel is getting."

Nelson leans back in his chair, smiling. "Has he given you the details of this so-called 'information'?"

She doesn't answer. He nods as if he expected that. "Mr. Ross *has* no information. I'm afraid you are mistaken. Raymond's death was an accident. If Mr. Ross has tricked you into paying for his services by some sort of misrepresentation, I'm sorry. You should be aware that you can't trust private investigators. They are all crooks, feeding on sorrow and desperation. I'm deeply sorry about Raymond. I know you are angry and want someone to blame, but--"

Toni jumps to her feet. "I don't need to hear your bullshit. I don't need your *sorry*. You think I don't know about the trouble between you and Raymond?"

She then starts outlining certain problems Nelson had with Raymond in the past. Nelson can see she's desperate and losing control. As Ross should have known, her erratic behavior has led her to a reckless maneuver. Nelson doesn't know if he has to worry about what she's told others about what she knows, but he can handle *this*. He lets her go on, maintaining his concerned expression.

"Please relax, Antoinette. I understand what you mean. Raymond and I had our differences, but I would not want you to think that was personal. Let me tell you that we understand each other. I think we can work something out."

She sits back in her chair, pulling out a cigarette, trying to stop shaking. Nelson continues quietly.

"There is no need for this. I can tell you have been neglected by others, like Ross. Really you have, or he would be here, right?"

She doesn't answer, but Nelson sees he hit a nerve. "But *I* can take care of you and get you what you need, yes? Is he really helping you? He doesn't talk to you that much, does he? He doesn't tell you what you need to know or is really concerned about your personal needs. You know that or *you* wouldn't be here. You have come to the right man. I think I can do much better for you than a lowlife bottom-feeding private investigator, right?"

Nelson hates smoking but finds an ashtray for her. Give her the sense he wants to placate her and her scheme. "I just don't want you to believe I ever had anything to do with Raymond's death. For all you know, Ross did and set *you* up. What do you know about him? Did he meet with Raymond before his death?"

Toni pauses in her smoking. "Yes...he did."

"Maybe he took advantage of your brother. Don't you find it strange he's always around, but never really helping you? Now he's working with the lawyer. That lawyer doesn't have your best interests at heart, does he?"

Toni looks away. She's in early withdrawal and can't process these ideas coherently. Her paranoia is prominent. Nelson gives her a minute to imagine Ross seducing and killing her brother, than taking money from her to investigate the death. Anything Ross ever said that she didn't like will make this scenario much more real.

"We will bring this matter to a more than satisfactory conclusion for you, and you can tell Ross to end his investigation. I'm sorry you are having a hard time right now. I know Raymond was taking care of you--are you having problems?"

"The insurance payout was denied."

Nelson laughs sympathetically. "I wish you had told me sooner. I guarantee you I can fix that. You don't need an inquest; I can call in some favors, my dear. Like I said, Cheng isn't going to help you. Lawyers are awful persons; they have no *soul*. He's only out to get what he can for the estate. He'd take the insurance too, if he could. And what is a nobody like Ross going to do with an insurance company? But you shouldn't worry anymore. I have the right contacts to get your policy paid out in no time. Don't talk to Ross if he contacts you. While I am working out a permanent solution, and I know people who can get you a *much better* job than the one you have now, and get the insurance check cut and sent out to you, you wouldn't be insulted if I tide you over with some money--just a small down payment to what I can arrange for later?"

She wavers, struggling internally. She needs the money. She needs the fix. He has said the right things if she just wants to believe. But somehow, she still turns her glare back to him although her words are slow. "No. You killed him...You think I'd take money from you?"

Why the fuck are you here, then? Fucking bitch. No, don't let it show. She can't leave. That is unquestioned. She can't leave. He puts on his most hurt demeanor.

"Antoinette, No, I swear to God. I swear on my mother. I had nothing to do with Raymond. I might know who did, though, because of what you mentioned before. There was someone else Raymond was investigating; look, can I talk to you about it? I will admit to you and you only I was afraid to talk about it, even to the police. This person has pull with the police."

She's shaking still, barely able to hold the cigarette. "Who the hell would that be?"

"Someone dangerous. Ross could never handle this. Maybe you and I can figure out what to do. I need a drink, though. This is *so* heavy. But you deserve to know, I owe you that. I didn't know you were being treated so badly. I'm getting a drink. You want anything? A glass of water? A glass of wine?"

And she nods. Maybe she still wants to believe him, and under the struggle of fighting the demons on her mind, she lets her guard down to allow him to get her a drink. She's beyond considering the safety of that choice.

In half an hour, it's over.

∞

Twenty-Four ♦ The Two of Pentacles

The Two of Pentacles represents a situation where one is struggling to maintain a balance and maintain a positive karma in work.

∞

I CALL KENT AGAIN, but still I get no answer. Now I stuff the papers in my backpack, with the previous feeling of calm turning into muted panic. His call to me I could write off to 'pocket dialing,' but the text...I need to go back and see what's going on in spite of his warning.

At Kent's apartment building I pause before ringing his buzzer. My same gut feeling that held me back earlier kicks in. I ring adjoining buzzers and announce I have a FedEx delivery. Whoever's expecting one at 8:30 at night lets me in. I go up the stairs to Kent's floor.

At the apartment door, I listen carefully, and hear muffled thumps inside. I know something has gone wrong. I gently, quietly, test the door. Not locked. When I push it open, I stop myself from shouting out. I expect anything at this point, but had hoped at worst to find Kent arguing with Arthur. But Kent is crumpled on his living room floor just beyond the vestibule. I see blood on his face. His eyes are open, frozen staring up at the ceiling. The thumps are coming from inside the office--someone tossing the place.

I know whoever is in the apartment killed Kent. I can't call the police. If he's intelligence, he'll have a line into the police. DC at its heart is a small town. I know nothing of mine is in the apartment, and I handled nothing other than the notes in my bag. I feel a deep sense of regret at seeing Kent. He knew he had made a mistake in calling Arthur, and stepped in for me by sending me out. I have his legacy.

The noise has suddenly stopped. I'm ready to back away.

A face suddenly pops in front of the vestibule. I barely register him--white, male, dark hair, bulky shoulders. He reaches inside his jacket.

I make for the stairs. Footsteps are behind me, but I'm already flying down three floors to the exit. I might or might not hear a zing of a bullet from a silenced gun.

On the street, I take a quick mental inventory of the situation. No way I'm staying in town tonight. I need to get to the train, to Union Station a little over two and a half miles away. I can't take a chance on waiting overnight and flying out in the morning.
I flag a taxi and take it to about a block from my hotel to be safe. My room is empty, and I gather my stuff together and leave, getting another cab to Union Station.

At Union Station, I head for Amtrak. The station is a large, beautiful place but at night it has many empty dark areas. Usually I love this station and the train cars. The train areas are distinctly arched, with recessed blocks in the ceiling. It has a European feel. The effect is spectacular by day, eerie at night.

Rush hour is long over and the dark places seem too cavernous. I check the times for the next train to New York. Thirty-five minutes from now.

I look for a different train, but the times don't get any better. In line for a ticket, I notice a figure in the shadows off to the side of ticket kiosk. The figure slips out of sight. My paranoia rises. I stare into the dark corner for a better look. I'm sure a shadow is stirring.

I feel too exposed to stay here. Maybe I can get the station police to go after this person. And then again, maybe I had better not contact the station police, as I would have to answer a few too many questions. Amtrak seems less like a good idea. Scanning the station, I see the stairway to the Metro, the city subway system.

Down the stairs, around the corner, I find a niche to wait and think. Now the train is out of the question; too much time to wait. I don't like the idea of Kent's "friend" being on the lookout for me. I need to review the Metro map.

Looking out the niche, I don't see anything. Another 200 feet down from the tunnels leading to various Metro lines is another staircase. The map for the station is near the stairs.

As I step away, suddenly something hits my back, hard, nearly knocking the breath out of me. Both my backpack and suitcase drop. An arm goes around my throat. In the initial shock, I instinctively know not to struggle and choke myself further; I go backwards with him, and throw my weight down at the same time. He is expecting me to strain against him so he staggers, and my weight brings him down and me on top of him. His grip loosens enough for me to be able to jab an elbow to jab into his ribs. He gasps sharply.

But now I'm on top and more in control. My fist goes into his abdomen, then his crotch. He's professional though, and can handle the pain. His right hand comes up with a switchblade, so fast I can barely jerk my head away in time. The blade scrapes my jaw line. I raise my hands and pound down on his arm with my fists gripped. The knife clatters away but he grabs for my shirt, bunching it to choke me. I feel the material rip. Stars float in my eyes. I dig for his face. We lock like that for precious seconds--him trying to choke off my air, me feeling my throat close, losing my vision. I dig my fingers in his face, scratching his eye sockets.

A train arrives in the distance, making the darkened ground rumble. The man tries to swing me around to slam my head on the concrete floor. I can hear steps far off, blood pounding in my ears. Could be the police. Could be passengers. Could be whoever might be working with this man.

Defending yourself means not panicking, and getting out of a comfort zone. This is why when I practice fighting with people, I have them come at me as swift as possible to sense their movements and evade. This person has knows too. He's too smart to try to punch roundhouse, but I can feel where he's trying to strike.

Blocking, I keep him back from me. He's careful not to let his hands linger with the missed punches, but that can't last long. Close enough to punch is close enough for *kotegaeshi,* a turning wristlock. One had on his wrist, and my forearm against his elbow. I yank him down. He doesn't exactly flip, but he goes down and I have my leg already snapping out to meet his rib cage.

That puts him down well enough for me to grab my bags and slip away.

In a nearby walkway, small groups of people are coming up from a subway line and I join their midst. I don't bother with looking at the map but just leave the station. Time for Plan C.

A nearby taxi takes me north to Bethesda. The ride gives me a chance to calm down. The driver is yelling at someone on his cell phone, but I don't care so long as he ignores me. I just keep an eye out the back of the taxi window to check for tails. At a shopping mall, I get out, and spend a few minutes inside. I change my ripped shirt in the bathroom; wipe the blood off my jaw; have coffee at a Dunkin Donuts to let my nerves and adrenaline settle down.

Joel calls me. When I answer, he can't speak.

"What's wrong?"

"I don't know how to say it..." He sounds shaken.

I pull myself together to calm him. "Okay. Take it easy. I'll be back in a few hours. I need to find a bus service to the city."

"What happened *there?*"

"I had problems, but I'm okay now. You tell me what's going on at your end first."

"Jesus. I followed that fucker to Brooklyn. No one in the car but him, I thought. He drove to Toni's, neighborhood. He kept driving around like he was looking for something. Finally, he pulls into an alley near a grungy bar. I was wondering what the fuck, you know? Was he trying to score?

"So like ten minutes later, he backs out and takes off. I went to the alley just to look real quick, and...she was there, Gabriel."

"*Toni?*"

"Yeah. She was just lying there. I went up to her--she was already dead. No gun or knife or anything."

"Oh my God." At this point, I feel like crying and move my coffee off to a more isolated table. "Oh my God. Oh my God. Oh my God"

"I'm sorry, Gabriel. You were right about her."

"Where are you now?"

"Here. Near the alley. I called the cops from a pay phone. Anonymous. Gave them Nelson's license plate."

I trained him well. "Go home. Don't let them find you there."

"Hell no. I hope they find that fucker and accidently beat him to death. Now what about you?"

"I'm all right for now. Let me get a bus for the City and I'll call you back. Go to my place."

Deep breath. Don't fall apart now. Don't fall apart. It takes me a couple of tries to get my fingers working correctly, but on my iPad, I find a bus service in Silver Spring, Maryland that offer trips back to New York City. Silver Springs is a little under ten miles away. I go outside the mall and find a cab service. An hour later, I just manage to catch the next bus leaving from the lot.

The bus ride is comfortably banal. I text Joel to turn on the webcam where he is. A few seconds later, I see him at my desk in one of my sweatshirts. He's looking at me closely. I realize I'm still bleeding down my neck. I hold up a hand, signal I'm going to instant message him instead of speaking. We've done this before. I type a short version of what happened. I wait for his response.

He reads it over and looks at me again.

-- *Where are you?*

--*On the bus. Looks like I'll be in after one.*

--*I'll pick u up from Penn?*

--*Yes. I'll text you when we're coming in.*

The ride serves to numb me and I doze a little, but don't really sleep. Periodically I startle myself awake, looking for attackers. Other passengers give me the fisheye, but no one tries to cut my head off. On a bus, people see a lot worse. At 1:40 a.m., I'm finally back in New York. I walk upstairs and outside, trying not to bump into people from sheer exhaustion. Look towards 34th Street and check my phone.

--*I'm on 9th Avenue.*

I walk down the block and look for my car. In the midst of traffic and police, I see him like an oasis double-parked. We hug each other in spite of several cars honking at us for holding up traffic. We get back inside.

"Goddamn." He shakes his head and looks at my jaw, freshly cut again.

"I know. I can't even feel like this is real anymore. Anything come back to you?"

"No. You taught me better than that." He grabs my hand. "I'm sorry about her. I really am. I'm sorry I didn't know what he was doing, or I would have broken in and done something."

"Please. We couldn't prevent that. I would have been in the same position. You were right she made her choice but she didn't deserve what happened to her. You did good--maybe this can be solved the right way, instead of being another suspicious accident."

On the way back, I tell him what Kent told me: his investigation, his findings, his trials and tribulations as a result. At home, I take everything out of my back on the floor. The bag with Kent's notes. I take the folder to my office and put in an empty drawer of my file cabinet. "I'm not telling anyone about these. This is his work. He was killed for it. Maybe I got him killed for it."

"We should review one of your philosophy books; if Toni had free choice, he had free choice too. From what you told me, I think maybe he was dead when he first investigated this, in a sense. It just finally caught up with him. Leave those for later." He gets up to check the lock the front door.

I watch him. "Quite a profound thought."

"Yeah, I'm a profound guy. Both of them had information they couldn't handle. And yet we're still here. The best thing we can do is not let their deaths be in vain, right? So, we gotta keep fighting, man."

He comes back to me. "You're tired beyond tired. Get in bed."

"I hate being ordered around."

"So you say. I've seen otherwise."

I can only smile at his attempt at humor. The adrenaline gives way to exhaustion. I see Archie is fine, sleeping on the sofa. Okay to go to bed. Joel follows. He helps peel off my clothes to my shorts and then sits beside me. He ruffles my hair and yawns. I see how tired he looks as well.

"I got you into another fine mess."

A smile. "It's what I'm here for."

"You're too good to me."

"I'll agree. Don't forget it. I guess we can sleep now. The cat's on guard duty." He lies down beside me. It's comforting, like when we were together. I'm surprised how easily I just lie down with him. I know it's confusing, maybe not fair to any of us. But I can't think about Alex right now. I don't want to explain or justify anything. I need sleep too much and I need someone with me. Not time yet to unravel the mystery.

∞

Twenty-Five ♦ The Three of Pentacles

The Three of Pentacles represents reinvigorating a skill, mastering a skill, taking control of a situation.

∞

Sunday, August 15
Alphabet City, Avenue A

I SPENT ALL SUNDAY MORNING thinking about what to do next. I kept expecting police to show up and arrest me for having been in Kent's apartment. I can't bring myself to call anyone else and tell them what's going on. Toni's death hits the news. She's not identified, but we know. I feel bad for her mother and son. I call Toni's number to try to reach them, but no one answers.

Joel knows that's killing me and has me show him the notes. Gradually I focus on what to do practically. I call Jason at the bookstore. He has some instructional manuals on Gregg shorthand. Joel and I go to pick them up and spend a blessed non death-related hour talking with Jason about books.

Back home, we wait for anything else to happen. I discover that Kent's info on the Nazis is in the top of his stack, luckily enough. But I'm still checking my phone and the news every few minutes.

"Call your lawyer." Joel is lying on the sofa. He had been trying to draw and gave it up. "It'll make you feel better to do something."

Jim is in a better mood for once, which makes me sorry to go into the DC tale on his day off.

"Oh my God," he interjects. "I was just going to change the numbers on my 'Gabriel Ross has had '30' days without a run-in with the law' to '31,' and now I have to start over again."

"Sorry about that, more than you know. The police should be deep into investigating Kent's murder by now."

"Let us see what the Internet has to say about it...*DC Man attacked by intruder, police say,* is one headline. According to the *Post*, he was probably robbed and killed by an 'intruder' who ransacked his apartment, probably someone who was looking to support a drug habit, according to an 'authority' in the metro police department."

"Something's off. The cops should have been calling me by virtue of my number being on Kent's phone."

"And yet they aren't. We'll keep watch on this. If you get a call, call me first thing. Until then, try not to be around anybody so they don't die off. Do not date my sister."

"That's very funny. I appreciate the tact."

"You want tact? Get into another line of work."

"No lecture about being safe, or don't you love me anymore?"

"You got my motion work done, so I'm happy. As a friend, I think you'll either break this wide open, or someone will break you wide open. I'm rather resigned over it; I said my piece. Just let me know where to send the ambulance or hearse or bail money."

∞

Monday, August 16
Washington Heights, 12:30 pm

I'm in north Manhattan for Danny's project. I feel somewhat better, even with death haunting me. Toni's cause of death is uncertain as yet, but the police are looking for a person of interest-- Nelson, I hope. Alex calls me as soon as her name hits the wire. He's relieved I wasn't around her; I don't say who was.

Spending the day following the film crew helps keep the dead at bay. No one really bothers us except at one building where a couple of drug dealers get nervous, but I talk to them and calm them down. The project has been extended to some buildings in the Bronx on a later date, and Danny invites me along. I'm non-committal at the moment.

When we're taking a break in the afternoon up near Ft. Tyron Park, Danny casually leads me to a park bench away from the rest of the crew. We sit with a couple of Cokes and cigarettes, ignoring park rules as usual. Danny watches me without comment.

His blatant observation gets on my nerves. "What the fuck with the eyeballing, man?"

Danny nods. "I noticed today your language has gotten worse."

"My language is always bad."

"Not so much naturally; you usually talk like a professor. But when you hang out with certain people, you pick up their speech patterns."

I shrug. I don't like where this is going.

"Alex called me yesterday."

"Really? I hope you and he had a nice talk about me behind my back."

As usual, Danny isn't the least bit ashamed. "Seeing him soon?"

"Tonight, if you must know."

"Good. I hope it's good. I like him. He's a person of good character, compassionate, smart..."

"And?"

"And not a street skell."

"Thanks. I'll let him know he passed your credit check. What's up your ass today? I'm here, we had a good day, nothing too terrible happened."

"You're always good about your work. But two things. First, something is seriously bothering you. I'll get to that later. The other has to do with making choices."

I know what his agenda is, really. Sighing, I light another cigarette. A person almost gets killed four fucking times trying to do the right thing, and still has to be lectured.

I say through the cigarette, "So, let's brass-tack this motherfucker: what did Alex ask you? And what did you tell him, so I know how much damage control I need tonight?"

Danny smiles grimly. "Imagine my surprise when he asked me who Joel was. Imagine my surprise that Joel is even *back* in your life. You've been hanging with him in the past week...strange you didn't tell me about that."

"Now imagine your shock when I tell you to mind your own fucking business."

"I've heard that one before. Let's just review the facts: who pulled you up off the floor when you were broken-hearted after you found out what that *pendejo* did to you. It may be two years later, but I remember pretty well sitting with you in your misery. After that, you wouldn't even try. A couple nice guys showed up, but you didn't give them a chance..."

"Please go on. Tell me the mythology of my life."

"The drama of Ignatz and Krazy Kat is back."

His old name for Joel and me. It hurt because I love old comics and Krazy Kat in particular, and Danny disapproving of us from the start--he claimed he saw parallels between the lovesick cat and the abusive mouse, and myself and Joel.

"That's unfair, Danny. You're being a dick."

"About men who fuck with my best friend, sure I am. Who get caught red-handed, shall we say, pimping out to Wall Street slime."

"I should have never brought you along on that time."

"When we followed him to the penthouse on Maiden Lane? Yeah, you should have, and that's why you did. I could see you somehow justifying it, denying it later. You needed the help to break with him then. And now he's back. So what's he doing now? Does he have a job?"

"He just got back."

"Still escorting?"

"No. He's changed. But we're friends. Working together."

"Oh, you're just friends?"

"It happens."

"To other people, yeah. You feel too much for that to really work with you. You worry me even more now. I thought just putting your life on the line with the killers you're investigating was the worst you could do. I was apparently wrong. You want to destroy your personal life as well."

I sigh again and turn to face him. "I swear to God I know better. I want things to work with Alex. I hope you didn't go into all that past history with him, it doesn't help."

He looks away, a bit embarrassed. "No. I just said he was your ex, nothing you wouldn't tell him. I didn't say anything else, I swear; you'll have to do that. I wouldn't put the fail on your thing with Alex. I'm hoping he has the *cojones* to keep you away from him."

"I know exactly what you think of Joel. If you're honest, you'll admit you never liked him when we were at our best in the relationship. I'm not defending what he did. But he did help me the last couple of days. And I needed *help*, not to be dressed-down."

If Danny's offended, he doesn't show it. "What Jim and I said, we said from love, asshole. Don't go playing misunderstood loner. Alex told me he gave you some trouble, too. He feels very bad over it, like he's letting you down."

"He isn't. I understand the politics of his job. I just don't like--"

"Being told what to do. What else is new? So Joel steps in like the Lone Ranger to do everything your big bad friends won't. You think I don't remember that little bit of manipulative bullshit from before. You have a tendency, Gabriel, to rush in where angels fear to tread. I admire that sometimes. Your chutzpah gets you success. But because of our messed-up childhoods, we can't appreciate our flaws too well. You don't see where you deliberately dare death to fuck with you."

I finish my Coke. The film crew watches us from a distance. Getting close to the time to leave, but Danny's not ready.

"What's that got to do with anything?"

"Your friends show you when you go too far. But Joel is the devil on your shoulder. He knows you hate like hell to be told anything--because of your dad. So he gives you that leeway. Fuck your friends. Do what you want. They're just holding you back. I might remind you this is not the first time you almost were killed. And he does this for his own amusement, to have control over you--not because he cares. He doesn't care about anyone. He should have left you alone but now he's back to tell you the same shit. Everyone's against you and only he supports you."

I get angry at Danny, and I don't want to. He has no idea what happened, no idea that Joel has been watching me with Veronica, which refutes his words. And what can I tell him about it that doesn't sound overly defensive? "I'd never say he was the perfect boyfriend. But sometimes I was right, and you were wrong. I always hear when I'm wrong, but no one ever wants to admit when I'm right. So I needed someone who was okay with what I do. I'm telling you now--*you're* wrong."

"Selective memory. I've always been honest with you. But you have your romantic ideas. And yet again, you're almost killed as you so generously tell me three days later--because of this bomb. When you delay telling me something, I know something's wrong and it's not just almost being blown up. Gabriel, he went along with you because he's a manipulative son of a bitch. He knows how to make you feel good and to play up how everyone's against you and only he understands you. If this were *anyone* else, you'd see it."

"So I have no judgment, is that what you're saying?"

"About him, no. He likes knowing someone can't resist him and will blow off that person for kicks. But *you* broke it off with him, not the other way around. He's not used to that. So yeah, he wants you back so he can prove a point to himself. Then he'll fuck with you again and take off, and you won't have him *or* Alex. Don't throw your life away."

We're silent for a moment. I hate this sort of thing and I'd just as soon end the conversation. But he's waiting for me to argue. I look at my phone to see if any messages will rescue me. I think in a way how stupid this argument is with so many persons to have died around me. I can't have time to even psychologically process it. But I go on nonetheless. He's right I don't like to be told what to do--even now.

"He apologized for what happened. We all make mistakes, Danny. He's still a strong person and a good man."

Danny turns this around in his head. He knows I wouldn't have mentioned it if I didn't think the apology was sincere. But we both sometimes have difficulty getting past old feelings.

"You see something I don't. Apologies don't mean much in his world. Don't let that lead you into something you'll regret."

"I'm not. You'll have to just trust me on that."

"I'll worry about it later. What is eating at you otherwise?"

I give him a very brief version of Toni being killed, and the trouble in DC. He takes another cigarette and we contemplate life again. I'm relieved to have been able to talk about it, but I'm shocked to see the hint of tears with Danny.

"Don't do that to me."

His voice is fierce. "How can I not? You've never been in something like this before. It's like death is following you. But I care about you. You're my best friend--you're more than that. You're my family."

"And you're mine. I've gotten in something deep; I hope I can get out. I think it'll be over soon. And I had help. He helped me."

Danny doesn't respond. He rubs his eyes. I put my hand on his shoulder and he embraces me. "Don't leave me, Gabriel. Don't disappear into some kind of minefield or mindfuck."

"Not going to happen."

∞

Monday, August 16, Continued

After the filming is over, I find out Cheng has left a message for me to come to his office.

"You've heard."

Yes. Toni has taken the normal from my life. Well, let's get real, Gabriel. There is no normal life, and in yours, a dead client is par for the course.

"Has anyone contacted you?"

"No." Cheng eyes me. "Should they?"

"I heard about a person of interest."

"Perhaps. I understand your suspicions about her death, but she has a history, Gabriel. Raymond knew it, I knew it, and you probably even knew it."

"Yes, I suppose so." I don't tell him what he doesn't need to know.

I call Greene and ask him if he can find out anything. Then I head out again, destination Brooklyn, Toni's address. I don't know who will be there, but I want to find out what happened to her. I feel some responsibility for her dying five weeks after her brother.

Greene calls back. "The detectives are looking for the guy who runs the Foundation. Some anonymous tip about his license number."

"Is he a suspect?"

"You know how that goes. They have to find him first. He wasn't at home, not at the office and not answering his phone."

"Thanks."

A short while later I knock on Toni's apartment door. An unfamiliar older woman answers. I tell her who I am. "Toni was my client."

The woman nods shortly. "I'm Marilyn, Julia's sister and Antoinette's aunt."

"Can I talk to you a minute?"

"I don't know what's going on here. In a matter of weeks, my niece and nephew are dead. My grandnephew is orphaned. My sister is a wreck; she's at home under sedation. She can't deal with this. On the verge of a nervous breakdown. I hope you can appreciate that."

"I can. I lost my family close together as well, but not like this. I know you must be wondering who the hell I am and why I'm here. I want to find out what happened. Toni had a troubled life, and her death doesn't seem right."

Marilyn looks over her shoulder in the apartment. "Adam's here." Her voice is lowered. "We've been seeing Toni suffer for years. No one was completely surprised by this, but it tears us apart. You think her death isn't right--don't you think that what you do just makes the grief worse?"

"I can't say." I raise my hands in supplication. "I'm not getting anything out of this. I just feel I need to do this for her."

Marilyn looks far sterner than her sister, just as Raymond was far stronger than Toni. She finally cracks the door open more. "If you make him upset, I swear to God I'll have you arrested."

I nod, and go past her into the apartment. It's spacious and pretty well decorated, if in a rather jumbled state with furniture slightly askew, papers and books piled helter-skelter, clothes everywhere. Marilyn appears to be a bit embarrassed about it, looking around as if she could cause the mess to disappear.

Adam is shell shocked and quiet. He eyes me sideways. First his uncle, then his mom. Just like what happened to me, except I was much older than he when my mother died--in 2003, and then Dominic a year later. But I remember feeling the same way he does. Just his is harder to deal with.

Marilyn waves me to sit at a kitchen table covered with papers, books, half-eaten snacks, electronic game devices. Adam gets up and follows me into the kitchen. I can't read him, but I know he has to be fucked up right now. I put my hand out to him. In response, he throws himself into my arms.

Marilyn's eyes narrow. What's up with this man she doesn't know? Why does her grandnephew trust a virtual stranger? I don't know myself. But the boy needs someone to cry against. His grandmother is broken down and Marilyn doesn't look like the hugging type. She doesn't complain though. I hold Adam and let him cry on me until he's exhausted. I'm almost ready to cry myself with my own grief over the people who have been lost, and that makes me want to value life that much more. Aside from all the strange happenings with me, I feel for him. He's innocent; he's going to need help to get through this.

Marilyn finally speaks. "You were looking into Antoinette's insurance claim."

"Yes. I guess you know why."

"I don't know what was going on, if it was a fantasy of hers or not. Raymond was a good man, though. But Antoinette seemed to feel you were holding up her money." She has a hint of reproach, either for my past actions or in case I'm about to give her a bill.

"I wasn't holding up her money; I was trying to help her get it. She wanted a loan, but that's unethical in my business. When she first hired me, I gave back the rest of her retainer. I know she was going through a difficult time. But I was on her side."

Some of the confusion has cleared for Marilyn. "I appreciate that. She wasn't always good at giving the whole story. So, why are you here? What is left to do for her now?"

"I want to know more of her circumstances immediately before she...well, she may have held back information I didn't know, for her own reasoning. I want to know was who she saw and what her actions were."

"Well, on Friday she asked if Adam could be with me for the weekend. Of course, I asked where she was going to go. She said she was speaking to someone, but she didn't say who it was."

"Did you ask?"

"No. Antoinette didn't like to tell me much about her life. We have different personalities. Julia had a tendency to believe whatever she said, but I thought it sounded funny. I know she wanted money, I couldn't help her as much..." Marilyn looks to Adam.

He's raised his head. "She was on pills, I know. I don't hate her for that, but I'm mad."

Marilyn clasps her hands together and continues. "She said she was doing something smart, taking control of the situation, and would explain later." She suddenly turns and picks up a coffee pot and offers me some.

Adam still watches me. "Do you think she did something wrong?"

I phrase my reply carefully. I don't want to criticize his mother; he doesn't need that. "I think she *thought* she was going to do the right thing, but met with the wrong person--someone with whom she wasn't fully aware of the danger."

"Who is he?"

I contemplate Adam him man to man. He has been through enough to earn respect. "I can't tell you who I think it is. Not to confound you, but because saying things without proof can get you in trouble."

"But you think someone did." His voice is flat.

"Yes, I find the circumstances too suspicious. I will try to find out. If I'm right, it has to do with Raymond's case. If I'm wrong, I'm sorry. I'm not trying to cause you more pain."

A small comfort to know your son or nephew or uncle didn't die from a self-inflicted sex injury, but was murdered, and your daughter or niece or mother did not die in an alley from a drug overdose, but was murdered.

He looks at me, unreadable, yet an understanding seems to be between us.

"I would like to know if there are any notes, computer records, anything that might indicate where she went before this happened."

They look around the room without getting up. The mess of the apartment stands out as a challenge. Marilyn sighs. "I don't know how she organized her life. Are you looking for anything in particular?"

"I'm not sure." I lean back with the mug of coffee. "It could be anything from a clearly articulated plan to a Post-It note with initials. Something recent. Did the police question you at all?"

"They asked some questions, I told them what I told you."

Marilyn and Adam both get up and offer to help search. We start in different places. I try a section of the living room that appears to be something of an office. Marilyn searches the cacophony in the kitchen, Adam the bedroom. I flip through a checkbook, a second cell phone, an address book, tons of papers, notes, grocery lists, letters to people sent and unsent.

"I found this." Adam comes up from behind me with a small legal pad. It's blank. "Look."

He turns it to the light of a table lamp. I can see the formation of what had been written on the page just above and ripped off. I take study it in the light then turn the page over, where the writing is more visible as raised letters. It appears to be notes to herself.

"She was always writing things out. I was writing some things for school on this the day before yesterday, and she borrowed it. So, this stuff is probably new."

I take a pencil and gently rub over the indentations in the page. *Responsible for death,* is one line. *Know what you know;* "know" was scratched out and replaced with *did.* Having worked with lawyers, as did Toni, ideas took shape. *Proof. Hated you. Knew you had taken money. Jury will believe.* And in the top left corner, *E Nelson.*

With their permission, I put the whole pad in an evidence bag I carry for that purpose.

She saw Nelson to have it out with him, because she didn't think I was moving fast enough. Something in what she said made him act instead of just bouncing her.

Knew you had taken money. That makes me think I was right she was privy to something about Nelson she hadn't told me. I couldn't make her choose the right action. But maybe some kind of justice can still play out.

This is all we can find, but it's enough for me. I promise Marilyn and Adam I'll get the evidence to the authorities. I don't want to tell them about Nelson right now, it's too much for them to handle, especially Adam. Adam asks me if he can talk to me in the future, and I'm okay with that as well. Marilyn says she'll let me know when the memorial service will take place.

I make a copy of the paper and take a photo of it, and then mail the writing pad to Cheng's office to add to the evidence. Meanwhile, later that evening Jim lets me know he has discreetly checked out the investigation in DC. The police are focusing on some transients in the area who are suspected of smash and grab incidences. This makes no sense and perfect sense to me. Whoever killed Kent doesn't want me arrested because I might bring focus on who really did it. I wonder what they're doing right now.

∞

TWENTY-SIX ♦ THE EIGHT OF PENTACLES

The Eight of Pentacles represents intrigue in business matters, a patience needed in preparing for a needed result.

∞

Monday, August 16, *Elsewhere*

JACOBS MEETS AGAIN with the Swiss man. Nelson is the topic of conversation, but he's not present. The Swiss man is leaving soon to return to Europe, and conveys his impatience with the escalating problems to Jacobs.

"This can't continue."

"I know he has gone too far at this point. I'm going to step in and take the situation away from him. It has to be done."

"What would be the next step...you need some new help?"

"I'm not dealing with it directly. But I have our man here. He arrived this morning. Mr. Zest. Zest is *the* professional. Nelson could have been like him if he were to last long enough."

The Swiss man lights a cigar and nods. He contemplates the smoke rising slowly in Jacobs' library. "A very good idea. And what will he do?"

"He's going to handle the situation expeditiously and with as little trouble as possible. He'll approach Ross. But not as Nelson did. Zest has a special way with these matters. I have the associate who's been helping Nelson briefing him now on all he knows about Ross and how Nelson handled it."

"And do you feel this will have the desired effect?"

"Logically. Taking him out is the next step, and I have no problems with that. But every action risks more exposure. He had his chance to stop this."

"I don't like it. If no problems have resulted from termination, stopping now seems a mistake, pointless."

"Zest is a good judge of that. Unlike Nelson, Zest has never failed. I wish I could have him work more often."

The Swiss leans over to tap his ashes. "Do you find yourself having difficulty in handling some of this work?"

Jacobs is caught by surprise. Any sign of weakness is not good at this level. Doubts are private, never expressed. He knows the consequences, even though he and the Swiss man are at the same level. "Nelson is a disappointment, but he seemed fine for many years."

"He handled the work for you."

Jacobs does not stir at the remark--he sees the implication, but can't show it. "A level of insularity is always necessary. As I understood, that was the philosophy from the beginning."

"Still, I have always thought that those in the circle should take on tasks themselves from time to time. That would establish character."

"Anything I need to do, I'll do it. But I would suggest that we aren't in an emergency situation."

"Emergencies aren't the issue." The Swiss shrugs and appears to drop the subject.
"What if Ross doesn't do as suggested?"

"Zest will handle it. Believe me. No questions exist with him."

"Fine. Then the remaining problem, I take it, is Nelson. What is your call?"

"It's sticky. The police are involved. He's hiding out right now; he called to try to arrange something. That gave me the excuse to have Zest here if he finds out. I suspect something else is going on, like drugs. I thought Nelson would have known better. But maybe that was his true nature. He's breaking down. Zest can handle that too. But ultimately, the question is whether Nelson can be redeemed is moot."

"His ambitions, you mean."

"Yes, so assuming we can get him off the hook with this woman's death, he'll still want to fulfill those ambitions. Even if he isn't taking drugs, even if he is just running into a rough patch--would he be satisfied with remaining where he is? No."

"I agree. He has taken too much on without clearing it first and now he has too much attention. I suspect he has been into more than we know. He will continue to do so until he is stopped. Is Zest going to take care of that as well?"

"He will do what is necessary. First Ross, then Nelson."

∞

TWENTY-SEVEN ♦ THE TOWER

The sixteenth card in the major arcana. The Tower represents disillusion, disaster, a sudden catastrophe from a hidden direction or an old enemy.

∞

Monday, August 16, Continued
Alphabet City, Avenue A, 9:00 pm

"YOU'VE BEEN THROUGH a war zone, like the soldiers I've interviewed."

Alex is sitting on the floor, more casually dressed in a denim shirt and jeans, black boots. I've come home from Brooklyn to meet him in my apartment. To give the situation a bit less of a heavy feel, I make some frozen margaritas.

He's been listening while I recount some of the lowlights of the last few days. Not everything but enough. "You haven't processed it all yet. It's too much. I think you need to step back and give yourself a mental break before you crack.'"

"It's not over. I don't know that I can."

I'm in shorts and a t-shirt, just sort of collapsed with my drink.

"I suppose an irony is that were it not for Raymond, we wouldn't have met."

He leans over and rubs my bare leg briefly. "I'm glad of it."

"Is your boss still giving you a hard time?"

"Not at the moment. I'm under watch, but things have settled down."

"I don't want to be the cause of your not getting the promotion."

"Well, they'll decide what they decide. You can't worry about it, that isn't going to change anything...I wanted to tell you, I'm sorry what I said about your work. There's just such a dichotomy between you as a person and the evil you deal with."

We contemplate each other.

He breaks the silence. "So where do we go from here?"

I'm not sure I can go into this. But then, life goes on and I have to live to spite death. I look at Alex. When Joel's with me, I feel one way. When I'm with Alex, I feel another. Right now, with him here I feel the closest to normalcy, maybe because Alex wants to be so removed from the ugliness of the world. "We go...where we want to. I think we've been honest with each other, but not open. But it's a start."

He smiles. "I think so. All right, we'll start something further."

The tension in the room lessens. Alex takes his shoes off. I get the sense he's planning to stick around.

We change the topic. I don't want to talk about what I'm doing next, because I'm not sure. He doesn't want to talk about it either. We talk of the other stories he's working on. He stretches and wanders around the room, pausing at the bedroom door. In watching him, I remember Joel slept over. He doesn't wear cologne, so no telltale scent. But then, nothing happened. Of course, I still feel guilty, and I swear Alex is surveying the room to determine if anything did happen.

"Help me change the sheets." I keep my voice light. See, if I ask him to help me, I must not have been doing anything wrong.

We make the bed with a certain sense of expectation. Archie tries to climb under each sheet and muck up the works.

"What are you doing tomorrow?"

"Following some leads."

"Do you need me to help?"

I smooth over the sheets. Archie has jumped aggressively in the middle of the bed, and starts washing himself to demonstrate his ownership. "I'm thinking to separate our work and personal life."

He frowns at that and walks over to put his hands on my chest. "I'm not afraid, Gabriel. I'm careful with my career. I've also thought this out. I was caught by surprise because I didn't think whatever you were looking at with this...Society could possibly extend into my work. I still don't know, but the implications were disturbing. Even the best reporter has few chances of finding a decent job, especially if forced out. But that doesn't mean I can't be aware of what you're doing, and that I wouldn't help."

"All right. I have a possible link to the Nazi guy. I need a reliable source to talk to who might be able to trace this, and maybe knows more about the Tertullians. Some so-called experts on Nazis really aren't good, just good at publicity. I'd like to find someone who did work quietly and with a solid reputation--it would help if not too far away. I can't fly to Europe--no, you aren't going to pay for me to do so."

"Okay, sounds like a plan."

The sheets get used.

I think afterwards we're bathed in relief this can still happen. I get a reasonable night's sleep. But I wake up early, and think about the people I've met who have been killed. I start to appreciate how my friend Rich, still serving in Iraq, feels with the possibility of death at any moment.

A brief flood of depression. How do I handle this and go on? Can I prevent any more deaths, or will I be the catalyst for more?

My cell phone rings as if hearing my thoughts. Not a known number.

"Mr. Ross? I think we should meet this morning. Columbus Circle. At the monument at the Merchant's Gate."

"I'm sorry, who the fuck are you, now?"

That wakes up Alex, who is instantly concerned.

"You can call me Zest. Don't spend time arguing about who I am and what I want. Just show up. You have plenty of motivation, such as what happened in DC."

The call ends.

Well, I guess I have an agenda for the day.

The time on the phone is 8 a.m. I get up. Alex sits up and grabs my arm. "What's going on now?"

"Some man who wants to meet up. From the Tertullians, I assume."

"Meet *where*?" Alex gets up as well. Seeing him naked in the sunlight, I regret having to leave.

"Columbus Circle. If I have to guess, he's going to threaten me, or try to blackmail me over what happened to Kent."

"And what you going to do?"

"Listen to him. Stall. I don't have to be ethical or honest with them."

"I can take the morning off and be your backup."

I'm heading for the shower. "I'm not using backup."

A half-hour later we've both showered. I even shave for the occasion. "Can you make, coffee, babe?"

"Sure, but don't leave just yet."

I look at myself carefully in the bathroom mirror as I shave. Fine lines of stress appear around my eyes. Moisturizer isn't going to help, being rid of these people will.

The day is going to be hot, but I'm wearing a jacket to cover my Sig Sauer. Black linen over black pants. As a compromise to comfort, I don't wear socks with the black loafers.

Alex hands me coffee. "You really want to go out there alone?"

"I'm not risking anyone today. I'll be on the lookout for any attempt in kidnapping, like a suspicious van hanging out. If all they want to do is talk, I'll talk."

"This could be an attempt to draw you out."

"Not in Columbus Circle. It might as well be in Times Square. If they don't have a helicopter to get away, it would be stupid to try."

"I don't like it. But I understand. You should have someone looking out for you, though. If not me...maybe your other friend."

Ouch. Inwardly, I flinch, but then stop. No, he means it. He's trying. His trying is a good sign. Don't fuck it up. "Not this time. But I will keep in touch with you. Have your phone on."

I arrive at Columbus Circle shortly before ten. The giant gilt-topped sculpture is in honor of the USS Maine. It's at the edge of Central Park, 59th Street. I stand right in front.

My phone rings. "This is Zest. I'm glad to see you were amenable to meeting."

"So, have at it. Where are you?"

"The weather is bit hot today. My having you go to the Circle is because I wanted you to see you are not in danger today. That's why you're where you are."

"I deeply appreciate that."

"Your sarcasm isn't going to help. I'd like to assume you are an intelligent person. But I deal with all sorts of personalities. You're not going to offend me. But we should talk indoors with more clement atmosphere. Go to the Met Museum. Meet me on the first floor in Medieval Art, Room 305."

"Cut me some slack, that's 20 blocks up and across the Goddamn park. At least make it the Natural History."

"Less trouble getting in Met. They won't check your person for weapons. You don't even have to pay if you want. Take a cab."

"And how will I know you?"

"Don't worry about that."

"Fine. Thanks for the insult about paying."

I hear what might be a tiny chuckle. "Sue me if you wish." He hangs up.

Sighing, I hail a taxi to head up to the 86th Street Transverse through Central Park and back to the East Side. Twenty minutes later, I get out in front of the Met.

The advantage of the Met is not standing in long lines for tickets; admission is 'suggested' as Zest helpfully pointed out. I still pay the full fare and move on to Medieval Art, an area I know well.

I have to admit being here is much more comfortable than in the 90-degree weather outside. I go inside Room 305, through the giant black gate that bisects the room.

A white man in his fifties comes up next to me. Gray hair, black eyes, cool manner. He rather resembles James Mason in *Lolita*. A homburg wouldn't be out of place on him. He has a full suit, handkerchief, tiepin and everything. We survey each other. His eyes flicker over me; he has a tiny wry smile. He's holding a cane, but I suspect not for a disability. He points to the left corner of the room. "Mr. Ross. There's a bench. Let's sit in front of your namesake."

We walk to the bench and sit in front of a giant hanging tapestry. It's an image of the Annunciation, with the Archangel Gabriel. Zest contemplates the image.

After a moment, he speaks again. "I know you're Buddhist. Are you familiar with the Christian mythology of Gabriel?" He has a low, pleasant voice. Educated. Not American but accent-less.

"Yes. And the Islamic. You want me to give you pointers on religious art? Be glad to."

His smile slowly widens. "Not the appropriate time. My only interest is whether religion plays a factor in this situation. With you I imagine not, at least with Christianity. I do know you're highly intelligent, and Nelson underestimated you. I do not, just so you know."

"Somehow, I think the same about you."

He smiles. "You'd be right. Under other circumstances, I'd like talking to you. But that isn't going to happen."

"So what *is* going to?"

"Again, we're here to show you aren't in danger today. But I think you are aware we know of you and what you're doing."

"I have nothing to say regarding that. But if Nelson is the best you can do--"

He shakes his head, still keeping the smile. "Nelson isn't part of what I have to say. You're dealing with me, although I doubt I'll see you again."

That's interesting. Nelson has screwed-up, of course. They know that. Which is good, as screw-ups often lead to a break in a case. And bad in that if Nelson, who is extremely dangerous, is gone, that means the Tertullians have sent in a designated hitter who probably can't be provoked. Zest must be that D.H.

I meet his eyes. "Why haven't you killed me?"

He doesn't even blink at that. "I wasn't brought in to do so-- unless I must. I don't deal in empty threats and I don't negotiate. Stop the investigation in this matter within the week. Make the case to Cheng that no further information can be found. He's paid you to this point. You tell everyone you are no longer working on the case. I'd start today."

I don't answer. He raises his eyebrows, turning his head to look at me.

"I heard you, Mr. Zest." I recognize this man is an entirely different level than Nelson. He has a quiet confidence; he's never going to tell anyone about phony degrees to impress them. His bona fides are completely in his bearing, his voice, and his eyes. Nelson thought he was serious, but Zest would be the dictionary definition of the seriousness.

"Good. I hope you can appreciate that I know your character. You aren't out of control, so you can appreciate what I have to say and I'm giving you the benefit of assuming you're smart enough to get who I am and that I mean what I say. I haven't had anyone close to you killed, or tortured and raped--like Ms. Gianni or Ms. Connor, or Mr. Pollan's wife for example. Because I know that sort of thing would only commit you against me.

"I don't have your ideals, but I respect them. That's how I differ from Nelson. I'd rather deal with this intelligently. I would have such terrible things done if necessary. I know you aren't close to your father; I wouldn't bother threatening him. Or your half-sister. But you don't want to be responsible for your friends. Not you. You have a conscience, Mr. Ross. Think of who you are close to. I know you would sacrifice yourself before you'd allow harm to come to them. But I wouldn't allow that. Mr. Martinez. Ms. Connor. Mr. Pollan and his family. Mr. Barclay. Mr. McFadden. Ms. Gianni. Mr. Jarvey. Even Ms. Booth's young son. I would do what I have to. By the time I'm finished, you'd gladly kill *yourself* from the guilt."

I listen to him tick off my friends one by one. He knows his game. He even knows about Joel, who rarely uses his last name, and my New Jersey friend Bob Jarvey. I feel cold in realizing he or someone with him has been researching me and my friends. All I can do is listen.

"You also can't do much good for the world if you're in prison. Mr. Pollan has checked to see why you haven't been contacted regarding Kent Varney. That's in abeyance. If I get a satisfactory result, the matter in DC in turn gets resolved satisfactorily. Otherwise, I assure you some evidence will be found linking you to his death. Do you disbelieve any of this, Mr. Ross?"

"No. I don't doubt your sincerity one iota."

"Good. I'm not drawing this out. You don't have to defend yourself about what you do, it's meaningless. In understanding philosophy as you have written of in your online articles, you know about autonomy and choice. So you understand what choice you have to make. Stop the investigation completely. Take Mr. Varney as an example for what happens in reviving investigations. Respect that fact that some matters can't be resolved and life goes on. Or, you can choose to continue and your friends will die and suffer, and you'll be incarcerated before you die."

I take a deep breath to steady my nerves. Under the fear is anger. I believe him absolutely and yet, I can't help myself. "I imagine you had a choice once--to work for these people or not. You ever regret that choice? I'll bet *your* autonomy is extremely restricted."

Zest stands up and smiles. "You don't want to know more about me, Gabriel."

I meet his eyes for several seconds, then quote Gerald Kersh. "'There are men whom one hates until a certain moment when one sees, through a chink in their armor, the writhing of something nailed down and in torment.'"

He studies me for a moment. I can't say he's taken aback, but he's listening more than someone in his position should. "I appreciate your sentiment, believe it or not. But you'll never be able to appreciate mine. Man to man, I hope I don't have to find out you made the wrong choice."

"And Nelson? He's on something you know. I'm guessing speed or coke. I don't think he can be controlled anymore."

Zest looks away thoughtfully. "You're not wrong. Don't worry about him. You need to worry about yourself." He nods at me politely and walks away.

I'm proud of myself for not having broken down in any way. My back is soaked in sweat, but I can handle that. I now have to figure how to best protect my friends.

∞

Twenty-Eight ♦ The Wheel of Fortune

The tenth card in the major arcana. The Wheel of Fortune represents sudden change, surprises, and a turning point. One thing must become another.

∞

Tuesday, August 17, Continued

I GO BACK HOME for a few minutes, and then I drive uptown to Allen Cheng's office. It happens this is the day I'm supposed to talk to his staff. He greets me affably and looks out the doorway to the large anteroom outside his office. "So, I guess you are about those interviews. Do you want to start with my assistant? I can have a list--"

"No. I do want to talk to you, though."

He's a little nonplussed. "Okay."

He sits a chair near me, rather than at his desk. "You look disturbed."

"I am. I'm ending the investigation." I set a folder on his desk with the expert reports and my own summary, carefully written.

His worried expression turns to shock. "Really?"

"I'm pretty sure that at this point I can't find out anything else. With Toni dead, the issue of her insurance becomes moot. As to Raymond, I think Ethan Nelson killed him as well as his sister, but I doubt the police will be able to do anything with it. Still, enough circumstantial evidence is here to challenge the cause of death if you want."

Allen opens the folder and flips through it briefly. "I didn't expect this from you. I thought I might have to tell you to be more cautious, but..."

"I've been threatened. To put it more bluntly, the people I love have been. I admire Raymond tremendously, and what happened to him was an injustice. But I'm not risking their lives to prove a point."

"Oh, my God. Did you report this to the police?"

"It's not reportable. It's why I'm backing away."

"Well, I'm so sorry...I can't say I blame you. Is there someone I could contact to help out?"

"Doubtful. Not the police, not a senator, probably not the President. I think I have a chance to rectify this if I just stop. They'll know if I do. I'm not sending you a bill for cataloguing Raymond's stuff. I apologize that it isn't finished, but I'm not going back in the apartment."

Allen leans on his desk, still trying to turn it over in his head. "But of course we'd pay you for what was done...what about the trip to DC? I can reimburse you..."

"Nothing there you can use."

"You must have used all the hours in the retainer, what do we owe..."

"Forget it."

Allen puts his hands flat on the desk. "Jesus, I don't know what to say. How is this going to affect your future work?"

"I don't care. You don't have to give me a recommendation. My reputation doesn't mean much right now. You can say what you need to. I'll be sending you an email confirmation of this meeting."

I get up and head for the door. He follows me.

"Listen, I didn't mean about your future work like I was going to trash you; I'm just concerned." He takes my arm. "You're serious about this."

"Yes."

"Well...are you okay?" He holds out his hand.

"Fine." I give him a brief shake and then I'm on my way. Outside the building, I go to a Starbucks, take out my iPad and send him the email I already had prepared.

Next I call Carl Mankiewitz. "Anything new on the story?"

"Some weird things are happening, what with Booth's sister."

"You got that right. How about printing an update?"

"You got a quote for me?"

"On background. The investigation seems to be stymied. No new leads have turned up. I don't think any more work is going to be done on the case."

"You mean...work from you."

"Yeah."

The same pause from Mankiewitz as I heard from Allen Cheng. "Really? That doesn't seem like what you'd do. The whole point is to find the cover-up--"

"And you can still argue that if you want. If you need to slag me in print, I don't care. I've heard worse. But I'd really like you to print something on me leaving it--even just a line or two."

"This for real? You're off the investigation, but you still want me to print something about it."

"I'm calling you about it, so it's real enough."

"That's fucked-up man. Why would you let it go?"

"I agree it's fucked up. I can't answer your question. You can ask it in the story if you need to. You can say I'm ten kinds of asshole if it helps. Bye for now."

I hang up, and call Danny. I tell him I'm ready to continue working on the film project, and I don't see any problems with other work getting in the way, particularly with Raymond's death as I've quit. He doesn't believe me at first. Then he's worried and wants to discuss it. "You sure you're okay--"

I cut him off. "I'm doing what's best, believe me. Let's just let it go." I hang up and then call a couple of regular insurance clients and check for upcoming assignments. Thank God, they are glad to hear from me. They have plenty of people to investigate for fraud. I make arrangements to pick up the files from their offices. Jim is my next call.

"Don't worry about DC. It's taken care of."

"Oh God, when you say that I know the shit's hit the fan."

"Yes and yes. Just drop it. Sometime this week, let's work on my response to the Licensing Bureau before they have a fit, okay?"

"Sure, no problem. You sure you're..."

I don't want to hear that again. "Yes." I hang up on him too. Now I sit for a minute in my car. I realize I'm shaking, and I need to get it under control. I've spoken to almost everyone I really need to. One more to go. But wait, before I do that I want to check on something.

I call Dr. Cole. "I have two things to ask," I tell him. "One, what's happening with Ms. Whitford?"

"Not good. She isn't in her house anymore. The doctor managed to get a restraining order against me--I don't understand how. I can't get any information. I do know this, her house people are gone. They were told to leave indefinitely a couple weeks ago, before you were there, and then were outright fired. The doctor or maybe the doctor's lawyer told them this. She also had a tenant on the top floor, a writer who lived alone. He was given a notice of eviction."

"So, something is going on with her and her place. Absolutely. Now the second question. Was there any problems in the Foundation about any missing money that Raymond may have looked into?"

A long pause from Cole. "How did you know about that?"

"My job, Dr. Cole, is finding things out."

"All right, I don't like talking about Foundation business but I trust you will keep this confidential. Raymond and I disagreed on how to handle this; I regret that now. This happened when there was a sale last year of a few pieces of art willed to the Foundation. The sale was a private auction. Raymond had been reviewing the receipts of this sale, shortly after he came back to the Foundation, and said around $45,000 was missing from the final price. Nelson first said this was the dealer's commission, and then he said the art didn't sell for as much as we first thought. Raymond was highly suspicious of this, but I had spoken to the dealer, who more or less confirmed Nelson's story. I had never known this dealer to have been dishonest."

"How do you feel now? Could that money have been embezzled?"

"I wouldn't like to think so, but I have to admit the explanation was not the best one. If the dealer hadn't confirmed that the amount was a mistake, I would have been far more suspicious."

"How well do you know the dealer?"

"By reputation. But I have started to realize that doesn't necessarily mean anything."

"Did you check with the buyer?"

"He's a man who lives in Europe. I got the impression actually that the man was buying for his mistress and wanted to keep the transaction discreet. I didn't pursue it."

"So it's not completely out of the question that Nelson and the dealer may have taken the money."

He sighs. "No, I suppose not. I don't have the contact information for the man, but I'll try if you look for Ms. Whitford."

"I can't do that. I'm ending the investigation."

"What the hell are you talking about?"

"I'm sorry concerning Ms. Whitford. I suggest checking to see if she's been stashed in a private treatment center somewhere. I suspect that is what Nelson's done. But I can't do it."

He too has a moment of silence at my news. "I have to say, Ross, I'm pretty damned disappointed in you."

"Me too. It doesn't matter about me. I know of some places upstate that have shady pill pushers. I'll give you a list."

"Why did you ask me about Nelson, then?"

"I'm sure you have heard the police are looking for him. He should be arrested, but if he isn't, your board *might* consider firing his ass." I hang up on him.

The next call is the hardest. I'm still shaking, but I keep it out of my voice. "Hi Alex."

"Hey, I was so worried about you. Thank God you called. What happened?"

"About what I figured, a warning. I should have called you before, but I needed a chance to sit and think."

"No problem, as long as you're okay."

"I am. I'm just...taking a moment to get used to the idea of stopping."

"Stopping?"

"I'm closing the case. I don't want to deal with it anymore."

Every person I speak to falls silent after my news. I suppose that says something about my integrity, if that matters.

"Gabriel, I don't know what this man said to you, but don't just..."

"The decision had to be made. We'll talk about it later. Everything will be okay. Just trust me. I'm not saying it's easy. But I realized it was the right thing to do. Sometimes you have to know when a job is over. It doesn't affect us; we'll get past it. Think about going for a weekend somewhere?"

"I'd love that, I'll admit. But I was looking for that Nazi expert, and I have a couple prospects I just emailed you about."

"I appreciate it, but forget it."

We keep up the small talk for a bit and then I gratefully bring the conversation to a close. No going back now. For a moment, the stress hits me and tears come to my eyes. Stop. Do this later. Still need to take care of business.

I've parked nearby a library branch, and have my books on Nazi war criminals in the car. I take them out and back to return, all of them.

I briefly stop for lunch. It's early afternoon and I don't have much appetite, but still I need to eat so I don't get sick from stress.

Then I go to FedEx Office, one of the larger ones with several self-serve copiers. First, I use one of their computers for a while. Looking up some things, checking emails, changing passwords. Then from my backpack I take out Kent's notes. I've separated larger papers from regular size. I start the first bundle in the feeder.

While that's going on, I check some notes I made while in the library, and take out a burner cell phone I bought earlier. The number is in the city, a man who lives in Brooklyn. I take a breath. Now or never. Dial the number.

"Hello?"

"Mr. Herrmann?"

"Yes, how may I help?"

"Mr. Herrmann, I was wondering if could talk to you about one of the war criminals you've been searching for. I'm a private investigator. I don't want to give details over the phone, but you could tell me if the information I have is reliable or not. And if you know anything regarding the Tertullian Society, I'd be interested in learning more."

∞

TWENTY-NINE ♦ THE HERMIT

The ninth card of the major arcana. The Hermit represents a person of wisdom who serves as the mentor to another, to spur a protégé on his or her journey.

∞

Tuesday, August 17, Continued
Bay Ridge, Brooklyn, 4:37 pm

THE DOOR OPENS. Herrmann is a man in his seventies. Over six feet tall with a full beard, black and gray. Somewhat overweight and an imposing presence like Orson Wells. He's smoking a cigar. He wears a rumpled long-sleeved button-down rust-colored shirt and corduroy pants. He looks me over for a minute.

"I take it you're Gabriel Ross." He has a moderate German accent.

"Yes, Mr. Hermann. I appreciate you taking the time to see me."

"Well. I'm retired but not really. I hear a good deal of bullshit information. If you're playing a game or working for some white supremacist organization, I'm going to have you prosecuted."

I just nod. Seems I get that threat every day, sometimes twice. He lets me in his apartment. A floor-through on an old brownstone in the Bay Ridge neighborhood, with nice high ceilings. Comfortable looking furniture, lots of books. And cats. Two out of what looks like six or seven come up to sniff me and I give them some love. He also has a couple of bulldogs that make their way over to get in on the action. Pretty soon, I'm completely preoccupied by playing with them. Hermann starts to sit, and then checks back on me.

"Do you like coffee, or tea? Don't let them take advantage of you."

"My pleasure. Tea would be nice, thank you."

Other cats, including a small tiger-striped kitten, stroll over to join the party. We all get to know each other. I'm tired. Before taking the train to Brooklyn, I traveled in various subway lines for half an hour, switching trains until I could feel I was safe from being followed. I don't have my phone or any electronic devices with me just in case. Hermann comes back with a tray and suddenly laughs.

"I see how it is. But this is a good sign. They usually know *tref* people."

I pull myself away from the menagerie to sit in a chair, with a small table and the tray between us. I have to remove the kitten from my backpack.

"Ha. Jonah will sleep in there if you don't watch out."

"No problem. I'll just have some explaining to do with my own cat tonight."

"You have a look about you, young man. Gabriel. Something's happened to you. You're haunted. So tell me what sort of information do you have, and what do you need?"

"What I have is this." I take out a couple of pages from a legal pad and hand them to him. "I translated this from some notes by a man who ultimately died for this information. I'm not telling you on the record, you can do with this what you will."

"*Schleiden*. My God. Eichmann's assistant."

"Someone seemed to think that this engineer Juan Linera might have stolen Schleiden's things. I'm thinking something else. He might actually *be* Schleiden. That wouldn't be out of line to take a Spanish name and start a new life. Plenty of Germanic Argentines, Peruvians, Bolivians. I did find a listing of employees in Standard Smelting in Cochabamba. He's long retired, but he might still be there."

Gathering the papers in my hand, I turn to face him. "I'm giving you this under a condition with your word of honor. If you know the Tertullians. I can't be connected with this. However you use it, I need for you to arrange that the information came from elsewhere."

"I can do that. I'll accept your conditions."

I give him the legal pad pages and a copy of a print out from my research in FedEx, computer time bought with a disposable credit card just for discretion. The handwritten pages are my translation of Kent's notes on Schleiden, basically the same thing that he had told me.

Hermann gets up to check his files. Not on computer, he has hard copies. "This engineer has not been mentioned before, not by any of my contacts." He brings the file back with him. "What do you mean when you say a man was killed for this?"

"I can't give you identifying details. I've been threatened off this myself. By the Tertullian Society."

He raises his head to look at me. "You know them?"

"I've gotten acquainted the hard way. In a sense, they're probably no worse than the Mafia. But one can one person do against that?"

"Yet you're here."

"If you read the news you'd know why."

He shrugs. "Not so much these days. Maybe I better start again."

I pick up my tea and spend some time telling him my entire story, from Teresa's funeral on to today. I don't know why, just something about him gives me the sense he's a well for secrets and I can have that as a gift. The cats and dogs settle around us as I speak. Hermann digs some treats from a drawer and gets several tails wagging and flicking.

After my story, he considers me thoughtfully. "Why did you give up? I suppose the answer is obvious, but you must have known you were under threat when you were assaulted."

"I didn't give up. I just told them I did. I'm trying to reduce casualties."

He smiles slowly and lights another cigar, offering me one out the box. Why not. The cigars bring a sense of ritual to our discussion. Herrmann leans back. "When I was younger, I did the same thing. Perhaps I'll tell you some time. It was a private but necessary subterfuge. This is a lonely business. After a while, no one wants to hear history anymore. Memories become faded; criminals become jokes. Hitler is a joke."

"Not to me."

"I see that. You are a staid young man. And this information on Juan Linera?"

"You have the network to check it out. Maybe the ZS?" Herrmann wasn't one of the names Alex had sent me, but I had found his name checking the others on the list. In some follow-up research on Herrmann I found out he had worked for the West German Central Office of the Land Judicial Authorities for the Investigation of National-Socialist Crimes (ZS) in the early 1960s. The ZS had been set up in German to investigate war crimes, particularly in concentration camps. Herrmann had found a few escaped Nazis. He was never much in the news as were other, more famous Nazi hunters, but from some interviews with him in recent years (such as on John Demjanjuk) I concluded his actions were quiet and earnest. And he is in New York. I can't risk going out of town.

"I can look into it. Let's hope this pans out. Maybe then your friend's sacrifice will be not be in vain. And so, you wanted to know about the Tertullian Society."

"Not much information around on them. I guess they weren't as interesting as the Illuminati."

"But much more sinister. We begin in 1908; a writer named Friedrich Schroeder started the group. At that time, a significant occult revival was taking place in Europe and I think over here as well. People like Yeats, Blavatsky, and Crowley. Some for good--spiritual development, some for evil purposes. Schroeder had researched ancient Germanic legends and combined them--wrongly--with Nietzschean principles and mysticism. Nietzsche was actually sympathetic to Jewish persons, and broke off his friendship with Wagner because of Wagner's anti-Semitism.

"This group was similar to the Thule Society. In fact, the two groups were rivals, and would cut each other dead on the street to get influence over prominent politicians. Hitler, of course, took any help he could and he was particularly attracted to those who flattered him and his grandiose music, architecture designs, government 'reforms.' He wanted to hear he would be a leader and a messiah to the German people. He played the Thule and the Tertullians against each other. Eckart died before Hitler rose to power, and so Schroeder had much longer influence and contact, even when Hitler was clearly making choices in strategy inimical to logic.

"Schroeder's writings on occultism, when you can find them, are about an interpretation of these collected myths and legends that certain people are secret masters of earth, and deserve to hold power over those who are lesser in quality. Social Darwinism we might say now. He believed both in the mystical aspect and in using the mystical aspect as a means for members of the secret organization to commit themselves. Psychologically, if you have to undergo a ritual to join a group, you will develop more attachment and loyalty to the group. The military and college fraternities act on this principle. Schroeder's rituals involved a symbolic death--like the mystery schools of ancient Egypt and Mesopotamia, drawing blood, perhaps even a form of sacrifice."

"Sounds like stuff I've heard before, like a Masonic group doing the Jack the Ripper killings as some kind of symbolism."

"For all we know, the Tertullians did such things and had others take the blame."

"Hard to prove their guilt in any event. Why are they named after Tertullian anyway? He was a Church father, not an occultist."

"Schroeder supposedly found a lost parchment Tertullian had authored. Maybe he did. At the time, the Dead Sea Scrolls were found, later on, bits and pieces were sold on the black market all the time. Schroeder may have bought something from Egypt long ago. Later the Nazis searched for various religious artifacts, and they did that from Schroeder's influence. According to the legend surrounding this document, Tertullian had actually started a school of Christianity that would eventually be adopted by some ancient Franks. Principles that advocated freedom for some to oppress others--philosophy and free thought was a means to chaos, as only better men had the right to control political power. On the surface, Tertullian was advocating for a unified Christianity, suppression of heresy and prohibition of women from preaching after his conversion in 197 CE. But the alleged document suggests he used Christianity as disinformation. Christianity could keep people pacified while the real power was at work. This was not Gnostic, but sort of an anti-Gnosticism."

"Still an opiate of the people."

"If it's true. But really, that doesn't matter. Even if Schroeder didn't believe it, it led to others' beliefs."

He pours us more tea. I pick up Jonah and hold him to my face, feeling his little heartbeat. One of the bulldogs grunts and puts his face on my feet, jealous. I scratch his head. "Like helping Nazis out after the war?"

"More disinformation. If people are looking for Odessa, they are chasing a ghost. I'm not saying it didn't exist, only that no one in power cared. Some Nazis went into science and helped with the Cold War. But the Cold War, nuclear science, going to the moon, these are just tools. Finance is what drives the Tertullians. Money always is power, and power is the goal."

"So the Society arranged for people to get into financial power?"

"I believe this to be so. After World War II, countries were restructuring themselves, even the US. Plenty of opportunity existed to get into banking, finance, politics, infrastructure. Developing laws and stirring fears to institute laws that are more draconian. Repression is a breeding ground for meritocracy, but a fascistic meritocracy."

"And today?"

"I think you've had a taste of what it's like today. Look at the austerity measures being instituted across Europe. That always encourages extreme positions in politics. It's had over 90 years to develop, and over 70 to be set in place. They aren't everywhere. They do not control the world. They aren't all-powerful, but they are powerful where they are. I have no doubt they have contacts and influence. Whether or not the mystic parts are still in place doesn't matter."

"So finding something, a conspiracy in which they are involved, would be very dangerous."

"You know that already. I think you were wise to let them think you gave up. I have no doubt they are involved in many conspiracies, regardless of countries or administrations, or kingdoms. Their loyalties rise above constructed politics."

He pauses to put down his file and close his eyes. "Gabriel, what are you going to do with this?"

"I don't know. My basic goal was to find the Nazi Raymond Booth heard about--Schleiden. Maybe that can be done. My other goal was to expose his murderer. This may lead to the Tertullians, but..."

"If you somehow found evidence of such, they would cut that person loose. It wouldn't be a fulcrum to the Society itself."

"I understand. I'm not prepared to try that. But I can't ignore it either."

"Did you need to talk about anything else? Forgive me, but I'm a bit weary after discussing these people."

"No, but I'd like to ask a favor."

He opens his eyes.

"I have a copy of some notes in shorthand. I'm working on translating them, but I'd like the copy to be somewhere out of my place. I don't want anything in my name. Can you hold it for me? Maybe with a note that it is to be returned to me or my representative upon request."

He smiles. "You just met me today."

"If I'm wrong, I'm wrong. I've told you enough to get myself killed if you are *boshaft*." "Malevolent" in German. I looked up the word special before coming over, sort of having this speech in mind.

He smiles. "*Das ist kein problem*. Do you have it with you?"

I take the stack out of the backpack. I have the copy in a plastic bag. He takes it. "I have an office safe suitable for this. Make your note, in case something happens to me. My lawyer would return it to you."

I write a note on my legal pad that the stack of papers is my property under the care of Bertrand Herrmann, to be returned to me upon request, or my representative. Herrmann has me add also upon his death. I sign it, and he signs it. "Do you want a code word, for your representative?"

"I think 'Jonah' would be good."

∞

Alex sleeps over that night. Of course, I tell him nothing of Herrmann, or Kent's notes. He has come over to comfort me about my decision to give up the case. I let him comfort me, because I'm afraid that if he finds out I was lying--even to protect him--he'll be gone.

The next day I'm at a loss for what to do. I don't want to talk to anybody, so I try to figure out how Nelson might have killed Raymond, and what sort evidence might be found to prove this.

A curt paragraph is published in the *Scene* along the lines of what I had discussed with Mankiewitz. He does not call me names. But the article says no real reason is given for my leaving the case. Good enough. A few hours later Jim leaves me a message saying he heard that a homeless man was arrested for Kent's murder. That tells me the Tertullians have gotten my messages. My friends are safe. Me, I don't know about.

∞

THIRTY ♦ THE FIVE OF PENTACLES

The Five of Pentacles represents losing what is close, business, security, persons. It is a severe test of resources.

∞

Wednesday, August 18, *Elsewhere*

ETHAN NELSON IS HIDING. He went to a hotel when he got the word he was being sought. He immediately called Jacobs. Jacobs had said he would help.

A friendly contact told Nelson Tuesday evening that Zest is in town. Confirmation of that came to him via word that Ross had dropped his investigation, quickly and publicly. Zest is supposed to be here to help Nelson, but he knows better.

Nelson waits in his room, dealing with his anger. He considers any number of actions. He has to reclaim his position.

He imagines his mind is at fever pitch the height of his intellectual capability. Jacobs must be able to understand his full worth. Something went wrong, outside influences. Nelson cannot imagine that all his work is not being appreciated. Did he not handle each situation competently, completely? Only Ross still being alive is holding him back.

The thought of failure is untenable. No, this issue has to be resolved somehow. Ross can't simply fool him and walk away. That has never happened. Now, Ross is more than a simple problem. He has imposed upon Nelson's life. There's no escape for him now. His choice in the matter is gone.

Finally, Nelson uses an untraceable cell phone to call Jacobs. He calls Jacobs at work, which is a distinct violation of protocol. But he feels Jacobs and Ross have forced him to decide the fate of his enemies and rivals.

After some time waiting on the phone, Jacobs answers. "What is this?"

He is angry, but Nelson does not pay attention.

"I think you have underestimated me. My loyalty can't be questioned. I have proven myself to you many times over. I can be a valuable asset to you and I suggest you take me seriously."

A pause on the other end. Jacobs must be thinking about what Nelson said. "We should talk. I can arrange for us to meet again."

"Why did you call in Zest?"

"You know better than to speak of business, or even to call me here. You know why he's here. For your help."

"Bullshit. You think I'm stupid? You're out of your mind. I'm worth twice of him. Do you know what I did to get the recommendation of my contact, the one who introduced me to you?"

His voice is getting loud. Jacob's voice becomes more soothing, quiet. "Don't read into this, Nelson. Zest is just a backup; he's not replacing you. I give you my word on that. Think about it. Have I ever not lived up to my word with you?"

Nelson considers. "No. But I think that someone's been spreading lies about me without understanding just how difficult this matter was with Booth. People who would like to see me fall. I can't let that happen. You can't trust Zest, he's a rogue."

"I'll give you a chance to state your case. Is that what you'd like? I understand, and I'm willing to listen. Let's meet so you can tell me what you think is going on."

"No." Nelson feels better, like he's regained control. Jacobs might be scared, having realized he made the wrong decision. He must wonder what Nelson knows and can the type of trouble he can bring if crossed.

"Not now. I'll meet with you after I take care of the problem. Ross is no longer going to *be* a problem. I'll have this done within 24 hours. Once that is over, you'll see how much better my work is for you and that I've proven my loyalty. Goddamn it, you had no right to question what I did! I have put up with the Society's shit for years...." He shakes his head trying to clear it. He needs to take something to calm down and fumbles for his pillbox. Jacobs prattles on the other end, more about meetings. Nelson is done with meetings.

"I'll call you when I've killed Ross. If I see Zest anywhere near me, I'll kill him too. He's dangerous and I'd be doing you a favor. He must know what I know. I've worked for you people for so long, and I could bring everything down with what I know. You'd all be on the street if I told what I know, and what I've done for you. You'd be in prison, or shot. The CIA would take you out."

"Don't go off the deep end. When we have a chance..."

Nelson doesn't listen. He hangs up and thinks about what he needs to do. That fucker Zest is surely going to try to hit him in his apartment, so he has to leave. Fine, he can go to another place that can serve more than one purpose.

Nelson puts together a few personal items to take with him until this is over, and leaves. He goes to his garage and gets his Pathfinder, and finalizes his plan in his head as he drives north.

Across the city, Jacobs puts down his phone. He does not let on to his assistants that anything is wrong. As soon as he's able, he steps outside his building for a call that can't be made inside.

"He called here, talking crazy."

"I suppose he's gone over the edge."

"Yes, he's losing it. He threatened me."

"Ross thinks he's on something."

"I do not doubt drugs are involved. He says he's going to kill Ross to prove his worth. And you if he sees you. He's talking about what he knows and could say--in public. He said he'll contact me again after he kills Ross, but obviously this has to stop now. Who knows what the hell he could do."

Zest chuckles to himself. Jacobs' panic doesn't transfer to him. If anything, he's amused.

"So that's what he feels he's going to do, slay the dragon. Well, it's time to take care of all this."

∞

THIRTY-ONE ◆ THE ACE OF CUPS

The Ace of Cups represents finding attunement in feelings, intuition, looking close to see what's around you that might develop, connections that need to be made.

∞

Wednesday, August 18, Continued
Alphabet City, Avenue A, 10:40 am

"MR. ZEST? What is he, a bar of soap?"

"He's not a joke. That's why I had to act like I was closing shop."

Joel is over at my place. It's during work hours, so no concern that Alex might show up. I can't handle that right now. I'm in an armchair, smoking. He's slouched on the floor with Archie.

I watch him thinking. He's concerned, as picks up my seriousness. But in the midst of that, something else is going on with him.

"And you chose to let little ol' me know what's going on, rather than tell me the Big Lie. Why is that?"

"I still need your help."

"Yeah, but from the context, you were lying to everyone else to protect them. But not me. A lesser man might think that you don't care if I'm exposed to danger."

I shake my head. "Not the case. You know I'd protect you with my life. You've been involved in too much for me to keep you out, and I trust you."

He sits up suddenly on his knees and rests his arms on my legs, looking directly at me. We stare at each other. He smiles. "I do know, because I'm not a lesser man. Ultimately, as you realize, I'm the only one you can trust. Clearly Harry Potter can't handle this situation or help you anymore."

"Zest is a whole 'nother level of badass, is what I'm saying. And we've already seen some serious badness."

Joel chuckles. "I get it. You're not fully clean unless you're Zestfully clean."

He laughs again when I frown at him for his inappropriate levity.

"For fuck's sake he threatened everyone I know, including you. He means it."

Joel's not as unaffected as he makes out. I know he has a wall within himself for defense. But now he's gazing at me with a contemplative expression. "I have more confidence in you than worry about Zest. Where do we go from here?"

The same thing Alex asked. The double meaning is unmistakable.

"You're my friend, and I'm glad I have your help. But we're not reviving our previous relationship. I'm involved with Alex. You and I have too many issues to get together again."

He just smiles. "I wasn't asking about that, in fact. I was asking about the investigation. But it's on your mind, isn't it--what's between us. In any case, we'll see how long the 'involvement' lasts when he finds out you couldn't trust him. Don't look at me like that; I'm not telling him. Fate is fate. The truth will come out at some point when he fails you again."

I start to get up but he leans on my legs. Sarah McLachlan is playing in the background. That makes the situation with Joel more surreal. I understand what Danny means about being caught up on his fantasy. He continues with his seduction.

"I wasn't going to discuss this now, but I'm not 'reviving' anything. Because we never really ended. The fact I'm here proves that. It's all semantics, as you used to say. Impress me with your words, baby."

I shake my head. "I need us both to do something better. I want you to go forward with your art, and I want to support you in that."

He raises an eyebrow. "And you? Are you going to give up your profession for him?"

"No...but I understand why he wants me to."

"When you stop it will be because you want to, not others. In the meantime, the help you give people shouldn't be overlooked. It may not be prestigious, it may be like having to spend time in Hell, but I find a beauty in your compassion.

"You and I are a true partnership. He can't possibly appreciate you like I do; you can't trust him like you do me, and you know it because here *we* are talking about what to do with your case, not you and him."

Damn it, he makes this hard by coming up with something deep. "That was about being cautious, not distrustful. I don't know what kind of pipelines the Tertullians have into the *Herald Standard.*"

He's not buying it. "Sounds pretty complicated to me. You don't seem to think he could carry off *pretending* to believe you. Whereas, playing your game is pretty much my specialty."

I move back from him. "I'm aware of that...but I can't do this again, be with you."

"Why? Why are you so sure?"

He has his intense, cat-like gaze on me, but I can't meet it. "Because I'm with Alex. I feel very strongly about him; I just can't turn away from that. And I can't get emotionally involved with more than one person--you know, my *feeling* too much? I loved you. But I can't risk you running away from me again. In any sense."

Joel goes back to the floor, and takes some sort of paper vine-like thing from his jacket pocket and starts playing with it. He doesn't respond to what I said, but I see his mind working.

I tell him, "That doesn't affect our friendship, or our working together, if you still want to help me. I'm going to work on some ideas I have about where evidence might be found tying Nelson to Raymond's murder. Raymond didn't die in his apartment, so he had to be held somewhere--dead or alive. I seriously doubt he was in Nelson's apartment. The door attendant would have seen him. He had to have some other place."

"Of course I'll help, Gabriel. What you said about me running away was wrong. I'm not like that. Or really, I'm not like that now. I'm not leaving you."

"I didn't intend to hurt you with what I said. That was pretty bad of me after what you've done this weekend."

"You didn't." He rolls over to look at me. "It's not important now. I hurt you before too. That's why you feel the way you do. You're uncomfortable with me. But if you weren't feeling something about us, you'd act very differently...*in*differently. I know I have to make up for the past. And I will. If you think I'm only concerned for myself... you're the only other person whose needs I'll respect before my own. Out of anyone I've been involved with, male or female, you're the one who means most to me. The one who really has something *there* with me. Yeah, it took fucking up to realize that. But I don't care if you go back with me or not; I'm still here for you."

I'm speechless for the moment. Too much to comprehend. He lays the red paper vine he's playing with on the table and gets up. "I'm going now; not because I'm upset--don't look like that--but I know right now I'm distracting you from thinking, and I don't want to. Let me know what you need me to do." He pauses, then walks over and kisses the top of my head before leaving.

When he's out the door, I look at the vine. It's in the shape of the endless Buddhist knot. I turn it over in my hands, and then put it on the table under the mandala painting.

I go back to my contemplation with some effort. Nelson kidnapped Raymond the same day I met him, and returned Raymond's body some time Sunday or early Monday morning two days later. He would have hidden the body close. No sense driving six hours to say, Syracuse, and back. So he went somewhere in the city—Long Island or lower Westchester. Jersey involves too many bridges, opportunities to be photographed and stopped by police. Manhattan is too busy--the kidnapping was risky enough. I like the idea of Long Island or Westchester. Since this was a Tertullian-connected problem, maybe he would have taken Raymond to some property linked with them. Maybe with the Foundation, since it could be a Tertullian front. But I think it's somewhere sparsely populated.

Property records for the five boroughs of the city are covered in an online database, as are Nassau and Suffolk Counties in Long Island, and Westchester County. Thank God, no driving to individual county clerk offices. The Foundation owns the building, but I don't see anything else. I try Nelson's name and don't find anything. But then I remember Dr. Cole saying Nelson had cleared out Eleanor's brownstone. I check that record.

The deed has been transferred to one Nathan Dain. I recognize the first and last names as being part of Nelson's previous identities. I search for that name in the other counties, and find one in Westchester County. The Westchester ownership is fairly recent, dating from Ethan's time as director. From the building permit on file, the deed and the plat, I find out it's a warehouse located near Campfire Lake. Pretty out of the way and yet close enough that Nelson could have risked transporting a body in a trunk. Maybe some trace evidence or something belonging to Raymond is still there.

∞

Thursday, August 19
Alphabet City, Avenue A, 6:15 am

Alex stayed over that evening. I plan a trip with Joel the morning when Alex leaves for work. But I'm pre-empted at sunrise when Nelson calls me instead. "Gabriel."

"What in the name of God do you want?" I talk quietly, so as not to awaken Alex. I slip out of bed and make my way to my office.

"I need to talk to you. I want your help."

"Are you kidding me?"

"No, I think you are the only person who can understand, who will believe, all I need to talk about."

"And why do you need to talk now?"

"Please listen. I know I have no right to ask you this..."

"Where are you?"

"I'm sure you understand I cannot tell you that."

"Well, what do you want?"

"You know something of what is going on here, with them."

"Who are "them," Nelson?"

"The Tertullian Society."

"If you say so."

"Don't play coy. They have set me up for murder."

My sympathy is at a low point. "So tell the police."

"Do you think the police will believe me?"

"No." Because *I* don't.

"What would you do in my position?"

"I don't know, honestly. How about turning yourself in?"

"I will, if I can get protection--witness protection program. But I can't just walk in, and time is running out. They'll listen to me if you're there to back me up. Then they will take what you say and pretend it's their own information. You can trust me on that, because I've seen that before. But who cares--we'll be safe. You won't have to be public about it."

I listen carefully to make sure Alex hasn't awakened before I answer. "Nelson, you've tried to have me killed or injured at least three times that I know of. Why would I help you?"

"I'm not going to deny that I have been a troubleshooter for the group. I did what I was told. They won't let this go. I know how they operate, and I can give valuable information that will help you personally."

"Why not just leave? Leave the country, change your identity."

"I will. At some point in the future. Right now, it's easier for *them* to let me take the heat for everything. If I go this way, with you, I can have them looking for certain people I know, and take the heat off me."

"Tell me where Eleanor Whitford is, then."

"I'll tell you, but not until we meet."

"What are you asking me to do?"

"I would like to meet with you to discuss how to approach this."

"I thought we were doing that."

"I'd rather meet face to face. Phones can be tapped."

I sigh. Now I hear Alex up and moving around. Time to end this. "Where do you want to meet?"

"You've heard of Solstice Park?"

"Yeah." Solstice Park is in Westchester County, in Yonkers. That confirms in part my idea about him.

"Very important you meet me alone, Gabriel. I can't take chances until I know I have some kind of safety with the police."

"Sure." Although I have no intention of doing so. "I understand."

"Look. I know that my apartment is under surveillance of some kind, as well as the brownstone, from what's in the papers. I'm not trying to do the right thing; you know I'm not the type. I'm trying to survive. I can't abide any cowboys."

"I understand. I'm not trying to trick you. I just want this over with as well."

We agree to meet later in two hours. Alex sticks his head in the door. "Everything okay?"

"Just a bill collector. I'm fine." But I'm edge until he leaves. As if he knows, he delays getting ready. I do my best to be casual. When Alex showers, I call Joel to play back up. Then I act like the good boyfriend. I must be all right at it because Alex leaves with a genuine good mood.

Ten minutes later, I'm out the door of the building. Joel is already there. "I saw Harry Potter leaving. That must have been tense."

"Shut up and let's go." He smiles and we get in my car. While driving, I tell him about the property information on the way up, and we plan how to handle meeting Nelson.

Around ten, we arrive at the entrance to Solstice Park. It was once a private estate in Yonkers, owned by one of the original New York robber barons, Caleb Carlson. Carlson was rumored to be interested in the occult. The park takes up a couple city blocks, surrounded by the Hudson River on one side, and stone walls around the other three. It has a private foundation of its own to support it and limited visiting hours, which does not include today.

However, the park is not hard to get into. A chain is across the driveway leading up to the tiny visitor's center. I duck under the chain, and I'm in. There are no cameras in the park.

I have a map of the park from an online historical society that I use to figure out my bearings. I have been instructed to meet Nelson near a long-unused fountain. Most of the park is overgrown forestry and crumbling stone monuments. The original house that was part of the estate is next door, now a private school.

Getting to the fountain takes around ten minutes. I have my phone in my pocket, primed to send a text that it's safe for Joel to follow in. He has my Sig Sauer in case Nelson tries anything at all. I don't expect Nelson is telling me the truth, but I hope to get some information from him.

The fountain is fairly large, ten feet in diameter. A female figure with an arrow and clutching a scroll rises from the center. I sit on the ledge.

A few minutes later, a rustle alerts me that Nelson has arrived. Still heavy with the cologne, and he sweats more than usual. His eyes are jumpy. Even though he's carefully dressed, I sense he's falling apart psychologically.

He doesn't try to shake hands which is okay with me. He sits a couple feet away, putting him at a slight angle. "Good to see you."

I can't respond likewise. "What should we discuss? I have limited means of helping you. Zest had a talk with me, if you didn't know."

"Fuck him, he thinks he knows everything. This is a very unfair set of circumstances. I've been valuable to the Tertullians for many years, and handled many troublesome problems for them that have required being above the law. I had their protection. Now I don't know what happened."

"Maybe you have a heavy hand with the problem-solving. Bombs aren't easy to cover-up."

He may be on the outs with the Tertullians, as Mr. Zest suggested. Even so, what could he offer the police, really? Even the FBI or even a Congressional investigation? If the Society is what it purports to be, contacts in major law enforcement and government are a given.

"Did you kill Raymond, Nelson?"

"I'll admit I...took care of Raymond. It wasn't my idea. I had to do what they wanted. My contact made that clear. I liked and admired Raymond."

I'm very sure he admired Raymond. "Who's your contact?"

"His name is Jacobs. At least that what I have to call him. You'd know who he is and I'll tell you later. I deserved better after many years of taking care of their problems. They treat me like an errand boy. You were pretty good at not getting killed, and they blamed me for that, too."

"So sorry."

"But you see why I'm talking to you then. I have nothing to lose. You are probably the only one who *could* help me."

"And Toni?"

My voice must have showed something. He lies carefully. "I didn't do that. They set her up in the office, and left me to take the fall."

Apparently, that's supposed to satisfy me. But of course, I know from Joel it's not true. I don't let on. "Do you have evidence of any of this? You know when we talk to the police, they are going to want more than just a pretty story. They could just write you off as trying to get out of an indictment through a fairy tale."

"*Fairy tale!*" He's enraged, but calms down with effort that leaves him sweating more. He's drawn to rub the scar under his eye. "You have a point. I have evidence; I'm not saying exactly what I have. But I'm not stupid. Long ago, I knew that there would be a reason to have support for what I'm saying. I have it, and I can access it."

"If you have it, why not just let Jacobs know? As I'm sure you know, the simplest way to avoid being wacked is to let your enemy know that you have XYZ in evidence, and if something happens to you, XYZ will be on the front page of the *New York Times*, *Wall Street Journal*, and other rags."

He turns to me, frowning. "It doesn't work that way. This isn't evidence that can be published. Even if it could, the people involved wouldn't shut down the whole global network. I consider myself smarter than simpler plans to leave evidence with attorneys or some other unethical persons to be published upon my death. My goal is not to be killed."

"Okay," I'm starting to get tired of his company. "Tell me about Raymond. You were the man in the photo I showed you, at the coffee shop. Am I right?"

"Yes. I knew what he was doing, that Whitford had talked about it with him. Hacking into a computer is not hard. I erased all his emails on it, but I saw he was going to hire you. I had planned how to take care of him already, but I had to act fast. That couldn't happen. I called him on Friday and told him I had some evidence of corruption in the Foundation, and only he could help me. I had to talk to him right now, that I was scared."

Amazingly, Nelson doesn't seem to realize that he's telling me he used the exact same line on Raymond he used on me.

"He met with me outside; he wouldn't let me in his place. But I came prepared. Slipped some stuff in his coffee and he was out. I kept him in a place of mine I use for things like this, until it was time to set up the scene."

"Is your place nearby?"

He shows surprise by my question, which confirms for me the Campfire Lake property is his. "Not now. I'll discuss that later."

"You had someone in the medical examiner's office, didn't you? No drugs turned up on the autopsy."

Nelson smiles. "Let's just say the person handling the autopsy was vulnerable. His name is Samuel Ides. He's an idiot. He hit someone with his car when he was drunk. The person with him at the time knew me. I figured I would use that someday, and this was the occasion. He made the report say what I wanted."

He places his hands casually on his legs. I watch his hands. I'm prepared for anything.

"You know anyone in the police we speak to?"

"Yeah. I have a person. You tell him you know inside information on persons who have control of the Foundation who have been complicit in a conspiracy for whatever--murder, theft, and so on. You know these persons have also been part of an ongoing conspiracy for whatever domestic or international *mishigos* that you know of, and you have cold hard evidence on this. Make it simple."

"It's not simple." He moves closer to me. "I want to trust you, but I don't think you believe me. I'll show you the evidence, and then you can help me with the police."

I move back from him. "Where is Eleanor Whitford?"

"She's all right. Many people would pay big to be on the kind of medication she's on now. My doctor is watching over her in a private clinic upstate. Like a rehab."

"Where?"

"I'll tell you later."

"What county at least?"

"Rockland. Can we go on, now? Have I proved myself yet? I'll show you the place where Raymond was killed."

That's very funny. He'll show me. Then kill me there. "In a minute. Who helped you with the bomb? And shooting at me?"

"Does it matter? You'll never find him. It wasn't me, if that's what you mean. You wounded him --you were lucky. He almost never misses. I doubt you ever realized how often he's watched you."

He's wrong about that too. "So we should be introduced. Who is he? Just a hired hand or a specialist?"

"Very special. He goes by a code name. Smoke, he calls himself. He's a ghost, really."

"Like you?"

He smiles. "Something like that."

"Whatever you say, Mr. Rane."

That makes him angry. "You...you *were* in my place. I knew something was wrong." His hands reach for me. "How do I know you aren't setting me up? What if you are working for them?"

No more subterfuge with him. He's up and grabbing for my neck.

The best defense is not to be there. I'm already moving to the side and have my arms up to block him, deflecting his forward blow. It knocks him off balance.

A shot goes near his feet. Nelson stumbles away and scans the area. "Who did you bring with you? Not the reporter. You probably have the other one--the one with you at Christensen's house."

I keep him at a distance, maintaining a defensive posture. "He isn't going to do anything to you unless you try to kill me. That's why I don't want you too close."

"You betrayed my *trust*." He practically spits at me, then suddenly gets up and leaves, so swiftly I can't grab him.

A moment later Joel comes out of the woods. "What happened with him?"

"Let's go back to the car." I take out my phone and stop the recorder. "He's freaking out big time. I don't like not knowing where he is."

We go back to my apartment. I have to rest for a minute and think. But I can't rest with Nelson bouncing around the city in a drug-fueled delusional state.

"Are you going to take that recording to the police?"

"I don't think I can use it. I still have to worry about Zest. But Nelson's actions show how desperate he was. He was probably planning to kill me after he 'showed me the evidence.' He would never go to the police. He just wanted me to think he would. We really need to do something about him."

"What do we do now?"

"Babe, the plan still holds. Going to the warehouse to check it out. Figure it out from there."

"Are you glad I was with you?"

"Of course I am. You're my lifesaver."

He's very pleased with this. He reaches for his cigarette but I take my pack out before he can light up. "I'm going to get some equipment together. You need to change into something for the woods.

He shrugs. "I can go home and come back."

"I'll meet you there, save some time. Then we'll head upstate. It's after eleven now."

"Get your stuff and come over. I'll have a pizza or something at my place. We need to eat first."

I agree to meet him in an hour, and he leaves.

After setting up my messenger bag, I lock up and head over to Chelsea.

At Joel's building I buzz his apartment, and he doesn't answer. I call and also get no answer. I don't like that. When he actually promises to be somewhere, he always keeps it. I use the key he gave me to get in. His place is on the third floor. Outside his apartment, I stop when I see that the door is cracked open.

That isn't right. Joel knows better than to ever leave a door open, even if he's expecting me. I go in I look around the plain living room, which leads straight back to a kitchen and then two bedrooms.

Two things cause me to be filled with adrenaline and fear. Joel's clove cigarettes are on the floor next to the apartment door, with a few spilled out of the pack. And I can smell Nelson's cologne.

∞

THIRTY-TWO ♦ JUDGMENT

The twentieth card in the major arcana. Judgment represents resurrection, a coming together of the past and present in a collision that will determine the fate of the participants.

∞

FIVE MINUTES LATER, I'm in my car, breaking laws to get to the Third Avenue Bridge leading to the Bronx, and from there racing for the Bronx River Parkway. Even with reckless driving, an hour creeps by. Nelson has to be going back to the warehouse. That's the only thing I can think of for this stunt. I'm angry with myself for letting Joel leave when Nelson's on the loose. Stupid. Nelson was waiting for him.

My cell phone rings.

"Gabriel."

It's Nelson. "Yeah?"

"I want to meet with you."

"Any particular reason?"

"I have your friend here. The whore you're so fond of."

I feel a cold sickness inside at being right and the pleasure in his voice. "What do you want?"

"I want you to come here and see if you can save his life. If you don't, he'll be dead soon. You know I can do that. But I'll trade you for him. He can leave; I don't care about him. You can then match wits for me if you think you can."

"Fine. If he's alive. If not, I'll tear you apart, I swear to God."

He sighs dramatically. "You don't understand how I work. I told you I don't care about him. It's you, since you think you know everything."

"Where do you want to meet?"

"Do you know Westchester County?"

I should, I'm twenty miles into it at the moment. But he doesn't know that. "Hold on, I'm getting a pen. Where in Westchester?"

"Go up the Taconic. Take the exit for Campfire Lake. Be at the turnout in the lake in two hours." He hangs up.

Good. Little does he know I'm a half-hour away, and nobody else is dying on my watch. From the Bronx River into to the Sprain Brook Parkway, which then becomes the Taconic State Parkway. I think of nothing but getting there. At Campfire Lake, I pull over and take a few minutes to study a map of the area. Still over an hour until his deadline.

The warehouse is on Brock Road, which ends half a mile past the lake. I see an old hunter's trail curves around parallel to Brock and just might be behind the building where Nelson is supposed to be waiting.

The lake itself has a small turn out where people can stand and look out over the tiny body of water. I park there and take out my Sig Sauer and head for the hunter's trail an eighth mile north. I find it rutted and overgrown, but clearly a trail. Walking quickly and quietly, I estimate where Brock road ends using a walking odometer. From my bag, I take a pair of long-distance Pentax binoculars and survey the area from a thicket of trees.

A dull gray structure about the size of a three-story warehouse is approximately 100 yards away. A metal fence runs around the back. I can see a similar fence at the front, with a gate open for a car to drive through. No windows or security cameras are on the back of the building.

I make my way to the gate, take a deep breath and jump for the top, about seven feet up. I try to grab with as little noise as possible. Heaving myself over, I drop down and head for the back of the building. The building seems odd in the middle of a rural area, but it's well hidden from Brock Road by the trees. I take off my bag and leave it on the ground with my jacket, just keeping my gun and pocket tools. I turn off the volume on my phone and put that in my pocket as well.

In afternoon light, I still feel vulnerable. I look around each corner of the building carefully. The building is as almost as large as an old one-movie theater. What I'm afraid of is that the place only has one entrance. I'd have to go in shooting.

I see that around the left side is a large generator. The power lines attach to the building just under a vent. I'm able to climb on the generator and reach the vent grate, which releases exhaust for air conditioning. Feeling a little like I'm in *Die Hard,* I hoist myself up to the shaft, which just barely allows me to crawl in. I have a choice of direction and go for the back of the building.

The first grate I come to, I look out the mesh carefully. Whatever room this is, it's dark and full of crates. My Leatherman tool pries the grate open and I carefully lay it down in the shaft and swing myself out, hanging by my arms. A wooden crate nearby serves as a means to get to the floor without dropping.

I hear no one in the room. No lights are on, but the room is carefully temperature controlled. I briefly use a pen light over the different crates. Several are for paintings. Others appear to be for antiques. It occurs to me this might be a warehouse for the art that the Foundation handles, or that Nelson steals and fences, maybe.

Cracking open the door, I take a couple of minutes to become acclimated. I see darkness in sort of a hallway, and faint light ahead.

The hallway is a wide catwalk around a larger first floor area. I move carefully but fast, to search as much as possible. More crates, or just empty. I start to panic.

Be cool, find Nelson, disable him, find Joel.

The staircase is ahead of me. It's metal. I look over the railing to the faint light below, which is coming through the windows in the garage-size double doors at the entrance of the front of the building. A dozen yards from there is a figure hunched over.

At first, I think the figure is Nelson. A change in light shimmering through shows me it's Joel; he's lying on the floor, and has his hands tied behind his back. I'm afraid he's dead, just like I found Raymond. I don't think I could live with myself if that happened.

Then I see his torso move a little. He's alive. I allow myself to breathe easier. I have to find where Nelson is now. I can't do anything with Joel until I know where Nelson is.

Rustles from somewhere down below. Not enough to see, but now I can use a trick. I pull out my cell phone as the rustles get closer. I find the last incoming number and call it.

The phone goes off below. I see where he is now. He's holding a gun and heading for the front garage-style door. He stops to answer the phone. I step out and silently go down the metal stairs in my sneakers.

"Yes?" He looks at the phone. "Gabriel?"

I'm on the floor, silent as a cat, moving behind him. He doesn't like getting the call. Suspicious, he looks around but can't see me in the shadows. I hear him sigh and he turns back and flicks off the safety. He passes within three feet of me but doesn't notice.

He reaches down and pulls up Joel by his collar, and points the gun at his head.

"Don't fucking *play games* with me, Gabriel."

For a moment, in the midst of my otherworldly sensations I see an outcome of Joel being killed in front of me. Or trying to save him and dying beside him. No. This can't happen. Won't happen.

My rage at Nelson overflows in me, and I tell myself to stay calm; I have to. This is the moment not to act rash. He's waiting for me, isn't doing anything until he knows I'm here, in order to make it hurt more.

Slowly I move again in the shadows, pacing myself and getting the sense of his actions. Before he turns to look around him, I feel him about to do so and seize upon the moment the gun is turned elsewhere. I raise my gun and slam it down on his head.

He staggers to the side, but doesn't fall. The drugs must have him hyper. But Joel reacts to our presence by rolling away. Nelson, infuriated, eyes full of hate, aims the gun at him again.

Without pausing, I jump in front of the gun and grab for his hand. The gun goes off, echoing horribly in the cavernous room. But the shot goes wild, hitting no one.

I pull his gun hand away from him, slip my fingers under his with my thumb on the back of his hand, and twist violently. The gun drops. As I kick it away, I shove my gun against his face.

My rage is so strong, I'm milliseconds from blowing his fucking brains out.

A voice behind me. "Gabriel. Hold on..."

I recognize the voice as Zest. Keeping the gun against Nelson's head, I use my other hand to dig at a pressure point in his shoulder and force him to his knees, then stand behind him, turning to look at Zest.

He's standing inside the entrance with his hands open by his sides, palms facing me. About ten feet from where Joel is. I know instinctively Zest is showing me he doesn't have a weapon.

Nelson moves a little and I grip his collar and yank to cut off his breath.

Zest doesn't react to that, staying in the same position. His expression is calm. "Don't shoot him."

I don't respond. I not only want to shoot Nelson, I want to kick the living fuck out of him first.

Zest holds my eyes. "Let me talk to you a minute. I'm *not* going to ask you to let him go. He's not going anywhere."

"Damned right he isn't."

Nelson begins speaking quickly. "Listen, Gabriel. You need to kill him. You know we're on the same side and I can help you. Zest is a cold motherfucker. You and I can work this out--I thought you were trying to kill me, I was wrong about you, but we can work together. Zest will fuck you up. Shoot him now and I'll help you. I was never trying to kill your boyfriend--"

I yank up on his collar savagely, cutting off his words, making him gag.

"Hold on." Zest is not looking at Nelson, only at me. "Don't do anything with him yet. I want to talk to you about this man to man."

"What's your point, because I'm not interested in clemency."

"I know. I told you, he's not going anywhere. But I want to do this differently. In a better way. First let me cut Mr. McFadden free; you'll feel better."

"Stay away from him or I'll shoot you, then Nelson. I don't miss, unlike your 'Smoke' person."

"I'm not moving and you know I don't doubt you. I have a Swiss Army knife, not a pistol. I'm not going to hurt Mr. McFadden."

"Don't try me, Goddamn it."

"Let him." This from Joel. His voice sounds guttural and strained, making me want to hurt Nelson more.

Nelson coughs, trying to get his voice back. "You going to trust him? From the Society? He's a hired gun. He'll tell you anything to get you to do what he wants. Don't let him near your friend. Just kill him, for Christ's sake."

Zest briefly looks at Nelson, but doesn't change expression. "You know better than to listen to him, Gabriel. Can I take out my knife to show you?"

I nod. Keeping one hand up, he slowly puts the other in his pants pocket and takes out the knife, holds it up. "I believe you about your shooting skills. I know what happened in New Jersey. This is a show of faith."

"Zest was brought in to kill both you and me. Don't fall for it." Nelson twists under my hand as he speaks, and I dig my fingers in harder.

"Gabriel, this is a different situation. I'm aware you gave up the case, and I'm not here about that, I want to assure you. This is about Nelson, now. Not you."

I glance at Joel. He nods.

"Cut him loose. That's all."

Zest carefully and slowly approaches Joel, and so I can see him, slices the plastic binds on Joel's wrists open. Joel puts his hands on the floor and slides away. He's not quite able to get up.

The sight of that makes me see red. Zest stands and returns to his previous posture, keeping his eyes on me.

"You're angry, but intelligent. I know you want to kill him, but it's not your thing. It's mine. I need to set it up. You have nothing to gain from this."

"And I believe you why?"

"First I want to tell you something. I'm not alone here. I'm not threatening you, just telling you. You won't see them. If you do anything to me, they'll know. You won't get out alive. Neither of you. I don't want to do that, and you're too smart to let that happen."

"You're going to believe his bullshit?" Nelson is sweating under my hands.

Zest talks over Nelson's words. "I was watching your place because I knew Nelson was coming for you. I was not going to let him kill you. Since you dropped the matter that does not give us any benefit, it only attracts attention. But he decided to follow Mr. McFadden, and I then followed him from there to here. I was not going to let him kill Mr. McFadden either; that would just have set you against us again. I know what Nelson was doing. Understand we have no more issue with you, Mr. Ross. But I need to do it this way, and you'd do best to let me handle it."

"Because you'll kill me otherwise."

"No. The situation is this: my associates know Nelson shot first the first time, before I came in. If they hear another shot they'll come in and kill you all. They'll have to. I don't want it to happen that way. We both have reasons for me to handle this. One reason is that while I understand your ire, this isn't you. You've won; killing him will only hurt you. It will kill you."

"I'm not worried about your people outside. I got this far. I'd take my chances."

Zest nods. "You'll risk yourself, I understand. Don't risk Mr. McFadden. He's in no shape to get out of here without you. I'll tell you again, you and I have no fight. My second reason is that this is a professional courtesy."

"We don't exactly have the same profession."

"So you might think. But I know that quote you gave me at the Met...call this the "chink in my armor"."

The implication of this. Doing him a favor.

"Between you and me, as professionals." His voice becomes soft. Nelson starts to protest and I tighten his collar again. But he can still talk.

"Gabriel...before you do that, you really have to think about what he's doing. He'd never let you out. You have all the power now, and I can get you out of here. I know those men he has outside and how to get away from them."

When I don't respond, Nelson's voice gets more desperate. "Don't let him do this to me, Gabriel. You're better than that."

"Don't talk to me, Nelson."

Zest continues, keeping my eyes. "Gabriel, you proved yourself before to doing what's right. I have a stun device in my pocket. Turn Nelson over to me. I *know* if you aren't worried about saving yourself, you don't wish to jeopardize Mr. McFadden. Between us as two professionals, you know what to do."

Nelson speaks over his shoulder, looking up over my gun. "Gabriel, you can't do this. I'll go with you to the police right now, after we get away. You of all people can't give me to him so he can *kill* me. You're too *good* for that."

He's still trying to get out of my grip but is staring right in my eyes. Zest waits, slipping the knife back in his pocket. His eyes are wary.

Joel is sitting up against the wall next to the front door. He can't do much more than that. He's waiting for me as well.

I look back at Zest. "Go ahead. Take him." Nelson tries to tear himself away from my hands, but I hold on until Zest reaches me, and then I shove him to the floor and step back as Zest turns the device on him. Nelson arcs back in a seizure, and then falls on the floor, twitching, then still.

Zest has his own pair of handcuffs in his pocket and snaps them on Nelson's wrists. He walks carefully to the door. "I'm signaling my associates that you can leave."

He steps outside briefly. I go and collect the stun gun and Nelson's gun, then return to Joel. He looks up at me, breathing hard. I touch his head briefly.

Zest comes back in. He checks Nelson, then turns to me, his hands still open.

"It's set for you to leave. If it makes you feel better, you can take the gun and the stun device. You both need to leave now, and do not come back to this place."

Without hesitation I stick the guns in my pockets, and help Joel to his feet. He tries to walk, but he's nearly dead weight. Zest holds the door while I help Joel up and out. Just outside the door I look around but nothing happens. Zest and I meet each other's eyes once more, and then he closes the door behind us.

∞

THIRTY-THREE ♦ TEMPERANCE

The fourteenth card in the major arcana. Temperance represents a swing in circumstances and balance being brought to life.

∞

Thursday, August 19, Continued

I CAN'T DRIVE FAST ENOUGH to get back to the Taconic.

Joel had done his best to try to walk to the car, but I had pretty much carried him. Nothing happened; we didn't see any sign of Zest's helpers. I put Joel in the Camry, and threw the guns in the water.

Once on the highway Joel keeps falling asleep against me. But I shake him repeatedly as we head back. I don't know what he was drugged with, and I don't want him to overdose like Toni.

"I'm taking you to the hospital in White Plains."

"I'm okay, man." He forces himself to sit up.

"Did he get you with a needle?"

"Yeah, right in my back. I didn't hear him at all. That's not..." he closes his eyes.

I elbow his ribs.

"Jesus, was that necessary?"

I pull the car over on a wide spot on the shoulder and lift his head up. His eyes are clear, but a little dilated. He watches while I study him. I'm listening to his breathing and heartbeat. He seems normal, but it's the gleam in his eye watching me watching him that tells me he's okay.

I get back on the road and back to my apartment nearly an hour and a half later.

Alex was supposed to be coming over, but I use my lying skills to convince him I have to go out of town on an emergency insurance assignment.

I have Joel lie on my bed, but keep him awake.

"You're not going to let me sleep?"

"I want the drugs to metabolize from your system. Look, even Archie's worried."

Joel smiles, but he's having trouble talking. "He knows I'm the only one who'll treat him right; if I'm gone, he's in trouble."

I have to keep watch over him, and I'm exhausted myself. But I keep shaking and teasing him awake. He fights with me each time.

"Stop digging in my ribs, man. Slap me or something." He looks up at me. I have my arm around him.

"I'm concerned, moron."

"Me too. I don't let people get the drop on me too often."

"I know. Nelson is a special category of person. Was, anyway."

"The last thing I wanted to do was get you--"

"You didn't. He was after me, and used you. I'm sorry about that."

"We're both sorry, and we're both still alive again."

We both helped each other in these situations, I think to myself. I let him sleep at dawn, when I can't stay up any longer myself.

Late in the morning, I wake up suddenly, and check on him. He looks in fairly good shape. He opens his eyes and looks at me.

"You okay?"

He rolls over closer to me. "You jumped in front of the gun."

"Of course."

"It's not an 'of course' it's just you. You were going to kill him."

"The thought crossed my mind."

He starts to say something else and stops. He studies me for a minute. "You were so angry." His voice is subdued.

"He was going to hurt you." I turn on the TV and lie back down with him for a while.

Later I take him back to his apartment, and he sketches me while I install a new set of locks on the door. I mostly hide out in my apartment the rest of the weekend, except when I'm checking on Joel. Veronica helps with that. I don't tell her everything, but enough for her to be there when I can't.

∞

Monday, August 23

Monday starts with a bang. Mankiewitz calls me. "You hear about Ethan Nelson, the director of Raymond Booth's nonprofit?"

"No, I've been meditating."

"Huh. Came in an hour ago. An anonymous tip was called into the police. Nelson hung himself from his shower rod, and left a note claiming responsibility for Booth and his sister."

"Will wonders never cease?"

"Any comment?"

"Yeah, I hope justice is done."

"Anything else, Ross? This rather vindicates you and everything you said before."

"Really? No one is suggesting I killed him to make myself look good? Whatever, I'll get my reward in Heaven."

I keep up with the story online over the next few days. Forensic investigation turns up some traces of clothes and hair evidence are found in the apartment. I have to admire Zest's work in that. No one's going to be looking in that warehouse. The suicide note claims Nelson killed Raymond because Raymond had found out he was embezzling money from the Foundation. Naturally, evidence of that was discovered as well in Nelson's office.

Mankiewitz keeps calling me for a comment, which I decline to give him. I admire his tenacity. He's another one with sharp instincts.

In a subsequent phone call, he expresses frustration. "Ross, what's up with you, man?"

"I have my reasons. You don't need me; you're doing well on your own with the story."

"Someone holding you back?"

"Not important. But I'll give you something on background. You're giving the medical examiner's office and the NYPD a hard time, and they deserve it. Look into Ides, Sam Ides. He handled Raymond's autopsy. I'm not saying the office knows; they may not. But Ides is bent and I'd pressure them into reviewing the paperwork."

"All right, man. If you change your mind about being on the record, let me know."

Mankiewitz and the Thin Blue Line make a push for an internal investigation the next day. No response at first from the ME's office, but a leak reveals that Ides faked the toxicology report. The original paperwork turns up showing Raymond had gamma-hydroxybutyric acid--liquid Ecstasy--in his blood.

The *Herald Standard* even follows up on the case. But Alex doesn't work on that story. I don't speak to any reporters period, other than Mankiewitz off the record. The *Scene* makes the point I was right from the beginning, which I appreciate even If I'm not saying anything.

I find out which rehab rip-off Eleanor is being stashed at, and drive up with Joel and Veronica to pull a little scam to get us inside, where we find Eleanor and smuggle her out. We drop her off in Dr. Cole's care back in New York City.

The ME's office decides to change the manner of Raymond's death to homicide. The Brooklyn ME's office determines that Toni's death is also homicide. The case is closed again. Marilyn calls on Friday to tell me Toni had been cremated after the autopsy was completed last Wednesday, a few days after her death, but a memorial service is scheduled for the following Friday. Julia is still having trouble dealing with the logistics out of her grief, and I offer to help.

Being in Brooklyn to help the Booth family also makes visiting Herrmann convenient. I've told him what happened with Nelson. A few days before the memorial service Herrmann asks me to come over again and have tea with him.

Inside Herrmann's place, I play with Jonah and the rest of the cats and dogs and then settle in. Herrmann offers me a cigarette. He's a Winston man.

"Did you know Linera recently died?"

"Had no idea. Natural causes?"

"It's hard to say. Because of your information, I was able to have a couple of colleagues down in Bolivia track him down. He didn't go out much--not surprising at his age. But he was found at the bottom of a rock outcropping, like he'd been for a walk and fell."

"Kind of convenient." I suspect Zest is clearing up loose ends.

"His funeral was public, because apparently he had been 'respected' in the community. My colleagues attended and were able to photograph Linera and get a DNA swab at the open-casket funeral--which wasn't easy. They almost were arrested. We just received the results which prove he was Schleiden."

Herrmann sets down his cup. "This will now be news. My colleagues are going to say they have been watching Linera for several years. You won't be involved, as I promised. The fact he was killed gave them a chance to get close when they otherwise would not."

"I appreciate that. How did you happen to have his DNA?"

"His daughter and wife were abandoned in Germany when he left. The daughter hated him and offered to keep her DNA on file if he was ever found."

Jonah jumps on my lap to dig his little claws into my shirt. I curl him in my arms and listen to his purring. Kittens cure all the evils in the world. "So going public is to expose his identity?"

Herrmann smiles, reaches over and grips my arm. "Better. I would have liked to see him extradited and tried. But he was never indicted because no one knew where he was. Germany was not likely to get involved. Bolivia cut diplomatic ties with Israel three years ago; no way would they let Linera be sent over, especially for a capital offense."

He pours tea. "But it turns out Schleiden was not a humble engineer. He still had the assets he stole from Germany and looted from Jewish victims. My colleagues were able to find that out from his will. Not that it said as such, but we are well aware of what was missing. Therefore, a legal action will be brought to repatriate the art and artifacts--ten million dollars' worth. Would you believe he shipped his thievery out of Germany before Hitler blew his brains out? In crates marked Red Cross humanitarian relief, no less. We don't know who the US contacts were who helped this terrible enterprise."

I smile to myself. If Zest was behind Linera's death, he was also responsible for the ensuing legal battle to be fought. Kind of ironic for a Nazi organization. "I'm guessing the Foundation. It was started in 1946. Maybe we can look into just who started that place and why."

I have been getting used to living without someone being killed every five minutes. My finances are slowly repairing. One or two ex-clients have come back. No problem with me; I don't hold grudges. Jim has begun handling my licensing investigation, which appears to be no big deal considering the source of the complaint. He puts in a motion for dismissal on the lawsuit. It probably won't work but Jim's looking forward to working on a jury with the good Reverend Bunton's stellar reputation.

Alex goes with me to Toni's memorial service in Park Slope. Marilyn wants me to speak and I keep it short, talking about how much she loved her family and how electric her personality was. True enough. Joel and Veronica attend the service together. They sit in the last row of chairs, whereas Alex and I were in the second. Veronica comes up alone and greets me and Alex before the service starts. He briefly glances back at Joel. I have not introduced them and not planning to for as long as I can put that off. But I'm sure Alex knows who he is. Joel pretends not to be looking at us.

After a few other people speak, those attending then move around to look at the photo albums and slideshow of Toni that's set up in one of the two rooms. Adam talks to me at that point about his feelings for his mom. He needs an ear to share his thoughts at such a bad point in his life. I offer some insight from when my own mom passed away.

"You'll always miss her. It gets better with time, but you'll miss her. It'll come suddenly sometimes. Missing her and being sad is okay, because it reminds you that you love her and she loved you."

He thinks about that. "Can I stay in touch with you?"

"Of course you can. If Julia is okay with it, you can call me or see me whenever you want."

He looks at me seriously. "Was that man who died the one who killed her?"

"Yes."

"Was he the only one?"

"More or less, Adam. Sometimes bigger forces are at work. I tell you about them another time."

"Can I help you find them some day?"

"Sure. You need to be a little older, but we'll look into it."

Julia is functioning, but Marilyn continues being the strength of the family. I've gotten on her good side with my help in setting this up. She stops and speaks to me privately. "The insurance company is considering reversing its decision on denying Raymond's policy payment."

"It's little comfort, but I'm glad."

She keeps my gaze. "I know you had a good deal to do with this. You tried to help her. I see you feel for her and I appreciate it."

Cheng has come to the service for a brief visit. He shakes my hand, but thankfully doesn't ask about my life choices. Nonetheless, he's concerned over me. "Are you okay?"

"I'll survive."

"I know you will, and I feel you deserve better than what happened....but, interesting that in spite of 'giving up' the case, the goals were accomplished."

"What can I tell you? Forces of fate were at work."

"Do you believe in fate?"

"I believe in forces."

I'm surprised when I later see Dr. Cole. He and Toni seemed at odds in life. He draws me aside. He doesn't seem to know where to start. He looks away several times, gathering himself. I wait, sensing something different.

"I have an idea why you ended the investigation. Not much, but enough."

Instinctively I step even further away from other people and so does he. "Let me guess. You looked into it yourself."

"To some extent, with the art issue I told you about. I wanted the board to investigate this more thoroughly. I was pretty adamant about it. Then my daughter had...a scare."

He now looks embarrassed. "I can't endanger her. I might just resign from this whole thing."

"I can't blame you. You're doing right to protect her."

He nods and walks away.

I'm suddenly exhausted at being reminded of the Tertullian Society. I gesture to Alex for him to come over. I lead him out to the lobby of the funeral parlor. "Can you get the car? I'm ready to leave."

"Of course." He kisses my cheek quickly and leaves.

Joel and Veronica come up to me. Veronica kisses me too, and walks away to leave me with Joel.

Joel goes to the window to look at the street. "I see you have Harry Potter well trained."

"Think what you need to, son."

"I will. At least he hasn't moved in yet."

"No one's moving with me. He did ask me to move in with *him.*"

"Really? He owns his place, too. What a catch."

"How do you know?"

"I learned how to do checks on people from you. Don't get your knickers in a twist. Like I said when I came back, I just like to know my competition."

I shake my head. "This isn't a matter of competition."

"So you say. Why didn't you take him up on it?"

"I like having my own place."

He smiles, playing with his tie.

I walk up beside him. "Don't read into it any more than that...are you feeling okay lately?"

"I'm fine, Gabriel. I'd be more worried about you. Yeah, you feel too much. I told you after the bomb in Jersey, the point is we survived. Same thing what happened in Westchester. It's over. You don't have to carry around the weight of the world for me. I don't want your friendship out of guilt."

"It's not guilt. I genuinely care."

"I know. Just don't convince yourself it's guilt and then back away." He turns to me. "So I guess Harry Potter didn't mind finding out you lied..."

Another smile when I don't respond. "Because you didn't tell him what happened, did you?"

"As you said, it's over."

"But you allowed him to think something that wasn't true, which is what you accused me of doing to you. And you're carrying the secret you can't tell him."

"I lied for protection."

"So did I. It was a mistake." He reaches out to place his hand on the back of my head. "You are the only man I really cared about in this way. The only one who I ever believed I was...something special. Maybe I distanced myself because of that."

I know why he was distant, what happened to him in his youth. I had a bad childhood but his was so much darker. The moment between us becomes difficult.

"I care about you Joel, but you can't fuck up my life." I look him in the eyes with what I hope is a stern expression. "I'm sorry we didn't talk it out before when we were together. I don't know why you can't buy that."

He shakes his head. "No, I can live with rejection. You have no idea how much I lived with. I just want you for you. You *know* going through this case crossed a boundary within you. You know things that other people died for. You know why you made the choice you did in that warehouse. You have to carry that around and it's a burden. You have to live in a different world than everyone else. I already know that world; I'm in it waiting for you. You need me with you to negotiate it." He looks out the window again.

"He's pulled up outside, you better leave."

I put my hand on his shoulder. He rests his face on my hand and closes his eyes. "You think you'll need me again? For your work?"

He lifts his head and takes my hand, gripping it tightly for a moment, then letting go.

I find myself saying, "Actually, I've got a new case I could use some help, if you want to come by tomorrow."

"I'll be there."

Before I walk out, I look back over my shoulder. He's still watching me. When he smiles, I can't help but smile back.

∞

THE END OF THE HANGED MAN.

GABRIEL AND JOEL RETURN IN *TWO-FACED WOMAN*.

GABRIEL'S WORLD EXTRAS: PREVIEW OF TWO-FACED WOMAN

WHO WILL CATCH YOU WHEN YOU'RE FALLING?

THE SECOND BOOK in the Gabriel's World Mystery/Thriller/LGBTQ+ series continues the story of Gabriel Ross, a strong, brilliant, intuitive private investigator in New York City. Gabriel's cases take him to dangerous places in his inner self and in the real world. On behalf of his clients, he seeks justice while risking his license, freedom, and life.

In this story, he's undergoing severe psychological trauma from events during the previous summer (detailed in the first book, The Hanged Man), while he immerses himself in the cases of two special women. Sophie Faulkner, a woman with a second self, has been falsely accused of murder. Geneva Lennon, a transgender woman, is searching for her true birth identity.

While working to help these women Gabriel also attempts to reclaim his spirituality and deal with his turbulent relationships. His boyfriend Alex is trying to change him and make him quit his profession. But Gabriel's loyal ex-boyfriend Joel is helping and protecting Gabriel on these cases, and he may convince Gabriel he's the love of Gabriel's life. Two-Faced Woman is set in duality: two loves, two clients, two realms (dreams and reality), and mixing the spiritual and the physical. And the danger is double-downed, with two brutal criminals who will make Gabriel face his biggest risk yet—what he has to become in order to take them on.

PRELUDE ♦ 64 ANTICIPATING COMPLETION (Wèi Jì)

Water over Fire: Life has provided setbacks. A new cycle is coming. One may still feel lacking in some way, but that is the necessary prelude to take responsibility to facilitate the new cycle. The fourth line (yang/nine) moves in this reading. Yang in a yin line means some difficulty in the journey, but the person should try to raise strength and fortitude.

∞

Saturday, November 27, 2010

Gabriel is back in the warehouse in Westchester. Joel is on his knees and Ethan Nelson pointing a gun at Joel's head, about to fire.

No, this can't happen...I rescued him. You're dead.

Gabriel tries to lift his Sig Sauer and hit Nelson across the head--like he did in in the warehouse, in August. But he can't move.

Nelson then turns and stares at Gabriel.

"I was going to kill your boyfriend."

He points the gun at Gabriel.

"I think I'll just kill you."

He pulls the trigger.

Gabriel doesn't feel the bullet hit his chest, but he falls backwards, away from Nelson, away from Joel.

Falling down further. Down into Hell.

Cold.

Blackness.

Alone.

∞

"No!"

My eyes open. I'm gripping my sheets.

I sit up slowly. The adrenaline throbs in my head and my chest. I'm covered in sweat.

It's a dream. You're alive. Joel is alive. Nelson is gone.

I feel nauseated now. The Xanax.

It's three in the morning. The bedroom is dark, but not entirely. A small lamp is on. I don't remember turning it on, but I also don't remember getting undressed and getting into bed.

I get up to go to the bathroom. A glimpse of my reflection in the wall mirror startles me. A 36-year-old man, in decent shape (when I don't work, I exercise, when I don't exercise I work) but who hasn't been eating well or sleeping very much. The reflection looks haunted.

I turn away from my double and start to leave my bedroom. Then I see the broken door frame. The wood around the lock is cracked and splintered. What the fuck?

Archie, my black and white tuxedo cat, is walking with me. He stops to look up.

Joel kicked the door in. Remember?

I don't remember, and yet I know it happened.

"But Joel doesn't do things like that," I tell the cat, who's washing his paw. "We were working."

Well, Joel was working--taking care of some reports for me. I wasn't supposed to be doing anything. That was the compromise I gave into with Alex.

The nausea overcomes me and I run for the bathroom. Since I haven't eaten anything that I know of in 24 hours, it's just dry heaves.

As I lean on the sink to leverage myself back up, I see the Xanax bottle in the wastebasket. Empty. It had held at least 24 out of a 30-count prescription.

Archie jumps on the bathtub rim; his tail snaps back and forth as he watches me.

You had just collapsed by the bed. "Here is as good as any place. I just don't want to think anymore." That's what you were saying to yourself.

Then a loud noise--that would be Joel kicking in the door. You're a private investigator, you can make deductions like that.

And some moments later, Joel shaking you. "How many? Tell me!"

"Four..."

My deductive powers tell me Joel flushed the remaining Xanax down the toilet.

I go back into the living room.

Everything in here room is calm. Case files are stacked neatly on the writing desk. My cigarettes are on the coffee table with my lighter on top of the box.

Another memory. Sitting in the side chair, while Joel's talking to me, and I'm trying to open the pack of Camels. I can't do it; my fingers won't work. So I crush the box and throw it on the floor.

That box isn't anywhere around. The one on the coffee table is new, but the cellophane is off. Someone went out to buy it.

I light up a cigarette out of the new pack.

I'm not in Hell. Not the supernatural one anyway.

The dream starts coming back to me. Nelson. *He was in my client's apartment. Raymond Booth. Nelson was strangling Raymond in front of me, and I couldn't move. I could only watch him.* That was the first part of the dream.

I move to the kitchen for some water, and open the window to feel the night air of the witching hour. Freezing cold, but it cools the sweat.

The Xanax is wearing off and now I won't sleep again. I go back to the living room.

Joel has completed the reports. I flip through them. He must have finished all this while I was passed out. Watching over me.

My personal cell phone is near the cigarettes. I check to see if anything is on the phone that could offer some illumination.

The last text, to Alex, says *--me too.*

What?

I scroll up to previous messages. I see the ones from the morning that I *do* remember. Alex asking me to not work for the day and just clear my head, so we could get past our argument. Then later in the morning reminding me I said I wouldn't work.

He also sent a text in the afternoon suggesting that he come over last night, instead of tomorrow, to talk. I don't remember that one, or the reply underneath.

--*Can't. Veronica has an emergency I need to help her with, nothing bad. I'll see you Monday.*

I didn't write that. Veronica, my best friend, didn't have an emergency yesterday. However, I catch the scent of her perfume in the apartment, and I see an empty pack of her brand of cigarettes, American Spirit, in the living room wastebasket. She was here.

Archie tries to jump in the wicker wastebasket, to snag the pack. *Of course, she was here. No doubt Joel called her and asked her to come over and help watch you. They put you to bed. Deduction.*

The text under that one says, *All right. Tell her hi. I love you, okay?*

--*me too*

I stare at that last text. Joel typed that, and the one about Veronica. To keep Alex from coming over and walking in on me passed out.

Archie comes over to look at the phone. *That's why the reply doesn't say 'I love you.' 'Me too' is the most Joel could make himself type.*

Archie navigates the coffee table, stepping around the pack of tarot cards. Those remind me of Toni, Raymond's sister.

In the dream, after killing Raymond, Nelson stabbed Toni in the back and dumped her outside my apartment door. I open the door to see her there, staring up at me with frozen eyes.

But Nelson had drugged Toni. Made it look like an overdose, and left her in an alley in Brooklyn. I never saw her there. Well, dreams don't always make sense. He hadn't strangled Raymond by hand with a garrote, either.

And then the last part of the dream, with Joel. And there, the dream was accurate. Nelson had kidnapped Joel, taken him to the warehouse, and held him there to lure me in. He was going to kill us both, but I had managed to get in the warehouse without Nelson knowing, and knock him away. Nelson is gone. Mr. Zest, professional troubleshooter for the Tertullian Society, took care of that. I doubt Zest has these kind of dreams, although he claimed he and I were simpatico.

Remembering the dream with Joel triggers my recall of the rest of the afternoon yesterday.

I'm wandering around the apartment. I can't concentrate, I can't read. I'm supposed to be relaxing because Alex and I are trying to get over our fight. About my working too much. And whom I work with.

And Joel, studying the files on the computer fraud case, looks over at me.

"What's wrong, Gabriel? Really?"

"Nothing. I'm fine."

"No, you're not. It's what went on this summer, right? It's been three months since Toni's funeral. I know you were more shaken up about that than you said."

"I suppose. I thought I was handling it. But two clients died. I feel like I could have done something..."

"Stop saying that. Stop with the guilt. Nobody could have handled that case better than you."

"I almost got you killed, too."

"Don't think about that anymore. Is that why you aren't working? So you can let all the demons in to visit? Nelson's not going to come back and shoot me. It's over. Not the first time I had a gun to my head, anyway."

I'm trying to open the cigarettes then, and stop, crumpling the box and throwing it. That shocks him enough to leave the files and walk over to me.

I look at him. "What happened to you before?"

"I shouldn't have said anything. Forget it. Just something that went down when I was younger..."

For a moment, I don't know what is real--if Joel is alive, and I'm just suffering, or if he's dead and this is a dream.

I want to just forget everything. Forget. I'm exhausted but I can't stop thinking. And my phone buzzes with another text. It's not Danny, my other best friend. He's still angry at me. It's Alex again, checking up on me.

I can't work, I can't bring my clients back to life, I can't bring my mom and my uncle back to life, and I can't placate anyone who's living right now.

I just want to be out.

And even though Joel is talking, I get up and lock myself in the bedroom. Find the bottle. A half tablet didn't do it when I got the prescription. Or a whole, or even two. Let's double-down, then. Wait for it to hit.

Pounding on the bedroom door.

Listening to Joel's voice on the other side, but not responding.

"Come on, I'm sorry about that." ...

"Fuck...Gabriel? Open up." ...

"Goddamn it, open the door!" ...

"Gabriel? I'm sorry...please. I know you're going through a bad time. I'm here for you. Please don't hide. Come out and talk to me. Or let me in. Something." ...

"You're scaring me. Please. Open the door." ...

"If you don't open it, I'll break it down." ...

And this is where I walked into the movie.

I lie on the sofa, with the TV on. Should I call or text Joel or Veronica, or Alex? Maybe the safer thing to do is nothing.

Archie settles on the pillow next to me. His expression seems both affectionate and stern.

You can put it off for now, brother, but you know you have to make changes.

ABOUT THE AUTHOR

Alex Fiano is a bi/genderqueer writer, teacher, artist, and LGBTQ+ advocate (particularly for youth) living in New York City.

[Cover images created in part with brushes from dead_brushes/brusheezy.com]